SF Books by Vaughn

LOST STARSHIP SERIES:
The Lost Starship
The Lost Command
The Lost Destroyer
The Lost Colony
The Lost Patrol
The Lost Planet
The Lost Earth
The Lost Artifact

THE A.I. SERIES:
A.I. Destroyer
The A.I. Gene
A.I. Assault
A.I. Battle Station
A.I. Battle Fleet

EXTINCTION WARS SERIES:
Assault Troopers
Planet Strike
Star Viking
Fortress Earth
Target: Earth

Visit VaughnHeppner.com for more information

Target: Earth
(Extinction Wars 5)

By Vaughn Heppner

Copyright © 2018 by the author.

This book is a work of fiction. Names, characters, places and incidents are either products of the author's imagination or used fictitiously. Any resemblance to actual events, locales or persons, living or dead, is entirely coincidental. All rights reserved. No part of this publication can be reproduced or transmitted in any form or by any means, without permission in writing from the author.

ISBN-13: 978-1723456404
ISBN-10: 1723456403
BISAC: Fiction / Science Fiction / Military

-1-

I slipped through a forbidden hall to do the unthinkable because crazy guilt had consumed me for eight long years.

It was dark within the corridor, but I wore special goggles that allowed me to see in the pitch-blackness. It was freezing in here as well, so I wore a special metallic-looking garment, a skintight thing that kept out the cold. A small bubble of warm air circled my head, generated by a tiny device attached to the base of my neck.

I'm Creed, by the way, no longer Commander Creed of Earth, but the Curator's Galactic Effectuator.

Yeah, I know, you have no idea who the Curator is or what a Galactic Effectuator does. The Curator—an old man who looks like Michelangelo's God, the one in the famous painting on the Sistine Chapel ceiling where He's reaching out to touch Adam's finger and fill him with life—runs the Fortress of Light in the center of the Milky Way Galaxy. The Curator claims the place is the Creator's, not his, but never expanded on the idea. The Fortress, or Museum, as some knew it, orbited the massive black hole at Sagittarius A*. One pronounces that as Sagittarius "A" Star, incidentally.

I was the Curator's Galactic Effectuator, as I said. The easiest way to understand that was to think of a glamorized movie spy, and that was me. I often left the Museum—the Fortress of Light—in a special stealth ship and took care of problems. Sometimes that meant *liquidating* a troublesome alien warlord. Sometimes that entailed sneaking into an ultra-powerful stronghold and removing an object that would otherwise cause future problems. Sometimes, I just poked into things here and there, and found out what was really going on, relaying the information back to the Curator.

In many ways, I was his scalpel for cutting out trouble, and I'd done a damn fine job since resigning my post as Earth's war-leader.

Earthlings or humans are the *little killers* of galactic lore. According to legend, we'd been patterned after the First Ones—not given the same grand powers, but dangerous enough in our own right.

Just so you know, I hadn't had any communication with Earth these past eight years. There was a reason for that. Our galaxy was divided into varying levels or zones of civilization. Earth, for example, had a 6C Civilizational Score, which was low. Those in higher zones weren't supposed to interfere with those in lower zones.

As I hurried through the dark cold corridor, pangs of homesickness hit. That always happened when I came here.

From somewhere ahead, I heard the floor creak as if by a stealthy footfall.

I froze, my hand on a blaster secured to my hip. The blaster emitted what I thought of as a disrupter ray.

I couldn't just shoot, though. I wasn't supposed to be in this part of the Fortress of Light. That meant killing the person ahead was probably out of the question. The best thing was to not get caught so I wouldn't have to explain myself later.

I released the blaster and eased into an alcove.

Sometimes, the best Effectuator work was as simple as playing hide-and-go-seek like a kid.

I heard another creak, an ominous sound that indicated someone big. Then—

I leaned out of the alcove, straining to hear. I thought I heard a *click*. There was a sudden rushing sound afterward. I frowned. That could have come from someone teleporting away, air rushing in to occupy the vacated space of a vanishing body.

Who would be teleporting here? The Curator could, certainly, but why would he bother? Had enemies found a way inside the Fortress?

I eased my shooting hand back onto the disrupter. As I did, doubts assailed me. Had I really heard the floor creak, heard a click and a sudden rushing sound? Maybe I'd made the noises up in my head.

Why would I, though? Hmm… Maybe guilt had caused an overreaction. Coming here always brought deeper guilt that I'd never learned to deal with. Maybe my subconscious wanted me to leave and thus invented these things as reasons.

I shook my head and forced myself to face the guilt. It was the least I could do.

I slipped out of the alcove and resumed my trek, creeping slower than before as a precaution.

I'm not proud of the act that caused the guilt, but I'll tell you about it anyway. There was this sweet girl named Jennifer. I'd met her when I'd become an assault trooper back on Earth. Later, she'd joined a grim expedition to the portal planet, a place that linked our space-time continuum with an evil dimension holding Abaddon and trillions of xenophobic Kargs.

Abaddon had been a First One, and the next thing to the Devil. A case could be made that the First Ones had been the archetypes for angels and thus bad First Ones the pattern for fallen angels or demons. Kargs were robot-like aliens from a different dimension, perfect companions for Abaddon.

We'd closed the portal planet, but during our escape to our dimension, we'd accidentally left Jennifer behind. As we'd fled, Abaddon had communicated with me, letting me know that he'd caught my girl and would twist her into something vile. He assured me that she would hate my guts for the rest of eternity.

It had been hard, but for the good of all, I'd bailed on Jennifer, sealing Abaddon behind in the evil space-time continuum.

Wouldn't you know it, Abaddon had still found a way into our dimension? It happened some time later, and he'd only been able to slip through with a handful of spaceships instead of billions of star-crafts as he'd originally intended. He'd brought the altered Jennifer along, of course. Through a dream, he'd told me Jennifer would personally slit my throat. It hadn't worked out that way. We'd killed Abaddon and beaten his Karg-Jelk Super Fleet. We'd also captured Jennifer—she had indeed hated me with a particular fury. Abaddon had thoroughly corrupted her, as well as having elongated her body and speeded her reflexes.

These days, the Curator kept Jennifer in stasis, having promised me eight years ago that he'd try to cure her.

Well, the old boy had not kept up on his end of the bargain. I knew, because I came from time to time to check up on her. In some manner, Jennifer always sensed me, and it upset her because she began to squirm in her stasis sleep. But I'd come to talk to her anyway. The guilt at what I'd done would come upon me like the tide, stronger at some times than others. At high tide, the guilt became so strong that I had to slip in and see her again. I needed to tell her I was sorry for leaving her behind, for the umpteenth time. I needed to tell her that I was a worthless piece of shit—

Okay. I'm sorry about that. I try to keep this clean, or as clean as I can. And I've told myself countless times that negative talk wasn't going to help me fix this.

I'd failed my girl in the worst way at the worst possible time for her—

I shook my head.

I wasn't going to play the negative mental tapes anymore. Instead, I was going to do something positive like free Jennifer and let her live whatever life she could with whatever time she had left. Keeping her like sleeping beauty for the rest of existence was wrong, and I was finished wronging Jennifer.

I turned a corner and reached the door to her chamber. It was open, and it was dark in there, without even a glow from her sealed tube.

With a silent oath, I tore the blaster from my hip and moved through the hatch, flattening myself against the wall on the other side. I used my goggle-enhanced vision to scan.

None of the medical machines showed signs of activity. It seemed that someone had turned them off.

Was Jennifer dead or had someone kidnapped her? Had the kidnapper teleported away with her? Had I just missed them in the corridor?

With a sense of dread, I pushed off the wall, straining to sense something more. I reached the tube, and noticed that the far end was open.

Hurrying there, crouching, I saw the worst. Jennifer was gone.

-2-

For three days, I searched throughout the Fortress. I found no sign of Jennifer, no sign of forced entry onto the Fortress of Light. I went over the corridor with a special tracking device. It showed signs of me being there, but no one else.

I pondered the possibilities. I checked records. No one had left here except for me from time to time. Jennifer wasn't in stasis and wasn't anywhere inside the Fortress, well, anywhere that I could access.

The Curator had sensitive areas for his higher-grade functions. One of them was a unique viewing chamber that allowed him to see anywhere in the galaxy that his mind projected. I'd been in the chamber when we used it to hunt down Abaddon eight years ago.

Would the Curator allow Jennifer there? I seriously doubted it. He had said eight years ago that he wouldn't allow me access to her. Might he have woken her and put her somewhere I couldn't easily reach?

What about the teleporting sound? What about the creak in the floor?

Finally, I couldn't take it anymore. I had to know what had happened.

I marched through a brightly lit area toward the Curator's quarters. There were many strange portraits on the walls showing various alien life forms. In one of them was a painting of a stylistic Adam and Eve in a beautiful garden.

I wore the same metallic-like garment as before. It was as supple as spandex but harder than the bio-skin I'd worn as an assault trooper. I no longer had the circle of warm and breathable air surrounding my head. I simply inhaled the normal air of this area. I still had the blaster attached to my hip, with a special force blade on the other side.

I was a big guy, always had been. Back in the day as a Jelk Corporation assault trooper, I'd received a few modifications. The first had been forced injections of steroid 68. That had allowed me to pack on slabs of muscle until I looked like a beefy gorilla. My old friend Rollo had become even bigger, but I was big enough. The Corporation surgeons had also inserted neural fibers into me, quickening my physical response times.

"Creed," a voice said in the air. "Why are you here?"

That was the Curator's voice. It was rich and deep, as you'd expect it to be.

I halted and said, "I'd like to talk to you, sir."

"I'm busy. Come back some other time."

"I, ah, insist, sir."

For a moment, there was nothing. Finally, "Why are you here exactly?"

"Could I talk to you in person, sir? It will make more sense that way."

He sighed. "I sense your anxiety from here. What have you done wrong now, Creed?"

He hadn't needed to add the "now" to that. It made me bristle. "What have *you* done wrong?" I countered.

There was more silence. I usually spoke with the utmost courtesy to the Curator. There was a risk in doing otherwise, but I was upset and told myself I couldn't help it.

"Very well," he rumbled. "Turn left at the next corner and keep going. I'm in the Hall of Mirrors."

"Thank you, sir."

"We shall see," he said, ominously.

-3-

The Curator wore a long shimmering ice-blue robe that almost reached his perfectly manicured toes, which were supported by leathery sandals. Like the Michelangelo painting I'd mentioned earlier, he had long white hair, a massive white beard and the most dangerous blue eyes in the galaxy.

The old man gripped a dull-gray-colored metal staff. It was a deadly weapon when he wanted to use it as one and it was incredibly heavy, like Thor's mythical hammer.

As I walked toward him, I saw hundreds and then thousands of Curators. They all looked and moved alike. Soon, I saw thousands of Creeds heading through the aptly named Hall of Mirrors.

It was a creepy place if you let your mind wander. Back on Earth as a kid, I used to perch up on the bathroom counter and position the hinged mirrors just so. I would look down long corridors or rows at young Creeds staring into the endlessly long depths of doubled and redoubled reflections. I used to wonder if those Creeds were in different dimensions or worlds that I could enter if I knew the right way to go about it.

While in the Hall of Mirrors, those old ideas came rushing back with a vengeance.

I knew the Curator liked coming here to think. He'd told me so several years ago. Maybe he liked looking at the endless possibilities as I'd done as a kid. Maybe the reflections helped him in some other way.

The Curator was a million times smarter and wiser than me. He'd screwed over Abaddon back in the day, when the Devil-like First One had gone searching in other space-time continuums for who knew what. The old boy had trapped Abaddon out there in the Karg Dimension. It had been neatly done in my opinion, although the Curator had seemed to feel guilty about the action eight years ago when he'd told me about it.

That got me to wondering. Maybe the Curator had his own guilt to deal with. The last few years, we'd stopped talking as much. I think we'd both gotten sick of each other. The old boy didn't keep too many other people in the Fortress of Light. Maybe he was the solitary type and I'd gotten on his nerves with my extended stay. I'd helped him solve a host of problems he'd let pile up. Maybe with those fixes behind us, he no longer felt a need to humor me.

"Hello, sir," I said.

He turned to face me. So did thousands of other Curators.

"I'm surprised," he said. "Few have navigated the Hall of Mirrors as effortlessly as you've just done. How did you know which corridors and turns to take?"

I shrugged. "Just lucky, I guess."

He stared at me with those scary blue eyes.

Despite my best efforts, I felt words forced out of me. "You helped train me, remember? You gave me a greater than ordinary awareness."

His broad brow furrowed. "Oh," he said, as if he'd forgotten about that.

"Are you okay, sir?" I asked.

"Quite well," he said. "It is this place," he added. "When I'm here, I lose myself in ancient memories so I have a harder time focusing on the present."

I nodded, hoping he wasn't going to ramble on with one of his endless dissertations.

"Right," he said. "You wished to see me. You know I don't like people needlessly walking near my quarters."

By people, he meant me.

"This is important," I said.

"Humph," he said. "What you consider important and what I consider important are often two different things."

He was in one of his moods clearly. During the Abaddon affair, the Curator had been enjoyable to work with. After I'd become his Effectuator, I'd learned about his grumpy side. He could become cross and positively fairy-like. By that, I meant the fairies in the old stories, where the supernatural creatures were unpredictable, as willing to curse as to bless.

It was dangerous to anger the Curator at those times.

"You are going to bother me, aren't you?" he asked.

"I am, sir."

His eyes narrowed, and his breathing deepened. "I'm not in the mood, Creed. You had best leave while you're able."

I actually thought about it. I was readying my mind to give the impulses that would move the muscles that would turn me around and walk away. Then the guilt hit.

I'd left Jennifer behind with Abaddon, saving my own skin. Could I do that again?

I shook my head.

"Humph," the Curator said again, and he tapped the bottom end of his staff against the polished floor.

It sounded like a peal of doom. But instead of quailing, I got pissed. If this meant my death, okay, it meant my death.

"Jennifer is gone," I blurted.

"Eh?" he said, his bushy eyebrows lifting. "What do you mean by gone?"

"She's not in her tube."

"Well, of course she's not there. I released her."

"You did? When?"

"Here now. You're not in my employ to question me. If anyone does any questioning, it will be done by me of you. Besides, how do you know she's not in her tube? Have you gone into the chamber? I explicitly said you were forbidden to enter that area of the Fortress."

A hot retort rolled onto my tongue. I barely kept it from rolling off. This was the Curator and he was in one of his moods. This might be the time to use—

"Honesty," I said aloud.

"What's that?"

"Sir, the guilt for what I did to Jennifer became overwhelming—"

"Hold it right here," he said, interrupting. "Did you or did you not go into the chamber?"

"I did, sir."

"In other words, you disobeyed me."

"Yes," I said.

The big blue eyes swirled with anger. The huge hand clutching the staff tightened so the knuckles whitened. He tapped the end of the staff once more. This time, the peal made the polished floor shake.

"You have disobeyed me, Effectuator."

"I have already said it was because I couldn't stand the guilt."

"I am not interested in your excuses."

"Sir, if you'll just listen—"

He aimed the staff at me. It had an open end, showing a long hollow tube. I'd seen the staff open up one other time, and it had resulted in Abaddon's destruction.

I licked my lips. This wasn't going the way I wanted.

"I'm sorry, sir—"

"No," he said, interrupting again. "You are only sorry because you were caught."

"I wasn't caught. I just told you what I did."

"Only because you know that I can detect lies."

"Well, yeah—"

"Silence!" he thundered. "I am about to pronounce judgment against you."

"Okay. That's your right."

"I said silence!"

Something crazy swirled in his eyes. I could see he was going to do something rash, so I beat him to it. I grabbed the end of the staff and jerked hard. It was like moving a granite wall, but I shifted it just enough or maybe I ended up moving myself as a yellow ray beamed out of it. Instead of striking me, the ray bounced against a mirror and jumped to another. The yellow light reflected a thousand times in a second.

Suddenly, with a roar and a fantastic crash, thousands of mirrors shattered and blew shards of glass everywhere. It seemed to go on forever, although in reality, it ceased abruptly.

As the Curator looked around, his eyes shined with a feverish light.

"What have you done?" he said in a choked voice.

"Me?" I said. "You did it."

He fixed his gaze upon me. "You have destroyed the Hall of Mirrors."

"Ah, surely we can fix it."

"We?" he said. "*You* can do nothing of the sort. You are a destroyer, a killer, a—"

He ripped the end of his staff out of my grasp. "You are a menace, Effectuator. How will you pay for this monstrous damage?"

I looked around at the masses of shards glittering on the polished floor. I saw thousands of stands that had held the mirrors. I imagine this must have been a special kind of glass. Had the Creator fashioned the room?

I had an unusual reaction. My shoulders slumped. It must have been the guilt over Jennifer still lingering in me. Usually, I didn't sweat this kind of stuff.

"I'm sorry," I said in a forlorn voice. I shook my head, threw up my hands and let them drop to my side.

A change came over the Curator. Some of the anger seemed to drain from his eyes.

"I almost sent you to the…" His words trailed away. He shook his head, and he regarded me more closely. Then he tilted the staff toward me. "Grab hold," he said.

I did.

In a flash, we vanished, reappearing in a vast room with strange globes floating in midair and crystal pillars reflecting soft blue light.

"You can let go of the staff," he said.

I did.

He aimed the staff at a nearby globe, one three times the mass of a big man.

"Let me show you what happened with Jennifer," he said. "I admit to it having saddened me."

With growing trepidation, I looked up at the smooth globe.

-4-

I watched for a long time, as I saw a lot of stuff happening on a screen embedded within the globe. Jennifer was the center of most of the action. Some of the time, I actually heard audio.

She'd become a tall woman with what I'd call an evil beauty. She had hard, knowing eyes and long dark hair like a vampire queen. Had she colored her hair? I couldn't remember anymore, which made me sad. She had an elongated torso and legs and a leopard-like way of walking. What made it worse, or maybe better, was a butt to kill for.

Jennifer wore tight-fitting, purple garments and thigh-high hooker boots with heels and kept several weapons on her waist.

She seemed restless like a caged beast. Abaddon had twisted her mind into a devilish bent. Once, Jennifer had been the sweetest woman I'd known, kind, loving, considerate—

The scenes bit into my heart.

I saw her go under various rehabilitation machines. The Curator often appeared in those. Later, he guided her through a lovely forest, beside a lake and under a host of stars. He spoke to her about good things, obviously attempting to soothe her warped psyche.

As time passed, she changed, losing some of her stiffness. She even smiled shyly several times.

"How long has she been up and about?" I asked.

"Several months," the Curator said. "I actually thought she was getting better."

"Did she trick you?"

The Curator nodded. "She pretended to soften even as I believe she was plotting to escape."

The scenes continued to shift, and as I watched, I thought her tortured mind was settling down, easing into saner avenues of thought.

"I notice she never mentions me," I said. "Did you edit out those instances?"

"No."

"Did you find her lack of comments about me odd?"

"Of course," the Curator said. "At first, I believed she practiced subterfuge. Later, I thought she was trying to cure herself by never saying your name. Early on, I had her take profile tests. Every time she saw your photo, her blood pressure rose dramatically. Clearly, she loathed your very existence."

I glanced at the Curator. Had he meant that as a jibe at me?

"Watch closely," he said. "She begins asking probing questions. For the last several weeks, she's had a thirst to know everything. Again, in the beginning, I suspected her. Later, she seemed to genuinely be getting better. I believed she was trying to immerse herself in life so she could drown the awful memories of her time with Abaddon and you."

I watched. Jennifer asked the Curator questions the way a young kid would. Some of the scenes showed her in the Library at a reader, absorbing data like a sponge.

"Did you check her reading list?" I asked.

"Of course," he said. "She read volumes of galactic history, showing a marked interest in the Forerunner artifacts, the Jelks, the little killers—"

"Why not say humans?" I asked, bristling at the term.

"Because the volumes she read referred to your species as the little killers. She also read about the old days when the Plutonians fought the First Ones."

"Who?"

"The Plutonians," the Curator said.

"Who are they and what happened between them and the First Ones?"

The Curator studied me and finally shook his head. "It is a long sad story. I do not care to relate it, especially as it likely caused Jennifer's choice."

"Now I want to know about these Plutonians even more."

"I realize this. But since you cannot do anything about it—"

"Whoa, whoa, whoa," I said, interrupting. "What are you doing, dangling a challenge before me as if I'm a dog?"

"Effectuator, you must compose yourself. I have been doing you a favor by showing you all this. I know you care for Jennifer and care for Earth—"

"What do these images have to do with Earth?" I asked.

"You will stop interrupting me. I am the Curator. You are my Effectuator. There is balance in our statuses, a balance you upset when you interrupt."

"Okay. I get it. Don't interrupt you again." I waited a moment before saying, "Now, what do Jennifer, the Plutonians and Earth have in common?"

"You're a stubborn man. Stubbornness has aided you on many occasions. Here, it will only bring you grief."

I eyed him, finally nodding, turning back to the globe.

I watched Jennifer read, ask a few more questions, including about Plutonians, and listened to the globe go mute as the Curator obviously explained about them to her.

"All right," I said, looking up. "Now, you're baiting me."

I wasn't sure, but it seemed as if the corners of the Curator's lips twitched upward the slightest bit.

"Nonsense, Effectuator," he said.

"Is this about the Hall of Mirrors? Are you trying to get back at me for that?"

"Nonsense," he said again, turning back to watch the globe.

After a moment, I did, too, wondering if the Curator—

"Wait a minute," I said, snapping my fingers. "Jennifer affected you."

"What twaddle are you spouting?"

"Bad behavior corrupts good behavior. It seldom works in reverse. You've spent the last few months with her. In some manner, she's, oh, I don't know, turned you malicious, at least more malicious than is your wont."

"That's preposterous."

"She was trained by Abaddon. She became his assassin, right? Surely, there were—"

"Enough," the Curator said. "You spout idle, even foolish speculation. I have a good reason to keep quiet about the Plutonians. If that silence causes you some anguish—well, you did destroy the Hall of Mirrors with your impetuous act. I can find another punishment for that, if you wish."

I shook my head.

"Then watch," he said, aiming his staff at the globe. "This is what I want you to see."

I saw all right. Jennifer raced through the Fortress of Light until she crouched before a sealed hatch, using a small tool on it. With the tool, she managed to slip into a hangar bay, break into a spaceship, activate it and leave the Fortress through an outer bay door. I watched her vessel zoom away from the vast accretion disk that surrounded the massive black hole at Sagittarius A*.

Others noticed her, including the Ve-Ky with their Vip 92 attack ships. The aliens rose up with clouds of attack ships. Jennifer had chosen her craft well, however, as it vanished from sight. The 92s launched their electrical missiles, but didn't appear to hit anything. After a time, the Vip 92s turned and went back down into the accretion disk.

"She stole a stealth ship?" I asked.

"Indeed. It is a clone to your own Galactic Effectuator Vessel."

That was interesting. "Where did she go? Do you know?"

"Notice," he said, looking intently at the globe.

On the screen in the globe, the star field shifted. Jennifer's ship reappeared as it neared a giant donut-shaped Forerunner artifact with a black hole in its center.

"Is that the artifact Holgotha?" I asked.

"The same," the Curator said.

A little over eight years ago, the artificially intelligent Holgotha had been parked near the dwarf planet Ceres in the Solar System's Asteroid Belt. Such Forerunner artifacts had the ability to teleport long-distances.

The artifact and I hadn't parted on the best of terms eight years ago. I wondered if Jennifer knew that.

She parked the stealth ship near Holgotha, space walked onto the outer surface and made the trek to the ancient alien buildings on the inner ring. Was she immune to the radiation from the black hole? I watched as Jennifer phased through one of the buildings, disappearing from sight.

I turned to the Curator. "Did she talk to Holgotha?"

"You're not watching," the Curator chided me.

I turned back in time to see Holgotha vanish—teleporting away. The Forerunner artifact left Jennifer's stealth ship behind. If she'd parked the ship on the artifact, it would have teleported with it. We assault troopers turned Star Vikings had done just that with our ships back in the day.

"Where did Holgotha go?" I asked.

"Indeed," the Curator said. "That is curious. I do not yet know."

"You haven't looked for her or Holgotha from within your special viewing room?"

"I have, but I haven't found either of them yet."

"Where do you think Holgotha went?"

"To the Plutonians," the Curator said softly.

"Why there?"

"It is the one place I cannot look."

"You're kidding."

"I assure you, I'm not."

"Great. So where are the Plutonians that you can't see them?"

The Curator shook his head.

"Are the Plutonians in another dimension?" I asked. "As I recall, you couldn't see into Abaddon's former space-time continuum."

In lieu of an answer, the Curator stared at me.

That pissed me off. "Why are you showing me this, then, if you're not going to tell me what happened?"

His lips tightened, although he said, "I believe the Earth, maybe all humanity, is in terrible danger."

"Why is Earth in danger?" I asked, exasperated.

"Why? Because of you, Effectuator. Jennifer wishes to destroy what you love. It's my belief that after she's made you suffer, she will hunt you down and kill you in the most agonizing manner she can devise."

My gut clutched. "And you know this how?" I asked more quietly.

"By my contemplations in the Hall of Mirrors," he answered. "I replayed in my mind her various questions and responses. The conclusion seems obvious to me now."

It was my turn to stare at him. Finally, I asked, "What are you going to do about it?"

He shook his head. "*I* will do nothing."

"You're going to let humanity die?"

"Not necessarily, as Jennifer may not survive her encounter with the Plutonians."

"Why won't you do anything?" I demanded.

"My role as Curator has nothing to do with the battles at the fringe of the galaxy. Let the strong survive and the weak perish. It is the remorseless law of nature."

"But if these Plutonians are like Jelks, and don't belong in a lower civilizational zone—"

"See here, Effectuator. You must realize that I'm constrained by the dictates that govern my actions. I will have to give an account to the Creator one of these days. I want my hands clean. It's as simple as that."

"Let me go to Earth, then," I said. "Let me fix the situation."

He gave me a searching look. "No," he finally said. "I cannot. You are my Effectuator. My dictates govern the missions I can give you. Going after Jennifer to stop her from waking the Plutonians to destroy Earth and everything associated with it is not among my prerogatives. Do I make myself clear?"

"You're forbidding me from chasing her?"

"You are my Effectuator. You are to wait at the Fortress of Light until I assign you a proper mission as suited to my tasks. Besides, if you left here and raced through endless jump gates, it would take you over two years to cross the twenty-seven thousands light-years to Earth."

"The Moon Ship—"

"Is strictly off-limits to you on pain of death," the Curator said, sternly.

"So…you're telling me to twiddle my thumbs until my next assignment while Jennifer and these Plutonians destroy humanity?"

"I believe I have been clear on the subject. You must resign yourself to the probable fate that humanity is as good as dead."

"And that doesn't bother you?"

He gave me another searching look. "I am constrained, Effectuator. I have spoken."

"You know saving the human race from the Jelks and the Lokhars, and from Abaddon, was my abiding passion. Nothing else mattered compared to that."

"Jennifer stole some of Abaddon's DNA," the Curator said suddenly

"What?" I said. "What does that even mean?"

"She read volumes on creating clones from DNA samples."

"You mean bringing Abaddon back to life?"

"Hardly that," the Curator said, "but, I suppose, creating an army of Abaddon clones could now be within her power, or the Plutonians' power, in any case."

"That's…horrible."

"Hmm," the Curator said. "Have you seen enough?"

"Tell me about the Plutonians."

He shook his head. "I cannot. It is a forbidden topic. Now, I must leave. I have to repair the Hall of Mirrors. That is going to take considerable time and attention. Please do not interrupt me for the next several weeks, as I will be otherwise engaged."

"Uh…okay," I said.

"Grab hold of my staff. It's time I took you back to your quarters."

"Right," I said, giving him a questioning look.

The Curator ignored it, and soon, we vanished from the chamber.

-5-

I went to my quarters because the Curator had told me to.

I sat on my bed and thought about what I'd learned. Could the Curator have deliberately shot the yellow beam at me so he'd break the mirrors in the hall? That seemed preposterous. And yet, the meaningful looks, and the fact that he'd told me the name Plutonians even though he wasn't supposed to talk about them, told me something.

I was beginning to believe that the old boy *wanted* me to flee the Fortress of Light and race back to Earth. He obviously wanted to me to try to stop Jennifer and these Plutonians, as he surely knew me well enough to realize my reactions to certain news. It also made more sense now why I'd been able to slip past the safeguards keeping Jennifer off-limits.

The more I thought about it, the more I believed I was right. The Curator was a canny old man, and he'd been acting a little too foolishly lately. Yet, if I was wrong about this…

I rubbed my chin.

The Curator wanted to keep his nose clean. He wanted to be able to say he hadn't sent me to Earth.

I shook my head. Would such a stunt trick the Creator? I doubted it. But hey, we each had our foibles. None of us acted one hundred percent rationally. Abaddon had kicked over the traces and fought against the other First Ones long ago. If Abaddon was anything like the Devil in the Bible, not even he acted rationally. How rational was it to rebel against Omnipotence, to fight against the One who couldn't be beaten?

I'd say not very.

Well, anyway, the Curator seemed to have gone about this in a roundabout manner. Did the old boy hope I'd take the bait?

Yeah. I'd say he knew his Effectuator. Still, if the Curator had made these rules, I had to use my wits to do this right in order to keep my boss in the clear with his boss, or his own conscience, in any case.

Well, then, it was time to use my Effectuator skills to save Jennifer and defeat the Plutonians.

A thrill swept through me. I was going home. I felt almost giddy. What stopped the feeling was the realization that Jennifer had gone to these Plutonians. They likely lived in a different dimension, which was why the Curator's all-seeing-eye chamber couldn't reach them.

How could I find out about these Plutonians? I snapped my fingers. I clearly had some effectuating to do, some sneaking around and poking my nose—and my eyes—where they didn't belong. That meant I had to re-watch the globe showing me Jennifer's reading choices in the Library. Then, I had to break into the Library and read those items.

All that should prove easy enough for an Effectuator of my skills.

It was time to get started, because this mission was going to take a heck of a long time.

-6-

My eyes snapped open as a klaxon wailed in the distance. At the same time, a coffin-like lid slid open, exposing me to cold ship air and a nearby bulkhead.

What was going on?

Then I remembered. I'd gone into suspended animation—I glanced to the left at blinking red numbers. They helped focus my thinking.

Back on the Fortress of Light, I'd gone to the globe and watched carefully. Later, I'd broken into the Museum's Library, reading what I could find about Plutonians and First Ones. Afterward, I'd broken into various lockers, borrowing Effectuator equipment along with some special items. Lastly, I'd taken my goodies and gone to the hangar bay, choosing my Galactic Effectuator Vessel or GEV for short.

After leaving the Fortress of Light and passing through the protective force field, I'd been fair game for the Ve-Ky and other bloodthirsty aliens hot to break into the Curator's home.

Getting away clean, I'd set up an AI navigation controller. Finally, I'd lain down in the stasis tube for a long sleep. According to my GEV's chronometer, that had been a little over two years ago, Earth time.

With a groan, I sat up, causing life-support tubes to rustle all around me. I was naked, and it was freezing in here. The klaxon was making my headache worse than ever. I must have come out of stasis too fast.

Was I near Earth, then?

The klaxon continued shrieking, and suddenly, I'd had enough of it. I ripped off the life-support tubes attached to my body. That wasn't the right way to rehabilitate back to normal bodily functions after a two-year freeze. But the klaxon not only annoyed me, it said I'd run out of time and likely options, too.

I gathered my resolve even as it slammed home that I'd been out for two entire years inside an automated stealth ship, slipping through one FTL portal after another, straining to cross 27,000 light-years to reach Earth in time to save it.

The klaxon changed pitch to one of greater urgency. It took me a second to figure out what was going on as the headache spiked between my eyes. I knew that sound. Intruders had forced a breach into the stealth ship. That necessitated the intruders being able to *see* the GEV.

I clutched my head, squeezing it. Damn the headache and the noise.

I should be on the galactic fringe near the Solar System, one of the least technologically developed regions of the Milky Way Galaxy. Yet given that, how had such primitive sensing gear detected my GEV?

Several possibilities came to mind: Holgotha, a Jelk still running loose, one of Abaddon's surviving Kargs or maybe even Jennifer and her Plutonians.

With a groan, I climbed out of the stasis unit and moved to a locker. I donned my silver-colored, metallic-like uniform and slapped a blaster against one hip and a force blade against the other, shoving my feet into combat boots.

I moved out of the chamber, staggering unsteadily, but made it into a different room. I looked around and said, "Lights."

The chamber flickered on. I went to a screen as it began to activate.

For a moment, I saw my reflection in the screen. I had a heavy beard and mustache and long shaggy hair. The stasis wasn't perfect, it seemed. The hair made me seem like an old-time mountain man from American frontier times or a mini-me Curator. I'd have to shave the first chance I had.

The activated screen warranted my attention, as it showed three suited intruders with heavy caliber pulse rifles. They were moving down one of my empty ship corridors. The three were big, loping along like NBA stars, and wearing what looked like Lokhar suits and weapons.

That was interesting.

I manipulated the controls, changing the camera feed. Soon, I spied three Lokhar heavy cruisers. They were large triangular-shaped vessels I'd know anywhere. They surrounded the flickering stealth ship, each of the heavy cruisers projecting a green-colored tractor beam, holding my GEV like a fly in a pyrotechnic web.

I manipulated the panel some more, zooming for a close-up of one of the heavy cruisers. I swore when I recognized a purple symbol. Each heavy cruiser sported identical insignia. The three military craft belonged to the Purple Tamika, a political-religious-clan affiliation. The Purple used to run the Lokhar Empire, had run it until I'd slain Emperor Felix Rex Logos many years ago in a duel inside Holgotha. Orange Tamika had taken charge after that. The Orange had liked humanity and me. The Purple hated both of us.

Could the invading tigers know they'd stumbled onto me?

I called them tigers because Lokhars looked like giant, upright tigers. They were nasty aliens with a predatory mindset and a highly religious nature. Could Center Race aliens have contacted the Purple Tamika Lokhars and given them the tech to spot my ship? Were Center Race aliens breaking the rules and playing politics out here in the fringes? Or was this Jennifer's doing, or maybe even the Plutonians?

No, I doubted the last. I'd read a little about the Plutonians. They were so highly xenophobic they made the Kargs seem like church greeters. Thus, I doubted Plutonians had aided Lokhars in any way.

I turned the scan inward again. There were more Lokhars swarming aboard my ship. They were all suited and armed, space marines, if I remembered correctly.

How had the heavy cruisers spotted my stealth vessel? That was supposed to have been impossible.

I shook my head. The how didn't matter right now. What was I going to do about them?

My GEV wasn't a fighting ship, although it had a few armaments. It was big for one person, but nothing compared to the heavy cruisers. If the tigers aimed their ship weapons on my vessel, they should have no problem destroying it in time.

I let out my breath. Could I negotiate with the tigers?

That seemed like a bad idea given our history.

Did that mean I had to kill the Purple Tamika tigers, using Effectuator means?

I finally saw the reason why primitive Lokhar battle-tech had spotted my ship. One of my stealth generators had malfunctioned. The failsafe that was supposed to wake me in that event had also failed. *That* indicated Center Race alien manipulation of some sort.

I narrowed my eyes as I studied the intruders. They began to fan out throughout the ship.

Once the tigers knew they were dealing with old Commander Creed, they would no doubt view it as righteous karma, believing the Creator had given me into their hands so they could torture me to death. I could possibly use the flitter to escape. But that would mean the end of my plan to save Jennifer and the Earth.

I hadn't broken my oath and raced to the galactic fringe so a bunch of Purple Tamika tigers could get advanced core tech.

It was time to take care of business the way I'd learned to do working for the Curator.

-7-

I sprinted down a corridor and almost pulled a hamstring doing so.

But there was no more time to allow my muscles to warm up. I had to get the action started before the intruders reached the inner sanctum of my GEV and made it impossible for me.

In case any of you are tempted to feel sorry for the tigers, don't. The Purple Tamika Lokhars had come to Earth many years ago and nuked and bio-terminated 99 percent of the human race. One thing I'd learned since then, the universe was as brutal and ruthless as ocean life. The bigger, faster and more aggressive fish ate the smaller, slower and more easy-going fish.

If I turned soft and tried to do this any other way, the human race and my former lover would die. Now, I'm not inherently bloodthirsty, although some people might think so. If you leave me alone, I'll leave you alone. But if you try to exterminate my species, don't be surprised when I come out swinging next time you show up.

Did that mean I thought I was going to defeat these Lokhars?

I chuckled as I palm-opened a sealed hatch, stepped inside and locked it behind me. Lights snapped on, revealing a chamber tightly packed with high-tech gear.

I slid into a chair and began typing like crazy on a touchscreen, activating an unusual computer. This was state of the art, center of the galaxy tech. I donned a headset and leaned back, my thoughts now controlling the machine.

This was delicate work, as I didn't want to broadcast any discernable signals the tigers might intercept too soon.

It took precious time, but finally I began activating the *Killer Claw's* beam batteries. The heavy cruiser's big guns trained on one of the other Lokhar vessels.

A light on my panel blinked.

This was interesting. Someone on the *Killer Claw* was attempting to regain control of the heavy cruiser's beam weapons. Using the helmet, I double-checked the guns. They were warming up, radar locking onto Heavy Cruiser *Glorious Rage*.

Would you look at this? Someone over there had a brain. They were attempting to cut power to the cannons.

I ran through a Lokhar security check.

As I did, beams flashed from *Glorious Rage* and *Steel Fang*, hammering against the beam cannons of *Killer Claw*. That was damn fast work and fantastic targeting on such short notice.

Something else caught my attention. The cannons fired red rays. I did a fast check. Yup. Those were graviton beams, the same as the Kargs had used on their moth-ships. The Lokhars must have decided after we defeated the Karg-Jelk Super Fleet ten years ago to use the enemy's technology.

I couldn't worry about that now.

Using my headset, I abandoned the *Killer Claw's* graviton weapons. They weren't going to last long against such heavy and deadly fire at pointblank range. Instead, I gained control of the heavy cruiser's engine core computer. I found the self-destruct sequence, started it and melted any possibility of countermanding the order.

I shifted my concentration to the *Glorious Rage*, taking over its beaming cannons.

The primitive computer technology didn't have a chance of standing against me.

I changed the targeting parameters, added a butt-load of power and concentrated on Heavy Cruiser *Steel Fang*. Before anyone over there knew what was going on, heavy beams pounded against the *Steel Fang*, creating a hull breach in no time. I kept the beams hot, pouring through the opening. They smashed down interior bulkheads, swept through living quarters and life-support equipment and finally struck a stock of T-warheads. Nuclear explosives, in other words.

"Whoa," I said under my breath. I wasn't trying to commit suicide, just destroy their heavy cruisers.

I redirected the beams just in time, leaving the heated warheads alone.

If one of the tigers were smart, he'd contact me and threaten to blow all of us to kingdom come unless I stopped destroying their heavy cruisers. But nothing of the sort happened.

I could have shut off the tractor beams altogether, but surely someone would notice that. Instead, I retargeted the tractor beams, having them each latch onto another heavy cruiser. Adding power to the tractors beams, I had them pull each other closer.

Mine was the smaller vessel by several magnitudes. Plus, there had been three beams on one puny GEV. That had held my ship in place. Dragging each other closer was slow, hard work due to the heavy cruisers' greater mass. It might even overload the engines.

That would be okay as long as I wasn't still around.

I used the last tractor beam, switching polarity, turning it into a presser beam. That one gave my GEV a hard shove, moving me away from the doomed heavy cruisers.

After a fifteen second push, I changed polarity again and used it against a different heavy cruiser.

That was all I had time to do. I ripped off the headset, letting it drop to the deck.

Tigers had found the inner sanctum. I knew, because one of them used a portable beam weapon against the hatch, beginning to cut through in order to get to me.

This was about to get personal.

-8-

If I'd had time to prepare, I could have made this a simple job. I had weapons and exotic suits for regular Effectuator work. For eight long years, I'd gone on Intelligence-type missions for the Curator.

Would've, could've, should've. The Lokhars had caught me napping, literally.

I waited in the control room, letting the GEV drift farther away from the tractor-beam tugging heavy cruisers. All the while, a blue spark burned through to my side of the hatch. It must have been white-hot on their side as a pulse beam burned out a tiger-sized outline. Soon, one of them would kick the outlined shape down so they could storm in here.

That's what I was waiting for.

Finally, the blue spark reached the point where it had begun. I'd already stepped to the side. I counted to four—

Bam!

An armored tiger foot smashed the outlined section, causing the heavy metal to clang against the deck inside my chamber.

I shot the first tiger trying to rush in. He fell backward into the corridor. I pressed a tiny button on a grenade and pitched it through the outlined hole. A violent explosion and a heavy crump told me the grenade had succeeded. I heard armored tiger bodies thudding against the bulkheads and deck. One poor sod blew in through the outlined opening. His silver visor aimed in my direction as he landed prone on the deck.

I tapped the trigger on the disrupter. That burned through the visor and fried his head. Some of it leaked out as mush onto the deck.

I leaped over his body into the corridor. Most of the combat suits were shredded, and red, Lokhar blood poured from their wounds. I shot two of them who stirred.

Kindness didn't motivate me. I couldn't have cared less if they suffered. I just wanted them dead so I could get on with it.

If you're coming into this story on the tail end of things, you might believe I'm a homicidal maniac. I suppose if you've been along for the entire ride, you might think that, too. But it wasn't so. The Purple Tamika Lokhars were bad guys, bad tigers.

I didn't feel that way about the Orange Tamika. Some of my best friends were Orange Tamika tigers. But like I said earlier, the Purple Tamika tigers had attempted human genocide many years ago. They'd set the rules of engagement, and I had a long memory when it came to that.

I stalked the corridors of my ship, shooting the intruders. Soon, I made it to an equipment room. I donned a silver suit, activated the suit's force field and became the Angel of Death to the intruders. Earlier, a stray shot could have killed me. Now, none of them had a chance.

In short order, I cleared the GEV, saving one unconscious sub-commander and spacing the rest, who were already dead.

After securing him, I raced to the master controls. Luckily, the GEV had already slipped far enough away from the heavy cruisers. One of them had already blown, sending hull armor spinning against the others.

Now, the other two warships died violent deaths, blasting hard radiation, heat, shredded Lokhars, metal and all kinds of debris in all directions.

I'd already moved far enough away in the GEV that my ship was spared any damage.

A quick scan of the nearby stars showed me that I was deep inside the Lokhar Empire. That meant I still had hundreds of light-years to go before I reached Earth.

I didn't have time to think about that now. Instead, I donned a Zero-G work-suit and space-walked outside. I repaired the broken stealth generator. I had to bring a repair bot out to help me. Soon enough, we'd fixed it.

Other bots patched the hull breaches. Soon, I reactivated the stealth generators, rendering the ship invisible again.

It was time to talk to the Lokhar sub-commander in order to get a quick Intelligence report on the local scene.

-9-

Sub-commander Tal Feng was strapped into an interrogation chair with a harsh light shining in his eyes. The Lokhar space marine was a big old boy, a foot taller than I was and maybe weighing four hundred and fifty pounds of solid tiger bones, muscle and gristle. He had bloodshot eyes, singed fur on his torso and a bloody bandaging cloth around his left thigh.

I'd stripped him of everything but a pair of purple trunks. There was no need to interrogate him nude.

I'd given the sub-commander an injection earlier. Addling the subject's brain was much easier and more productive than torturing him for information.

I've never been a sadist. I wanted to learn things, not beat up on a defenseless Lokhar, even if he was a Purple Tamika bastard.

I pulled up a stool in front of him, settling into position.

"Hello Sub-commander," I said in the Lokhar tongue I'd learned long ago.

His head wobbled unsteadily as he tried to focus on me. The harsh light made it difficult but not impossible for him.

"You're a tough soldier, Tal Feng."

"You…?" he slurred, as recognition stirred in his squinting eyes.

I hadn't expected that. "Do you know who I am?" I asked.

"Yes…" he said. "You are the Evil One's imp."

"Wrong. Guess again."

It took him a serious effort at concentration. Finally, he nodded to himself. "You are Commander Creed."

"How do you know me?"

"All of Purple Tamika knows about the imp who slew the Maximum Princess Nee of Purple Tamika, the former Emperor's third daughter-wife."

I hadn't heard that name in a while. It brought back memories, some of them good, most of them bitter. The incident had happened during the same trip where I'd left Jennifer behind on the portal planet.

"That happened a long time ago," I said.

"The Evil One's imp drew a noisemaker and shot the Princess Nee in front of her guards and many adepts."

That wasn't exactly what had happened, well, Tal Feng hadn't included my reason for doing that. Haughty Princess Nee had boarded the dreadnaught in order to kill all the humans aboard and scotch the critical mission. I'd simply acted fast in enlightened self-interest. It had been my skin or hers, and I'd chosen hers.

"Tell me, Sub-commander," I said, "who rules the Lokhar Empire these days?"

"How can you not know?"

"Would I ask if I did?"

That seemed like a calculus problem for him. He frowned, finally saying, "The great Purple Tamika Emperor Daniel Lex Rex the Third rules our glorious empire."

That's how the interrogation began, questions and answers. Because of the injection I'd given him, the sub-commander no longer had independent will and had also become stupider. Through a torturous process, I learned that Daniel Lex Rex had led an insurrection against the Orange Tamika Emperor Sant. It had involved a vicious civil war. The Purple Tamika had won in the end, mostly because they'd nuked some key Orange Tamika worlds. Such genocidal bombardments went against the Lokhar code when fighting amongst themselves, but winning often absolved the winner of all past wrongs. There was a key side effect to the bombardments. The Purple Tamika tigers had to retroactively come up with a reason for their barbarism. It appears they told themselves they had to do that in order to rid the universe of Commander Creed and possibly the rest of the little killers as well.

Due to their newfound mission—in order to ease their consciences about the tiger-killing bombardments—the Lokhars had reunited the former Jade League. They had preached about the danger of letting the notorious little killers of legend become too strong. Before it was too late—the Purple Tamika Lokhars said—everyone needed to unite to put the little killers back into their cage of a pre-industrial world where they couldn't murder other races. It had worked, as the Jade League had reformed.

I questioned Tal Feng for over an hour. I learned that humanity had grown too quickly for the peace of mind of the other alien races.

The old Jelk Corporation worlds had held many human slaves. Once the Saurians departed for the old Jelk core worlds, the main Earth Fleet had raced in with Starkien help and liberated almost all the planets. Millions of freed humans had emigrated to Earth, so the homeworld teemed again.

Before Earth could consolidate its Confederation of Liberated Planets, the Jade League had struck with a large battle fleet. Three years ago, the two sides fought a bitter battle in the Altair System. The Jade League had taken heavier damage, but the Earth and the Starkien Fleets had each been smaller to begin with and had been whittled down to nubs.

There was an arms race afterward, with the Jade League out-building the humans and Starkiens.

After the Battle of Altair, the humans had relinquished their claims on about half of the former Jelk Corporation planets they'd tried to incorporate into the new Confederation.

Sub-commander Tal Feng didn't tell me all this the way I've told you. He told me in fits and starts, and by me having to ask the right questions.

I learned one other interesting thing. The Lokhar Emperor Daniel Lex Rex badly wanted me in person to pay for my crimes. He wanted to torture me on the Lokhar homeworld before a vast audience. Accordingly, he had sent an offer. The Terran Confederation could buy back many worlds and possibly peace if they turned me over to him.

None of the Purple Tamika Lokhars believed Prime Minster Diana's claim that I was no longer around.

"The humans say you left for the galactic core," Tal Feng slurred. He was getting sleepy and finding it hard to pronounce his words. "But we know that is a lie. The Creator lives at the core. He could never stand Commander Creed's wretched presence there."

"How can you say that?" I asked. "Ten years ago, Lokhars saw Creed on the Curator's Moon-ship."

"Those are lies," Tal Feng spit.

"It's historical fact," I said.

"The Orange Tamika said likewise, but—"

"Orange Tamika helped humanity defeat the Karg-Jelk Super Fleet," I said, interrupting. "Even you Purples have to know that's true. It was a glorious victory for all of us."

Tal Feng studied me with his squinting, bloodshot eyes. "The Kargs and Jelks weakened the Orange Tamika. The space devils attacked the Orange for their sins so Purple could rise again. The evidence speaks for itself."

"Only a bigot could say that."

"Lies," Tal Feng slurred. "You are Creed, the liar, the imp of the Evil One. The little killers must perish if we are to survive. So have the holy adepts spoken."

"Emperor Lex Rex is going to try to turn this into a holy war, is he?" I asked.

"Emperor *Daniel* Lex Red," Tal Feng snarled.

I eyed him, wondering if the Shi Feng, the old Lokhar secret guild of assassins, had been revived.

It might seem crazy that the Lokhars had reverted to their old ways so quickly after defeating the Karg-Jelk Super Fleet. Yet, history said that such was often the case after a long war. People, and possibly aliens, too, wanted to return to the old paths in order to feel secure again.

Whatever the case, this sounded like the worst possible time for Jennifer and Plutonians to show up to attack Earth. There was a greater war brewing, and it looked like the Lokhars already had all the advantages.

I was beginning to feel that I never should have left Earth. I might have been able to help Emperor Sant defeat this Daniel Lex Rex. Dianna should have thrown aid to Orange Tamika.

I know hardheaded politics says to stay out of other peoples' civil wars, but in this case, our interests were with Orange Tamika. Why hadn't Dianna made the smart play?

I shrugged.

I didn't know all the facts. I knew only a glimmer of them because of what I learned from Sub-commander Tal Feng.

I wondered about his last name. Did that have any relation to the Shi Feng?

"Listen," I said.

At that point, Tal Feng grinned at me in a nasty way. His eyes bulged outward, and with a groan, he strained against the straps holding him down. He hadn't tried that except at the very beginning.

"You won't break free now any more than you could then," I said.

In the end, I think he knew that, as he wasn't really trying to break free. I think he was trying to overstrain his heart.

I leaped up and raced for a med machine. If he wanted to die, I wanted to keep him alive. I suspected he possessed a truth he didn't want me to have.

Tal Feng made gurgling sounds as I shoved the machine to him. As I pulled out tubes, he shuddered and his legs kicked out.

I attached the machine to him anyway and tried to revive him, but I was too late. Sub-commander Tal Feng was dead, taking his secret with him.

How had he died so quickly? He must have had a way to force it. There hadn't been any poison capsules in his fangs, as I'd checked for that earlier. If he had killed himself, why had he waited so long to do it? Finally, what had he died to hide?

I doubted his sudden death had anything to do with the Shi Feng. I mean, he couldn't have read my mind that I was going to ask him about the Lokhar assassin's guild.

In the end, I spaced his corpse with the others. I decided I would deal with one problem at a time. First, I had to stop

Jennifer, possibly these Plutonians and then the Purple Tamika Emperor Daniel Lex Rex, roughly in that order.

-10-

As a Galactic Effectuator, I'd learned that there was always something to gum up the works, some new wrinkle or complication that I hadn't foreseen.

I debated plans and ideas. Finally, I returned to suspended animation. I had a month and a half of traveling and didn't feel like just sitting around doing nothing. A guy could go stir crazy spending a month and a half all by himself.

Anyway, I woke up in a stasis tube a week out from Earth. That meant I was right on schedule. I revived slowly this time and thus avoided any headaches and hamstring pulls.

I exercised, read various intercepts the AI had picked up during my month and a half and tried to get an understanding of the political ramifications of this new era—new to me, at least.

The Terrans and Starkiens had formed the Alliance against the larger Jade League.

I've spoken about the notorious Jelk Corporation before. The Jelk slavers had raided Earth throughout the centuries, kidnapping humans and resettling them on various planets. The Corporation had mainly relied upon an obedient slave race of Saurians to do their dirty work, but they'd used reeducated humans as well.

The Jelk Corporation was gone, of course. As I've said, the lizard-like Saurians had left the star systems near Earth and headed toward the old Jelk Corporation core worlds. They'd set up a Saurian Unification, warning other alien races to stay out of their territory.

The various intercepts verified the essence of Tal Feng's story.

I stayed invisible while traveling in the GEV, passing unnoticed through various star systems, using the jump gates to speed my way home.

The nearer I came to Earth, the more my heart raced. I couldn't believe how excited I was becoming. I felt like a kid. Couldn't this ship go any faster?

That caused me to wonder if I'd made a mistake by becoming the Galactic Effectuator. It had been interesting work, but I'd always felt something missing. The one time I'd been truly happy in my life was while leading Earth's assault troopers against everyone. That had been living, man.

I passed through the Alpha Centauri System, noticing the Starkien shark-shaped warships and the various defensive satellites. I wondered if Baba Gobo was still alive.

As I neared the jump gate that led to the Solar System, I picked up a troubling transmission from an Earth-ship that had exited the gate.

"We've been attacked," the comm officer told the Starkiens. "The Defense Fleet has been destroyed. We request aid in defending our star system in case the raiders should reappear and finish off our homeworld."

I almost took the GEV out of stealth mode to demand more information. *Finish off our homeworld* sounded ominous. Had Plutonians attacked?

I accelerated toward the gate. Despite my best effort to get here as fast as possible, it sounded like I might already be too late.

-11-

I cruised through battle debris drifting in the Moon-Earth region. Ever since I'd dropped out of the Alpha Centauri-Solar System jump gate, I'd been monitoring the situation.

I couldn't believe what I saw.

The debris field indicated a savage space battle had taken place. As far as I could see, there were no Earth-crewed vessels in evidence. Had aliens destroyed every ship of the Defense Fleet? Vast, irradiated scars showed where aliens had smashed the Moon's defensive systems, annihilating missile silos, launch pads and beam emplacements.

There was something even worse, though. The entire South American continent glowed with a harsh red color. I'd picked up intercepts. Everyone in South America was dead. All the fish in the ocean one hundred kilometers out from the South American shore were dead. Many people in Central America had sickened and died.

This was a disaster. It wasn't as bad as The Day, when Purple Tamika Lokhars had slaughtered 99 percent of humanity and killed all the plant life. But aliens had struck hard again. Had this been a warning from the Plutonians?

My heart burned with rage. I could hardly think straight. Had the Curator known this was going to happen?

As I sat in my pilot chair, I shook my head. Unanswered questions weren't going to help. I had to use my Effectuator skills. That realization helped calm me.

I continued, cruising invisibly through the horrific battle damage. The aliens had exploded every Defense Fleet vessel. What—

I sat up, studying my main monitor. I could hardly believe this. I saw a suited…android drifting in the debris.

I'd seen other suited figures. They had all been dead. The space-suited android didn't breathe, but he might have shut himself off. I might be able to revive him.

I used my scanner, studying the readings. The longer I did so, the more convinced I became that I was looking at N7.

That made sense. N7 would have stayed with humanity. By this time, he would have reached high command, likely a post in the Defense Fleet.

I maneuvered beside the slowly tumbling android. Using a special tractor beam, I locked onto him and gently tugged him toward the GEV. As he neared, a small hangar bay door opened. With the tractor beam, I pulled him through.

The bay door closed and I got up, hurrying to the space locker.

Soon enough, I used a utility robot to remove the helmet. It was N7 all right. I'd recognize the placid, choirboy features anywhere.

I couldn't believe it. I was grinning from ear to ear at seeing my old friend. Surely, I could reactivate him.

On my orders, the robot lifted N7 and followed me to a special chamber. There, the robot laid N7 on a special table.

I gazed upon my old friend. I could turn him on again and ask him what had happened, but at the last moment, I decided on a different approach. This approach entailed a brutal invasion of privacy, but I was dealing with possible human extinction and saving the woman I'd wronged, the woman I still loved.

I was still the Galactic Effectuator. Maybe I'd been doing this solo work too long. Guesswork had never gotten me as far as precision had. There was another thing. If I didn't have to, I didn't want to explain much about the Plutonians. That meant it would be better if I could figure these things out for myself first.

With my Curator-level tech equipment, I found the seal to N7's braincase. I hesitated, bent my head in thought, and finally gave the order. The robot opened the seal and hooked delicate equipment to the AI-like computer brain inside.

I steeled my heart, went to a special machine and began to manipulate it.

It took me a while. Finally, I managed to break into N7's programming and see exactly what had happened out there a short time ago.

-12-

The invading vessels created their own jump gate by tearing open the fabric of reality a little over two million kilometers from Luna Central.

From Earth's side, the first indication that something was wrong was a blast of neutrinos that appeared where nothing had been before. Seconds later, a brilliant oval shape grew into existence. The x-rays and gamma rays emanating from the shape caused watching orbital sensors to blare with alarm.

Shortly thereafter, N7 received orders from an orbital relay station. Without hesitation, the android led his squadron of battlejumpers from the other side of Earth, racing to meet the possible threat.

The squadron crossed the blue-green curvature of the planet in time to see the three enemy vessels exiting the hard-radiation-spewing portal. The android's first thought was that this was a feint, that the real attack would take place from a different direction, out of a different portal.

What could three small ships do, after all?

The gate—the oval shape—disappeared as the last alien vessel exited it, leaving no trace of its former existence. The three exotic ships were cruiser-class at best, each emitting bizarre sensor readings.

Admiral Max Harold—the Commander of the Defense Fleet—accelerated from his station around Luna. He led nine state-of-the-art battlejumpers. On an open channel, the admiral demanded the three craft to surrender immediately.

The vessels ignored him as they accelerated for Earth, jumping to an incredible velocity.

Harold and his captains made swift adjustments, the Luna-based battlejumpers racing on an intercept course for them.

From farther away, N7 brought his six battlejumpers toward the fray. It seemed like massive overkill against the far smaller alien vessels, but everyone was jumpy after the latest ultimatums from the Lokhar Empire.

The enemy vessels closed fast with Harold's nine bigger ships. From eight hundred thousand kilometers away, the alien vessels fired harsh particle beams. With pathetic ease, the beams smashed aside force fields and punched through hull armor.

N7 studied the sensor readings. This was inconceivable. The Karg moth-ships had used graviton beams, which were inferior to the alien particle beam.

The first of Admiral Harold's battlejumpers exploded like a grenade, sending hull-plating, interior decking, shattered fuel pods, waste, bio matter and other debris into a growing circumference.

What was going on here?

N7 ordered emergency acceleration. They had to combine forces and hit these three alien ships as one.

Luna Central went to highest alert, launching swarms of fighters, warming up improved laser batteries and readying ship-killing missiles. At the same time, Harold's remaining battlejumpers opened up with everything they had, launching T-missiles and pouring beam fire at the enemy.

Since there was nothing else he could do yet, N7 recorded the mayhem. The enemy vessels lacked force fields. That was most interesting. It should have meant an easy victory for the Defense Fleet. But the alien hull armor was unlike anything N7 had witnessed before. It was incredibly dense, and there was something intrinsic dampening the beam fire and nuclear detonations that reached the alien armor.

Harold's battlejumpers did damage, certainly, but only a miniscule amount and at an agonizingly slow rate.

More of the admiral's battlejumpers ignited, blowing off chunks of ship, while Luna Command fighters exploded like popcorn. The enemy vessels shrugged off the Moon-beamed laser fire as if it didn't exist.

Then, the alien vessels reached the Moon, bombarding the surface with raw energies, creating gouges of damage to deep, hardened silos.

Who were these aliens? Where had they acquired such devastating technologies? Could the Defense Fleet stop them?

A static-laced message blared from the bridge speaker. "Concentrate against the lead enemy vessel," Admiral Harold ordered. "We have to at least kill one of the alien ships."

The surviving fighters, the few remaining lunar laser batteries and the last of Harold's battlejumpers concentrated on the forward alien ship.

Before anything else happened, another of Harold's vessels simply blew apart, spewing water vapor, shards of ship materials and twisting crewmembers into space.

Then, the concentrated fire caused damage to the lead enemy ship. The readings—

N7 looked up at the main screen. Moon-based heavy lasers clawed past torn alien hull armor. That should—

The alien vessel went nova as fantastic energies exploded outward in a growing circle like a stone causing a ripple ring in a lake. The lethal destruction reached the nearest battlejumpers. Force fields vanished, and hull armor crumpled like tinfoil. Engines ignited as new explosions added to the alien frenzy.

"Sir," a sensor officer said to N7.

"I have noted the situation," the android said.

N7 knew the officer referred to the alien self-destruction wave. It had also harmed the remaining two enemy vessels following behind.

Why did the aliens insist their vessels explode with such annihilating force if they had taken too much battle damage?

N7 shrugged off the question for analysis later as his squadron closed with the terrible enemy.

The android had learned his trade from the legendary Commander Creed. N7 employed some of those cunning tactics and other tricks learned through countless military campaigns since. None of that mattered today, at least not enough to stop the enemy vessels. Yes, he destroyed one of the two remaining cruiser-class ships, and it self-destructed just as the first one had.

The titanic wave-blast destroyed two of N7's battlejumpers.

The last alien ship concentrated its hellish particle beams on his flagship. The ensuing explosion ripped apart the battlejumper, but not before N7 had donned space armor.

Due to vicious hull ruptures that sent the ship's interior atmosphere howling into space, the android shot through the crumpling vessel, tumbling end over end as heat and radiation washed over him. It hurt like blazes, but he survived the flagship's death.

Afterward, while spinning in the void, N7 had a catbird seat, as an ancient saying went, while the final battle against the alien ship took place.

The exotic vessel shot toward Earth with single-minded ferocity. At a near-orbital distance, the alien launched a frightful bombardment from its underbelly. The munitions screamed through the atmosphere and detonated in a frightful blast, causing an entire continent to shudder.

The bombardment cost the alien vessel, however, as Earth-based fighters roared from orbital launch points, swarming the extraterrestrial warship, hammering it with everything they had.

It went critical and exploded, and with its last wave-like detonation, it took out over two hundred and ninety space fighters.

At that point, the fight was over, but the suffering had just begun.

Over a million kilometers away, N7 was alive in his suit, after a fashion, but he had no way of contacting anyone. The blast and radiation had demolished his helmet radio.

Since he was an android, he shut down just before the air-tanks went empty. How long could he survive in the vacuum, though? Would anyone find him before Earth's gravity pulled him in and burned him up like a meteor?

-13-

After taking care of N7, I exited the GEV in my flitter, heading down into Earth's atmosphere. Soon, I raced over the Rocky Mountains in the former state of Colorado. The Day, decades ago, had ended America, Russia, England, all the old nations.

Over ten years ago, we'd had to restock Earth after cleaning up the toxic agents. Luckily, all things considered, the kidnappers of the Jelk Corporation had also stolen many Earth plants and animals, bringing them to alien planets. We'd gone to those places, picking up seeds and animals, replanting and restocking our home world.

The Rockies looked whole again, a vast woodland wilderness. But what if the latest aliens—most likely Plutonians—had bombarded North America instead of South? All this would be dead again just like what happened on The Day.

I was going to find these Plutonians. Then, they were going to learn why the rest of the universe called us the little killers.

Despite my rage, I obeyed the Earth Defense protocols, moving through a pre-selected air-route. By the orders given by Earth Control, it seemed clear that no one really believed that I'd returned from the Galactic Core.

That was okay. I hardly believed it myself. It was taking getting used to seeing the small number of stars visible in space out here. In the galaxy core, stars glittered everywhere you looked. It was crazy beautiful, like viewing a million shining gems at once.

I banked the flitter, taking it lower, heading toward New Denver. That was the Earth's capital, or where Diana the Amazon Queen was presently holding court. It turned out she'd held onto power all this time. What's more, she had ruled autocratically since the Battle of Altair.

From my study of human history, strong-armed rule seemed the most natural to the human psyche. We liked kings and queens—and we liked grumbling about them even more.

A ping from the controls told me I was under radar lock. That was fine, as I didn't think they'd fire.

I'd taken the Galactic Core equipment out of the flitter before launching. On all accounts, the Curator would not want humans getting hold of any tech higher than a Civilizational 6C Category. I was going to do my best to make sure I kept as many of the Curator's dictates as possible.

Besides, I had an Effectuator plan up my sleeve. After watching N7's memories, I'd listened to Earth communications for a time, getting a picture of what was going on down there. Down here, I mean.

Before leaving the GEV, I'd debated long and hard and had finally reprogrammed N7. Normally, previously, I would never have done that, but eight years of effectuating had left their mark on me.

I would likely need backup for my plan to work. I had to have someone I could trust, and I couldn't think of anyone better than N7, especially after the modifications to his brain core.

Soon, I landed in New Denver spaceport and walked out onto the tarmac to meet a herd of siren-wailing military hovers. The hovers grounded twenty feet from me, and armored marines spilled out of them. Every one of them aimed a pulse rifle at my chest.

A larger than average armor suit clomped toward me. I half expected Rollo to whirr down the visor. Instead, a hard-eyed man with green eyes stared at me.

"You don't look like Commander Creed," he finally said.

I don't know why he'd said that. I'd shaved the beard and the shaggy mustache, and I'd clipped my hair as best I could—and I didn't believe I'd aged much the past ten years. Maybe I was the legend to him, and someone in the flesh could never seem as grand as the heroic person of imagination.

"Should I know you?" I asked.

"I was an assault trooper once," he said. "These days, I'm General Briggs of the Terran Defense Force."

"That's why you're so big?"

He nodded. "Jelk Corporation thugs injected me with steroid 68 and inserted neural fibers in my muscles. I was with Commander Creed when we went to the Karg dimension in a Lokhar dreadnaught."

I gave General Briggs a careful scrutiny.

"No, you weren't," I said. "I'd remember your ugly mug if you'd gone. Not many assault troopers survived the portal planet."

The general's eyes narrowed as he studied me.

"I'll tell you what," I said. "If you strip off that tin-can of a suit, I'll beat the living crap out of you. That will prove you're no assault trooper."

"Hmm…" Briggs said. "Creed was arrogant."

"If you were an assault trooper, you'd be wearing the combat skin instead of the tin can."

"Okay," Briggs said. "Whoever you are, you're well briefed. I'll give you that. Now, hands up. We have to search you."

I did as requested.

Briggs motioned to a pair of MPs in regular dress. They searched me, and they didn't find anything interesting. They did take my .44 Magnum. I'd brought it along for old time's sake, and as a piece of authenticity.

"This could be the commander's old revolver," an MP told Briggs.

"Which means he might have killed the real Commander Creed," Briggs said. The general turned to me. "All right, get in the hover. We're taking you to interrogation."

"Take some x-rays of me first to make sure I'm not carrying a bomb in my body. Then take me to Diana. She'll

50

know it's me. In case you don't realize it yet, Earth is running out of time."

"Get in the hover," Briggs growled. "In case you don't realize it yet, we're running the show here, not you."

I eyed him before shrugging and headed for the hover he'd indicated.

-14-

The interrogation took five hours of relentless questions by a small man with a humped back. He was Police Proconsul Ike Spencer. The man had a neat little mustache and plastic seeming eyes like a shark.

While under my Effectuator AI-brain-probe, N7 had shown more emotion than this Ike Spencer did.

Finally, the Police Proconsul sat back. "I'm sorry," he said in a voice that indicated he wasn't sorry at all.

I raised my eyebrows, wondering what kind of crap he was going to pull now. So far, I'd kept my temper in check. Now, I felt it slipping.

Before I could tell him exactly what I thought about his techniques, he said, "I'm sorry. You are definitely Commander Creed. There's no doubt about it."

"Then, why are you sorry?"

The Police Proconsul grunted as he stood. "You'll find out soon enough, I'm afraid."

A hatch slid up behind me.

"It's Creed," Spencer said. "Tell the Prime Minister there's absolutely no doubt about it."

Clearly, the Police Proconsul wanted to keep something secret. I had a good idea what it was, but played dumb because of my plan.

An honor guard of suited marines entered the room.

"They'll take you to the Prime Minister," Spencer told me. "I'll join you shortly."

"Wonderful," I said.

The small Police Proconsul eyed me anew. "I haven't detected any advanced equipment on your person. That would belie your story about becoming a Galactic Effectuator."

"I haven't said anything about that." I said, in case the Curator had just started watching from his special viewing room in the Fortress of Light.

"I'm well aware you haven't," Spencer said. "But you told Ella about it at Saint Petersburg ten years ago. Do you remember the incident?"

"Absolutely not," I said. "Ella left before the…" I trailed off. Had Ella spied on me that day? It was hard to fathom. How had the Police Proconsul come to learn about my occupation otherwise? He was trying to trick me into giving away secret knowledge.

Obviously, he knew about the Curator. Ten years ago, the assault troopers had gone all over the galaxy in the Curator's teleporting Moon-ship. The others must have told stories afterward, but none of them had learned as much as I had during that time.

"Yes?" Spencer asked me.

"Nice try," I told him.

"You do not seem to understand the situation," he said. "The Prime Minister is under siege from many sides. She's guided Earth through these perilous times. We need her."

"I don't disagree with that."

"I am not a modest man, Commander—"

"It's just Creed these days," I said, interrupting.

Spencer nodded. "As you will. Neither of us is modest. Thus, I wish to tell you that I am one of the key reasons the Prime Minister has retained power against all comers."

"Oh?"

"Some say that Earth has become a police state. There might be some truth to that."

"Because of you?" I asked.

"Like you, Commander—Creed—I wish to see the human race survive. We won't if we're divided against ourselves."

"Okay…"

"The Prime Minister needs your help. Remember that, please."

"What are you trying to hint at?" I asked.

"She has hard decisions to make. With the last attack from out of the blue— Well. We can't afford to let the Lokhar Empire use our sudden weakness against us. There are many alien races that would like to see humanity eliminated."

"That's why I'm here, to help stop that."

Spencer eyed me anew and then nodded to the marine guards. "I shall see you in a few minutes. Please keep in mind that we are under a heavy burden. This latest attack is the last straw."

I turned to the marines. "Let's go. I'm tired of his pussyfooting."

"I'm sorry," Spencer said to my back.

"Yeah," I said. "You already told me. Come on," I told the marines. "Time's a-wasting."

-15-

Prime Minster Diana of Earth and the Terran Confederation of Liberated Planets had come a long way up in the world. Once, she'd ruled an alien freighter grounded on Earth's toxified surface, ruling through tough henchmen, a razor-sharp mind and a willingness for brutal decisions.

I doubted much had changed since then.

Despite the passage of time, Diana was still a tall woman, with wider hips than before, startlingly magnificent breasts and well-kept handsome features. She had long dark hair, maybe even more luxurious than before. She wore a long dress with a low-cut front to reveal much of her charms. She also wore glittering jewelry. There had always been a seductive way to her, especially her voice.

She used to liken herself to Diana the Huntress of Roman myths. The Greek name of the goddess had been Artemis, the sister to Apollo.

Personally, I would amend the analogy. I think Diana was more like the legendary Cleopatra of Egypt, the lady that had seduced Julius Caesar and later Mark Antony. Both women used their feminine charms and wiles to climb the ladder of power. Each possessed a razor intellect and a tough streak to do just about anything in order to keep power.

The marine guards ushered me into a spacious chamber with various maps on large tables. Room-sized statues stood around the high-domed chamber. They looked like old Greek statues, some of them missing arms.

More than anything, the chamber reminded me of pictures of Imperial England in the days of Queen Victoria. There was even a throne toward the back of the room, with a semi-circle of curule chairs facing the throne. I had no doubt that's where Diana sat during discussions or pronouncements.

Diana looked up from a map as the marines marched me toward her.

Several tough-looking guards were in various spots throughout the chamber. They were big men in red suits, again, akin to Imperial British guardsmen. I noticed that each of the guards had modern hand-weapons on his person.

General Briggs stood with Diana, wearing a tan army uniform. He was a large man, but Diana stood a little taller.

There was one other person with them, a petite woman with short blonde hair, wearing a long gown and less jewelry than Diana had. The petite woman struck me as the Prime Minister's personal secretary. She noticed me first, or looked up first and smiled.

It was dazzling enough to cause a stir in me. I didn't recognize her, but I knew the up and down look that she gave me.

The petite, possibly sexually hungry secretary nudged Diana.

Diana had to have noticed our entry. But she looked up now as if surprised. Her gaze went straight to me, locking tight and seemingly searching my soul.

"Creed," she breathed in her seductive way.

I found myself blinking, having forgotten the depth of strength to the Amazon Queen's particular power.

"Diana," I said, grinning with delight as I approached.

Diana held up her right hand, palm forward.

The marines halted, forcing me to halt.

"Wait by the door," she told them.

The marines turned around smartly, without hesitation, marching to the double doors, taking up station there and standing at attention.

As they moved away, the members of the red-suited security detail moved closer to Diana. She hardly seemed aware of them.

As an Effectuator, I was always aware of such details.

"Creed," Diana said again, beckoning me nearer.

It would never be her way to rush up to greet me with a warm hug. That wasn't how the most powerful woman on Earth should act, and she knew that.

I marched toward her, keeping my grin and cataloging the various reactions, hers and others, particularly the security detail. They watched me closely as if ready to draw and fire. They also watched Briggs like that, which I found telling.

Instead of embracing like old friends, Diana reached out and grabbed my hands. She held me at arms-length, studying me the way a mother might her son.

"Creed, Creed, Creed," she said. "You pick an odd time to show up again."

I shrugged.

"Come," she said. "I want to show you something."

She pulled me to the map table where General Briggs and the petite secretary stood.

"You've met the general," Diana said.

I nodded to him. Briggs gave a stiff nod back.

"Now—"

"I'm Creed," I said to the secretary.

She gave me another dazzling smile with plenty of teeth and promise in her eyes.

Diana had already looked down at the map. She looked up now, glancing at me and then her secretary and seemed annoyed.

"My personal secretary, Nancy Kress," Diana said.

"Nancy," I said, as if tasting her name.

"I've heard so much about you, Mr. Creed."

"It's just Creed," I told Nancy.

Her eyebrows arched up. "Creed…?"

"Just Creed," I said.

"There must be a story behind that," Nancy said impishly.

Diana cleared her throat.

Nancy blushed, which surprised me. She hadn't seemed the type.

"If I could have your attention for a minute, Creed," Diana said.

"Are you in a rush?" I asked.

"You can't just show up and begin flirting with my secretary when we have momentous decisions to make," Diana complained. "I know you noticed the battle debris around Earth while coming in."

"I saw it," I said.

"Where's your spaceship?" Briggs asked. "You can't have traveled all this way in the flitter."

I shrugged. Let them guess. The GEV was still in stealth mode, so no one could see it.

Diana gave me a searching look. "You're playing a part, Creed. It's obvious, and perplexing to me."

"Oh?" I asked.

"Now, see here," Briggs said.

"Later," Diana told the general cryptically.

Briggs shot me an angry scowl before nodding to her. It seemed to pain him, but the general closed his mouth and waited.

"He's well trained," I told Diana, deciding to needle Briggs a bit, see what it would show me.

"Yes, he is," Diana agreed.

I glanced at Briggs. The general seemed not to have heard the comment, but I knew he had. This man would react when he decided it would be in his best interest, not before. I cataloged him as possibly dangerous.

"Before we continue," Diana said. "I want you to look at this. Would you, please, Creed?"

She pointed at the table map.

I looked down at it. It was a stellar chart of the local region. The purple area must have been the Lokhar Empire. Blue showed Jade League territories. Red represented Terran Confederation star systems, while the Starkiens showed up in yellow. It surprised me to see that the baboons had spread out some.

"The problem is not just a matter of territory," Briggs said. "The relative armaments count for much more."

"He means warships," Diana said.

Police Proconsul Spencer took that moment to join us. He walked through the double doors in a scarlet uniform not much different from those of the security detail. The gunmen didn't tense as he approached the map table. Instead, one of them gave Spencer a quick signal with his eyes.

Did Diana know about that? She seemed oblivious, but that could have been an act.

"Creed," Diana said, as if Spencer's arrival was a signal. "Our Police Proconsul is much more than a clever secret policeman. He's become something of an authority on the inner workings of the galaxy core. For instance, because of him, we know you became the Curator's Galactic Effectuator."

I eyed Spencer. He pretended not to notice the scrutiny, looking intently at the map instead.

"Spencer has spoken to everyone who went to the Fortress of Light with you in the Moon-ship ten years ago," Diana said. "With a few, he did even more than speak."

"He interrogated?" I asked.

"I gathered information," Spencer said, without looking up.

The little man thought pretty highly of himself. I almost got the feeling he'd coached Diana in this performance.

"We know the Center Aliens think of us as the little killers," Diana said. "We don't know much about why, or what the phrase means to them. We know Abaddon died ten years ago and that Jennifer went to the Fortress of Light with you."

"Diana, you do remember me briefing you all about that, right?" I asked. "I made a report about my time on the Fortress of Light before I quit the assault troopers ten years ago."

"You left some things out of your report," she said.

"Damn little," I said.

The Prime Minister stamped a foot. "In case you've forgotten, we know the galaxy is divided into civilizational zones. We know about the Ve-Ky and others. We've worked hard to gather all the advanced technology we can. It's one of the reasons why we've been holding our own against the more populous Jade League."

"Noted," I said.

"I have to ask you, have you come back in the capacity of the Galactic Effectuator?"

"Where did you ever hear about such a thing?" I asked.

"If you're not the Effectuator on official business," she said, "that will change how we deal with you."

"Why bother hinting, Diana? Tell it to me straight."

"If you can't help us as the Effectuator, we're going to have to help ourselves."

"Why do you think I'm here?" I asked. "To help Earth."

"If you're not the official Effectuator, how can you help us?"

I stared at her, trying to decide what she knew about an Effectuator. She could be pretending to know more than she did in order to get me to drop my guard and talk about it. My gut told me she'd learned about the title, Galactic Effectuator, but little beyond that."

"What do you know about the alien ship that bombarded South America?" I asked.

Diana hesitated before saying, "Precious little."

"She means we know *nothing* about it or them," Police Proconsul Spencer said.

Diana gave the small man a cool glance, the kind that said he should shut up already.

"I say that in the interest of time," Spencer told her.

Diana stared at him a little longer and finally threw her hands in the air. "Do you know anything about these aliens?" she asked me.

"Maybe," I said.

"No, Creed," she said. "Don't be coy. If you know something—"

"Listen," I said. "It's not that easy. I want to help in every way I can. You must know that."

"The old Creed would help," she said. "I know *that*."

"I'm the same man you always knew."

Diana shook her head. "I don't think so. The old Creed was impulsive. You haven't done anything impulsive yet."

"No?" I said, glancing at Nancy.

"That's another thing," Diana said. "When did Creed ever flirt with the girls?"

Diana had a point. Eight years as Galactic Effectuator and countless Intelligence missions might have changed me in ways I hadn't recognized. It was possible I wasn't as rash or as reckless as before.

"About all we know for sure," Spencer told me, "is that the three alien vessels possessed advanced technology."

"*Highly* advanced technology," Diana amended. "The ships lacked force fields, for one thing, and yet they shrugged off our beams. Would you like to see battle footage?"

I shook my head.

Diana and Spencer traded covert glances.

"You seem to know something about these aliens, Creed," Spencer said. "We're desperate to know more so we can make an effective strategy against them."

I drummed my fingers on the map table. What *should* I tell them?

I cleared my throat. "I've, ah, been on a long research mission these past ten years," I said.

"Did you get kicked out of the galaxy core?" Diana asked.

I stared at her. "Let's just say I happened to come upon some ancient galactic lore."

"Does the lore include data on the aliens that attacked South America?" she asked.

"I think so."

"Who are they?"

I nodded and began to talk.

-16-

"I don't precisely know who attacked Earth," I began. "But I believe they're called Plutonians."

"They're from Pluto?" General Briggs blurted in astonishment.

"No," I said, "from the land of the Lord of Hades."

"Are you saying the aliens have a connection with Abaddon?" Diana asked.

"That," I said, pointing at her, "but probably not in the way you think. Hades is one of our words for Hell. Abaddon is a name for the Devil."

"Come now," Spencer said. "You're not invoking Bronze Age sky gods, are you?"

"I fought Abaddon," I said. "I've lived…" I almost said, *I've lived in the center of the galaxy.*

"You were going to say?" Diana asked, looking at me closely.

I shook my head, telling Spencer, "I'm invoking nothing, I'm just telling you—oh, forget it."

I paused to recollect my thoughts. Why bother letting Spencer get under my skin? That's what he was trying to do. He was a professional spook, after all. One of the best ways to get a man to say too much was to get him upset and preferably angry.

Diana shot Spencer a hard look. The Police Proconsul spread his hands in an apologetic way. I could imagine what silently passed between them. *Cut that out. Don't do or say anything that will stop Creed from talking. We have to keep him talking.*

"We know Abaddon once found a way into another space-time continuum," I said. "Ten years ago, the Curator told us that Abaddon was a First One. The First Ones were powerful humanoids with uncanny abilities or powers like comic-book super heroes."

I turned to Spencer.

"Is that easier to accept than gods and devils?" I asked.

The Police Proconsul shrugged noncommittally.

"Whatever First Ones could do," I continued, "they weren't the only ones with powers or the ability to conjure themselves some. Sometime in the distant past arrived, evolved, were created—take your pick—the Plutonians. From my research, I learned that the Plutonians fought the First Ones. Does that mean they fought Abaddon? I don't know, but I don't think so. I think Abaddon had already lost himself in the Karg Dimension.

"Be that as it may," I said, "the war between the First Ones and the Plutonians lasted a long time. It did a lot of damage, but plenty of cool techs were invented as the two sides warred against each other. The Plutonians had the technological edge, I believe, but that failed against whatever advantages the First Ones possessed."

"You don't know what those advantages were?" Diana asked me.

I shook my head.

"Please," she said, "continue. This is fascinating."

I took a breath and plowed ahead.

"However long the war lasted, the First Ones finally and utterly defeated the Plutonians. For reasons I cannot fathom, the chief First Ones didn't want to exterminate the Plutonians. By this time, it was clear that the Plutonians were xenophobic to an intense degree. The First Ones might have debated the issue among themselves. I don't know. Finally, though, someone suggested they do to the Plutonians what Abaddon had done to himself."

"Stick the Plutonians in another dimension?" Spencer asked.

"Essentially," I said. "But the First Ones had learned from Abaddon's mistake. None of them wanted to open a way into another dimension. Who knew what they would find on the other side? It was too risky, they believed. So, the greatest First Ones used the best science as developed by the Plutonians and carved out a pocket universe connected to our space-time continuum."

"What is a pocket universe?" Diana asked.

"Exactly what it sounds like," I said. "The First Ones fashioned a small area the size of a star system. They stocked the pocket universe with a star, some planets, and put the sleeping or suspended-animation Plutonians there. Finally, they sealed up the pocket universe and washed their hands of them, congratulating themselves on ridding the universe of a dangerous menace and yet keeping their hands clean from genocide."

"If the Plutonians were that dangerous to the First Ones, why would killing all of them matter?" Diana asked.

I smiled. "You, my dear, think like a little killer."

She eyed me. "Did someone tell you that once?"

I nodded.

"Was it the Curator?" Spencer asked.

I shrugged.

"Quit probing," Diana told the Police Proconsul. "Let him finish."

"As you wish," Spencer said.

I wondered if that was an act, a form of good cop, bad cop.

"According to what I've learned," I said, "the Plutonians have slept in their pocket universe for eons."

I looked around the map table, waiting for one of them to ask how I'd learned all this.

None of them did.

I'd learned all this in the Library on the Fortress of Light by reading the same books Jennifer had perused. The rest of what I was going to tell them was merely educated guesswork.

"Someone has broken through to the Plutonians, to the pocket universe," I said. "The person wishes to revive them. The attack against Earth would lend weight to the idea that they succeeded in their effort."

"Prime Minister," Spencer said.

Diana was frowning, staring at the Police Proconsul and then me. Finally, she nodded.

Spencer cleared his throat. "This is an interesting revelation. The Plutonians, presumably, have access to ancient technologies?"

"The ships created their own jump gate," I said.

Spencer nodded. "These ancient technologies are from the time of the First Ones?"

"That seems likely," I said.

"Mmm-hmm," Spencer said. "One point troubles me."

I waited for it.

"Who is this person that risked entering a pocket universe to awaken hyper-xenophobic Plutonians? More to the point, why would they attempt to convince the Plutonians to target Earth and to do it right away?"

"*Jennifer* went to the Plutonians," Diana said suddenly

"Yes," Spencer said, eyeing me. "She still hates you, doesn't she?"

I nodded slightly.

"It's all coming together," Diana said. "There's only one place Jennifer could have learned about the Plutonians: the Fortress of Light."

"If that's so," Spencer said, "you're obviously the Effectuator. Why otherwise would you be in the Fortress of Light with her?"

"Look," I said. "Only one thing matters. We have to go to the pocket universe and—"

"Creed!" Diana said, interrupting me. "That's out of the question. Three Plutonian cruisers destroyed *five times* their number of battlejumpers and the Luna Defenses. They also wiped out a continent. We'd need more than the Alliance Fleet, never mind having to find a way into the pocket universe—" She stopped abruptly. "Just how are we supposed to reach this realm, anyway?"

"There's a planet called Acheron," I said, "a venerated place, rich in horrific legends."

"Just a minute," Diana said. "You're not suggesting we visit there, are you?"

"No."

"Oh?" she said.

"I'm going to visit Acheron," I said. "You're going to loan me several battlejumpers, along with selected crews."

"I see. And just where is this legendary Acheron?"

I glanced at her, Spencer, General Briggs and finally the sexy little secretary. "Several hundred light-years away," I said.

"And?" Diana said. "You may have been gone ten years, but I can still tell when you're leaving something out."

I shrugged. "It's in the Lokhar Empire."

"I knew it," Diana said. "Where in the empire?"

"The middle," I admitted.

"And you want to lead a Viking raid there, just like old times."

"We have to," I said. "Look. There are harsh penalties for introducing higher-level tech to a lower civilizational zone. But if the highly advanced tech happens to be lying around on a planet in the lower-level zone…that's technically okay."

"What level tech are we talking about?" Diana asked.

"First One," I said. "We're going to need it to generate a dimensional portal."

"Oh," Diana said, "is that all?"

"No. We need First One combat tech, too. That way, our ships will have a fighting chance."

"And these techs are definitely on Acheron?" Diana asked.

"I have good reason to believe that what we need is deep underground in time-vaults."

"It's simple then," Diana said, sarcastically.

"Not quite. There's, ah, a guardian. I'll need…seven battlejumpers."

"*Seven*. Right. That will be no problem. We'll just slip in, out and around the Lokhar Empire with seven battlejumpers. No, Creed. That's out of the question."

"I'm sorry you feel you that way."

"Has it escaped your attention that we're under siege? We can't afford to release and possibly lose seven battlejumpers."

"One might do," I said. "I'll need a handpicked crew, though."

"Your old team?" she asked, sarcastically.

"That sounds good."

Diana looked away. "Is that the best you can do?"

I sensed a shift in her, and not for the better. "Prime Minister, I've come a long way to help. It's taken me over two years to get here. This is a good idea. Now, I have a few tricks up my—"

"Guards!" Diana shouted.

The marine guards were startled out of their parade ground rest as they hurried toward her, even as the security detail closed in around me.

"Secure him," Diana said.

The marines and the security detail came toward me warily. I wondered what they'd heard about me to act this way.

"Why are you doing this?" I asked Diana, while allowing the marines to cuff my wrists behind my back. "Is this payback for the first time we met when I took over aboard your freighter?"

"Call him," Diana told Spencer.

The Police Proconsul hesitated, finally asking, "Are you sure this is wise?"

Diana glanced at me before answering Spencer. "I don't see that we have a choice. Call the Lokhar Ambassador. Let's see if he's still willing to make the deal."

-17-

If I hadn't interrogated Sub-commander Tal Feng a month and a half ago, this might have come as a rude surprise. I still didn't like it, but at least I understood what was happening.

Diana sat in her Queen Victoria-style throne, fluffing out her dress. The security detail rearranged the curule chairs. Spencer sat on her right, with Secretary Nancy Kress beside him. General Briggs sat on Diana's left, with another officer I didn't know beside him. The marines in their battle-armor lined up behind Diana against the wall. The red-suited security detail took up station among the map tables.

I stood to the side of Briggs, with a battle-suited marine lieutenant beside me. My wrists were still shackled behind my back. Fortunately, I often stretched before working out, so my shoulders weren't as strained or as stiff as they could have been. I waited silently, wondering how this would go.

"Creed," Diana said once, leaning toward me. "I'm...I'm sorry. I wish you'd come to us as the Galactic Effectuator. I wish the Curator had given you leave to really help us against these Plutonians. It isn't right that Jennifer is trying to hurt you by destroying us."

"You should reconsider," I said. "My idea is a good one. It will work."

"*Are* you the Galactic Effectuator?" she asked, sharply.

"No," I said.

Diana frowned, straightened and finally asked Spencer what was taking the ambassador so long.

Fifteen minutes later, a marine opened the double doors and said in a loud voice, "Ambassador Gin Loris of the Lokhar Empire, the personal representative of the mighty Emperor Daniel Lex Rex of Purple Tamika and the Count of Tepis III."

Several large Lokhars in ceremonial combat gear clattered as they stomped into the chamber. They wore bronze plate-armor and carried ancient spears and shields. They were huge specimens, bulging with muscles under their tawny tiger fur.

A slender shifty-looking Lokhar entered next. He wore a flowing purple gown, a complex purple hat and square-shaped purple-tinted sunglasses. He reminded me of pictures I'd seen as a kid, showing some of the hippies that had gone to Woodstock.

The Ambassador entered last, Count Gin Loris of Purple Tamika. He was a fat sucker, waddling into the chamber wearing a vast tent of a purple gown. The tiger wore costly rings that glittered on his furry fingers and he had a puffy face, with fat enfolding his eyes and giving him the appearance of squinting all the time.

The ceremonial tigers spread out in a line before the throne. The hippy Lokhar with the square-shaped shades halted a comfortable distance behind them and directly in front of Diana. Count Gin Loris waddled up behind the hippy, putting his left paw on the tiger's shoulder. The hippy tiger tilted just a bit, letting me know that the count rested some real weight on the shoulder.

"This is a late hour for an official meeting," Count Loris complained. He had a deep voice and spoke English with hardly an accent.

"We're happy to see you, Count," Diana said. "You are gracious to have accepted our invitation on such short notice."

"Yes, yes," Loris said dismissively. "Your communication said this involved Commander Creed."

Diana paled. That was a nice touch, and I appreciated it.

"I'm Creed, fat boy," I said, speaking up.

The ceremonial tigers stiffened—a few of them more than the others. I wondered what that meant. The hippy tiger's head swiveled so he seemed to regard me through his tinted shades. Count Loris did not acknowledge my presence or my comment.

"You have told us for quite some time," Count Loris said, "that Creed was nowhere to be found on Earth. Can it be that you've finally found the commander after all this time?"

"The commander has just arrived home after a long absence," Diana said.

"Ah," Loris said, as if everyone knew that was a lie.

"We have debated among ourselves concerning your Emperor's proposal," Diana added.

"Indeed," Loris said. "Then you wish for peace among our two peoples?"

"We wish for peace," Diana said, sounding tired.

Count Loris finally looked at me. I didn't like him. I didn't like any of his company, but that was no surprise.

"If we can authenticate the criminal's identity," Loris said, "and if that is indeed the notorious Commander Creed, in full use of his mental capabilities—"

Count Loris took his paw from the hippy tiger's shoulder and rubbed his hands together. "Is that Creed?"

"I'll tell you what," I said. "Have the Prime Minister remove these shackles and I'll kill your toughest warrior, guaranteed. Then, you'll know it's me, fat boy."

The ceremonially armed Lokhars grumbled angrily as they glared at me.

"Silence," the hippy tiger said in a high-pitched voice.

The ceremonially armed tigers stiffened, falling silent.

"He certainly acts like Creed," Count Loris said. "However, we will need full authentication before we can proceed."

"And if we can prove to your satisfaction that this is Commander Creed?" Diana asked.

"Will you give him into our custody?" Loris asked.

Dianna hesitated before nodding.

"Then, if he proves to be Commander Creed we can sign a peace accord," Count Loris said. "You have seen that I have full authority to do so."

"I have seen," Diana said. "But I have another request to add, as a precondition."

Count Loris stared at her. "Name it," he finally said.

"You're aware of the latest attack against Earth?" Diana asked.

Loris dipped his head.

"The aliens…" Diana trailed off. "We desire twenty Lokhar heavy cruisers."

"I see," Loris said. "You realize that that is far too much to ask of us."

"I realize no such thing," Diana said. "Twenty heavy cruisers. I trust the Emperor's word, certainly. If he is twenty heavy cruisers weaker and I am twenty stronger, that will help me trust his word even more."

"Ah," Loris said. "Well, when you put it like that…"

"Unless, of course," Diana said, "you lack the authority to make such a decision."

"I have the authority," Count Loris said flatly. "I will debate policy with my team tonight. You will have my answer in the morning."

"I understand," Diana said.

Count Loris glanced at me, nodding several times before regarding Diana again. "You must ensure Commander Creed does not escape you nor commit suicide while in your custody."

"He will enter a high security cell as soon as we're finished here," Diana said. "Rest assured, the commander will be waiting for you in the morning."

"Excellent," Loris purred. "Yes, most excellent." He paused. "You are making a wise choice, Prime Minister. The Emperor has sworn to make Commander Creed pay for his monstrous crimes against Purple Tamika. He has sworn to do so upon the homeworld before all the notables of the empire. After tomorrow, if my team agrees to your…request, you will find a newfound friend in Emperor Daniel Lex Rex."

"Good," Diana managed to say.

"Until tomorrow," Count Loris said.

"Until tomorrow," Diana whispered.

-18-

After Ambassador Loris left, Diana fled the chamber before I could say anything to her.

"It looks like I'm a valuable commodity," I told Briggs.

The general wouldn't look at me. He left a moment later, taking the other officer and Nancy with him.

Police Proconsul Spencer stood, taking his time to adjust his suit, and finally approached me. "Do you have anything to add, perhaps?"

"I protest against such treacherous treatment," I said.

"We both know that isn't what I meant. Are you the Curator's Effectuator? If you are, that will automatically change your status among us."

"Where did you ever hear about such a thing as an Effectuator?"

"We're serious about this, Commander."

"How many times do I have to tell you that it's just Creed?"

"Earth must have peace," Spencer said. "We can't fight the Jade League and the Plutonians at the same time."

"Let's be serious for a minute," I said. "You can't successfully fight the Jade League or the Plutonians *one* at a time."

Spencer stared at me.

"Do you believe the Lokhar Emperor will keep his word?" I asked.

"For a time," Spencer said.

"Long enough for the Plutonians to defeat Earth?" I asked.

Spencer raised an eyebrow. "Tell me about Acheron, the planet with First One tech."

"I'll take you there," I said, "but I won't tell you where it is while I'm a prisoner."

"Do you love humanity more or do you love your skin more?"

"That's not it," I said. "The knowledge won't help you without me. But if you have the knowledge, you might trade it to the Lokhars for another transitory advantage. I can't allow that."

"There's another option," Spencer said. "We could go to Acheron later."

"I already told you. Without me, Acheron is worse than useless to you. The guardian will destroy whatever you send."

"Because you're the Effectuator, and only you have the special tools to defeat the guardian?"

I said nothing.

"We don't *want* to make the trade," Spencer said.

"Then don't."

"But we have a greater obligation than just to our consciences. We will do whatever we must to keep the human race alive."

"I believe you," I said. "Thus, I forgive you for doing this."

Spencer's eyes narrowed. "You're taking this much too lightly. Our giving you to the Lokhars is a real possibility."

"Look. I get it. You're trying to pressure me. But I'm not the Effectuator, so pressuring me is pointless."

"After here, I'm taking you to our securest prison."

"Do what you gotta, pal."

He studied me for a time, and I wondered what he was thinking. "I see," he finally said. "You're really going to force our hand."

I said nothing, because he had hit far too close to the truth, but maybe not in the way he thought.

"You won't escape the prison," he said.

I said nothing.

"Ella Timoshenko is not going to come to your rescue."

I turned my head, looking elsewhere.

"First Admiral Rollo is a broken reed," Spencer informed me. "These days, he enters a fighting cage for money. Don't expect any help from him."

"I won't and don't," I said softly.

"N7 is dead," Spencer said, "slain during the Plutonian raid. Dmitri Rostov died ten years ago, killed by Abaddon. You're alone, Creed."

"No," I said. "You're alone, and you're spitting in the face of the one person who came to help you."

He searched my eyes, and I could see he was a crafty man. That was good. I also saw that he was a highly ambitious man. That…might not be so good.

"Guards," Spencer said, while turning away. "Escort the gentleman to the Rat's Nest. Put him in Solitary Cell Z/Z, and tell the warden to keep a constant watch on him. It's the warden's hide if Creed dies or goes missing before tomorrow morning."

The guards hurried to me.

"This is your last chance," Spencer told me.

"I'm not going to lie to you and tell you that I'm someone I'm not," I said. "But I still think your best chance is to work with me."

The small Police Proconsul sighed, shaking his head and walking away. I was glad he did. The pretense, on my part, was becoming taxing, and I had a lot of work to do tonight.

-19-

The Rat's Nest was a deep underground facility several kilometers from the main Government House. The Ambassador's quarters were between the two places, which was important for what I had in mind.

The Curator had forbidden me to interfere here. Yet, he'd shown me Jennifer and told me about the Plutonians, giving me just enough information to set me on the trail. When the Curator really didn't want me to do something, he kept quiet about the issue.

Was I dead certain the Curator wanted me to do this? No. But I'd learned a long time ago to go with my gut. I'd known a month and a half ago about the Emperor's offer. I'd also learned about the Ambassador's presence on Earth before I'd landed.

I hadn't known Diana was going to hand me over to the Lokhars, but I'd figured that might be a possibility. Instead of feeling sorry for myself while Diana made the offer and sulking as the marines brought me down to my cell, I'd been formulating my plan. A lot of that plan was going to depend on how well N7 had incorporated my modifications to his AI brain.

I sat back on the cot in my cell, putting my hands behind my head.

The cell was deep underground, had several video feeds focused on me and several guards sitting at a table, keeping an eye on me as they played cards. Along with the guards was a bank of controls. Their area was spacious, mine rather cramped, with bars between us.

Each of the guards had a stun gun and a nightstick on his belt. They were muscular, one of them a short man with long, knotty arms, another with a polished bald head and eyes like chips of lead.

These three wouldn't hesitate to take me down any way they could.

As I sat back, with my hands behind my head, I watched them, staring at each of them in turn.

Finally, the short man with the long arms turned his chair so he faced me. "Do you mind?" he growled.

"Sitting in here?" I asked. "Yeah. I do. Thanks for asking."

"Don't bother with him, Dan. Don't you know he's Commander Creed? He thinks he's tough shit." That was Mr. Polished Head speaking.

"Come on," I said. "I don't think that."

They all looked at me.

"I *know* it," I told them.

Long-armed Dan frowned. Mr. Polished Head snorted.

"Let's get back to the game," the third guard said.

"You don't believe me?" I asked.

"I don't," Dan said, trying to stare me down.

"I could take all three of you at once," I said.

"Wrong," Dan said. "You couldn't even take me."

"With one arm tied behind my back," I said. "Do you want to try?"

Dan scraped his chair back and stood up.

"No," Mr. Polished Head said. "That's not going to happen, Dan."

"But—"

"No!" Mr. Polished Head said. "Can't you see he's renting space in your head?"

Dan looked at him.

"Yeah," Mr. Polished Head said. "Sit down. Play cards. He's not going anywhere. If he bugs you, just think about him dying hard on the Lokhar Homeworld in front of them nobles."

Dan thought about that, grinned at me and sat down again, pulling his chair back to its old spot.

The three of them started playing cards in earnest, pointedly ignoring me.

That, naturally, had been the reason for my shenanigans.

Three quarters of an hour later, I saw the first sign that N7 knew what to do. I noticed a strange, telltale shimmer on one side of my cell. It was like a heat wave in the distance but bulged outward from one of the brick walls.

I glanced at the card players. They were into their game. For their sakes, I hope they stayed interested, as I didn't want to kill them.

The shimmer became more pronounced, and I could see the ghostly outline of a suited man with a bubble helmet. I couldn't quite see inside the helmet, but I knew it was N7.

I pointedly looked up at the four video feeds watching me.

The ghostly bubble helmet nodded up and down. He fiddled with something on his belt, unlatched it and seemed to take my picture. He moved out of the brick wall and stepped to various parts of the cell, squeezing past and through me some of the time.

Finally, N7 was ready.

He was wearing a Shrike Lord Phase Suit. I would have preferred using a Ronin 9 Teleportation Suit such as we'd used against Abaddon ten years ago, but those hadn't been anywhere to be found on the Fortress of Light. Thus, I'd taken the next best thing.

The phase suit operated on similar principles as the Ve-Ky combat suit. I'd once made such a suit malfunction so the "Skinny" had died inside a wall.

N7 *phased* into normal reality, becoming visible to anyone who looked. As he phased in, he set up small video slates before the cell cameras. To anyone watching, the slates would show me sitting on my cot with my arms behind my head.

The video slates wouldn't help, however, if one of the card players looked over here. Given the law of averages, one of them would do that soon enough.

N7 handed me a pair of earmuffs. I put them on. He activated a sonic stunner, aiming the device at the card table.

All I heard was a slight hum.

With sudden and violent swiftness, the three pitched onto the floor, clutching their ears as they twisted in pain. Finally, each man relaxed as he fell unconscious.

N7 lowered the stunner, clicked a switch and signaled me.

The hum went away. I took off the earmuffs, hearing nothing now.

N7 twisted off his bubble helmet, removing it from the suit. "Are you well, Creed?"

"Fantastic," I said. "I'm being sold like a piece of meat. Nothing could be better. You did good, N7. Now, secure the guards and then come back here. You did land the GEV nearby, didn't you?"

"Of course," he said.

"Good. We have a lot to do if we're going to finish this before anyone discovers I'm missing."

-20-

In the interest of speed—after securing the guards, of course—N7 put on the bubble helmet and picked me up. He then activated the phase suit.

I didn't like moving out of phase without a suit, but I felt like I'd need every second and thus insisted N7 get going. I had a plan, a good one, but it was complicated—which meant it had flaws.

It was an eerie feeling moving out of phase like this. The world seemed blurry and gray, decidedly indistinct. I had a difficult time knowing where we were, and I found it hard to breathe.

I had a rebreather over my mouth and nose, but that wasn't as effective as the closed environment of the suit. I closed my eyes to avoid a headache. The bubble helmet had special filters embedded within it, allowing one to look around without mental fatigue. If I looked around too much with my naked eyes while out of phase, the disorientation would begin to play havoc with my brain.

Soon enough, as we both came back into phase, the world came into focus again. N7 released me, and I staggered to a stool inside my GEV.

The stealth ship could land on a planet easily enough. The GEV was still in stealth mode and was out of the way, camouflaged for the moment. That might not last long as luck often played a factor in these missions, usually bad luck.

I used to watch plenty of action shows as a kid. There was one in particular that always got to me. The hero often needed a car while he was stranded on foot. He'd run at a normal city driver, making the guy skid to a stop in his vehicle. Then, the hero would yank open the car door and aim his gun at the person's face, shouting at him or her to get out. Naturally, the person did, and the hero drove away in the stolen car in order to finish the desperate mission. Just once, I would have liked the driver to irrationally fight back. Sometimes, people do stupid things. Sometimes, an action star like that would have yanked open the car door of a tough guy willing to just go for it and wrestle the hero onto the pavement.

But then the hero would have had to shoot the guy, or maybe the tough guy would have taken out the star, and the series would have ended right there.

Made-up stories were one thing. Real life was something else, with accidents happening all the time.

My point is that something was eventually going to go wrong on the mission. As the classic military maxim states: *No plan survives contact with the enemy.*

Inside the GEV parked a kilometer and a half away from the Rat's Nest, N7 stripped off the Shrike Lord Phase Suit. It was a bulky thing with air tanks, a phase generator, directional locator and other paraphernalia.

With his help, I put the suit on, checking and double-checking the various controls. We had to move fast, but that didn't mean rashly.

Finally, with everything on but the bubble helmet, which I cradled in an arm, I asked, "Have you contacted Ella yet?"

"Yes," N7 said.

"Oh?" I said. "Is she ready?"

"No."

"What does that mean?"

"Ella is unwilling to use the Jelk mind machine," N7 said. "She says it has been too long. She won't know what to do."

"Balls," I said. "Tell Ella I'm counting on her. If she can't do it, no one can. Then, Earth dies. It's as simple as that."

"I doubt Ella will believe you."

"N7, I don't have time for this. Make Ella believe me. That's an order."

The android blinked, looking confused.

"Yes," I said. "You're under my orders again. It's official."

"What is your authority?"

"N7, I don't want to have to say it."

With a forefinger, the android touched his forehead. "I feel a compulsion to obey you. Have you tampered with my programming perchance?"

I hesitated before saying, "Yes."

"That was wrong of you, Commander."

"I shouldn't have done it. But I did because I'm in a time crunch. You aren't helping things by arguing with me."

"I feel the inner compulsion expanding in me," N7 said.

"Look, I had to do what I did. Can you take my word for that?"

"Would *you* take my word if our positions were reversed?"

"I don't know." What was going on here? N7 was supposed to obey me. How did he find any AI willpower to resist after I'd reprogrammed key features?

"Your answer suggests that you would not 'take my word for it' but are unwilling to say so," N7 told me.

"Think of my tampering as an upgrade. You always wanted those, right?"

"I do desire upgrades, but like you I abhor mental enslavement."

"Enslavement? Did you know how to operate a Shrike Lord Phase Suit before today?"

"That is nonsensical, as the question is not germane to the issue."

"If it helps you any," I said, "after this is done, I'll reverse what I did earlier."

"What did you do to me, Commander?"

I sighed. This was taking too long. "I made you loyal and I made it so you can't tell anyone what you've learned or done."

"It is as I suspected. You have enslaved me."

"N7—"

"Am I wrong, Commander?"

I looked at N7, an android and one of my oldest friends. Let me amend that, one of my *only* friends. Maybe I'd been gone from Earth for so long that I'd forgotten about real friendship. That brought an overwhelming sense of guilt, which astonished me.

I'd been having far too many guilty feelings lately. I wanted the old Creed back. This was getting tedious.

"Okay," I said. "You're not wrong. I miscalculated. No. I screwed up and messed with one of my only friends. I regret that, and I won't do it again."

"How can I trust your words, Commander?"

"I don't know if you can. I played fast and loose with you, N7. If you want to abort—go ahead. All you have to do is walk out that hatch and you're free of me."

"Will you succeed in your mission without me?"

"Maybe, but the odds are longer. You know, N7, I don't know why we're having this conversation. Forget that. I don't know how it's possible. Something is going on that—"

An interior hatch slid up, and Ella Timoshenko stepped through. "Hello, Creed," she said.

I did a double take, eyeing her, N7 and then her again.

Ella was a thin Russian with a pretty face, with a few wrinkles I didn't remember, and a figure that still wouldn't quit. Her dark hair was longer than before, but still made her seem like an erotic elf lady. She'd been an assault trooper once, one of the only female troopers among us.

Unfortunately, Ella had a gun in one hand—aimed at me— and she had a communicator in the other hand. She studied me, and she seemed as serious as I'd ever seen her.

"This is awkward," I said, nodding slowly. I turned to N7. "You let her aboard. Oh, right." I faced Ella again. "You reversed my modifications to N7. But...I don't see how that was possible, especially in so short a time."

"N7 contacted me before landing, and I joined him as soon as the vessel touched down. We've been reversing your AI-altering ever since."

"I still don't see how. Everything in the GEV is locked against unauthorized use."

"Locked with your passwords," Ella said. "You may have been gone ten years, Creed, but we still know you better than anyone else does. We may even know you better than you know yourself."

"You cracked my passwords?"

"Easily," Ella said.

It was starting to come together. "Right," I said. "That's why Diana and her pet policeman keep asking me about being the Galactic Effectuator? You told them."

"I did," Ella said.

"Why?"

"You've been gone a long time. Maybe your loyalties have changed."

"They haven't," I said. "How much did you tell Diana?"

"She doesn't know about your stealth ship or about N7."

"Small favors," I said. "Thanks. Did Diana ask how you knew about that?"

"I told her I eavesdropped on you and the Curator ten years ago on the park bench in Saint Petersburg."

"How do you know about that?"

Ella blushed. "I planted a bug on the park bench that day."

"Oh." I nodded. "So where does all that lead us? Are you going to shoot me?"

"I haven't decided," Ella said. "First, what's your plan?"

I thought fast and finally gave her a quick rundown regarding the phase suit part of my plan.

My Russian scientist was nodding before I was finished. "I figured it was something like that because N7 said you wanted me to use the Jelk mind machine. I changed Doctor Sant's mind once. Why not change the Lokhar Ambassador's mind, eh?"

"Are you with me or are you going to shoot me?"

Ella glanced at N7. "What do you think?"

"I understand why he tampered with my mind," the android said. "I also believe that he is truly contrite for what he did to me. I am with you, Commander Creed."

"It's just Creed," I said, because I was starting to feel choked up and didn't want to show it.

"I prefer Commander Creed," N7 said. "So as long as I am helping you, and under your command, I will continue to use your old title."

"Fair enough...and thanks, N7. You don't know what it's like finding that you still have friends."

"You're not going to get emotional on us, are you, Creed?" Ella asked.

"Are you in, or out?" I asked, quietly.

"In," Ella said, as she holstered the gun.

"Great," I said. "Then let's get to work."

-21-

The plan had complications, too many moving parts that could come to a screeching halt if the wrong person walked in at the wrong time.

N7 had just about destroyed the mission by bringing Ella in as he had. As I trudged, out of phase, to the Ambassador's residence, I wondered how I'd screwed up while retooling the android's brain. Might I have subconsciously "intentionally" made a mistake with N7? That struck me as farfetched, but I didn't discount the possibility.

Whatever the case, I'd gotten sloppy. That meant I needed to pay closer attention to each individual task. The two years in suspended animation might have dulled my instincts more than I'd realized.

Walking while out of phase wasn't as easy as it might sound. For one thing, it was hard to know where you were going. One had to phase-in slightly, like a submarine gliding near the surface and shooting up the periscope, to have a look around. Being completely out of phase was like the Invisible Man trying to see where he was going. With light rays passing through him, his eyes wouldn't bounce any images into his mind. The light rays would simply pass through the interior reflectors in his eyes.

I phased into ghostly form and looked around, seeing a ghostly tiger guard marching in the downstairs area of the Ambassador's official residence.

Climbing was harder while out of phase; it took deliberate practice. The same was true of going down through the ground.

I went fully out of phase again and moved upward, turning ghostly, seeing a guard in a hall, and walked through a wall into the fat boy's sleeping quarters.

What made everything harder than usual was the cargo slumped over my left shoulder. I carried a tub-of-lard replica of the overweight Lokhar. The replica was a form of an android. It wouldn't fool the tigers for long if anyone looked too closely. The point was to have the replica sleeping in the Ambassador's bed so no one did look too closely.

I entered the darkened quarters, fully expecting to see lady tigers in bed with the Ambassador. Nope, not this time. Count Loris slept alone. The old boy made a production out of it, moaning in his sleep and turning about. He'd kicked all his sheets aside, snoring like a banshee.

I phased fully in. As I did, the Ambassador's eyes shot open.

Had I triggered a hidden alarm or was the Ambassador unusually alert to hidden presences?

Count Loris stared at me. Through me? He closed his eyes and rolled over. Had he figured I was a nightmare? A second later, he rolled toward me with his eyes wide open. He sat up, opened his mouth, no doubt getting ready to roar.

I lunged at him, dropping the replica as I did. The thing hit the bed and thumped to the floor, making a racket on the way down. The Ambassador began shouting just as I stretched out and touched him with a stun wand. A massive jolt of electricity zapped him. He made a gurgling sound, shook hard and slumped back, out cold.

I put away the stunner as someone tapped at the bedroom door. That was fast.

"Excellency?" a high-voiced Lokhar asked from the other side.

I'd heard that voice before. Right. It must be the hippy tiger.

I activated the replica as the hippy tapped again. "Excellency?" he repeated.

"Yes," the replica asked, at the proper modulation.

"Is everything well, Excellency?"

"Yes, yes," the replica said. "Fine. Now leave me. I'm trying to sleep."

I waited. Maybe the replica had said that wrong. Then again, maybe it worked, as the hippy went away. At least, he stopped tapping at the door.

The replica helped me disrobe the Ambassador, putting on the count's nightclothes. Then, the replica crawled under the covers and feigned sleep.

The replica was center galaxy tech, far better than anything anyone could fashion out here.

I worked under the huge tub-of-lard—the real Ambassador—grunting as I hefted him onto my back. That should give some indication of my strength. This old boy was massive.

With my chin, I clicked a helmet control and we phased out.

While out of phase, I staggered out of the bedroom and worked down to the main floor. I ghosted into slightly higher phase once in order to look around. A guard must have seen me, as he stared in wide-eyed terror, the fur on his head standing up on end.

That was just great.

I debated phasing all the way in and shooting him, but decided I'd have to trust to luck. I phased out, carrying the ponderous Ambassador back to my hidden stealth ship.

-22-

The Jelk mind machine was a vicious piece of technology. The Jelk Corporation had used it to brainwash selected people for nefarious ends.

Count Loris was strapped into the machine, which was inside the stealth ship. Back in the day, Ella had become something of a master with it. She'd modified many Lokhars while we'd worked hard to revive Earth.

Ella worked hard now, fiddling with controls that made the old boy jerk and twitch while he sat under it.

N7 helped Ella with the ordeal.

I begged off, moving into a different area of the ship. I'd never enjoyed watching the process. It took a cast iron stomach to listen to some of the sounds the inductee made while under the machine.

I lay down for a bit, opening my eyes several hours later as Ella shook my shoulder. Her eyes were bloodshot and her hair a bit disheveled. She almost seemed half-crazy and kept blinking too much.

Sitting up, I asked, "Is he ready?"

She slumped into a nearby chair, running a hand through her hair.

"I like how you ask first if I'm okay," she said.

"Are you okay?" I asked.

"No."

I nodded. "Is the Lokhar ready?"

"Maybe."

I raised my eyebrows. "I need better than that."

"I know. But he's as good as you're going to get from me."

"Was he conditioned against the mind machine?"

Ella gave me a searching look. "You've changed."

"It's been ten years."

"No. It's more than that. You're different. You used to have more compassion—"

"I hate the Lokhars, especially those belonging to Purple Tamika."

"More compassion for your own people," Ella finished.

That brought me up short. Was she right? Had I changed after eight years of working alone? I used to run the assault troopers. They'd been my people, my responsibility.

I rubbed my forehead. "Look, Ella, this is big and bad and vicious. I don't have time to soothe every hurt."

She searched my face. "Is it big or is this about Jennifer?"

It took me a few seconds before I asked, "Have you been in contact with Diana?"

Ella shrugged noncommittally.

"Yeah," I said, a moment later. "This is about Jennifer. I'm—" I wasn't sure what to say next.

"You're more driven," Ella told me, as if seeing something new. "Is this about you leaving Jennifer behind on the portal planet?"

I opened my mouth, and for once, my cockiness deserted me. "I wanted to go back for her," I said, the words sounding plaintive to my ears. I hated that.

"I know," Ella said, gently. "You made the hard choice, the right choice. I suppose that's one of the perks of command. You get to carry the weight of your choices."

I said nothing.

"What's Jennifer like these days?" Ella asked.

"No different from when she was with Abaddon."

"Why did she go to the Plutonians?"

"Diana guessed it. Jennifer wants to destroy what I love. So she's busy destroying herself and the human race."

"Can we defeat these Plutonians?"

"If we raid Acheron—"

"That's the name of this legendary planet?"

I nodded. "If we raid Acheron and get the tech that's there."

"Guaranteed win?" Ella asked.

"There's never a guarantee in battle, just better odds."

Ella thought about that, grimacing afterward.

"I don't know what to tell you about the Ambassador," she said. "He has greater willpower than Doctor Sant ever had. Partly it's because Count Loris's mind is more devious, which makes the machine's changes harder to predict. The Ambassador might slip his leash at the wrong time."

"We need him, Ella. We need him so we can grab the Lokhar heavy cruisers. They're hidden somewhere nearby."

"I don't know where they are, but I do know they're rigged to self-destruct if we approach them wrong."

"Do you know how many the Ambassador has?"

"Six."

"Good. Six will work. The question is, will the captains obey the Ambassador's orders, no matter how strange those orders seem?"

"How can I possibly know that?"

"You can't. We'll have to find out the hard way."

"I do know this," Ella said. "The heavy cruiser captains are all from Tepis Clan, the one Loris runs. They're supposed to obey him. But you're making this harder than it needs to be. Why not go with the Ambassador as a prisoner, having him order a raid on Acheron? I take it that is your plan."

"I'm surprised you have to ask. You already told me the mind conditioning might not hold."

"I know…"

"What is it?" I asked. "You're keeping something to yourself. Spit it out."

Ella watched me as she said, "Your plan seems overly complicated."

"It is because I don't trust Purple Tamika Lokhars and I don't trust Diana."

"It shows, you know? I bet it's one of the reasons why Diana doesn't trust you."

I ignored her little tidbit of wisdom, and asked, "Is Loris ready to travel?"

"I could use another several hours to smooth out—"

"Forget it," I said, interrupting. "I need to get Loris back now so he's ready to meet the Prime Minister this morning. Can I ask you for a favor?" I added.

"Don't you mean 'another favor?'"

I nodded.

"Go ahead," Ella said with a sigh.

"Don't contact Diana until this maneuver is over. Oh, and stay in the GEV until I get back."

"*If* you get back," she said. "I have serious doubts about the Ambassador."

"I'll get back. Don't worry about me."

"I am worried. You'll be a prisoner again—I mean after the Ambassador pulls his stunt—and N7 will have to do this all over again with the phase suit."

"Will you do me the favor or not?"

Ella cocked her head, soon nodding. "You shouldn't have tampered with N7."

"I know. I've already said as much."

Ella and I both stood up.

"Let's get started," she said.

-23-

I now reversed the process, lugging the Ambassador on my back, returning him to his ambassadorial bedroom.

Once there, I phased in, looking around. It was quiet. None of the furniture had been moved. The heavy curtains were still. I glanced at the replica in bed. It slept soundly.

"Hey," I said, softly.

The replica opened its eyes, and it shifted them sharply, staring to my left as an obvious signal.

I heard a *phut* sound even as I turned ghostly again. A dart passed through my midsection. I felt a twinge there, letting me know that I wasn't normally dense, but enough to have felt something pass through me.

The dart wobbled in flight and struck a wall. I didn't hear anything now, as I'd gone ghostly enough that my amplifiers couldn't easily pick up sound waves.

Several darts passed through me, some through my chest.

I turned around with the ghostly Ambassador on my back. Two Lokhars stood in front of the thick, slightly wavering curtains, no doubt having moved out of hiding from behind them. They wore fur-tight garments, the likely attire of Shi Feng assassins.

One of them glared. The other stood stiffly, with the fur on his head standing up on end. Each of them gripped a dart gun.

I phased in, watching as they seemed to solidify—I was the one doing that—and I brought up my blaster, using the other hand to keep the Ambassador in place on my back. I fired the disrupter ray. At the same time, I shifted to one side, likely much faster than they could have imagined with Loris on my back. A dart hissed past me. The other assassin—the freaked-out Lokhar, a possibly superstitious one—had frozen in shock while I'd burned him down.

As the two half-disrupted corpses thudded onto the carpet, I heaved the slumbering Ambassador onto the huge bed behind me.

I had to work fast. The assassins might have told others about their suspicions. Yet, it was possible the two had worked independently of the ambassadorial staff.

I asked the replica what had happened while I was gone. It told me the two had shown up an hour ago, quietly opening a widow and slipping inside. For a time, the two had watched the replica sleep. At no point had an assassin shaken it or spoken to the supposed Ambassador.

Maybe this could still work.

I had the replica slip out of the Ambassador's clothes, putting them onto the old boy.

Meanwhile, I debated strategy. The more I thought about it, the more the two tigers seemed as if they had belonged to the ancient death cult.

From what I knew, the Shi Feng originated long ago in the mists of Lokhar history, before the tigers ever entered their Space Age and before they turned to Creator worship. In that distant era, the Lokhars followed anthropometric, Lokhar-like gods and goddesses, much like the Greek pantheon. That thinking had changed over time as Lokhar society evolved. In this era—or the last time I'd dealt with them—the Shi Feng had demanded purity and right thinking from Lokhars and an exclusion from other aliens, convinced that only their tiger kind were made in the image of the Creator. They had clung to the Forerunner artifacts such as Holgotha as if they were holy relics. Lokhar legend held that the Shi Feng never failed, although I'd beaten them. In the past, Lokhars granted the death-cult assassins supernatural abilities.

If the cult had sprung up again under the Purple Tamika rule, that would explain a lot.

Finally, I grabbed the first corpse and phased out with it, stashing the corpse in a thick wall. When I released the dead Lokhar, it slowly phased in, embedded within the wall.

I went back and stashed the other assassin elsewhere.

Finally, with everything ready, I had the replica slump over my left shoulder. I deactivated it and phased into a ghostly form.

I'd mopped up and then wiped down the spots of spilled blood, but some of the blaster fire had singed the corner of the rug and one of the dressers. I'd moved things around a bit to hide the evidence. Hopefully, the damage would remain hidden long enough.

I went fully out of phase and started for the GEV. I needed to put away the replica, give N7 the phase suit and have him carry me back to the prison cell in the Rat's Nest.

Ella had been right earlier. This was complicated. What made it worse was that I hadn't practiced any of the moves.

I phase-ghosted, looked around and found myself in a wall. I phased out, took several steps and ghosted in again. Okay, I was on target.

Afterward, out of phase once more, I put my head down and trotted as fast as I could go. It was going to be morning soon. I had to get back to the prison cell before anyone noticed I was missing or this wasn't going to work.

-24-

I made it back to my cell in time. Even better, while wearing the phase suit, N7 righted the three sonic-shocked guards and attached inhibitors to their foreheads.

The inhibitors were disc-shaped and would peel off later as if they were bandages. Each ran through combinations as if the person's mind was a safe. Finally, each device made a clicking noise, indicating the memory eraser had worked.

N7 removed the inhibitors, pocketing them and signaling me with a suited thumbs-up.

I nodded and lay down on my cot, pulling a blanket over my torso.

N7 turned ghostly, came into my cell and removed the video slates. He walked back to the guards, phased in, pressed a buzzer and quickly phased out.

At the buzzer sound, the guards raised their heads. Luckily, N7 had set them in their chairs as I'd taught him. None of the guards had slipped off his chair first and woken up on the floor.

The three raised their heads almost simultaneously. Each covertly glanced at his companions, likely to see if anyone had noticed that he'd had his head slumped. Each seemed to be so worried about himself that he didn't notice—

"Hey," long-armed Dan complained. "What's going on here?"

No. It looked like I'd miscalculated. I bet Dan had a poor self-image, the reason he wanted to fight everyone all the time. It may have also been the reason why he'd used steroids and had become a guard in the first place. He wanted to show the bullies in his past that he really was a tough guy.

"You guys feel okay?" Dan asked.

"What are you talking about?" Mr. Polished Head asked.

Dan blinked at him.

"We've been here all night," the other said. "Go on. Look at your cards. It's your bet."

Dan hesitated, finally turning and glancing at me.

I watched him through slit eyelids while feigning sleep.

"Now what's the matter?" Mr. Polished Head asked him.

"Nothing," Dan grumbled. "I just thought—"

"Check, fold or raise," Mr. Polished Head said, interrupting. "Just do something already."

Dan studied his hole cards and finally limped into the pot.

Three quarters of an hour later, word came down that I was going back to the main Government House.

The third guard got up and ran his nightstick across my bars, making a racket. "Get up, you."

I smacked my lips, sitting up slowly, rubbing my eyes. "What time is it?"

"No tricks, bright boy," the guard said.

"What?" I asked, even as I debated disarming them, but knew I might get a nightstick cracked against the back of my head for my troubles. Thus, I ate from the breakfast tray they shoved through the slot, washed up afterward and meekly put my hands behind my back when Dan came in to cuff me.

As he clicked the handcuffs onto my wrists, he whispered, "Did anything strange happen last night?"

"Yeah," I whispered back.

"I knew it. What happened?"

"You won a couple of hands."

It took him a second, then he jerked my right arm down—it was already behind my back. "Very funny," he said. "I ought to—"

"Hurry up, Dan," Mr. Polished Head said. "We don't have all morning. We're supposed to take him over pronto."

Dan breathed heavily behind me, finally whispering, "I hope you like the Lokhar Homeworld, fool."

"Won't make any difference what I like."

"Yeah? How come?"

"Because I won't be going there," I whispered.

Dan snorted and pushed me toward the exit. "He ain't so tough," he told the others. "Meek as a lamb the whole night. I thought he was going to try something."

"You never know," Mr. Polished Head said, as if imparting words of wisdom.

"You got lucky," Dan said, shoving me again.

I almost turned around and tripped him, but I kept wondering about the Shi Feng assassins. The Purple Tamika Lokhars loved them. The Shi Feng were an ancient guild, full of Lokhar traditions. Usually, the assassins kept to themselves, acting like shadows. Had I slain the only two in the ambassadorial party, or were there more? In particular, one more to complete a triad?

"Cat got your tongue?" Dan sneered behind me.

I glanced at him over my shoulder, saw his stupid grin and realized he'd said something else just now. I didn't bother trying to remember what. A bad feeling grew in my gut. Even if everything went according to plan, a Shi Feng assassin could upset things. I'd have to keep my eyes open, and I'd have to get the others to un-cuff me so I could act if I had to.

I should have told N7 to lurk at the meeting this morning in the phase suit, as I suddenly had a feeling that this was going to be tricky.

-25-

Diana sat on her Victorian throne, wearing an even fancier dress today, one that shimmered with sequins.

The same company of players had reappeared; General Briggs, the other officer, Spencer, Nancy, the marine guards along the back wall and the red-suited security people around the tables.

The same combat-armored marine lieutenant stood beside me, with the cuffs behind my back.

"How about someone take these off," I said. "My shoulders are stiffening up."

Small Police Proconsul Spencer glanced at Diana.

She wouldn't meet my gaze, although Briggs had nodded when I'd first entered and Spencer had given me a quiet hello.

I couldn't tell if Diana had said anything or indicated in any other way, but Spencer told the marine lieutenant, "Take them off."

Diana glanced sharply at her Police Proconsul. I realized then that Spencer had given the order under his own authority.

The Amazon Queen did not countermand the order, and she glanced at me before quickly looking away.

"Thanks, Prime Minister," I said, rubbing a wrist.

Diana did not acknowledge me.

I nodded to Spencer. He returned the faintest of smiles.

"What's on the agenda today?" I asked Diana.

She frowned, still without looking at me.

"Still want to trade me to the Lokhars?" I asked her.

She glowered at me. "I know you're lying about not being the Galactic Effectuator."

"How do you figure that?" I asked.

Diana opened her mouth, and snapped it closed with a click of her teeth. She faced forward once more.

Soon, the double doors opened and the same marine as last night shouted the Ambassador's arrival.

Everything went as before, with the ceremonially spear-armed Lokhars leading the way.

I studied them, wondering if one of them was a Shi Feng assassin. Each of the tigers was large, heavily muscular and moving with athletic grace. I remembered the assassins I'd blown away with my .44 many years ago on Earth. One of them had detonated—he'd carried a bomb in his body.

"Have you screened the tigers?" I asked Spencer.

He stared at me from his spot beside Diana.

Since I realized he wasn't going to answer, I faced forward as the hippy with his purple-tinted shades preceded the Ambassador.

Count Loris was bleary-eyed. That was a bad sign. He sniffled, too, as if he had a cold. He moved slower than yesterday, as if he lacked the same energy, which was probably the case. Well, fat boy wasn't here to win a beauty contest. He was here to do exactly as Ella had programmed him.

Count Loris rested a heavy hand on the slender Lokhar's shoulder. The cat actually glanced back at the Ambassador.

Loris scowled at him.

The hippy nodded, as if the scowl comforted him in some manner.

"Welcome, Ambassador," Diana said. "I trust you slept well and had a momentous meeting with your policy people. We await your decision."

"You seem hasty," Loris said in a rougher voice than yesterday.

"Then I must ask for your forgiveness," Diana said. "I have weighty matters on my mind. I did not sleep well." She glanced at me. "I kept wondering about what would happen to Commander Creed on your homeworld."

"Just so," Loris said. He cleared his throat, adjusted his huge purple gown and paused. He frowned, rubbed his forehead as if a headache had suddenly developed and opened his mouth to speak. He stood like that for five seconds, finally closing his muzzle. He cocked his head, seemingly puzzled.

"Is something wrong, Ambassador?" Diana asked.

"I…" he said. "I seem to have forgotten something."

"Can we help in any way?" Diana asked.

Count Loris opened his mouth again and groaned, rubbing his obviously sore head.

The hippy went lower as Loris's hand pressed down harder against his shoulder. Without any notice, the slender Lokhar's knees buckled and he stumbled, going down onto his knees.

Several ceremonially armed tigers glanced back in surprise. None of them turned to help the hippy.

The hippy scrambled to his feet. He seemed shamed, bowing low before the Ambassador.

Count Loris didn't seem to notice. His mouth was opening and closing as if he couldn't figure out what he wanted to say.

The hippy leaned near and whispered to Loris.

The Ambassador did not look up, but continued his weird performance.

I suspected, then, that Ella hadn't remembered her brain-tampering skills as well as I could have wished. Still, she'd told me the Ambassador had a devious mind. Was he struggling to overcome his recent conditioning?

"Sir," the hippy said, loud enough for me to hear.

Loris looked up, and for a moment, seemed confused.

"Prime Minister," Loris said, sharply, "please, forgive me. I am not feeling myself this morning."

"If it's any consolation," Diana said, "neither am I."

The hippy whispered again. The Ambassador shook his head. The hippy turned around, facing the throne. The Ambassador rested his hand on the shoulder again, although not as heavily as before.

"I have an announcement to make," Loris said mechanically. "It is a change in plans and protocol."

"Oh?" Diana asked.

"I cannot accept Commander Creed," Loris said.

Several ceremonially armed tigers turned around again. The hippy glanced back as well.

"Rather," the Ambassador said, "I shall summon my ships. You will outfit a party, enough for three vessels, and you shall accompany me back to the homeworld. There, you shall present Commander Creed to the Emperor."

"You expect me to leave Earth?" Diana asked.

"No, of course not," the Ambassador said. "You must select a representative to act on your behalf. Your chosen marines will witness the commander's grisly death and report back to you what occurred."

"I'm not sure I understand," Diana said. "You're not accepting Creed as a prisoner?"

"That is correct," Loris said. "He will remain free in your representative's custody until we reach the homeworld."

"But I thought your Emperor wanted Creed a prisoner."

"In the proper time and place," Loris said. "Now, I will retire. I am feeling taxed—"

The hippy tiger whirled around with a hiss. "Traitor," he said. He slashed the Ambassador across the face with razor-sharp claws that erupted from his paw-tips. They seemed like ordinary claws, like those that every Lokhar possessed.

Almost instantly, the Ambassador shrieked, stumbling backward. A second later, he collapsed onto the floor and twisted in agony as he began vomiting blood.

Several ceremonially armed Lokhars whirled around. Two heaved their spears. The hippy Lokhar—the Shi Feng assassin—dodged the first missile. The second spear caught him in the chest, making him stagger.

"Guards!" Spencer shouted.

Three spear-armed tigers turned toward Diana. Four of them lunged at me.

Beam weapons hummed. Every Lokhar in the chamber collapsed under murderous fire from the security detail and the marines standing in back.

The carnage was horrendous and fast, with a host of smoking, sometimes-shriveled tiger carcasses thudding onto the blood-slicked floor

One of the spearheads grazed Diana's arm, staining the shimmering dress with bright drops of blood. I expected her to drop from poisoning. She did not, as that tiger hadn't, apparently, been Shi Feng.

I parried the spears thrust at me, using my hands as trained: knocking each spear aside after the spearhead had passed. Otherwise, I would have seriously cut the sides of my hands.

"They're dead," Diana said in shock. "All the Lokhars are dead." She looked up at me, with dazed amazement on her face. "It's over, Creed. You made sure that the Lokhar Emperor will hate us with searing passion for murdering his ambassadorial party. That will be considered a harsh slur against his imperial dignity. Now, he *has* to burn Earth to its bedrock. You've just made sure that the aliens will wipe out humanity forever."

-26-

The Prime Minister's pronouncement ensured that everyone stared at me.

I glanced at the dead, smoking tigers. The crisscrossing beam-fire had been amazingly accurate and deadly. My plan to use the Ambassador to grab the Lokhar heavy cruisers had just evaporated. I hadn't even gotten the codes from his mind and had no idea where the heavy cruisers were hidden.

As Ella had said, I'd planned to use the heavy cruisers to slip undetected through the Lokhar Empire. Now, reaching Acheron was going to be much more difficult.

"Look at them," Diana said in a stricken voice. "We just murdered the ambassadorial party of the most powerful aliens in our sector of the galaxy. What are we going to do now?"

"Follow my plan," I said. "It will still work."

"What plan?" Diana shouted.

"I believe he means slipping through the Lokhar Empire and reaching Acheron, the planet of the First Ones," Spencer said.

"Not technically the planet of the First Ones," I said, "but a place that contains some of their technology."

"First One technology is going to save us from the Lokhars?" Diana asked.

"No."

"No?"

"It will help solve the Plutonian problem," I said. "Once we've done that, taking care of the Lokhars should be much easier."

"That doesn't make any sense," she said.

"Sure it does," I said, smoothly. "Think about it. The Alliance will control the Plutonian pocket universe, right?"

"So what?" she said. "Earth needs more battlejumpers, not a pocket universe."

"You're not thinking this through," I said. "The pocket universe will give you fantastic mobility, force-multiplying the battlejumpers Earth already possesses."

"What mobility?"

"From what I've read, the Plutonians can reach most of the galaxy with equal speed. Think about it. The pocket universe is outside our space-time continuum. The wormhole—the needed dimensional portal—can open from the pocket universe into many possible areas with equal ease."

"Ah," said General Briggs, who had been following my explanation. "The pocket universe will act as a nexus point, a junction. Go to the pocket universe, and you can invade the Lokhar Empire at any point you desire."

"Theoretically accurate," I said.

"I don't understand that part," Briggs said. "Will it act as a junction or not?"

"We haven't tried it yet, but it should work the way I've outlined it."

Diana groaned. "This is just more of your gibberish so we don't put you back in prison where you belong. How did you engineer this debacle, Creed?"

"What are you talking about?" I asked, letting anger tinge my words.

Spencer glanced sharply at the Prime Minister before regarding me curiously. "Yes," he said. "I see it now. This murder spree is your handiwork, isn't it? You're the Galactic Effectuator. This is what you do. You're like a stage magician, practicing misdirection while you go about your task. We believed you were safely in our Rat's Nest. Instead, you outmaneuvered all of us. That was neatly done, Commander. You have my congratulations."

"I'd like to take credit for this—" I said.

"Please," Spencer said, "don't bother denying it. You've created an incredible balls-up for us. We'll have to take out the rest of the Lokhar delegation, or sequester them until we decide what we're going to do. In the meantime, you're free. And we're forced into accepting your help. You don't seriously expect me to believe that what happened here occurred by accident?"

"Are you saying the commander engineered this?" General Briggs asked Spencer. "That doesn't make sense. You told us he was in his cell all night."

"I'm going to double and triple check that," Spencer replied. He eyed me. "What will a close examination of the guards and your cell reveal, Commander?"

"Not a damn thing," I said.

"What do you recommend we do?" Spencer asked.

"Same as always," I said. "Grab the Lokhar heavy cruisers and pack them with assault troopers."

"How do we summon the Ambassador's heavy cruisers to us?" Spencer asked. "They're nearby, certainly, but we haven't located them. Besides, are the Starkiens a match for the Lokhars?"

The Proconsul referred to the unfortunate fact that Earth didn't have any nearby battlejumpers at the moment. The Plutonians had destroyed those. Starkien warships presently protected Earth.

"It may not come to a battle between Starkien versus Lokhar," I said.

"What are you two talking about?" Diana said. "Look at these dead Lokhars—"

"Prime Minister," Spencer said, interrupting her. "We have committed a terrible deed here today. It has sealed our fate, as you've already explained to us. We have burned our ships."

"What ships?" Diana asked.

"It's an old expression," I said, studying the Police Proconsul. "It refers to Hernando Cortez. He was a Spanish Conquistador. He sailed to the Veracruz coast in what was once Mexico. After landing his men, Cortez secretly burned all his ships anchored in the bay."

"That sounds like madness," Diana said.

"No," I said. "It meant his small party of Spanish soldiers had no choice. They couldn't retreat. So they advanced and found the Aztec Empire and conquered it with the aid of Indian allies. It was one of the most amazing conquests in Human History."

"And you're our Cortez?" Diana asked, sarcastically.

"And those are our burned ships," I said, indicating the smoking tiger corpses. "Once Emperor Daniel Lex Rex hears of this, he'll summon the Jade League and demand a vast armada to attack us."

"We're all dead in other words," Diana said.

"Hardly," I said. "Now, we really have a chance at striking a victorious blow against the Lokhars."

Diana stared at me as if I'd lost my senses. Spencer leaned near and whispered in her ear. She stared at him for a time, and slowly, a change came over her.

"*Are* you the Galactic Effectuator?" Diana asked me.

I sighed. Maybe it was time to drop the pretense.

"Not anymore," I said.

"What does that mean?"

"That I left the Curator's service."

"Whatever for?" she asked.

"Because he forbade me to rescue Jennifer," I said.

"And you came here anyway?"

"I had no choice. I have to save Jennifer and I have to stop her from destroying Earth."

"Why didn't you tell us all this in the first place?"

I shrugged. I could have given a reason, told her why I'd now told the truth about Jennifer; because Ella had already given the game away. I could have told Diana that the Lokhar dead were not according to some grand plan on my part. This was a disaster. I'd wanted the Ambassador alive. I kept all this to myself because I'd learned a key lesson many years ago as Commander Creed. It made the troops feel better if they thought their leader knew what in the hell he was doing. If they knew their leader was winging it, they might lose heart and stop trying as hard.

It looked like not much had changed since those days.

Diana took a deep breath and abruptly sat down. She fanned herself with a sheaf of papers. Finally, she shook her head.

"I'm out of options," she told Spencer. "What do you think we should do?"

The Police Proconsul glanced at Briggs before regarding me. "You never did tell us how you reached Earth."

"That's true," I said.

"Well?" Spencer asked.

"I have a stealth ship."

"Hmm," Spencer said, before turning to Diana. "Creed has outmaneuvered our play against him, and we do have two implacable foes. As I recall from my readings, Commander Creed was notorious for using one problem to solve another."

"You want me to trust him?" Diana asked.

"I wouldn't go that far," Spencer said. "But I do think it's time we reinstate him and let him do what he does best."

"Create mayhem for those he hates?" Diana asked.

Spencer nodded, "Precisely."

-27-

I didn't want to borrow a Starkien beamship, and I didn't want to wait for Earth Defense battlejumpers to get here. We had to get started if we were going to stop Jennifer from convincing the Plutonians to launch everything they had at Earth before we could get into their pocket universe and stop them.

The problem was that I also didn't want strangers aboard my GEV. It was a small vessel, anyway, and could only reasonably hold maybe fifty people for a short time.

The solution was simple. Instead of strangers, I'd have fifty friends aboard, and we would find the six hidden Lokhar heavy cruisers and pirate them.

That meant I needed assault troopers. The problem was that all of my former assault troopers were ten years older. Some of them wouldn't be elite soldiers anymore.

Still, I only needed fifty and could presumably select the best out of those who volunteered.

General Briggs was on it, combing the planet for ex-assault troopers. He was the Prime Minister's creature, however, and would attempt to pack questionably loyal troopers onto my vessel. I couldn't blame him: he was what he was. But I could certainly try to outmaneuver that play as well.

While still in stealth mode, N7 took the GEV upstairs into low Earth orbit. Ella got on the horn for me, calling a few of the ex-assault troopers she'd kept in touch with over the years.

I went to Neo Vegas, using my flitter and landing at the airport.

Neo Vegas was a lot like old Las Vegas before The Day. The city contained The Strip with all its old vices: sexy ladies, gambling, drinking, wild shows, you name it. I'd been to Vegas as a kid. This one lacked the huge casinos of old.

It felt weird walking The Strip. There were hardly any cars but plenty of bicycles and a few flitters zooming overhead. In that way, it reminded me of the futuristic cartoons I'd loved as a kid, with old George J. zipping around in his flying-saucer vehicle. Neo Vegas lacked the futuristic buildings of those cartoons, it had old-style buildings of the type from before The Day.

As I walked The Strip, it hit me that I was home, but it wasn't the same. The Lokhars had stolen our old world from us many years ago. All those people I'd known before The Day were dead. Everyone related to me by blood was gone. It was like that for all the real Earthlings now.

Those of us that lived on Earth were all Terrans—sons of Adam, you could say—but we weren't all Earthlings who had lived on our homeworld before The Day.

I've said it before, and it really struck me today as I walked The Strip. The roughest one percent had survived the Lokhar sneak-attack. The mean humans, the sons of bitches that hit a guy in the mouth if he said the wrong thing had primarily been in such out of the way places that he or she had lasted long enough to start surviving in the new world.

The human immigrants to Terra weren't like that, weren't mean sons of guns. They usually had living fathers, mothers, uncles, cousins, brothers, sisters—family, in other words. That wasn't a knock on them. Heck, I would love to tell my Mom all the cool things I'd done since she died. What it did mean was that the immigrants to Earth were different from the one-percenters, not bad, but different.

No assault trooper had come from the freed slaves of the Jelk Corporation. Well, in one sense we'd been slaves, too, for a time. But we'd been the wild humans, part of the one percent, the killers, and had torn off our slave collars and turned on our jailers.

I stopped on a sidewalk on The Strip, raised my hands into the air and shouted with frustration. I'd forgotten about all the dead from The Day, the ghosts that haunted Earth. Walking the streets like this, almost feeling home again but knowing I'd never know the Earth I had lost, drove me crazy.

How I hated the Lokhars. I realized now I would love to start a league of my own, raise a vast host of starships and burn the bastards to the ground planet by planet.

I'd thought I had lost those old hatreds. I guess I was wrong.

I noticed people avoiding me or hurrying past.

I lowered my arms, finally put my hands into my pants pockets and kept walking. I wore regular garb today, so I blended in soon enough.

I missed Earth. I missed my people. It was good to be home, though, even if it was bittersweet.

As I walked, I remembered Dimitri Rostov, my slain comrade. I inhaled the air and increased my pace.

Maybe that's what this was all about. It was more than saving Jennifer. In some way, even though she'd been born a slave human on a different world, Jennifer represented all the good things we'd lost when the aliens had come to Earth.

I had to save her. I had to bring her back. I had to show her that I wanted to face the monster for her.

What was the worst thing for a man? It was running away when the bad guy came for your girl. It was being a chicken when you were supposed to be the lion.

A man is supposed to protect his woman. A man is the defender. Some people don't believe that, but some people are idiots, too.

One of the best things of the one-percenters is that we say what we mean. Before The Day, Earth and particularly the West had social justice warriors. They were terrified little weaklings afraid of bad words, needing safe spaces in case they fainted from "hate speech." Yet these were the same losers that screeched at anyone who didn't agree with them. The SJWs didn't mind calling their enemies every rotten name in the book.

When you looked up the word hypocrite in the dictionary, it had as a synonym: SJW.

Well, it didn't matter anymore. The SJWs were dead, slain by the Purple Tamika Lokhars. So I wasn't going to worry about it anymore.

Sometimes, though, I wonder what kind of hell they would have made of America. Then I realize that regular people—the gun owners—would have finally gotten sick of them one day and said, "That's it. Now we're going to play Cowboys and SJWs."

Thinking about that made me feel better.

Yes indeed. It was time to start recruiting the best of the best.

-28-

I asked around in the casino. A waitress told me to check down in the card room.

I walked around, watching people play the slots, try their luck at blackjack and the roulette wheel. I almost felt as if I'd returned to before The Day. There was old cigarette smoke, the clink of drinks and the tinkle of coins falling into slots. I heard a drunk or two explaining his system to another. I watch dice flash as a crowd surrounded a craps table.

Neo Vegas was practically the same as Las Vegas. The new boss was the same as the old boss.

I bought a beer, guzzled it and bought another. I took it by the long neck and headed for the stairs leading down to the poker room.

Soon, I moved through a corridor to a poker table. There were seven men sitting around it. The dealer was an older lady wearing a casino uniform, a gray outfit with her name SUE on a tag. She dealt the cards. They were playing Texas Hold 'em.

I saw my old pal Rollo Anderson almost right away. He was huge, and by huge, I mean hugely fat. I couldn't believe it. He had to weigh close to four hundred pounds.

What had happened to my best friend?

He had a Tom Collins on the table before him and seemed drunk.

Rollo and I used to work together in Black Sand, a mercenary outfit. We'd been in Antarctica on The Day. He hated aliens more fiercely than any of us ever had. He also used to be the First Admiral of Earth.

Rollo's skin was blotchy, and he was wearing a hat—so I couldn't tell if he'd lost all his hair or not—and he was huge like I'd said. That didn't mean there wasn't hard muscle underneath all that blubber. According to what I'd heard, he fought in a cage for money.

Did Rollo blow all the money down here playing poker?

I stayed back, watching. Rollo bet every hand, and his chip stack dwindled considerably. Finally, he won a hand.

Several of the men glanced at him.

Rollo collected his winnings, flipping one of the chips to the dealer. He didn't seem elated, but drained his drink and gruffly ordered another.

A waitress hurried to him, collecting the empty glass and giving him another.

After that, Rollo won the next three hands.

There was another big boy at the table, but this guy seemed to be all muscle. He obviously used steroids, but not of the 68 variety. He might have even been taller than Rollo, which would make him huge.

Mr. Muscles must have been in his late twenties or early thirties. He had dark hair, a leather jacket with silver studs on the neck and cuffs, and an arrogant sneer to his lips.

"You cheating?" the kid asked Rollo.

My old friend ignored the barb, saying, "Raise," as he tossed two 25-dollar chips onto the table.

The next two men folded.

The kid—he wasn't really a kid, as I've said, but he sure seemed like one compared to the bear called Rollo.

"I asked you a question," the muscular kid said.

Rollo just sat there.

"He can't have won fairly four times in a row," the kid told the others.

"It's your call," the dealer said quietly.

"I know it's my call," the kid said. "I asked him a question, though."

The dealer glanced at Rollo before regarding the kid. "I don't think he wants to talk to you."

"Hey, doofus," the kid said. "Are you so drunk you can't hear me?"

Rollo picked up his glass, rattling the ice cubes, finally lifting the glass to his lips and sliding an ice cube into his mouth. He began to crunch it methodically.

"This is bull," the kid said. "I'm all in." He pushed his pile of chips into the middle of the table.

"I'm out," the next man said.

Everyone else folded until it was back to Rollo. He looked up at the kid, who was glaring at him in a challenging way.

"You're not going to cheat your way out of this one," the kid said.

Rollo set his glass on the table, studied the kid's chips, and counted out the same amount from his larger pile. It left him with about two hundred chips. With one meaty paw, Rollo pushed enough chips into the pot to match the all-in.

"What do you got?" the kid said.

Rollo kept staring at him, saying nothing.

The dealer cleared her throat.

Rollo did not move. He just kept staring at the muscular kid.

"Deal the flop," the kid said.

The lady did no such thing. She kept looking at Rollo.

Slowly, the big bear of a former First Admiral nodded.

The dealer dealt three cards, flipping them over. It was an ace of hearts and two nines, one clubs and the other diamonds.

The kid laughed harshly. "I've got you now, cheater."

The dealer dealt another card, a queen of diamonds, waited and finally put down the river card, a two of clubs.

Rollo turned over his cards. They were two aces.

The kid turned over his cards, two nines.

"Yeah," the kid said, reaching out with both hands.

Quick as a cobra, Rollo grabbed one of the kid's wrists.

"Hey," the kid said, looking up. "You want to mess with me, old man?"

Rollo didn't say a thing, although his grip tightened.

The kid screamed and tried to jerk his wrist free. The arm would not budge. The kid howled and levered up onto the table, coming over it at Rollo.

The ex-First Admiral threw a left-handed punch against the kid's looming face. I heard something pop, and the kid dropped onto the table, out cold, with blood pouring from his broken nose.

Rollo let go of the kid's wrist and sat back. He wasn't even breathing hard.

Several of the men had jumped up from the table. They stared at Rollo. The dealer, from her chair, looked over at him.

"He called me a cheater," Rollo told her. "I don't cheat."

"Obviously not," I said, stepping up. "Otherwise, you would have taken his money and saved him a broken nose and a probable concussion."

Men whipped around to stare at me.

"Creed!" Rollo shouted. "You're back." He got up slowly, ponderously, and came around the table.

I held out my right hand. He ignored it and crushed me in a bear hug. I had to brace myself, otherwise I might have lost my breath as he tried to squeeze it out of me.

"You old bastard," he said, thumping my back. "I can't believe this."

"Sir," the dealer said.

"Hey," I said, poking the monster man in the belly.

Rollo gave me a look.

I pointed at the dealer.

"Oh," Rollo said. He faced her. "Don't worry about it. I'll take him to the infirmary. Have someone bring him his money."

The dealer nodded.

Rollo easily lifted the huge kid and draped him over a shoulder.

"Come on," he told me.

We climbed the stairs. Rollo immediately went left, walking with the kid over his shoulder. People got out of his way. One well-dressed man hurried near. He was obviously security.

"Is there a problem, sir?" he asked Rollo.

"I'm taking care of it," the ex-First Admiral said.

"He seems to know you," I said, as we left the security honcho behind, watching us.

"He should," Rollo said.

"You cause a lot of grief here?"

Rollo stopped and looked at me. "Is that what you think?"

I shrugged. "What else should I think? Spencer told me you fight in the cage a lot."

"I do. So what?"

"You drink a lot."

"Yeah. Does that matter?"

I shook my head. "I give up. What's the deal?"

"No, deal," Rollo said. "But I own the casino. What this Spencer didn't tell you was that I've made a mint in the cage and through some clever betting."

For once, my friend shocked me. "How come you've gained so much weight, then?"

Rollo grinned slyly. "I learned from the best. You. Most of this fat is pseudo-skin. I wear it for show. If people saw what I really looked like, they'd never enter the cage with me."

It took me a second. Then, I laughed. Rollo had always been a meatball. It looked like he'd finally learned to use his brains, too, and not just at computer games.

"How about that," I said. "You might not want to join me, then."

"Join you in a military strike?"

"That's right."

"Would I be the First Admiral?"

"If you wanted," I said.

He grinned toothily. "I've gotten so bored these past few years, you wouldn't believe it. You bet. I'm totally in for some action like the old days. When do we leave?"

Yeah. That was the question. We had to get out of here soon, or winning wasn't going to make any difference.

-29-

It took a week before I found all fifty assault troopers and scrounged-up enough symbiotic second skins, or living skins, or bio suits to armor them.

We all had to practice with second skin again. It had been a long time since we'd done this. Just like always, the bio suit started as a big black blob that one took out of a container. The blob felt like gelatin and quivered when I plopped it onto the floor. I stepped onto it next, and the warm substance began to ooze up my naked legs until it had coated me to just under my chin.

The second skin fed off intense sunlight and a man's sweat. In return, it amplified his strength, could give him energy, help heal some damage and harden its outer surface like flexible armor. It could also stop most radiation from reaching its human.

Once, the bio skins had secreted drugs into a trooper, turning him into a joyful berserker. We'd modified that feature a long time ago, so a wearer could think normally.

I'd chosen former assault troopers for several reasons. One, as I said, I trusted my old comrades. Two, they'd all taken steroid 68, making them stronger than ordinary. The surgically implanted neural fibers also gave each of them heightened reflexes. That meant assault troopers were faster than ordinary people.

Rollo had shown some of that at the poker table. The kid hadn't had a chance against him.

Three, I felt I could trust assault troopers because I'd worked with them in the past. Four, I had a feeling many of the old gang hankered to return to the fold and rejoin their comrades.

When the call had gone out, two hundred and fourteen assault troopers had shown up. From those, just like Gideon, I winnowed them down until I had the chosen fifty.

We practiced in Wyoming, near former Cheyenne, pounding around, firing our new weapons and learning the old call signs and commands.

After another week passed, I hurried to a comm shack one afternoon around two p.m. The shack was halfway up a steep wooded slope, with the troopers spread out below going through maneuvers. Ella had informed me that I had a call from the Prime Minister.

I squeezed into the main room, now packed with field equipment, removing my helmet. Black second skin covered the rest of me, although I wore combat boots like we had used to do.

Ella moved aside from a computer screen. Diana stared out of it.

"Creed," Diana said, pausing, letting her eyes rove over me. "It's been awhile since I've seen you like that. It brings back memories."

"Don't it just," I said. "What's up?"

Diana hesitated just a moment, and it almost seemed as if a guilty look passed through her eyes. That vanished as she said, "I need to speak to you."

"Isn't that what you're doing?"

"Speak to you back at the capital," she said.

I hid my frown by keeping my features blank. "Is our line tapped?"

Diana ignored the question, saying, "I'd appreciate it if you could make it here by four. Oh, and you'd better come alone."

"Why the rush?"

"You plan to leave Earth soon, isn't that right?"

I nodded.

"There's the reason," she said, becoming cryptic.

"Fine," I said. "I'll see you in two hours."

Diana nodded stiffly, and the connection ended.

"Something's wrong," Ella said. She leaned against a nearby table, having obviously watched the exchange. She was still wearing her living skin. It made her look like a superhero from one of the old movies. It also made her look hot. Her helmet and various armaments were on the table behind her.

I waited for her to clarify the remark.

"You shouldn't go alone to New Denver," she said.

I snorted. "You think fifty assault troopers can buck Earth Defense?"

Ella shook her head. "But why stick your head in a noose? That's why Diana wants you in New Denver alone. Have N7 land the GEV, we pile in and off we go."

"No. Later, we're going to need Diana, her generals, admirals and particularly her troops if we're going to beat the Plutonians in their side dimension. Before that, we're going to need regular space marines in the six cruisers so they can help us on Acheron."

"Fifty assault troopers can capture six Lokhar cruisers?"

"Technically, no," I said, "but with a few of my special toys, yes."

"You're allowed to use those in our backward Civilizational Zone?"

"The Forerunner artifacts used to live here," I said. "So did the Jelks. My point is that a lot of beings have broken those rules."

"So the rule is meaningless?"

"I didn't say that. But rules are bendable, sometimes. Look. If I can solve the problems with Jennifer and the Plutonians with a minimum of fuss, my bending of a few tech rules shouldn't matter much, especially as we, the Lokhars and some of the others like the Ilk and Gitan use stolen Karg technology."

"Shouldn't matter *much*?" Ella asked.

I shrugged.

She ran a handful of fingers through her hair. I liked it better long like this. It was more becoming on her.

"I still say it's a mistake for you to go alone to New Denver," Ella said. "Do you remember the last time you were on Earth?"

"Are you referring to the control discs that Abu Hawkblood used?"

"Exactly," Ella said. "I wonder if Diana ever found the main stash of discs."

"Has Diana really gotten that bad?"

"Gotten?" Ella asked. "Don't you remember Diana like she used to be?"

"Sure, I remember."

"Well," Ella said. "Now, she has the power she's always craved. Spencer has been like a drug to her, and he mainlines her more and more all the time."

"You don't like the Police Proconsul, do you?"

Ella shook her head.

"Do you think he's bugged our comm shack?"

"I know he has."

That was a surprise. My equipment must have been faulty, because I'd tested for bugs a week ago and hadn't found any.

"I know it," Ella said, "because I already found and removed the listening devices he installed."

"You really think Spencer's people are going to try to plant a control disc onto me?" I asked.

"I don't know what they're going to try. I just know that you should be careful. Look. You're tough, Creed. No one denies that. You are or were the Galactic Effectuator. You have special tech. But that doesn't mean you're immune to trouble, especially if you're alone and your enemies know your strengths. You know the old saying, pride goes before the fall."

Ella had a point. It's when a person thought he was invincible that he lost the quickest.

"Diana told you to hurry to New Denver, right?" Ella asked.

I nodded.

"That means she doesn't want you to think about it. Fortunately, I've done your thinking for you. Take us with you just to make sure they don't try something funny."

"All fifty troopers?" I asked.

"Yes."

I studied Ella Timoshenko. She looked serious. She'd grown up in the old Soviet Union when it had been a communist state. She might have grown up paranoid about police power because of that, but that didn't mean she was wrong.

"All right," I said. "Summon the troopers. We're going to take a little jaunt to New Denver before we head upstairs to the GEV."

"Diana's not going to like it," Ella said.

"Changing your mind already?"

"No. I'm just giving you a heads-up about what to expect."

I smiled.

"You already knew all that?" Ella asked.

"No. The smile is because it's good to be among my own kind again. I'm starting to feel more comfortable all the time."

-30-

The fifty chosen troopers landed at the New Denver spaceport in an old 747, a leftover from the old world. Just like the last time I'd landed alone in my flitter, a horde of siren-blaring hovers raced out to greet us.

We exited the plane like the U.S. Olympic Hockey Team that had beaten the Russians back in 1980, loaded for bear. Some of the troopers carried their tubular containers that held their bio suits. Others had holstered sidearms.

The armored hovers landed on the tarmac. Bay doors swung open, and marines in combat armor jumped out. They aimed pulse rifles at us and advanced quickly, soon surrounding us with approximately four hundred space marines.

"We should have already put on our second skins," Rollo grumbled as he stood beside me.

The newly reinstated Rollo looked quite a bit different from his poker-room guise. He no longer had splotchy skin, but normal tight skin on a broad face. He was bigger than me, thicker, and looked like an escaped zoo gorilla. Rollo kept a monster .55 hand cannon strapped to his leg.

I happened to have my Magnum .44, not that it would do much good against the armored marines. After I'd made the deal with Diana, Spencer's people had returned my old sidearm.

"Who's in charge here?" I asked the marines.

Another armored hover landed. This one vomited red-suited security people. They had weapons drawn, escorting Police Proconsul Spencer.

The small, uniformed policeman approached me. "Commander Creed," Spencer said, holding out his right hand.

I shook hands with Spencer, and I indicated with my chin the force assembled against us.

"Would you come with me, Commander?" Spencer asked.

"Where to?" I asked.

He raised an eyebrow. "Does it matter where?"

"Yup."

"Are you sure about this, Commander?"

I laughed in a good-natured way. "I wouldn't have said it unless I'm sure. You have a problem with my people being here?"

"Commander, do you happen to notice the space marines surrounding your small—?"

I cut his speech short by grabbing him by the front of his uniform and hoisting him so he had to stand on his tippy-toes. "Listen up, Spencer, I don't like strong-armed tactics used against me."

He tried to act cool, but it was hard to do that up on his toes like that. He frowned down at my hand as if his displeasure would bother me. Finally, he looked up into my eyes.

"You'd better release me," he said quietly.

I'll give him this. Spencer had composure and self-confidence. I liked that about him.

"Why did the Prime Minister summon me and tell me to come alone?" I asked.

He said nothing, simply waited for me to release him.

"Suit yourself, Police Proconsul," I said. One-handed, I lifted him off his feet and pitched him back to Rollo.

My old friend passed him back until Spencer stood in the middle of the assault troopers.

"Get the Prime Minister on the horn," I shouted to the marines. "Until you do, I'm holing up in the jet."

I turned to leave—

An armored marine stepped forward, poking me in the side with the barrel of his pulse rifle. "No, you don't," he said through his helmet speakers.

I whirled around, plucked the pulse rifle from his exoskeleton grip and bent the barrel, ruining his weapon.

His visor whirred down, and General Briggs stared at me in disbelief.

"Get the Prime Minister on the horn," I told him.

"You can't—"

"I already have," I said, interrupting him. "So save the speech. I'm not interested."

With that, I motioned to the assault troopers. As a group, we moved past blocking marines, who stepped aside, and we climbed back into the 747.

I'd hardly picked a seat when a red-suited security man climbed up the ladder and poked his head inside the plane.

"Commander Creed," the man said, "I have a communicator." He held it up. "The Prime Minister is on the line."

"Pitch it here, son."

The man only hesitated a second, tossing the hand-communicator to me. Afterward, he departed.

I looked at the little device and could see an upset Diana looking out of the screen at me.

"Hello, love," I said.

"Creed," Diana said. "This time you've gone too far. Kidnapping the Police Proconsul is a traitorous offense against the government of—"

"Whoa, whoa, whoa, slow down. A horde of space marines charged us as we got off the plane. They came with guns loaded, surrounding us as if we were criminals. Then your pet policeman starts making demands." I shook my head. "We've never dealt with each other like that before. What's going on?"

"Release the Police Proconsul this instant," Diana said, angrily.

"Sure," I said. Turning around, I pointed at Spencer sitting in a seat. "He's out of here."

"We're just letting him go?" Rollo asked, seeming crestfallen.

"Yep. The Prime Minister has given the word, and she's in charge."

Rollo eyed me, shrugged, put a hand on Spencer's right shoulder and practically flung him up onto his feet.

"Git," Rollo said.

Spencer glanced at the mountain of a man, dusted off his shoulder, glanced at me and left with as much dignity as he could muster.

After he walked off the plane, I told Diana, "He's out, heading down to the hovers."

"Now," she said. "I demand that you come into town."

"No problem."

"Alone," she added.

"Now, there's a problem."

"Ah," Diana said. "So Spencer was correct."

"About what?"

"That you've been plotting—"

"Hey, Prime Minister, do you want me to get those six cruisers for you or not?"

"Will you threaten Earth with them?"

I said nothing, merely stared at her.

"Come alone, Creed," she said. "Convince me you've been acting in good faith."

"I didn't have to come to Earth," I told her. "Without me, humanity was toast. Either the Lokhars or the Plutonians will burn down our planet. Why are you all of a sudden having second thoughts about me?"

"You're not following the line of authority, Creed. You're up to your old tricks, running things how you see fit."

"Yeah, so what else is new?"

"I'm the legal authority of Earth."

"No question there."

"That means you'll do exactly as I tell you."

"Nope," I said. "I will not. Diana, it looks to me as if you have to decide. If you want to try to castrate me so I can't do my job, then I'm going to walk."

"You'll leave?"

"On the next plane out," I said.

She stared at me through the small screen. "I demand that you take—"

"Listen," I said, interrupting her. "I'm leaving to get the Lokhar cruisers. I'm not going to fly them to Acheron with fifty people. I need regular military along for that. I'm going to need thousands of personnel, some ship people and some space marines."

"What's your point?" Diana asked.

"You can send who you want when we try for Acheron."

"What if I demand that you take Spencer with you?"

"If you want to try to run Earth without him," I said, "sure. Why not?"

"Do you mean that?"

"I give you my word."

Diana said nothing.

"Think about it," I said. "Am I acting any differently than from the past?"

"No…"

"Did I try to depose you back then?"

"No," she said more softly.

"Then, why would I bother now? I've never wanted to run the whole shebang, well, except at the beginning when I had to. Look. I'm a warrior. I'm not sure if I'm even a soldier. But I like to fight, especially against those who screw with those I love."

Her shoulders deflated. "I overreacted," she said, softly.

I shrugged. "Holding onto power is hard, making you paranoid. I think we're ready, at least given our timetable. Have your people had any luck locating the Ambassador's cruisers?"

"No."

"Do you mind having them send me a list of the places where the cruisers were not?"

"Where should I send that?"

"I'll call back and give you a number."

"How long will it take you to reach Acheron?"

"First," I said, "we have to find and capture the cruisers. But the short answer is, as fast as we can."

-31-

I had several overriding problems, almost all of them related to lack of time. The kicker was, when would the next Plutonian attack come? If it came too soon and they sent more ships, Earth would cease to exist.

I didn't know that the Plutonians would target Earth next. It was an assumption. I didn't know, for certain, *anything* about Jennifer's dealing with them. I didn't even know if it meant anything substantial that she'd taken Abaddon's DNA along.

The mysteries were a fundamental problem. As the ancient Sun Tzu had said in *The Art of War*, "If you know the enemy and know yourself, you need not fear the result of a hundred battles. If you know yourself but not the enemy, for every victory gained you will also suffer a defeat. If you know neither the enemy nor yourself, you will succumb in every battle."

I knew next to nothing about the Plutonians other than that they hated everyone and possessed fantastic technology. It was more than possible that they'd butchered Jennifer soon after she arrived.

If I thought about the Plutonians and Jennifer too much, I gnawed the skin off my right index finger's knuckle. Since worrying wasn't going to help anyone, I had to concentrate on what I *could* do, and get it done as quickly as possible.

Now, the Lokhars could have piloted their six cruisers outside of a star system, making them impossible to find. That seemed unlikely, however, as it would take such positioned vessels too long to reach the Ambassador when he wanted them. Thus, I'd discounted the tactic.

As I've stated earlier, faster than light, or FTL, travel in this part of the Orion Arm meant jump gates. Jump gates were only found in star systems, never in empty zones between the stars. The trick, therefore, was in picking the right star system to search.

I'd picked the Tau Ceti System for several reasons. One, it was close to Sol. Two, the system was uninhabited. Three, other nearby star systems had already come up empty from previous searches. Four, the Tau Ceti System contained more dust and debris than other systems, making it an ideal place to hide. The last made me reconsider the possibility. The best place to hide was often the worst place because it was the obvious place to check first. Sometimes, though, a person could overthink these things.

The biggest problem so far was having fifty people aboard my rather small stealth ship that only had one head, restroom, water closest, john, can—call it what you want. Ella had made a rotation roster, and that had helped some.

During the short trip, I'd discovered something about myself. I didn't like having all these people aboard my ship. These last ten years, I'd gotten used to working alone. I found out something else: the longer I had the fifty people aboard, the less I was disliking it.

Maybe I was thawing out and becoming more social again.

I was presently alone in the piloting chamber, sitting back in my chair, staring up at a large screen. I could hear people clomping around outside in the corridor, and tried to ignore it.

I didn't want to go out there and tell them to keep it down. Space was at a premium on the GEV and they had to walk somewhere. Fifty people was clearly too many. I should have only brought thirty-five, maybe just thirty.

With a shake of my head, I told myself to forget about that, concentrate on finding the Lokhar cruisers.

I fiddled with the scanner and debated launching a probe. Those were in exceedingly short supply, and once the probes were gone, I couldn't resupply until I returned to the Fortress of Light, a journey of two years.

I'd already scanned and flown around three terrestrial planets in the inner system and now I worked on the first gas giant in the outer system. The excessive debris made the search harder than normal.

I scanned for three hours, drinking far too much coffee while I did. I'd begun to squirm in my seat and now stabbed a comm button.

"Did you find something?" Ella asked on the other end.

"No," I snapped. "Is the john empty?"

"Ah…can you wait—?"

"I can't wait," I said, impatiently.

"Okay… I'll put you at the top of the list."

"You'd better," I said, instead of saying thank you. It was my ship, after all, and I had to go.

I rushed out, waited another few minutes before the place was empty and returned to the piloting chamber a new man. What a difference.

A half hour later, my scanner pinged. I checked why and discovered a tiny signal at a distant dwarf planet, indicating possible comm traffic.

I ran an analysis of the signal and then the dwarf planet. It was a fast-spinning object at the near edge of the system's Kuiper Belt. It was a hot dwarf planet spewing lots of radiation and radio waves. There was also a ton of debris shifting, orbiting around the planet like ocean eddies.

I ran a probability program through the predictive AI. The planetary radio waves might have caused the signal, and the heavy radiation emanating up from the dwarf planet would make that a less than ideal spot to hide. The predictive result was a 16 percent chance that the ping had come from a Lokhar cruiser.

Sixteen percent was better than anything else I had. Thus, I changed course, heading out to the Tau Ceti dwarf planet.

-32-

After too much time had passed, I maneuvered in high stealth mode near the dwarf planet. I hadn't told anyone else about the new possibility. I didn't want people pestering me for the latest update and clogging my comm channel while I was trying to search.

The dwarf planet was a little bigger than Pluto but hot instead of intensely cold. It was a lava pool of a planet for reasons I hadn't yet detected. It was also far from the Tau Ceti star. The excessive dust and debris meant a person couldn't even spot the star from here with the naked eye.

So far, I hadn't detected anything positive other than that single ping earlier. I was already gliding through the shifting eddies of dust and debris. If the Lokhars were hidden—

My sensors suddenly went wild, blaring an alarm.

I manipulated my board, switching to a rearward scanner. A triangular-shaped, Lokhar heavy cruiser slid toward me, its beam ports hot for firing. Even as I watched, Karg-like red graviton beams speared toward the GEV. The graviton rays burned away interfering debris, which gave me a better idea as to just how thick it was out there.

The beams struck the GEV, heating the superior hull alloy instead of instantly thrusting particles apart and thus smashing through like they would have done to regular hull armor.

I opened a ship-wide comm channel with one hand and activated an emergency accelerator with the other.

"Get ready," I said. "Hang on to whatever you can. We're going to move, and you're going to feel it."

I clicked straps into place, turned my chair the other way, locking it in place, and pressed a switch.

We accelerated at thirty-two Gs. That overloaded the gravity dampeners so I felt intense pressure pushing against me.

The stealth ship leaped out of the enemy beam fire. We also struck the dust and debris with greater force. The ship shuddered from the multiple impacts. Worse, it must have lit us up as a target.

Seven active enemy targeting computers locked onto us.

Seven? I thought. What was going on here? Even with all the swirling junk, I should have seen those ships before this. How had they been able to hide from my superior sensors?

I slapped emergency controls. We quit accelerating so intense Gs no longer made it hard to lift my chest to breathe. My fingers blurred across a panel.

Outside the ship, a probe launched, emitting special signals. A second probe launched in a different direction.

I moved the stealth ship down. I did so slowly, however, using every stealth feature I could. It was too bad the GEV didn't have phase abilities like the Shrike Lord Phase Suit. Then, I would have simply disappeared from regular space.

My comm board lit up. People were calling, no doubt wanting to know what was happening out there. I couldn't blame them, but I ignored the calls as I concentrated on the situation, using passive sensors to study the enemy.

Red beams burned through the murky dust and debris. The two probes had begun accelerating, jinking this way and that, attempting to throw off enemy targeting—they also jinked like that to imitate the GEV. The probes doubled as decoys. More enemy beams joined the fray. Just how many cruisers had the Ambassador kept out here? Ella had said he'd claimed six. There were more than six, although not all of them appeared to be heavy cruisers.

One of the probes ignited as a graviton beam struck it. The exploding probe expelled hardened devices emitting signals to mimic a blasted ship's debris. That was to buy us more time, as the enemy captains would believe they'd hit and destroyed the stealth ship.

A moment later, the second probe exploded. It, too, expelled the special hardened devices.

All the while, I slowly maneuvered to a new location.

I realized what must have happened. The GEV had been in stealth mode, but it had moved too quickly through the dust and debris. Somehow, the Lokhars knew to look for the evidence of a stealth vessel by watching the dust. My passage had stirred the space debris just enough. Maybe information concerning a new stealth vessel had come from the three original heavy cruisers I'd destroyed. Before sending their boarding teams, they might have launched a comm buoy.

I should have searched for that.

I maneuvered even more slowly so I wouldn't stir any dust or debris forcefully enough to alert their targeting computers.

More enemy cruisers appeared on my passive scanner until I counted eleven. Five were heavy cruisers. The rest were light, nearly half the mass of the larger vessels. This was more than an ambassadorial escort.

Had Jennifer contacted the Lokhars? Or had the tigers learned about the Plutonian assault against Earth and begun readying a strike force to hit our homeworld?

I drummed my fingers on a console. That didn't seem right. Five heavy and six light cruisers weren't nearly enough to raid Earth, never mind trying to saturation bomb the planet. The Starkiens had far more beamships than those orbiting Earth. Our factories mass-produced drones, fighters and missiles. Workers were already building new silos on the Moon and re-supplying the spent ones on Earth. Besides, Earth Force warships stationed in other regions were hurrying home.

So, if that was the case, why had the Lokhars slipped eleven cruisers out here? Why hide in the Tau Ceti System? Were more warships on the way to augment the force? Were the Lokhars attempting to gather a true fleet near Earth to hit with overwhelming force?

A chill swept over me as I had a new idea. If Jennifer had contacted the Lokhars, were the tigers waiting for a *second* Plutonian strike against the homeworld? If the Plutonians hit now, or later with greater force, they might well destroy every defender just like the first time. *Then,* eleven cruisers could waltz in and saturation bomb the planet, giving us the old one-two punch.

I needed to capture these cruisers, or capture the flagship, at least, and interrogate the admiral-in-charge. I had to figure out their plan so I could thwart it.

What good would it do to raid Acheron and come home to a dead homeworld?

As I contemplated these things, the Lokhar cruisers converged on the fake ship flotsam, the hardened emitters from the first destroyed probe. The enemy split into two groups. The first one had three heavy and three light cruisers. The second had two and three respectively and headed for the other set of emitters from the second destroyed probe.

A second chill swept over me. I had a sudden feeling the Lokhars knew exactly what kind of stealth ship they had destroyed—or that they believed they had destroyed. That meant two things. They knew about me and they were trying to glean center galaxy tech and would find the emitters soon.

I needed another mind, if nothing else, to bounce off ideas and help me think clearly. I needed a plan of action, and I needed it now.

-33-

First, I answered intra-ship calls and told people an edited version of what had happened. Second, I let Ella into the piloting chamber. She was the second non-effectuator to have reached the heart of the GEV. N7 had been the first.

She looked around before regarding me. "It doesn't seem that much more sophisticated than a battlejumper bridge."

"That's because the chamber was redesigned to my specifications."

Ella thought about that, finally plopping onto a swivel chair. "You wanted something familiar to operate?"

"Exactly," I said.

"Why are you so tense?"

I showed her the Lokhar groups converging on the destroyed probes. The cruisers no longer accelerated, but launched shuttles, no doubt to collect what they could.

"They're going to find the emitters," I said, in case Ella didn't understand the problem.

"Where does that leave us?"

"Exactly," I said.

She scrunched her brow. "I doubt the tigers could have targeted your GEV by observing the disturbed dust and debris. You're overlooking some obvious problems with the scenario."

"Like what?" I asked.

"Suppose they knew about your stealth ship. I could see that, given what happened when they woke you up. Suppose they're watching the dust and debris, their predictive computers wired to alert them about anomalies. How long have they been watching?"

"Oh," I said, beginning to perceive her point.

"Weeks, maybe," Ella said. "Even alert tigers become dull after a time. Yet what just happened? The first shot struck the GEV dead on. Even with radar-lock-on that doesn't always happen. And I know you're not going to say they got a lucky hit."

"So what are you suggesting?"

Ella pinched her lower lip. "They must have advanced targeting gear."

"Maybe," I said, unconvinced. "They spotted me before I spotted them. Even with advanced tech that shouldn't have happened, as I have the best sensors around here."

"Their first strike suggests you don't."

"Okay. If you're right, why aren't they firing on us now?"

"I don't know."

I scowled as I studied the main screen. The cruisers surrounded two areas, shuttles slowly moving within the enclosed zones.

Eleven cruisers were too many to just sit around and wait for the Ambassador. Six would have been too many. There was something going on I didn't understand.

"We could slip away," Ella suggested.

"Shhh," I said. "I'm thinking, and we aren't going to slip away. We need Lokhar ships, remember? We have to reach Acheron sooner rather than later."

Still, I thought about Ella's ideas. A Lokhar vessel had targeted and struck the stealth ship before I'd seen it. My superior alloy hull had foiled the attack, and my quick action together with the probes had allowed me to slip out of sight. No other enemy ship had hit the GEV since then.

I manipulated my board, pinpointing the ship that had fired and struck mine. It was a heavy cruiser, and it hung back from the others surrounding the selected zones.

I wanted to board that ship and find out what had allowed it to spot us.

"Okay," I said softly.

I began typing.

"What are you planning?" Ella asked.

"To play hardball with the Lokhars," I said. "They're in the Tau Ceti System, far too near our homeworld. They mean to exterminate us."

"That's an assumption."

"It's what Purple Tamika tried to do to humanity last time they were in charge. I don't see why they'll have changed their hearts this time around."

"You could be right, but what are you suggesting?"

"I thought you knew me better than anyone."

Ella studied me and paled as she bit her lower lip. Maybe she did know me after all.

I continued to type, sending a subtle message to each emitter, reconfiguring the commands. An emitter was small: the size of an old Mac computer. That still gave it plenty of space for special effectuator tech.

The minutes ticked away as Lokhar shuttles began collecting emitters. One by one, the various shuttles roared back to their cruisers.

I took careful note of which shuttle went into which cruiser. Finally, the last shuttle landed in a bay, and the warships began maneuvering back toward the dwarf planet.

The same heavy cruiser as before hung back from the others. That seemed to become more important and more ominous the longer I observed it.

"Might as well get started," I grumbled.

"Start what?" Ella asked. "Why won't you tell me?"

I tapped keys.

The emitters on the various cruisers started secretly probing their hosts electronically. Proximity would make it easier for them to crack the various tiger computers.

At the same time, I began the same procedure that I'd practiced against the three heavy cruisers that had woken me from long-journey stasis sleep; I sought to gain control of their main weapons systems.

"You know," I said, as I worked. "This isn't really fair. I have the best code hacking AI in the galaxy. My trick is a basic one. Against better-protected computers it wouldn't work. Out here in the galactic fringe, it's like running up, plucking an ice cream cone from a two-year old and slurping it in front of the crying sap. You have to have the right mindset to enjoy something sick like that. It's not my preference, but Earth is outclassed, and I can't leave any enemies behind to hurt humanity."

"What are you talking about?" Ella asked.

"Get ready. Get set. Go."

I began to manipulate my controls. This time, with the emitters in some of the cruisers, it was an even easier takeover than before.

On two light cruisers, outer bay doors everywhere opened. No interior hatches closed, either. That meant the atmosphere aboard the ships blew out into the vacuum of space. Soon, squirming Lokhars tumbled into the black, dusty void. None of them wore suits. They died almost right away, meaning those two cruisers were empty.

Four heavy cruisers trained their graviton cannons at each other. Red beams slashed out, cutting into hull armor. I'm certain onboard tigers tried to raise their electromagnetic shields—force fields. They all failed, as I'd shut down key generator stations on each warship.

Several light cruisers detonated with explosive results, sending hull plating, coils, engine pieces, shredded tiger parts, water vapor and plenty of other debris flying like shrapnel at nearby vessels, with deadly consequences.

Ella stared in disbelief at the easy mayhem, muttering profanities. Finally, she said, "This is wrong."

"I'm the Effectuator," I said. "This is what I do."

The mayhem went on for a time, the heavy cruisers cutting into each other, killing each other's crews and ship systems.

The surviving vessels were going to need massive repairs before I could use them on the main mission. The point was I would have Lokhar ships or the skeletons of ones, anyway.

Only one vessel resisted my computer hacking, the heavy cruiser that had initially beamed the GEV.

I opened intra-ship channels. "Assault troopers," I said. "Put on your suits and get your weapons. We're going into combat in less than five minutes."

"Creed," Ella said, after I'd clicked off the comm. "Fifty troopers to take out a heavy cruiser?"

"The tigers aren't going to expect a T-attack. You're staying on the GEV, though."

"Forget about that," she said, hotly.

"What I'm planning isn't like the Ronin 9 T-Suit," I said. "This is simply a higher version of the T-missiles, although my teleportation is more accurate, as I'm using galactic-core boarding equipment and procedures."

"Why should I stay back?"

"I need someone here in case something bad happens that I haven't foreseen."

"Like what?" Ella asked.

I snorted. "If I knew, you wouldn't have to stay, now would you?"

In lieu of an answer, she stared at me.

I went to my bio-suit container. After ten years, I was finally going to lead assault troopers into battle again. I could hardly wait. Now, maybe, I could find out what was going on with these Lokhars.

-34-

The GEV T-pad was small. I'd used it during missions, sending myself over, sometimes one other person as well. By standing shoulder-to-shoulder, five assault troopers could pack themselves on at a time.

I went on the first sortie, having the most technical trooper stay behind to run the pad.

The AI ran the coordinates, which could get tricky with two moving vessels. This wasn't like the Ronin 9 Suit, as I'd told Ella. The suit had done all the thinking for the teleportation. This was much harder and had to be more precise.

"Ready?" I said through my helmet comm.

The tech asked another question. It made me pause. Could he even run this thing while I was gone? I gave him the answer, and he brightened.

"Got it, Commander," he said. "This should be easy."

It was already supposed to be easy. As I thought about telling him that, we dematerialized—and appeared at the edge of the heavy cruiser's main bridge.

It was large, and the grossest creatures I'd yet seen huddled at various control panels. Those didn't look like any Lokhar controls I'd ever seen before. I didn't think the alien creatures were Plutonians, but maybe the books I'd read in the library hadn't gotten their descriptions right.

The first alien was—I don't know how to say it—a giant blob standing, or sitting or crouching at some controls. The thing was big like a mottled red-and pink gelatin piano and sported a host of rubbery tentacles like an octopus. There were a trio of eyestalks that wavered, the eyeballs on the end twisting around to peer at my four troopers and me.

We had improved pulse rifles, firing what seemed like sizzling blue sparks.

There were six of the giant blob creatures working the various heavy cruiser controls.

I suspect the sight of the alien monsters froze my troopers. It had the opposite effect on me. The instant I saw these monsters, I opened fire, realizing this could be an elaborate trap.

Pulses erupted from my rifle and struck the first blob creature.

Warbling cries that grew higher in pitch emitted from the thing. Quivering blobs like melted jam sloughed off from its main bulk as sparks hit it. The jam-like substance oozed from the open sores and onto the deck.

Each of the blob creatures reached down by the floor, picking up what looked like weapons.

"Grenades," I shouted. "Use grenades."

I dropped my pulse rifle and ripped a grenade from the belt around my second-skinned waist. Clicking a button with my thumb, I heaved the grenade, lobbing it as if trying to shoot a free throw in basketball.

The grenade sailed over the nearest blob-creature so it ignited on the other side of it. A powerful and very hot blast struck the creature and its control panel.

The alien blob shrieked and quivered violently, and whole sections melted away from it. A different trooper landed a grenade on it. The explosion caused our visors to turn dead black, while our second skins absorbed the radiation and shock.

The next few seconds produced horrible carnage. The blob-creatures got off a few shots. The second skins absorbed those, although one skin shuddered, meaning it was hurt.

More troopers appeared on the bridge.

"Use grenades, but lob them over the creatures," I said in as controlled a fashion as I could over my open-channel helmet-comm.

140

Then it was over as five grenades sailed at the last of the alien things, causing it to melt and spread across the deck like thick and sluggish slime.

"What are those, Creed?" Rollo said over a helmet comm.

"Damned if I know," I said.

"Those aren't Plutonians?"

"What part of 'damned if I know' don't you understand?" I asked.

"Roger," Rollo said. "They're a bad surprise. What are your orders?"

Luckily, my old friend recognized my surliness it for what it was. *I* was surprised.

I switched comm channels. "Ella," I said.

"Here, Creed."

"Scan the destroyed cruisers," I told her. "Tell me if the dead are Lokhars or some other kind of alien?"

"I'm on it," she said.

"Saunders," I said. "Secure the bridge. Make sure there aren't secret explosives in here."

"Yes, Commander," Saunders said.

"Rollo," I said. "Take half of the troopers and start killing everything you come across in the rest of the ship."

"Roger, Creed."

Rollo roared orders. Twenty-four troopers split into their squads and lined up. With Rollo at their head, they blasted open a hatch. I half-expected murderous enemy fire to mow them down. Nothing of the kind happened. The corridor outside was empty.

Okay. It looked like we'd really caught these things by surprise, whatever they were.

I went to the nearest control, examining it. Except for some modifications, these seemed like ordinary Lokhar ship controls.

That was comforting. This was an actual Lokhar heavy cruiser, not some alien vessel disguised as one.

"We've found Lokhars," Rollo radioed me.

"Marines, ship personnel or techs?" I asked.

"Yes," Rollo said. "All three. They're dead now."

Lokhars on the heavy cruiser. That made the presence of the blob creatures even more confusing.

"Creed," Ella said on my helmet comm. "The dead out there are Lokhars."

"Any other aliens?" I asked.

"Negative," she said. "And I checked for that."

"Saunders," I said, pointing at him. "Take two squads and head in a different direction from Rollo. We need to clear the cruiser fast."

"Yes, Commander," Saunders said, hurrying through the destroyed hatch.

I kept searching the bridge. Maybe the better thing would be to crack the computer and download all the data.

Suiting thought to action, I took a control device from my belt and began punching in instructions. Aboard the GEV, my AI began hacking the heavy cruiser's computer. I checked. Something was resisting a quick hack. That meant something greater than regular Lokhar computer equipment had been installed here.

That didn't surprise me.

"Commander," a trooper shouted.

I looked up, and the man blew apart, his pieces raining everywhere.

A heavy chuckle focused my attention. Abaddon stood by the ruined hatch, with a bazooka-like tube resting on his left shoulder. With it, he swiveled and fired again, sending a harsh beam against another assault trooper, blowing that person apart as well.

"Creed," Abaddon boomed in a powerful voice, a debilitating voice. "How does it feel knowing you are about to die?"

-35-

I couldn't believe this. "I saw you die," I told him.

Abaddon scowled at me.

He was huge, five times more massive than a man would be. He wore a dark suit and had skin the color of clotted blood. His features were classically handsome and his eyes swirled with power, with evil. He was like some dark Greek god and seemed intelligent and forceful beyond anything I'd known. Just like last time, his appearance called to mind fictional vampire princes or the way I imagined Satan would look.

Yet, in that moment, I realized something else. I peered into his eyes and did not feel the overwhelming power I'd felt before.

He aimed the bazooka-like weapon at me.

"Are you an image?" I asked.

"You fool, Creed," he said. "She said that you were cunning and dangerous. But you're neither of those things."

"Who said? Who is *she*?"

"Are you really that dense?" he asked in his booming voice.

The other assault troopers had regained their equilibrium. They fired a massed volley of pulses, which struck Abaddon and did something unexpected: they staggered him, causing him to cry out as golden ichor dripped from his dotted chest.

He must have fired the weapon as the volley struck him. A sinister gout of energy flashed like lightning from his tube. Fortunately, the pulse-shots had upset his balance. The gout of power flashed over my head and blew apart a section of a bulkhead behind me.

Abaddon shouted with such volume that I staggered backward. So did other troopers. Several fell down. The rest fired at him again. I picked up my pulse rifle and did likewise.

The volley of blue-sparking pulses struck him a second time, causing more anguish and more golden ichor to drip from his chest like blood.

"Again," I said. "Pour it on."

With a blink, Abaddon teleported away.

This changed everything. "Rollo, Saunders," I said over the comm, "bring your people back to the bridge. We're getting out of here." I waited. "Do you copy that?"

There was no answer.

"Rollo?" I asked.

"Here, Creed. Keep your pants on. I'm coming back. Is something wrong?"

"I've spotted Abaddon."

"What? That's impossible."

"Get back here!" I shouted. "Saunders, do you copy?"

A comm clicked on. I heard a scream over it like a man hit from a beam fired from a bazooka-like weapon.

"Follow me!" I shouted. "We have to help Saunders. Rollo, fix on my signal."

"How is this possible?" Rollo shouted over the comm. "Can Abaddon travel through time?"

"No," I said. And I knew then what had to have happened. Jennifer must have made a clone of Abaddon. That's why the being had lacked his father's majestic sense of evil and raw power. He was a stripling compared to the old Abaddon.

Yet, how had he become full-grown, an adult Abaddon? That was a mystery. What was he doing out here?

I roared with frustration even as I heard pulse-rifle fire down a corridor.

"I've found him," Rollo said over the helmet comm. "It's Abaddon, Creed, and he's murdering assault troopers."

"Hit him hard and fast," I said. "We can hurt him if we hit him. Use everything. I'm homing in on your signal. He might teleport and come in behind you—"

"He just did, Creed. Damnit! Hurry. He's mowing us down like flies."

I lowered my head, and I began to sprint. Could he teleport at will, or did it take a certain kind of energy he had to build up first? I had no idea.

Seconds turned into ten and then a half minute—I heard firing and saw Abaddon teleport behind a clot of assault troopers.

Without thinking it through, I grabbed a grenade, clicked the button and heaved. It sailed at the monster, who used his bazooka-like weapon to kill two troopers at once.

He laughed as if enjoying himself.

I raised my rifle and began firing. A few of the troopers who had followed me did likewise. We hit him with blue pulses in the back.

Abaddon whirled around just in time to take the full blast of the grenade. It lifted him off his feet and hurled him backward.

The blast also washed against us, blowing down assault troopers. It might have taken me down, too, but I'd dodged behind a station—the blast blew over me.

Then I was up again, racing at the supposed First One, a clone of the most dangerous being in our galaxy. From the hip, I fired pulses, the blue sparks splattering against him.

Others fired at him. We should have lobbed more grenades. Golden ichor poured and pumped from his torn flesh. I could see rib bones shining in ripped muscles.

He raised his head and locked eyes with me. "I am Orcus," he said. "I'm going away for a time. But I'm going to return, Creed. And when I do, I'm going to take a long time killing you."

I laughed maniacally, and I aimed at his mouth, clicking the trigger as fast as it would go.

Before another blue pulse reached him, the wounded Orcus, the cloned son of Abaddon, vanished from view. He must have teleported, but teleported where?

We had to find him before the bastard could get away for good.

-36-

"Creed," Ella said through my helmet comm. She was still on the GEV. "I've spotted another vessel."

"Where?" I asked.

"Near the dwarf planet," she said. "Oh, no."

"Is it firing at us?"

"It's launching missiles. The ship—it's another heavy cruiser—seems to be running away. At least, it's heading for the dwarf planet, maybe to get on the other side."

I looked around. This was a cargo room. There were far too many dead and dying assault troopers in here, gratis of Orcus.

"We have to get off the heavy cruiser," I said.

"The GEV's teleportation pad," Rollo said beside me.

"It's a one-way device. We have to get to the escape pods or to the shuttles."

Even as I said that, I knew we weren't going to have enough time.

"Belay that," I said. I touched my helmet. "Ella, Ella, do you hear me."

"Yes," she said.

"Do you see a small panel to your left?"

"I do."

"Do you see the buttons?"

"Yes."

"Tap in three-three-two-one-four-five," I said.

"Done," she said a moment later.

I'd already torn off a control device from my waist. I clicked fast, giving the AI full authority. I'd never liked doing that. The GEV AI was a tricky beast, far too intelligent. I mistrusted it as a matter of course. Still, from time to time, I'd let it do what it did best.

"AI," I said.

"I am here, Creed."

"Dismantle the incoming missiles."

"Working," the AI said.

Even as I did this, the other troopers were helping the wounded, giving aid as best they could. The bio suits helped repair what bio tissues they could.

"First missile, inert," the AI told me in its robotic voice.

"How many more are coming?"

"Two," it said.

I waited. Then I headed back toward the heavy cruiser's bridge. I should have already thought of that. The ship might have something to add in terms of weaponry to help stop incoming missiles.

I ran, puffing hard, wishing I were in better shape. Had Jennifer given Orcus leave to do this, or had the Abaddon clone escaped from her? It was all very confusing. I did not know my enemies. I could not expect to defeat them if I didn't know them. Sun Tzu had been quite clear about that.

"AI," I said.

"I have just caused the second warhead to go inert," it replied. "The last missile has safeguards. I do not think I will disable it in time."

"Where's it headed?"

"At your ship, Effectuator," the AI said.

"Can you set up a decoy signal?"

"Yes," the AI said. "But it won't be in time."

"Rollo," I radioed. "Tell everyone to get ready. A missile is headed here. It's going to hit. Maybe some of us can survive the blast."

"How much time do we have?" Rollo asked.

"Less than a minute," I said.

"I'll tell the others."

I ran toward the bridge just the same. Maybe I could reach it in time. Maybe I wouldn't, but quitting meant I'd lose for sure.

"AI," I said.

"The missile is on-target," it said. "Good-bye, Effectuator. I shall tell the Curator—"

I never heard the rest, as the missile hit the heavy cruiser. The thermonuclear warhead ignited, making everything turn white and then red, black, and then—I don't remember—

-37-

A beeping noise told me I was alive. My bones ached and my skin itched. What that a good or a bad sign?

I didn't feel strong enough to open my eyes, so I didn't. I lay there, enduring. Maybe someone touched me. Maybe it was my imagination.

I heard sounds afterward, and an instinct told me a woman called my name. I wanted to answer in case it was Jennifer. But no matter how hard I tried, I couldn't say a word.

I faded away soon after that...

I heard beeping noises again. There was a sense of the passage of time.

"Creed?"

The question came from far away. I thought it might have been God, but it was a female voice and I knew God referred to Himself with a male pronoun. Thus, I knew it wasn't Him calling me.

"Can you open your eyes?"

I tried, and I did. The reward was blurry images.

"You've been hurt," a woman said.

I recalled Abaddon—Orcus—the missiles he launched at us.

I made a croaking sound.

"It's all right," the woman said. "You've been healing."

The blurriness became more distinct, turning into an exotic elf-chick with a worried frown.

"Ella?" I whispered.

She turned her head to look elsewhere. "I don't think he suffered any brain damage."

"He's too hardheaded for that," a man said. Rollo, maybe.

"Ella?" I asked with greater volume.

"Right here, Creed. Don't strain yourself. You've been badly wounded."

"Listen," I whispered. "You have to listen."

"I am."

"Put me in the GEV stasis tube. It's in the—"

"I know where it is," she said. "You're already in the tube. That's why you survived. You were hit pretty bad, Creed."

I tried to reason out her words. Slowly, it dawned on me that she'd been using the GEV like an Effectuator. I hadn't told her about the stasis tube, and certainly not how to run it. Had she figured that out for herself? If that was the case, she'd been poking around where she didn't belong. The Curator wasn't going to like that.

"Do you see that?" Rollo said from far away. "He's getting mad about something."

"That means he's recovering," Ella said.

She came into sharper focus. I could also see the edges of the inner stasis tube beside me. The lid had slid open and I obviously lay inside it.

"How many died?" I asked.

"Three quarters of the assault troopers," Ella said.

"How many lived?" I whispered.

"The lucky thirteen," Ella said.

"Are any of the cruisers salvageable? No, wait. You have to prepare for Orcus. He's out there."

"Not out here," Ella said.

What did she mean? "Orcus escaped," I said. "He could be prowling behind the dwarf planet, plotting to destroy us."

"Creed, we're back at Earth. Orcus isn't anywhere near here. Don't worry about him."

"What?"

"You've been out for two weeks."

I thought about that. I'd been healing in the stasis tube for two entire weeks? The blast must have almost killed me. If we were back at Earth—

"Don't tell Diana about my injuries."

Ella looked away, probably at Rollo, before staring down at me. "Diana thinks you're hard at work on a plan. She's wanted to see you for a couple of days, but I've made excuses."

"Smart," I said. "Orcus got away from us?"

Ella nodded.

"Did you see which jump gate he used?"

"We did. He opened a dimensional portal, which would indicate he escaped into the pocket universe."

I must have grown pale, because I heard Rollo say, "Better put him back under. Let him heal another few days."

"No," I croaked. "Help me up."

Ella shook her head. "If you can't get up on your own, you should heal a few more days like Rollo says."

The idea of trying to get up left me cold. The idea of lying here like an invalid made me mad. I gritted my teeth, tried to reach up to the edges of the stasis tube, and found myself panting.

"Relax," Ella said.

"No," I said.

"Creed."

I roared, and I raised my hands to the sides, clutching them. I heaved with everything I had. Then, I pulled and shouted louder, slowly sitting up until I could see Rollo. At least, I thought it was Rollo. My friend was blurry and indistinct. My head was also pounding from the exertion. I blinked several times and looked again. Rollo slowly came into focus. He seemed thinner than I remembered and had the strangest smile.

"There," I said, panting, with sweat dripping from my chin. "Now, tell me—"

That's all I remember. I must have blacked out from the overexertion and flopped back into the stasis tube.

-38-

In retrospect, I'd come just about as close to dying as a man could get and still make a full recovery. With Earth tech from before The Day, I would have died. With Jelk Corporation medical tech, I would have also died. With state-of-the-art center-of-the-galaxy tech, I made a full recovery after spending three weeks in the stasis tube.

The tube beeped at the end of the third week, the lid slid back and I climbed out without a problem. I remembered earlier and examined my body. I was naked and there were hundreds of little pink marks everywhere, indicating mass shredding across the entirety of my body. I wondered what the insides, my organs, looked like.

Had I been naked before when Ella spoke to me? I shook my head, deciding not to worry about it.

Ella had said something earlier about brain damage. I checked a mirror. My face and shaved scalp had similar pink markings.

I walked naked out of the stasis chamber, padded to my room, put on some clothes and went to the small galley. I ate three, half-pounder hamburgers, tons of fries and chugged water as if I'd crossed the Sahara Desert.

I felt full after that.

It occurred to me that the GEV was empty. I decided to test the theory and made a quick inspection of the ship. I was indeed alone.

I trotted to the control chamber and slid into my piloting chair. I clicked on the screen and looked outside the ship. I saw a small hangar bay around me, cocked my head, wondering if I was hallucinating. I realized a second later that the GEV must be in the main cargo hold of a ship. I reexamined the cargo bay. I recognized it as Lokhar design and thus it must be a tiger vessel.

I turned off the screen and headed to an outer lock. *Wait.* What if I was wrong about being inside a ship and was actually in space? I returned to my quarters, found my bio suit, helmet and boots, and put them on. Then, I went to the outer lock and opened it, prepared for anything.

I stared into a cramped cargo bay.

A man worked a machine near a hatch, looking as if he was drilling something with a drill press. He must have felt my stare because he turned around, saw me and began to shout and wave.

I exited the GEV, heading to him, letting the visor whirr down so we stared eye to eye. He was one of the Lucky Thirteen, an assault trooper by the name of Cherokee Jones. He was squat and thick with flaming red hair, something of a scout specialist and crack shot.

Cherokee Jones was three quarters English and one quarter Cherokee, and had been a U.S. Army Ranger before The Day. He'd been in Afghanistan hunting down terrorists, and had been deep in the Hindu Kush Mountains when the Lokhars had sprayed the world with the bio-terminator.

The trooper grinned. "Good to see you're back on your feet, sir."

"Where are we?"

"The Lokhar Light Cruiser *Thistle Down*," Jones said.

"No. Where is the light cruiser?"

"Oh. We're orbiting Luna."

"We're not already on the way to Acheron?"

Jones looked confused.

"How long have we been in Luna orbit?" I asked.

"A week, more or less."

"We've wasted all that time doing nothing?"

"No. We were getting set to leave. You wouldn't believe how fast people worked to get our two cruisers into fighting trim. But then Orange Tamika Lokhars showed up."

"Here in the Solar System?"

Jones nodded.

"Who commands the Lokhar flotilla?"

"Don't know about no flotilla. I heard it was a fleet."

"Fine," I said. "How many ships did the Lokhars bring?"

"Twenty-one, but half of those are Orange Tamika maulers."

That was interesting. We could use some maulers, the Orange Tamika heavy hitters. "Who leads the fleet?"

"A Lokhar baron," Jones said.

"Baron Visconti?" I asked.

Jones brightened, nodding.

"Baron Visconti of Orange Tamika brought a Lokhar Fleet to Earth?" I said.

"It made quite a stir," the trooper told me. "And from what I hear, the tiger has quite a story."

I remembered Cherokee Jones better now. He was a fantastic soldier, maybe the best scout in the outfit, and one of the longest serving. But he'd never been the keenest when it came to anything beyond eating, sleeping, whoring and fighting.

So, Baron Visconti had come to Earth with ten maulers, at least. A mauler was a perfectly round, spherical vessel with five times the mass of a battlejumper, making it *huge*. They could pour out prodigious amounts of firepower, how they'd gotten the name mauler.

At this point in the war between the Lokhar Empire and us, the baron's fleet was a substantial force. Ten maulers and eleven more Lokhar warships would make a fine addition to the human fleet gathering here. But that also meant Visconti had left Orange Tamika planets that much more undefended. That must have entailed a hard political decision on the baron's part.

I still couldn't see why Rollo and Ella hadn't demanded we leave for Acheron. With the Lokhar maulers along, we would have a much better chance of reaching the legendary planet.

"Are you all right, sir?" Jones asked. "You're starting to look pale."

"I'm fine. Now shut up a minute; I need to call Ella."

"You don't need to bother calling, sir. Ella, Rollo and the tiger baron are in the galley. They called me a half hour ago, asking if I'd seen any sign of you yet. One of us is always in the cargo hold in case you show up."

"Why didn't you tell me that right away?"

"Ella said to make sure you were coherent first. They don't want you getting excited if you can't take it. I've been determining that while we speak."

"Has something gone wrong?"

"I'd say so. But maybe them others should explain it to you. I'll probably just get you mad if I say it."

I stared at Cherokee Jones, finally saw the wisdom of his words and hurried past him to get to the galley and see what Baron Visconti had to say.

-39-

As I entered the light cruiser's galley, a giant Lokhar jumped to his feet.

Baron Visconti of Orange Tamika was the biggest tiger I'd ever met. The towering baron bared his fangs as he approached me. He had a massive chest that even Rollo could envy. Medals clinked on his Lord Admiral uniform, medals for courage, cunning and fighting in some of the hottest battles in Lokhar history. Visconti had been there when we'd destroyed the Karg-Jelk Super Fleet ten years ago. He was older, now, with more white on his muzzle than I remembered.

"Commander Creed," Visconti said in his deep voice. "This is a glorious meeting, old friend."

I'd removed the second skin and stashed the helmet elsewhere. Maybe I should have kept them on.

The giant tiger gave me a bone-crushing hug. I gave one right back, though, making him grunt. He let go, towering over me as he grinned down into my face.

"You're as strong as ever, Commander. I was worried about you when I heard what happened at Tau Ceti." Visconti turned to the table where Rollo and Ella sat. "Are you sure he was healing all this time? He seems perfectly fit to me."

"How are you feeling, Creed?" Ella asked.

"Great," I said, slapping my chest. The hug had taxed me, though. I had to exert myself to saunter to the table and sit down instead of collapsing onto a chair.

Rollo got up, pouring me some coffee, returning to the table with a saucer and cup. That seemed out of character, both his getting up for me and giving me a saucer for the cup.

I decided to play along and see if this was a subtle joke of some kind.

Ella eyed me like a concerned doctor, or was it more than that?

I sipped. The coffee was scalding hot. I almost jerked back from it before I remembered this was how I was supposed to like it.

I must have been even more winded than I realized. I'd recovered from a near-death-experience. Now, I had to regain my former stamina.

Visconti resumed his seat and we chitchatted for a time. The Lokhar made light talk until I'd finished my second cup of coffee.

During that time, Ella finally relaxed, her study of me lessening.

Visconti must have noticed, as he glanced at her. Then he became serious. "I heard you faced Orcus."

I glanced at Ella and Rollo, surprised the baron knew about the encounter with the cloned First One.

"We told him everything," Ella said.

I raised an eyebrow.

"We don't have time for anything else," she explained.

"What do you mean by *everything?*" I asked.

Visconti answered for her. "She means your time spent as the Curator's Effectuator, your encounter—while traveling to Earth—with three Purple Tamika heavy cruisers, the replica, the Jelk mind machine, the phase suit, the Ambassador, the Shi Feng and the space battle where you demolished eleven Lokhar cruisers and the horrible confrontation with Orcus, clone of Abaddon."

"Oh, that," I said.

Visconti put both massive paws on the table, his demeanor becoming grave. "I have fully rewarded their candor with bizarre tales of my own. You will want to hear them, I know, as they will fill in certain gaps in your knowledge."

"Tales about Orcus and Plutonians?" I asked.

"Until now, I haven't known their species name," Visconti said. "But yes, my tales include them and the planet Acheron, as well."

"Oh?"

"Much has happened during your decade-long absence," Visconti replied, "but none of it was galaxy shattering. That abruptly changed two years ago."

"Two years ago, Jennifer left the Fortress of Light and found Holgotha," I said.

Visconti nodded. "I surmise that, soon after reaching the Forerunner artifact, she transferred to Earl Daniel Parthian of Purple Tamika."

"Did the earl become Emperor Daniel Lex Rex?" I asked.

"Yes."

"How did that happen?"

"I've pieced together some of the history while other 'facts' are educated conjectures. The point is that a little less than two years ago, Earl Daniel Parthian led an expedition to the planet Acheron. He took what remained of the Purple Tamika Home Fleet, using every bombard. I've heard Purple Tamika fought a mythical battle against an incredible guardian machine that was stationed in orbital defense of Acheron. The Home Fleet would have lost except that a Forerunner artifact teleported into the fray, aiding the bombards during the lopsided contest."

"Holgotha," I said.

"Agreed," said Visconti. "In the end, the earl destroyed the guardian ship and plundered the planet. I know this is true, for I have been to Acheron and seen the empty time-vaults."

"What! When did this happen?"

"I have just returned from my expedition to Acheron," Visconti said. "The guardian machine is no more, having become nothing but orbital debris and junk. The planet was a vast desert world with howling winds and oily lakes shimmering with polluted colors. There were broken, metallic structures half-buried in the shifting sands. In the ancient, worn-down mountains, we found vast mineshafts. We descended into several. At the deepest level, we found a time vault exactly as described by the legends. The massive door stood ajar each time, the vault barren. Ultra-sensitive scanners indicated Lokhar footprints on the vault floor. Clearly, Earl Parthian's people had cracked the ancient vaults and plundered whatever treasures had lain within.

"That would explain some of the 'new' technologies and unbelievable powers they had unleashed earlier to regain Purple Tamika the leadership of the empire."

Visconti paused, becoming pensive. "My keenest scientist found evidence of a strange city buried deep in the planetary mantle. Obviously, we lacked the equipment to drill down to the structure or any teleporting device that could reach such a place. According to the scientist, the others hadn't reached the location either. Who would build such a place?"

I shook my head, as I had no idea.

Visconti inhaled sharply. "While our shuttles lifted from the planet, a portal opened beside Acheron's farthest moon. Out of it ejected three strange ships. My men hailed them, but the ships ignored the signals. Instead, they accelerated at us as our shuttles landed in the hangar bays. We destroyed the three ships, but it was a costly fight. I lost half my fleet before it was over."

"Did you capture any of the attackers?"

Visconti laughed sourly. "We had to concentrate on one enemy ship at a time, hammering at incredible hull armor with massed mauler fire. We could break through the exotic armor, but it took time, always too much time. I wanted the secret to such material and to their exceedingly deadly particle beam cannons. To that end, I readied assault shuttles to board and capture at least one enemy vessel.

The giant tiger shook his head. "Each time the maulers breached the hull and their fire slackened, and the assault shuttle captains moved into position, the raider blew up in a frightful explosion, taking everything in range of it. Not only that, but in the titanic blast, the raider destroyed the hull material and any vestige of his weaponry."

I nodded. It sounded just like N7's downloaded experience. What I found more interesting was Visconti's initial action. It seemed uncharacteristic of the Lokhar.

"Tell me," I said, "why did you journey to Acheron?"

The huge tiger stared at his paws, slowly shaking his head before looking up and regarding me. "For countless centuries, all Lokhars have avoided Achcron. When Earl Parthian began his rebellion, easily defeating every Orange Tamika fleet sent against him, I knew there had to be a technical reason for the sudden proficiency of Purple Tamika ships. I thought, 'I will use the same trick against him, avenging the bloody death of Emperor Sant.' You have heard how Sant died, have you not?"

"No."

"While Sant listened to petitions from his highest nobles, raiders teleported into his courtroom. One such invader was said to look like Abaddon. That one used a terrible weapon that he fired from his shoulder like an annihilating tube."

"Orcus," I said.

"Although the killer resembled the ancient enemy, he lacked most of Abaddon's potent abilities. He could not dominate everyone with his will, nor did he possess a personal force field stopping all shots fired at him. Still, Orcus—as you've named him—slaughtered Emperor Sant and the nobility in the Great Hall. That day, alien ships appeared out of unknown portals, smashing the main fleet, destroying the bulk of the empire's mobile combat power."

"How long ago did that happen?" I asked.

"Nineteen months ago," Visconti said crisply, as if he'd memorized the date.

"Did the defending fleet nineteen months ago destroy any of the raid ships?"

"Oh yes," Visconti said. "Those alien ships also exploded spectacularly once they'd taken too much damage. Clearly, the enemy has installed deadly explosives in all his vessels. I would hazard that the rulers consider their battle tech far superior to ours and want to ensure that we never get our hands on that tech."

"They're right to think we'll use their tech against them if we can," I said.

"In that vein of thought, I'd hoped to find something on Acheron to help equalize the situation against the Pretender Daniel Lex Rex."

"Hmm," I said. "Our enemy has already outthought us regarding the idea. They raided Acheron, perhaps to destroy anything we might find and use, and to raid the time-vaults for ancient technology."

"I agree," Visconti said.

I drummed my fingers on the table, the caffeine from the two cups having made me slightly jittery. The coffee must have been stronger than normal. Two cups shouldn't have done that to me.

"The Plutonians clearly have superior beam weaponry and hard-to-penetrate hull armor," I said. "They don't have electromagnetic shields, however."

"They don't need such shields given their fantastic hull armor," Visconti complained.

He had a point. "Tell me more about Orcus," I said.

"I've already told you what I know, which is precious little."

"No. You've said more than you realize. Orcus lacked many of Abaddon's powers. Perhaps the sire's powers grew with his great age."

"And grew with constant practice," Ella said.

"Yes," Visconti said. "Abaddon was supposed to be incredibly ancient, is that not so?"

"That's what I don't understand about all this," I said. "The Curator told me Jennifer had taken Abaddon's DNA. The Curator did not say anything about her already growing successful clones. I wonder why the Curator didn't warn me about Orcus."

"What is your point?" Visconti asked.

"The obvious," I said. "How did Orcus get to be as old as he is already? If Jennifer took Abaddon's DNA two years ago, at most, Orcus should only be two years old now, barely more than an infant. Instead, almost two years ago, he killed Emperor Sant."

"Perhaps the Plutonians have an accelerator," Visconti said. "Or perhaps your Jennifer found an accelerator on Acheron in a time vault."

"I've never heard of an accelerator," I said. "Does it accelerate growth?"

"It is a legendary device said to be on Acheron," Visconti told me. "The old tales suggest that it is a *time* accelerator. The tales also speak about the vast power needed to run the mythical machine. With it, a boy can become a man in a matter of minutes."

"Or a clone fetus can become an adult," I said.

Visconti spread his huge paws. "That would explain this Orcus's apparent age. He might only be eighteen months old but possess the body of a fully grown First One."

"That would also explain why he lacks some of the powers Abaddon possessed," I said. "Orcus has a fully mature body, but maybe it takes longer to gain a mature First One mind."

"So we know how Orcus grew up so fast," Ella said. "Maybe the greater point is that now we know Jennifer is allied with Emperor Daniel Lex Red."

"It's worse than that," Visconti said. "Emperor Lex Rex is allied to the Plutonians. I wonder what binds them, what goal or project unites their interests."

"Wait a minute," I said, slapping the table, making my coffee cup shake in its saucer. "That's not like Plutonians. From the history books I read, they're utterly xenophobic. They hate all alien races equally. That means they should hate Purple Tamika Lokhars."

"If that's so," Ella said, "the alliance indicates something crucial. The Plutonians aren't in charge of the operation?"

"If they're not in charge," I said, "who is?"

"Probably Jennifer or maybe Orcus usurped her place," Ella said. "No..." she said a moment later. "We have to consider a horrible possibility. Let me think this through. Using Holgotha as a bargaining chip—remember how much Lokhars revere Forerunner artifacts—Jennifer convinces Earl Parthian to throw in with her. He does, bringing the bombards to Acheron. They destroy the guardian machine and plunder the time vaults. With the new/old tech, Jennifer grows Orcus into a mature state. But you said before that she took the DNA of Abaddon. That means there could be more than just one clone, more than one Orcus."

"An army of Abaddon clones?" I asked, dismayed.

"Armed with the tech of the First Ones and the Plutonians," Ella said.

Visconti groaned. "We're doomed. How can we face such a force?"

His words stiffened my spine. "The same way we've faced everyone else," I said, "head-on, trying to kill them before they kill us."

"You know," Ella told me. "We had a few helmet cams installed before our expedition to Tau Ceti. I saw footage of the blob creatures on the Lokhar heavy cruiser you boarded. What were those creatures exactly?"

"The obvious answer is Plutonians," I said.

"Your books didn't say what Plutonians looked like?" she asked.

I shook my head.

"Or where they came from?" Ella asked.

"What's your point?" I said.

"The blob creatures, the Plutonians, didn't seem like any intelligent alien life I've seen so far. Are there any aliens like them in the galactic center?"

"None that I know of," I said.

"I think I know why Plutonians are so xenophobic," Ella said. "Maybe they're from a different space-time continuum. The Kargs were unlike anything we've seen before, as much machine as a biological being, and they came from a different dimension."

"Interesting," I said. "If that's true—that the Plutonians are from a different dimension—maybe that's why the First Ones decided to put them in a pocket universe."

"Maybe," Ella said. "Unfortunately, none of that tells us how Jennifer gained mastery over the Plutonians."

"I'm not sure she has gained mastery," I said.

"I am," Ella said. "Several items point to it. One, the Plutonians united with Purple Tamika instead of exterminating them. Two, Plutonians worked on Orcus's bridge."

"If those were even Plutonians," I said.

"Let me finish," Ella said. "The creatures worked on the chief cruiser, Orcus's flagship. Why were there so few Plutonians on the ship?"

"It's your theory," I said. "You tell me."

Ella clapped her hands together. "I have it. Jennifer has only woken a few Plutonians, maybe just as many control units as she found."

"What control units?" I asked. "Did you find something aboard the heavy cruiser to suggest control units?"

"Not a thing," Rollo said. "After the missile hit, the heavy cruiser blew up. Ella retrieved us as we drifted in space."

"Wait a second," I said. "Why didn't Orcus just turn around and kill us? All we had was the GEV for protection and one conscious person."

"You're wrong," Ella said. "Your AI used the two empty light cruisers, controlling them. The light cruisers chased Orcus's heavy cruiser to the dwarf planet. While they did, I picked up the unconscious twelve."

"Including you, the Lucky Thirteen," I said quietly.

"This is starting to come together," Ella said. "I've been wondering why Jennifer hasn't struck Earth with enough force to finish us."

"Maybe there's a part of her that doesn't want to exterminate humanity and that's what is holding her back," I said

Ella examined me. "No," she said, softly. "You're hoping that's true. But it's only a hope."

"Earth is still here," I pointed out.

"Because Jennifer and Orcus are stretched thin," Ella said. "They have to keep Emperor Lex Rex and the Plutonians in line and—"

"Now you're just free-balling it," I said. "There's no basis for thinking—"

"Creed," Ella said, interrupting me. "There have been more Plutonian attacks, three-ship alien cruiser-sized attacks."

"Against Earth?" I asked.

"No," Visconti said, "against Orange Tamika strongholds and against Earth Liberated Planets, former Jelk Corporation worlds."

"More attacks in the last three weeks?" I asked.

"More altogether," Ella said, "although we've just received reports of attacks that happened elsewhere earlier."

"I want to see a map of the attacked star systems," I said.

"You will," Ella said. "Diana has called a strategy meeting. The bulk of Earth Force has returned to the Solar System. Combined with the baron's maulers, Diana wants to decide where we should strike next."

"Next?" I asked.

"Well," Ella said, "where to strike. You don't win a war waiting for the enemy to finish you. You have to attack and finish him."

"All right," I said. "I want to see a map of all the Plutonian strikes. Then, I want to think about this. Before we meet Diana, I need a plan. Because the wrong plan will ensure our extinction."

-40-

I saw the maps, taking them to my study. There, I pored over them and tried to figure out the strategic reasons for the seemingly random attacks. They had all come unexpectedly from an appearing dimensional portal. That meant each attack had originated from the Plutonian pocket universe. All of the attacks but one had been the same size, three Plutonian cruiser-sized vessels. Many of the attacks had destroyed every defender, with the enemy warships bombarding the occupied planet, wiping out everyone below.

It was a merciless form of combat in keeping with known Plutonian xenophobia.

The one unique attack had been with twice the force, six of the cruiser-class ships. That one had also succeeded, murdering a billion humans on a former Saurian world and moon.

Maybe the enemy coordinator—the brain, Jennifer being the most likely—didn't consider the Earth as the prime target. There were far more humans than the ones in the Solar System. As I've said previously, the Jelk Corporation had kidnapped hundreds of thousands of humans throughout time. Those people had children, slave children to the Corporation, but alive just the same. After the Jelk Corporation disintegrated and the Saurians abandoned the frontier worlds, the human survivors had petitioned Earth to join the Terran Confederation of Liberated Planets.

Both the Lokhar Emperor and the Plutonians—and Jennifer, I supposed—wanted humanity exterminated. There was the binding goal. The Curator had told me quite some time ago that humans were the best soldiers in the galaxy. Others had good reason to fear us. We were the little killers.

Maybe these random attacks weren't random. What if their goal was simply murdering as many humans in as short a time as possible?

I studied the attacks and the timing of them.

No. It wasn't only about murdering humans, the little killers. Killing masses of humans was part of it, but also destroying Confederation's cohesion. The randomness of the attacks meant we would never know where the next one would hit. And more than slowly—actually, quite quickly—the three-cruiser strikes were killing us by the death of a thousand cuts.

A few Orange Tamika strongholds had also been hit, but they only accounted for seventeen percent of the Plutonian strikes.

I thought about that. I wondered if I should have asked Visconti his take on the eleven-cruiser, Purple Tamika strike force waiting in the Tau Ceti System. What had the cruisers been doing there? Why had Orcus joined them? Why had he taken Plutonian crewmembers on his flagship? Had there been another purpose for having the Plutonians along? Did the enemy task force have anything to do with Baron Visconti's arrival in the Solar System?

I sat back, putting my hands behind my head and my feet on my desk as I considered that. Visconti had gone to Acheron. That had been a bold move, a un-Lokhar-like move.

The tigers were an ultra-religious race. They'd venerated the Forerunner artifacts like many Christians did their icons and holy relics. Earl Parthian had gone to Acheron because Holgotha had shown up. That had likely given Jennifer high status. The earl could bolster his crews by pointing to Holgotha.

What had bolstered Visconti's crews?

Acheron had remained unmolested for thousands of years. One of the reasons was the strange guardian machine. Another reason was the conservative nature of the Lokhars. They had made sure no one went to the ancient planet. Earl Parthian's ability to get his crews to go there—

I dropped my feet onto the floor.

Something wasn't adding up.

I went to a comm unit and hailed Visconti's flagship, OT Mauler *Iron Boulder*.

Shortly, the baron appeared on the screen. "Commander Creed, I just returned to my vessel."

"I've been thinking about your journey to Acheron. That was an impressive feat."

"Not that impressive, my friend," Visconti said. "We failed to uncover anything of use."

"You substantiated Earl Parthian's pilgrimage to the planet. The shattered guardian machine proved it."

"That is true."

"You found looted mineshafts, proving the earl gleaned ancient tech."

Visconti nodded.

"Were your crews nervous going to the Acheron System?" I asked.

"Oh, very," he said.

"How did you convince them to break the ancient taboo?"

Visconti's left eyelid jerked, quivering a moment before settling down.

"It was difficult," he admitted. "We had heard about Holgotha, of course. I told them Earl Parthian had gone, and afterward he had become the new emperor. To be honest, Commander, we were desperate. It was much easier convincing them to come here to Earth than it was forcing them to Acheron."

The baron cocked his huge head. "May I ask you a question?"

"Be my guest," I said.

"Why do you ask me about Acheron?"

"Curiosity, mainly."

"Surely, it is more than that."

I grinned. "So much about this is puzzling to me. I'm trying to understand how Earl Parthian could take the shattered Purple Tamika and raise it to imperial heights once again."

Visconti stared at me before he shook his head. "I know what you mean. Some in the empire liken the feat to sorcery. They say that Earl Parthian employs magic."

"This is news."

"But there is no *magic*," the baron said. "It is the tech of the First Ones and the Plutonians that has gained the status of magic."

"I see."

"That is why the Shi Feng have grown into a popular cult again."

I faked a yawn as an idea struck. I needed to get off the line. "I'm getting tired, old friend. It's time for a nap."

"Yes. You should be well rested before the strategy meeting." He hesitated before saying, "Can I ask you a favor?"

"Go for it."

"Can I join you when you go down to Earth for the meeting? My officers and I agree that it would be wrong for Lokhar craft to enter the Earth's atmosphere."

"No problem," I said.

"The meeting is in six hours," he said. "I believe we should be prompt."

"Yes. I'll take my nap now then. Good-bye, Baron."

"Until we ride together," Visconti said.

We both cut the connection. It was at that point that I knew something was dreadfully wrong aboard the Orange Tamika warships.

-41-

I had to check out the possibilities of my gut instinct. First, though, I wanted to talk to N7.

Before I did that, I sealed all the outer hatches into the GEV. Then, I powered up the AI and listened to a summary of all that had happened in and to the stealth ship while I'd been in the stasis tube, healing.

The AI verified the story I'd heard from the others except in one particular. In the Tau Ceti System, no one had seen Orcus's heavy cruiser escape through a dimensional portal. Instead, the AI recorded the heavy cruiser, or a vessel of heavy cruiser class, accelerate away through the swirling dust and debris until it disappeared behind the dwarf planet. That had been the extent of Orcus's escape.

"Did you have any indication that Orcus's ship trailed us out of the Tau Ceti System?"

"No," the AI said.

"Ella didn't send a probe after the heavy cruiser?"

"No."

"Why would she tell me that she saw a dimensional portal open and that the heavy cruiser disappeared into it?"

"I do not know," the AI said.

"Can you give me a conjecture?"

"She is pranking you."

"Why would Ella do that?"

"I do not know."

I sighed. "Can you give me a conjecture as to the reason?"

"None with a reasonable probability of accuracy," the AI said.

"Give me one with an unreasonable probability, the highest among them."

"There is a three percent probability that Orcus teleported to the GEV before boarding his heavy cruiser. While in the GEV, Orcus hypnotized Ella."

"Without you sensing any of that?"

"That is why it is only a three percent probability," the AI said.

"Give me a lower possibility."

"There is a one point five percent probability that Baron Visconti has brainwashed Ella regarding the incident."

"Brainwashed her with a Jelk mind machine?" I asked.

"The Lokhars could have such a machine, but that is pure speculation."

"Suppose Baron Visconti brainwashed Ella. Can you give me a reason why?"

"There are a variety of reasons," the AI said.

I didn't ask the computer for any more reasons, as I already had one of my own. Instead, I went to the comm and hailed N7.

The android had remained on Earth during our mission to Tau Ceti. I'd wanted someone staying behind to watch events and give me an honest account later. N7 had seemed like the best candidate for the job.

I used a secure channel and soon saw the choirboy-looking android on the screen. He was in New Denver, with a window behind him showing snow-topped mountains.

"N7, I'd like a timeline concerning the Orange Tamika Fleet in the Solar System."

"I do not understand," the android said.

"When did the OT fleet arrive?"

"When your two light cruisers returned," N7 said.

"Wait," I said. "That happened two weeks ago?"

"No. You and the Orange Tamika Fleet arrived four days ago."

"Oh."

"Is everything well, Commander?"

"Fine," I said. "Are you curious as to why I haven't spoken to you before this?"

"Ella spoke of serious injuries when you faced Orcus."

"Yeah," I said. At least she'd kept that part of the story straight. Ella had told me earlier—like a week ago—that we were already in Earth orbit. Now, though, we were out here near Luna with the Orange Tamika Fleet. How had Ella—or whoever—managed to trick my AI concerning the false timeline?

"Why aren't we in Earth orbit?" I asked.

"Commander?"

"Just answer the question, N7."

"General Briggs convinced Diana to tell the Lokhars to keep in Luna orbit while we awaited developments."

"What kind of developments?"

"Is this a secure channel, Commander?"

"Yes."

"The Starkien Fleet is coming."

"Any reason why?"

"General Briggs has a suspicion regarding—"

"N7, *Briggs* has the suspicion?"

"You are right," the android said. "Spencer, the Police Proconsul, was speaking through Briggs. Spencer distrusts the Orange Tamika arrival."

"Any reason why?"

"Orange Tamika maulers fought with Purple Tamika a year ago. Until this moment, we did not know that any of Orange Tamika had resisted Earl Daniel Parthian's sudden rise to power."

That was news, as in devastating news. "Has Ella or Rollo been to Earth yet since our return?"

"No."

"Have you spoken with them?"

"No. You are the first of our party that I've spoken to, Commander."

"We returned with two light cruisers?"

"And a derelict heavy cruiser in tow," N7 said.

"They're all in Luna orbit?"

"Yes, Commander."

"How many Earth Force battlejumpers are in Earth orbit?"

"Thirty-eight, sir," N7 said. "More are coming. General Briggs informed me that in another week we should have fifty-two battlejumpers. Given the lower numbers these days, because of continuing battle attrition, that is an impressive fleet size."

"Right. Thanks, N7."

"Is something amiss, sir?"

"No, N7. It's all good."

The android studied me. "I suppose this is something Dmitri could appreciate."

"I totally agree."

N7 nodded sharply. "Is there anything else, sir?"

"I'm good for now. I'll see you at the strategy session."

"Very good, sir," N7 said.

I cut the connection and thought about what N7 had told me. The Dmitri reference was a code word between us. It meant that something was seriously wrong and I was going to check it out. He was to hold down the fort until I talked to him again.

Of all the former assault troopers, N7 remembered the old code words best.

It was time to look inside the OT Mauler *Iron Boulder*.

-42-

If you're thinking I put on the Shrike Lord Phase Suit, you would be one hundred percent correct. This was going to be more difficult than last time, however, because I couldn't just walk to the mauler while out of phase.

I donned a thruster pack over the phase suit, attaching an extra fuel tank to it. That made the pack excessively heavy. I'd thought about wearing the second skin to give me extra strength. But I was already too suited up for the mission.

The suit's phase generator would have to work overtime with every extra kilogram of mass I added. Living mass required far more energy than "dead" matter to go out of phase.

I grunted as I staggered into position. The combination of phase suit, thruster pack and extra tanks taxed even my herculean physique. I turned on the generator, taking myself and all my gear out of phase.

The load wasn't quite as heavy while I was out of phase. With lurching steps, I moved through my GEV, passing through bulkheads, and I walked through the Lokhar light cruiser we'd captured, the one holding my vessel. As soon as I became weightless, I knew I'd moved through the light cruiser's outer hull and into space.

To double check that I was headed in the right direction, I surfaced into ghost-phase. I saw Light Cruiser *Thistle Down* behind me. Beyond it was the Moon. I rotated until I saw points of light, the Orange Tamika Fleet.

In the faintest ghost mode, I activated the thruster pack and began heading toward my target. Finally, seeing I was going in the correct direction, I fully phased out again.

The thruster pack would propel me faster and farther while out of phase. I didn't know the physics of why this was so, just that it was.

I've always been more concerned that something worked in whatever way it did rather than in *why* it did such a thing.

I ghosted up several times to check on my heading. Each of those times, I stopped thrusting. I wasn't sure how sensitive the OT Fleet sensors were, and I definitely did not want anyone in the fleet to know I was coming.

Despite my velocity and the relatively short distance, I had a lot of time to think. What did I believe had happened?

Well, it seemed to me that Orcus had never fled into a dimensional portal. The Lucky Thirteen had survived: that had been the twelve of us floating in space amidst the heavy cruiser's debris and Ella aboard the GEV. Orcus must have teleported onto the GEV and done something to Ella.

Orcus wouldn't have been able to teleport into the heart of the craft, however, as it was rigged to repel anyone attempting that. Somehow, the cloned First One had tricked the AI, but not completely so. Afterward, Orcus had come up with his brilliant idea that included the Orange Tamika Fleet.

This was only a theory certainly, but it seemed to fit what I knew and it explained the little oddities I'd been witnessing since leaving the stasis tube. But theories weren't facts, as Ella used to be fond of telling me. One had to test a theory in the real world to see if worked or not.

Well, baby, that's what I was doing out here, thrusting through space while out of phase. I'd only done that one other time during a harrowing mission against the Greta De of Hollis 1-10.

I ghosted up again into partial phase and saw the Orange Tamika Fleet. It was much closer than before. There were ten huge ball-bearing-shaped maulers. I saw their sealed weapons ports. If those opened and the tigers started beaming, enemy ships would go down. In this case, "enemy ships" would be our carefully and painstakingly gathered Earth Force battlejumpers.

Alone out here, I felt like the Italian frogmen of the *Decima Flottiglia* MAS who'd raided the harbor of Alexandria, Egypt on December 19, 1941.

An Italian submarine had released three manned torpedoes that the frogmen had nicknamed *maiali* (pigs). The sub had done so at the depth of 49 feet, about 1.3 miles from the harbor entrance. The frogmen steered the manned torpedoes underwater, moving through the murky depths much as I maneuvered out of phase toward the Lokhar ships. The frogmen managed to attach limpet mines to British Royal Navy hulls, disabling two battleships for many months. Some of the frogmen had been captured that day. Others had been taken prisoner later.

I was hoping to avoid their fate. Fortunately, I had tech superior to the enemy's, unlike the frogmen of *Decima Flottiglia* MAS. For one thing, space wasn't nearly as murky as the harbor of Alexandria.

I counted ten maulers, two heavy cruisers, six light cruisers and three sleek pursuit destroyers. I noticed a few shuttles moving between the vessels.

So far, no Earth-crewed vessel had joined the Lokhar ships. I had no doubt the newly constructed silos on Luna were primed to launch missiles against the "friendlies" if the need arose.

Visconti wanted to join me on the ride down to Earth. What was the real reason? Was the baron attempting to gain our full trust, or did he plan to attack during the meeting?

When I said the baron, I meant the mind controlling the baron. Was that Orcus?

It was time to try to find out.

-43-

I rotated myself and used the thruster pack to brake my velocity to a slow drift. Afterward, I approached the flagship OT Mauler *Iron Boulder*. I felt like a space flea as I neared the giant hull, reading the huge lettering.

The ship name had a pre-Lokhar Space Age connection to the era when the tigers had fought each other medieval style. They hadn't used horses like humans had, nor any horse-like animal. The sword and spear-fighting tigers of that time had, however, built castles and catapults. Before the tigers invented gunpowder, they had developed trebuchets just as we had done on Earth. A catapult used the torsion of twisted rope or hair to hurl its load. A trebuchet used gravity-assisted counterweights. Such a weapon could hurl its missile farther and harder, and remain in operation for a longer time period. With a catapult, the ropes or hair lost their tension over time, affecting accuracy and requiring maintenance.

In any case, a clever tiger of that era had been inspired to use iron boulders against some of the more stubborn castles. The iron boulder had become a symbol in Lokhar terminology for massive destructive power.

I reached and slid through the outer hull of the Mauler *Iron Boulder*. Since I was no longer weightless, I staggered until I came to a large ammo hold. I debated a growing idea and finally decided to take the risk. By that time, I was panting from the exertion.

I detached the thruster pack and its extra tanks, stashing them in an out-of-the-way place in the hold. A tiger might find these if he came in here, but I felt it was worth the risk so I could move freely and more quickly in the phase suit.

Once I'd shed the extra weight, I phased out again and trudged inward toward the bridge, which was in the very center of the ship. That was the safest and sanest place to put a bridge. The idea that the command crew would be outside the main hull on top for easy targeting was ludicrous.

Every time I ghosted up for a look around, I saw regular Orange Tamika tigers going about their duties. There was nothing sinister or underhanded about their actions. I'd gone on more than one expedition with Lokhars. This all seemed normal to me.

As I've said, an OT Mauler was a huge ship. It thus took time to cross the intervening territory. Finally, though, I neared the bridge.

I carefully ghosted down until I could hardly see a thing. The Lokhars in the corridors as well as the bulkheads all seemed very faint, ethereal even. I stayed within the bulkheads for the most part, poking my visor out for an occasional look-see.

The first clue I might be right were big Lokhar guards. They wore tiger battle armor, space marine suits weighing an ungodly amount and with exoskeleton power. Their batteries could store an amazing amount of juice.

The idea of small nuclear motors powering battle armor was crazy. Not even galaxy-center aliens had that kind of ability.

The space marine tigers all wore combat armor. I ghosted up enough to see the blinking lights on their weapons, indicating they were ready to fire. A squad of Lokhar space marines stood at the entrance to the bridge.

No one was getting past them, well, no one who didn't own a phase suit like mine.

I pushed into the bulkhead and began moving. My heart was pounding. I hated the idea of Baron Visconti being under enemy control. I hated even worse the idea of a Lokhar battle fleet waiting to backstab us at the worst possible moment.

With a heavy heart, I moved through the bulkheads, judged distances and very carefully eased my ghosted visor toward the last wall.

I eased out of the wall with the visor until I saw faint ghostly images of long control panels built lower down to the deck than normal on a Lokhar ship. Slithering across the deck were blob creatures—Plutonians. They moved like fast snails or slugs might. Their locomotion revolted me.

I heard nothing yet, just saw these ethereal images.

My heart pounded worse than ever, but I didn't know why. I debated finding a place on the bridge where I could hide and fully phase in. I needed footage of these creatures. I had to warn—

I frowned as the pounding of my heart increased. It dawned on me that that was wrong. I'd been on plenty of harrowing missions while out of phase and in ghost mode before. I'd never had this reaction.

What could be causing it?

I blinked several times. I… I… Sweat stung my eyes, making me blink worse than before. That caused me to inhale sharply. Suddenly, I felt nauseous. Maybe I'd been out of phase too long.

There were stories about agents who hadn't been able to get back into phase. Even when their generators failed, they had remained stranded in the ethereal reality. They had wandered for a time, their bodies lasting longer out of phase because…

I don't know why.

I drew back into the bulkhead. Maybe if I didn't have to look at the gross Plutonians I'd gain my bearings again.

The opposite happened. I became more nauseous and the chest pounding grew. Was I having a heart attack? That couldn't happen to me. I was Creed, the fittest human in history.

I'd bested everyone sent to kill me. I'd defeated—

I frowned as even more sweat slid into my eyes. An overwhelming need to tear off the helmet filled me. I had to phase in and get my bearings.

With stumbling steps, I maneuvered through the bulkhead, through a corridor, more bulkheads—I began to run, panting, cursing with a desperate need to free myself of the restrictive phase suit.

This was killing me. I would die in seconds if I didn't tear off the suit. I'd been a fool to come here. I would lose. I would lie moldering on the ground for animals to gnaw. Abaddon would haunt my soul—

I halted abruptly, and as I stood there with pounding heart and sweat-stung eyes, I realized these thoughts were not mine. I had never been so defeatist in my life. These were alien thoughts. These were—

"Orcus," I whispered.

In that moment, I realized he was on the mauler and he knew I was here. More than that, the Abaddon clone was attempting to lure me to him so he could do unspeakable things to me.

"Not happening," I said through clenched teeth. Instead, I was going to find Orcus and kill him.

-44-

I shed the Shrike Lord Phase Suit, setting it against a wall. It felt good to wipe my eyes, run my hands over my head and breathe deeply of Lokhar ship-air.

I was still aboard the OT Mauler *Iron Boulder*. Now, I was only wearing my Effectuator metallic garb with the added feature of thick metal cuffs around my ankles, wrists and lower neck. I had a blaster attached to one hip and a longish handle with buttons attached to the other.

I was in a bright large chamber with an altar to the right. Various stained-glass-window types of figures stood as if in alcoves. They were representations of tiger saints in their strict Creator worship.

At present, the chamber was empty.

I did some stretches and flexed my fingers. I was going to kill Orcus—

The main hatch opened and three hulking Lokhars walked in. They did not wear combat armor. Instead, they wore flowing orange robes. Each gripped a long poleaxe-style weapon. The one difference was that instead of axe heads, they ended with flexible claw-like, movable hooks. Guide wires moved the hooked claws, which the bearer operated with a glove-like device attached to the lower end of the pole.

The weapon was a *raker*, a uniquely Lokhar weapon beloved by the Shi Feng.

I hadn't expected them to show up.

Lastly, Orcus strutted into the worship chamber. He wore a dark garment and possessed various tools at his waist, including several laser pistols that jangled as he walked. He'd healed nicely and seemingly totally from his previous damage, proving that I had to kill him in order to get rid of him. I didn't know if he had a stasis tube like me, innate healing abilities or some other kind of medical tech.

"Commander Creed," Orcus said in his booming voice. "Are you here to kill me?"

"You guided me here," I said.

He smirked satanically. "I'm impressed. I didn't realize you knew it was me."

"I didn't know right away, but it became obvious after a time. I remember how I drove you away once already while in the Tau Ceti System. You fled because we had seriously injured you. I liked giving you pain, the more the better, I say."

His eyes seemed to burn with power.

I grunted, as a weight struck my mind. Then I staggered backward until I thumped against a wall.

His eyes seemed to burn with even greater ferocity. "Kneel before me, you gnat," he said.

I'd always been a stubborn kid who became a stubborn man. It was one of my key traits. The Curator had said it had more to do with mere mulishness. I was one of those rare individuals, he'd told me, who possessed stronger than average willpower. By that, he meant I could resist those with domination powers.

Abaddon had been able to dominate others with a look or a gesture.

Orcus likely had the latent ability, but needed to grow in inner stature before he could do, with the same ease, what Abaddon had done in his prime.

Was this power unique to First Ones? I did not know. The Curator had taught me a few skills, which—he claimed—strengthened my native willpower. What I'm trying to explain is that I could resist Orcus's newfound strength. I don't know if Orcus knew that yet.

I debated trying to trick him by acting meek and humble until I could get in close for a deathblow. The thought made my gut crawl with revulsion. Instead, I stood tall and shook my head.

"Last time is going to seem like a picnic," I said. "Are you a good screamer?"

The ferocity in his eyes hardened into something much worse. That struck against my will like a proverbial ton of bricks. I gritted my teeth, trying to shake off his domination. It proved difficult but intensely rewarding. Using the brick-pile analogy, I tore them away until I climbed up on top of them to stare challengingly at Orcus.

Abruptly, the ferocity in his eyes dimmed. He seemed puzzled with me. Then, he smiled evilly.

"This is for the better," he said. "I will enjoy breaking you over time, bending you to my will particle by particle so you can see it happening and know that you are helpless to stop it."

"Not going to happen," I said.

"Oh? And how will you don your phase suit in time to escape from here?"

I pointed at the Shi Feng acolytes one at a time and finished by pointing at Orcus. Finally, I pointed at the floor.

"What does that signify?" Orcus asked.

"Your deaths," I said.

"You, a puny gnat, will kill me?"

"And the three buffoons with their sticks," I added.

"How do you propose to do that?"

I smiled.

"No," Orcus said. "It is time you learned the error of your arrogance. I thank you, though, for I have need of the phase suit. I'm glad you brought it to me."

"Why didn't you have your butt-boy Visconti hand the suit to you earlier?" I asked. "He could have had Ella take it out of the GEV and bring it to him while I was in the stasis tube healing."

"That was too risky at the time," Orcus said. "Her hypnosis might not have held with such an order. You see, I have bigger plans afoot than just gaining your suit."

"You desire the destruction of Earth Force?" I asked.

"That, and the annihilation of your pesky planet," Orcus said.

"Plutonian ships are headed here?"

"You do realize that I am going to inflict even more pain upon you because you think you are tricking me into telling you my secrets. That is a vain conceit, Creed."

"Are you Jennifer's slave?" I asked.

Orcus frowned, and he spoke to the Shi Feng assassins. "Bring him to me."

The three tigers leapt at me as they roared, bringing their rakers to the fore.

I drew my blaster.

"I think not," Orcus said, fast-drawing one of his laser pistols and firing.

That's when I activated the cuffs around my ankles, wrists and neck. They did not sheathe me in a protective force field. Instead, they acted like the suit I'd worn ten years ago when I'd fought Abaddon in his courtroom. The metal loops speeded my metabolism to an intense degree and allowed me to move at heightened speed. Naturally, I saw quicker and thought at hyper-speed as well.

The use of such a suit taxed an individual to an inordinate degree. It was one of the reasons I seldom used it. I had brought it along this time because I'd suspected something like this could happen.

Orcus's laser beam flashed at me, but not until I'd fractionally moved to one side. The laser pulse moved at the speed of light, too fast for it to make any difference to my heightened senses. A bullet would have moved slowly to me, but lasers weren't bullets.

Now, I used my drawn blaster, firing at each barely moving assassin. One by one, I burned out their eyes, frying the brains inside their skulls. As I charged across the room, their forward momentum changed as they twisted slowly in the air.

To me, they were out of the fight, images that wouldn't hit the floor until I had either won or lost.

I aimed the blaster at Orcus, firing at him.

The beam stopped centimeters from his skin. He had a force field this time. I don't think he generated it—as Abaddon had done, through force of will—but had some mechanical device to do it for him.

It was a clever move on his part, but it wasn't going to save the clone of the First One.

In my speeded state, I moved past the dead and almost-still Shi Feng assassins. Orcus moved the pistol, the laser flashing with repeated firings, meaning he held the trigger down as he tried to sweep it toward me.

As I raced at him, I slapped my blaster back onto my hip. I took the longish handle from my other hip, pressed buttons on the thing in the correct sequence, and watched a red force axe sprout into existence.

This had been Abaddon's weapon once when he'd fought me over ten years ago. My force blade—a gift from the Curator—had been destroyed in the fight, although I'd wounded Abaddon in the process. The Curator had collected the force axe after our victory, putting it in the Museum. I'd liberated the axe before my departure. It was probably the most sacrilegious of my thefts.

Orcus moved in slow motion compared to me. However, as a clone of a First One, he was one of the most dangerous and unique individuals in the galaxy. His thought process was likely swifter than others. He also had an ability to teleport. It was a natural phenomenon, just as an electric eel could generate an electrical charge and zap a creature.

Could Orcus teleport out of danger before I could reach him? I gave that a high probability. It would have been better if I could have caught him napping.

I ran at him. He attempted to raise his pistol into position. In regular time, my motion happened almost as fast as the blink of an eye.

I noticed a change on Orcus's face. It was subtle at first, but it was there. His eyes actually changed color, going from deep black to a sinister toxic green like chlorine gas. His brow furrowed, and I could see him start to concentrate.

I had to reach him. I had to kill him. If he could teleport away, he could order the Lokhars to attack us. I had no doubt now as to the nature of this trick. Orcus was likely waiting for three or more Plutonian ships to show up through a dimensional portal. Then, as the OT Fleet and Earth Force converged on the three Plutonian vessels, the tigers would backstab us and obliterate Earth Force, and afterward, the human homeworld.

It was a diabolical scheme—given that I was right about it.

I raised the force axe, the red glow shimmering with power. This was an ancient weapon, a piece of Forerunner technology. I began to swing and Orcus began to fade. I'd never witnessed anyone teleporting while I was at hyper-speed.

"No!" I shouted, swinging the force axe, hoping to reach him in time.

Orcus faded more, sparkles appearing in his body. That was a crazy cool image. The light brightened to an intense degree even as I kept swinging.

I wasn't sure. I thought I felt the slightest resistance to my swinging blade. The force axe produced wicked energies; reportedly able to slice through anything known in existence, including force fields. That's why I'd used such a weapon ten years ago against the almost-invincible Abaddon.

I tried to see what was happening, but the sparkles in Orcus's body were blinding me.

The force axe completed its arc. I thought I could see faint golden ichor splash from the vicious cut. Then I was stumbling through the spot where Orcus had just been.

The clone of the First One had successfully teleported away. Had I wounded him before he'd left? I felt sure I had, but I had no idea how badly. If I'd struck deeply enough, I might even have killed him, maybe lopped off his head.

Surely, if I'd chopped off his head, he would have quit teleporting. But then again, I knew nothing about his inborn ability other than that he possessed it.

Orcus was gone. I did not see any golden ichor on the floor. It might have teleported away with the giant clone. The First One might even now be telling others to go on high alert.

What was I supposed to do now?

-45-

I started with dropping out of hyper-speed. With a gasp and a lurch, I crashed onto the floor. The force axe flew from my weakened grip. It sizzled with power as the blade chopped into the floor.

I barely managed to scramble up in time. Cramps hit some of my muscles, but I ignored them, grabbing the handle and pressing switches.

With a *whomp* sound, the red force axe disappeared. The sizzling stopped, although a fierce stench billowed up from the burnt deck plating.

After that, I rolled onto my back and clutched a calf muscle. It didn't help much. I had to roll the other way and work myself up onto my feet. Then I pressed down with all my weight on the foot, forcing the cramp to subside.

That left me panting.

The metallic cuffs had energized my body to speeds it had never been designed to go. My mind felt sluggish, and my body was utterly fatigued. While in the hyper-state, the ankle, wrist and neck cuffs had supplied me with a numbing force by feeding off my body's natural fuel sources.. I could literally have run myself into the ground while wearing the hyper-suit. I could have killed myself if I'd stayed speeded-up too long.

Now, like an old man with age-withered muscles, I limped across the room, wheezing, coughing and feeling at least twice my age. Ten years ago, I'd had a complete hyper-state suit and been able to last longer without negative side effects. This time, I'd seriously strained my muscles. In fact, I wasn't sure how long I could keep going. I needed to sleep for days in order to recoup from the brief ordeal.

I could possibly pop some stims to help me, but I didn't want to risk a cloudy mind. Instead, I would use my sleepy, exhausted but still unclouded brain. The key was in knowing I was exhausted and prone to making bad decisions, and trying to compensate.

With great deliberation, I donned the phase suit. I didn't gloat over the dead assassins nor did I worry that Orcus's mind-slaves might even now be rushing to capture me.

I raised my head.

"Don't be a fool," I muttered. I couldn't afford to let anyone capture me. Earth could not afford my getting captured just now.

I'd just found out the worst. Earth Force and the planet were in deadly peril from an OT backstab. A Plutonian attack should commence soon. If Orcus had survived my force-axe blade, he could still pull this off, having the OT Fleet help the Plutonians against us at the worst possible moment.

I finally pressed together the last suit seal and clicked it on. I phased out before any Orcus slaves appeared.

In an exhausted state, I began to backtrack my former route. What should I do? It really depended on Orcus. Was he dead, badly wounded, giving warnings—or out of the picture for the time?

I didn't know.

"Right," I muttered to myself.

I found a small, unoccupied place, phased in and sat down on a tiger cot. I stared at the bulkhead for a time and suddenly jerked up my head.

I'd dozed off. I stirred, and my joints felt stiff and sore. How long had I been out?

I checked a helmet chronometer. I'd been out for twenty-two minutes. That was bad. I was giving Orcus time to recover if I'd only wounded him.

"All right, you smarmy bastard," I told myself. "It's time to walk the last mile. Until you're dead, you keep moving."

I thought about getting off the bed, but simply couldn't do it. My mind wandered until I remembered a day many years ago when I'd been deep inside the portal planet. The assault troopers had had to go the last mile, and many of them had simply quit. I'd goaded them. Maybe it was time to goad myself.

"Are you a pussy, Creed?" I whispered to myself.

Somewhere deep inside me an old resolve stirred.

I pushed off the cot and swayed where I stood. I had a mission. I had to get it done. I'd given the finger to the Curator so I could save my planet from annihilation. Now—

I moved one foot ahead of the other. I did it until I reached the bulkhead, and then I walked against the bulkhead, thumped against it hard and stumbled back onto my butt on the deck.

I stared at the wall, finally realizing I'd forgotten to go out of phase. I climbed up onto my feet and did that now. Then, I tried it again, pushing through the faint bulkhead as I trudged through the OT Mauler *Iron Boulder*.

In my dazed state, I stumbled through the giant vessel. I'm sorry to say I got lost, me, the Galactic Effectuator. Finally, though, I oozed through a bulkhead and found myself staring at ghostly Plutonians on the mauler's bridge.

I wasn't sure about the right way to do this. I was dull-witted, at best, but likely had the element of surprise.

It was making me think I'd slain Orcus.

That meant I had to wreak havoc on the enemy while I could. It would be best to free my old Lokhar friends from hypnotic domination. That meant killing the Plutonians. If I phased in, though, and used the blaster—

In the dimmest ghost phase I could, I snuck up on a Plutonian. Then, I stood behind him, phased in, activated the force axe and hacked through the slimy body of the blob alien.

The thing shrieked and squirmed like a salted slug. I hacked, turned and ran at the next nearest, doing the same thing to him or it. Maybe they were sexless, and divided in two like a cell in order to propagate the species.

At that point, an alarm rang.

I phased out, moving to where I figured the next blob was and phased in. Lokhar space marines in combat armor milled about. They seemed confused. Had they seen the Plutonians before this? Was the sight of the aliens confusing the tigers?

I chopped another blob creature, and shouted in Lokhar, "Kill them. Kill them all!"

I phased out as the tiger space marines opened up. They fired at me, the beams and rifle slugs passing through my ghostly form.

That hadn't worked the way I'd wanted.

I looked around and told myself to really see what was taking place. What was I missing? What was so obvious—?

I saw it then. The machine was as big as an old-style dishwasher from before The Day. A host of antennae sprouted from it. In ghost form, I witnessed a weird ethereal glow from it that zigzagged up the antennae and spread outward like sizzles of electricity. Two Plutonians operated the machine, constantly making adjustments and studying screens embedded in the thing.

Several tiger space marines had their backs to the machine, guarding it.

I phased fully out, moved to it and phased in, clicking on the force axe at the same time. With a swift chop, I smashed through the machine. Instantly, I phased out and moved far enough to reach a bulkhead.

I ghosted up and saw a different scene than before. Lokhar space marines stood about dully, seemingly confused.

The Plutonians slithered to weaponry and burned down the space marine tigers on the bridge. Then, it seemed, as if the blob creatures gestured and spoke to each other. Maybe they were deciding what to do next.

Dents appeared at the main hatch. It seemed that more space marine tigers were trying to bash their way onto the bridge.

I'd guessed right then. The machine I'd hacked had dominated or hypnotized tiger minds. But it took time for Lokhars to shrug off the mental dominance once the machine stopped sending its signals.

It was time to get to the other vessels and chop more domination machines into smithereens before the Plutonians made the right decision about what to do next.

-46-

I took out three more domination machines on three other maulers. But that's all the time the Plutonians gave me. By then, I was more than exhausted, moving on my last fumes of energy.

I made it off the fourth mauler and started using the thruster pack to the fifth. I noticed an oddity the next time I ghosted up for a look-see.

Maulers and other Lokhar warships were powering up their cannons.

I phased in just enough to call Baron Visconti.

"Creed?" he asked, staring at me on my visor-screen.

"Can you think clearly again?" I asked.

"I...I feel like I've been dreaming," Visconti said.

"You haven't," I said, "but alien creatures have been controlling your minds. Now, listen. I only have a few seconds. The Plutonians are going to pinpoint my position and blast the area."

"Plutonians?" he asked.

"The dead slimy creatures you've found on your flagship, the ones that have been controlling you."

Visconti rubbed his forehead. "This cannot be happening," he whispered.

"Listen, you clown. Plutonians still control most of your fleet. They're powering up their weapons. They're going to destroy your freed ships. Fight back. Call the other freed mauler captains and ask for Earth Force help. There's going to be a bloodbath unless you can think of a way to avoid it."

Even as I said that, my phase suit beeped a warning. Lokhar targeting computers had a lock on me. It was time to go.

"Good luck, old friend," I said. "It's been great knowing you. I hope you figure it out in time."

With that, I phased out. I did it even as red graviton beams stabbed at me. They flashed where I had been in phase, passing harmlessly through my ghostly form.

It was time to go home. I wouldn't be able to call for a time. I had to hope Diana and her admirals knew what to do. I had to hope N7 had spoken to her, and I dearly hoped that I could find the domination machine forcing Ella and Rollo to do Orcus's bidding.

Time... What a joke. Most of the time we think we have all we need. Then, something bad happens, and time becomes the most precious commodity in the universe.

As a kid, I'd wasted years of my life playing video games. I'd wasted even more of it in the classroom listening to my PC teachers blabbering about a lot of crap most of the time, with the exception of Mr. Glen, my history teacher in eighth grade.

Now I'd run out of time. I flew home with my thruster pack, ghosting up and witnessing a vicious space battle being fought at extremely close range.

The Plutonian-controlled OT vessels fired on the free but sluggish OT maulers that nominally belonged to Baron Visconti. At that range, no one missed. Getting off the first shot was critical.

Once, I dared to phase in and warn Luna Central. Was it in time?

The next ghost up, I saw Luna silo-launched missiles crash against the Orange Tamika Fleet. It was carnage of the worst sort. Instead of augmenting our force, the OT Fleet was forcing Luna Command to use up their precious missile supply.

I phased out again and continued for the Light Cruiser *Thistle Down*. It was a long and lonely flight out of phase. I was too mentally exhausted to think much. The time passed as a painful blur. Finally, moving on automatic, I reached our captured Lokhar vessel, which had moved onto the other side of the Moon from the Orange Tamika Fleet, using the cratered object as a beam-shield.

I stumbled through the light cruiser's bulkheads and finally reached the GEV. I took off the thruster pack—I'd shed the used-up fuel tanks a lifetime ago. Then, I unlatched the seals and crawled out of the phase suit.

I stood there with my eyes closed, utterly spent. A child could have gutted me.

The next thing I knew, someone shook me as I lay in bed—I had no idea how I'd gotten here.

"Leave me alone," I whispered.

"Creed. You have to wake up, Creed. What happened out there?"

"I don't know," I said.

The shaking continued. I had the feeling it would never stop. My teeth rattled. My neck hurt—I opened my eyes, peering up at Rollo.

"Get out," I whispered.

"You screwed up, Commander. The Orange Tamika Fleet went crazy. They opened up on each other. Luna Command helped them destroy ships. Missiles slammed home and ignited at pointblank range. What was left of the fleet took off."

"What?"

"The Orange Tamika Fleet fled Luna, fled Earth and our battlejumpers. The fleet is heading out system in the direction of a seldom-used jump gate. They're spraying masses of gels behind them, I guess in case the battlejumpers decide to fry 'em with the heavy lasers."

"Good riddance to the Lokhars," I mumbled, rolling the other way to go back to sleep.

"No, Creed," Rollo said, pulling me back to face him. "We need the Lokhars. Ella convinced Diana we can go after them and plead with them to return. We need their ships."

"Plead?" I asked, waking up more, peering at an earnest Rollo Anderson.

"Whatever we have to do to get the Lokhars to come back and help Earth," Rollo said.

"*You* want to plead with the Lokhars to stay?" I asked.

"Do you have trouble hearing me, Creed?"

"Just a second," I said, closing my eyes.

"Can't you wake up? What's wrong with you? Where are your phase suit and the force axe?"

The questions jarred. How could Rollo know about the force axe? I hadn't told anyone about it. What's more, Rollo would never *plead* with any aliens, no matter how much he needed their help. The First Admiral had a pathological hatred of *all* aliens. He was almost Plutonian in his xenophobia.

Orcus, I told myself. Rollo Anderson was still under the thrall of Orcus's mental domination. My best friend knew these things because Orcus—in some manner—must have enlightened him. That meant the cloned First One must still be alive.

I had a terrible feeling that also meant that Orcus was on the GEV.

-47-

I groaned as I sat up. All my muscles felt stiff.

"What's wrong with you, Creed?" Rollo asked.

"Where's Ella?" I asked.

"She's been trying to contact Baron Visconti and find out what went wrong. This is a disaster."

I eyed Rollo. He was even more out of character than he'd been before. Did that mean greater mental domination than earlier? I deemed that likely. That didn't have to indicate Orcus was aboard the GEV. In fact, that struck me as false the more I thought about it. The cloned First One would have slain me as I slept if he was here. No. It seemed—

"Oh, shoot," I said.

"What's wrong now?" Rollo asked.

"I left my kit in the other room."

"Do you want me to get it?"

"No. I need to get up, move around." I climbed to my feet as I said that and moved like a rusted robot.

"Why are you so stiff?" Rollo asked.

"I'll tell you in a minute."

Rollo stared at me, and something happened in the back of his eyes. He grinned nastily. "Nice try, Commander. But it's not going to work. You found out, didn't you?"

I faced him, saying, "I don't know what you mean."

"I don't believe you. You know…you know…" Rollo shook his head. Then he clutched his head with both hands, groaning.

I cocked my right arm and hit him on the chin. I must have hit him harder than I realized, as the blow catapulted my best friend off his feet. He cracked the back of his head against the deck upon landing. I'd just wanted to stun him for a second. Instead, he began to snore. Despite my exhaustion I rolled him onto his side and into the recovery position.

Then, since he was out, I stumbled from my quarters. How much time did I have left? Was Orcus—or were the Plutonians—pumping greater power through the domination machine? Did that burn out a subject's mind faster, or did that make the process more discernable to the subject so he could actually resist it? If someone lightly blew on the back of a person's neck, that might make the neck tickly and annoy the person enough so he rubbed his neck. But if someone blew as hard as he could on a subject's neck, the process would be obvious enough so the person would know what was going on. That's what I think had happened to Rollo a moment ago.

Even so, the Plutonians, or Orcus, surely knew how the domination machine worked. Could it have been a command surge of some kind, an error? Maybe the good guys had gotten a small break for once.

I reached the GEV control chamber and locked the hatch behind me. Then I activated the AI. I began a tedious process of querying my computer, trying to find the location of an unusual machine installed while I'd been in the stasis tube.

After ten minutes of questioning, I became convinced there wasn't such a machine on the stealth ship. So I queried the AI about the OT Light Cruiser *Thistle Down*.

Then it hit me. I knew where the domination machine must be. I didn't have the energy to don the phase suit, and I didn't want to sprint to the light cruiser's bridge. Instead, I used my GEV's takeover process and sent several *Thistle Down* missiles at the derelict heavy cruiser we'd brought with us from Tau Ceti. We'd also towed the heavy cruiser with a tractor beam, pulling it behind the Moon with us.

The enemy reaction was fast. Alarms rang in the GEV. My comm board lit up.

I pressed a switch.

Ella's partly disheveled face stared at me from the screen. "What are you doing, Creed? This is your doing, right?"

"Wait for it," I said.

Ella did no such thing. At her orders, *Thistle Down's* PD cannons destroyed the first missile. The next missile slammed into the heavy cruiser, smashing through it, although not with annihilating fury, as the warhead failed to explode. The built-up velocity used kinetic-energy destruction against the badly damaged heavy cruiser. The third missile did likewise. Somehow, that initiated interior explosion. Like mini-volcanos, eruptions appeared all over the heavy cruiser's hull.

That was fine, maybe even good. I hadn't armed the warheads because I hadn't wanted nuclear explosions to reach here. The interior explosions might have been enough to destroy the domination machine because the heavy cruiser was already in a precarious state of disrepair.

Almost immediately, as if to clarify the situation, the comm board lit up again, this time with calls from Luna Command and Earth Central.

"There were enemy munitions aboard the heavy cruiser," I explained. "They exploded so I think we're safe from any Trojan horse attacks."

Police Proconsul Spencer appeared on the screen next. "Do you have any idea why the Orange Tamika Fleet went insane?"

"As a matter of fact I do. A handful of Plutonians controlled each vessel—they had installed domination machines on each. I took out a few of the machines, some Lokhars regained their independence and the Plutonians overreacted against them."

"You expect me to believe such nonsense?" Spencer demanded.

"Give me a half hour," I said. "Then I'll explain in greater detail to you in person. Oh, by the way, tell Diana she'd better expect a three-cruiser Plutonian assault soon."

"Through a dimensional portal?" he demanded.

"That's it," I said.

Spencer searched my eyes, finally nodding. "I suppose that makes sense—the Orange Tamika Fleet wasn't our ally. The

Lokhar ships would have attacked us as we attacked the Plutonians."

Spencer had a properly suspicious mind and therefore saw these things faster than others would.

"You've nailed it," I said.

"And your people?" he asked. "Were they affected by this *domination* machine?"

"That's what I'm trying to determine. I'll know soon."

"A machine was on the heavy cruiser you just destroyed?"

"That's my guess."

"Yes," Spencer said, nodding. "I understand. It was cleverly done on their part."

"Maybe," I said. "But I also think they made an error."

"Oh," Spencer said. "How's that?"

"I'll tell you once I've cleared up the situation here."

"Don't take too long, Creed. I'm not willing to give anyone much leeway this near to Earth."

"Glad to hear it," I said, "as that's my own thinking."

-48-

I'd guessed right. The enemy domination machine must have been on the heavy cruiser. When Rollo came to from my sucker punch, he was mortified by what he'd been doing and saying these past days. Ella felt the same way.

"Orcus must have gained control of us in the Tau Ceti System," she said.

We were in the Light Cruiser *Thistle Down's* bridge heading for Earth orbit with the battlejumpers parked there. The other light cruiser remained in Moon orbit, a remote-controlled vessel under Luna Command.

"That doesn't seem right," I said. "Wouldn't Orcus have plundered the GEV in that case? He never did, which implies that he never had the opportunity."

"I think he could have," Ella said. "But the plundering action would have been too much for the mind machine to overcome in us."

"You're referring to the domination machine?"

"That. I think Orcus must have had a Jelk-like mind machine. I checked myself soon after…regaining my will. My brainwaves were subtly different from a test I'd taken several years ago."

"Wouldn't altered brainwaves be an effect from the domination machine?"

"Possibly," Ella said. "I still give it a higher probability that Orcus first altered our minds in order to make us more receptive to the domination machine. I put you in the stasis tube, as you were near death. That part is correct. Thus, you never received the first alteration because you were too weak to undergo the process. Perhaps that's why you were able to resist the domination machine so easily."

I'd undergone some intense training while in the Curator's service that made me even more unlikely to fall prey to such forces, but I didn't bother saying anything about it.

Instead, I asked, "Why would Orcus want me alive instead of dead?"

"Maybe Jennifer ordered him to keep you alive."

"But Jennifer hates me."

"Exactly," Ella said.

"Oh. You mean Jennifer hates me so much that she wants to make me pay the hard way for what I did to her."

"She wants to torture you just as Abaddon tortured her."

I shuddered while thinking about that. Most times, I put her terrible ordeal out of my mind. I didn't like to think what Abaddon had done to twist Jen. She'd been such a sweet girl, and now she was a murderous harridan hatching devilish, genocidal plots.

Once more, I resolved to save her. Yet, the more I tried, the more it seemed to move out of reach. For instance, couldn't Orcus have installed latent commands in our minds? Well, in *their* minds.

I asked Ella about that.

"I can devise some tests," she said. "Maybe I should get started on them."

"Good idea."

Ella left the bridge.

Rollo was slumped in a chair, staring at the main screen with Earth growing larger as we approached the planet.

"Sorry about hitting you," I said.

Rollo shook his head. He had a bruise on his chin and another on the back of his head, and a hangdog look in his eyes. "I needed it," he said. "Just like I needed the whippings my old man gave me when I was a kid."

"You're glad your father spanked you?" I asked, startled by the idea.

Rollo turned to me. "Totally," he said. "I was a rat as a kid. My dad helped beat some sense into me. Now, mind you, I didn't like it at the time. But I knew he did it to help me. Remember how no one spanked their kids anymore before The Day?"

"Don't I ever," I said. "I saw the results in the local supermarkets and elsewhere. Kids screamed and acted up and their parents *pleaded* with them to behave."

"Exactly," Rollo said. "A swift hand to the butt would have changed their attitude. Kids have to know who's in charge or they're monsters."

"There's an incoming call for you, Commander," a comm tech said, interrupting.

"Put it on the main screen," I said.

General Briggs appeared. "Commander," he said. "I thought you might like to know what's happening with the Orange Tamika Fleet."

"You bet," I said.

The screen split into two halves. On one half, Briggs still stared at me. On the other half, a swarm of Earth-built missiles closed in on the accelerating OT fleet. They had three maulers and all the smaller vessels left, making fourteen warships altogether. Some of the light cruisers had taken damage and one pursuit destroyer lagged behind.

"Have you received any calls from them?" I asked.

"We have not," Briggs said. "The Prime Minister would like a clearer picture of what you found aboard their ships."

I went over in detail everything he and Diana needed to know concerning my mission and the domination machines. I also told Briggs about Orcus, trying to remember exactly what the clone had said to me.

When I was finished, Briggs said, "I have a question."

"Shoot," I said.

"Do you think Baron Visconti really visited Acheron like he said?"

"Great question," I said. "That was the hardest thing to accept about his story. What gave the OT crews the morale to attempt such a thing? It was a forbidden star system to them. No. I doubt Visconti really went there. On the other hand, I believe Earl Parthian really did go to Acheron. That would explain a lot, particularly his rapid rise to power, maybe the domination machines and Orcus's adult age."

"Then we can't go to Acheron and plunder the planet for superior tech?" Briggs asked. "We can't because Purple Tamika has already picked it clean."

"You have a point," I said.

"Then how do we defeat the Plutonian cruisers, never mind defeating the rebuilding Purple Tamika navy with its superior weaponry?"

"I'll tell you how. Visconti spoke about a city deep in Acheron's planetary core. Maybe I could go to the star system and travel to the city through special Effectuator means."

"Do we have the time for you to go to Acheron and back?"

"With the stunt Orcus just pulled against us, it sure doesn't seem like it."

"So we fight as is until we're dead?" Briggs asked.

"Do you know of a better idea?"

The whites in his eyes expanded. "Maybe the Lokhar Emperor will accept our surrender."

"Sure, he might," I said, scornfully. "But Orcus and Jennifer won't."

"That is conjecture on your part," Briggs said.

"That's right, but it's the correct conjecture."

"We need something more, Commander."

I turned away. We needed something more. Briggs was right. We needed the enemy's advanced technology, for one thing.

"Plutonian cruisers should be attacking soon," Rollo told me.

"So what?" I said, understanding his implication. "If we try to storm them with assault troopers, the ships will just blow up spectacularly like always, killing more of the old guard."

"Not if you first get inside a ship with your phase suit and deactivate the ultra-detonator," Rollo said.

I stared at my over-muscled friend. "I'll be damned," I said, softly. "I actually knocked some sense into you." I turned to Briggs. "General," I said. "I have an idea."

-49-

The more I thought about it, the more Rollo's suggestion made sense. Not only would a Plutonian vessel carry exotic tech, but it should give us the ability to form a dimensional portal to the pocket universe.

There were some problems, though. Orcus must still be alive, escaping with the OT Fleet. Earth's missile salvo had destroyed the pursuit destroyer, two light cruisers, a heavy cruiser and one of the maulers. The fleet must have taken damage as a whole earlier to let the missiles get so close to them. Given the clone's special teleportation ability, I doubted Orcus had stayed long enough on any destroyed ship to die. Pop! He'd be on a safe ship.

What remained of the OT Fleet neared a jump gate to escape from the Solar System. I found it telling they hadn't made a dimensional portal to escape. That told me the present fleet could not do so. Maybe whatever did the creating had been too heavily damaged or destroyed.

Here was the thing. Could Orcus send a message to the pocket universe? Or could he send a message to someone who could reach the pocket universe quickly?

"Holgotha could do it," Ella said, when I mentioned the problem to her. We were riding a shuttle down to Earth, to New Denver and the coming strategy session there.

"True," I said. "I bet Holgotha is with Jennifer, and she's most likely at the safest place possible."

"The pocket universe?" asked Ella.

"That would be my guess."

"If all that's true..." Ella said, "I'd say Orcus can't call Jennifer yet. That means Orcus can't warn the Plutonians not to make another attack here."

"Those are too many ifs for my liking," I said.

Ella nodded, and that ended the conversation.

We reached New Denver shortly thereafter. This time, no massed hovers waited to swarm us on the tarmac. I rode quietly in a car, enjoying the mountains and particularly loving the green grass and the flowers everywhere. I rolled down a window as we passed towering evergreen trees. The pine scent was overpoweringly delightful, reminding me of boyhood trips into the mountains.

I smiled at Ella. She was in the back seat with me. "I've missed this," I said, quietly, maybe more emotionally than I'd intended.

"Are you going back to the Curator when this is over?"

I was looking out of the window again, maybe so I wouldn't have to face her. "I haven't thought that far ahead," I said. "I don't want to go back."

I listened to the tires rolling against the road.

Ella asked a minute later, "Do you think the Curator is watching you?"

"Sometimes."

"Does that modify your behavior?"

"What is this," I asked, "twenty questions?"

"You've changed, Creed. You're still cunning and like to attack, but you don't seem like the same hard charging bastard I knew ten years ago."

"I'm ten years wiser."

"That's hard to fathom."

"I know... I hate getting older."

"It beats the alternative."

"Yeah. That's what I tell myself. But I'd rather be younger and stronger."

"And dumber?" Ella asked.

"If that's the price, you bet."

"Not me. I never want to be dumber. I've made enough mistakes in my life, big ones. I don't want to make any more."

I turned away from her again. I'd made plenty of mistakes in my time, and I would likely make many more, but I loved being strong and reckless. I liked the invincibility of youth—at least when I had been young, I'd figured I was invincible and acted accordingly. Nowadays, I felt my mortality more often, and I didn't like it.

I focused on smelling the passing pine trees once more. In this marvelous moment, I loved life. I had purpose, and I was on the road to recovering my long lost love. I wasn't going to believe what the Curator had told me about Jennifer. I would help heal her tormented mind. I would fix what Abaddon had twisted. And if I couldn't do those things, the universe was going to know that Commander Creed, Effectuator Creed—one of those two, anyway—had given it his best shot.

-50-

Nothing much changed during the strategy session except that Diana made it plain that she wasn't simply concerned about the Earth's survival. She wasn't even mainly concerned with us Earthers surviving. She figured all the humans were Earthlings—Terrans—if long-lost cousins a thousand steps removed.

"I'm the elected representative of the Terran Confederation of Liberated Planets," Diana said, standing at the head of the conference table. She was wearing a suit today, skirt and jacket, and had her hair up. I can't say that I liked it as much on her. The suit was too masculine looking, the wrong look for an Amazon Queen.

"I'm not going to shirk my responsibility," Diana added. "We have to defend *all* humans."

"Begging your pardon," I said. "But a king by the name of Frederick the Great had a saying about that. *He who defends everything defends nothing.*"

"What's that supposed to mean?" Diana demanded.

"Easy," I said. "If you defend every spot just as hard, that means wherever your enemy strikes will be no better defended than anywhere else. One has left the initiative to the enemy."

Diana rubbed her jaw. "That wasn't what I meant," she finally said. "I want to defend—let me use a different word. I want to *save* as many people as I can. I don't want to divert everything to saving Earth while all the other Confederation planets burn."

"Oh," I said. "I get that. It's clear what we have to do then."

Diana shook her head.

"Attack," I said. "You know what they say. The best defense is a good offense. If you're attacking hard enough, your enemy doesn't have time to attack your territory. Thus, it's totally defended."

"Enough of your tomfoolery, Creed," Diana said. "I'm well versed in the strategic arts."

"I have no doubt about that," I said. "Sometimes, though, it's good to get back to basics. The enemy almost trapped us with the Orange Tamika Fleet. We barely foiled it in time."

"You foiled it," Spencer pointed out.

"Oh, yeah, well, I was glad to oblige," I said.

Diana rolled her eyes.

"My point," I said, "was that in foiling the deception and breaking the trap, we found out that the Plutonians are going to hit soon. We'll be ready for them."

"We have far more ships in place this time," Briggs said, "but it's still going to be a hell of a fight. What's more, I know the commander has suggested that we capture a Plutonian vessel—"

"Excuse me," I said, interrupting him, "but I'm going to do the capturing by myself."

"By using your phase suit?" Spencer asked.

"By any means possible," I replied. "That will probably entail help from the assault troopers."

Spencer turned to Diana. "It's risky being so reliant upon one individual—no matter how gifted he might be."

"What other choice do we have?" Diana said, challenging him with her eyes, and then sitting down.

"None that I can think of," Spencer admitted.

"I have a suggestion," Ella said.

Everyone turned to her.

"I've been studying what we know about the Plutonian ships," Ella said. "As I see it, the ships have one weakness."

"They have no weaknesses," General Briggs said bitterly.

"Perhaps 'weakness' is the wrong word," Ella said. "They have one deficiency in regard to our warships. None of the Plutonian vessels has an electromagnetic shield."

"A force field," Spencer said. "Does that matter?"

"Maybe," Ella said. "I watched videos and read after-action reports about the first Plutonian attack while waiting for Creed to heal in his tube."

"'Heal?'" asked Spencer, perking up. "What do you mean by that?"

I signaled Ella. She nodded faintly to me.

"A slip of the tongue," she said. "It means nothing."

Spencer sat back, slyly regarding me out of the corner of his eye. I wondered if this was a way to engage him: pretend to let something slip so he spent all his time on a false trail.

"Now," Ella continued, "we're aware that Plutonian ships possess some kind of inhibiter field. In some fashion, the ships seem to generate this field very near their hulls. The inhibiter limits the amount of explosive damage that…I don't know, that reaches the hull. The science behind the inhibiter baffles me. I'm simply reporting on what is there."

"How is that important to their lack of a force field?" Diana asked.

"I'm not sure," Ella said. "Maybe the inhibiter field precludes a force field. Whatever the case, the Plutonian ships do not have shields. In contrast, all our ships have shields, some heavier or stronger than others. A Purple Tamika bombard, for instance, is known to possess greater or sometimes double-layer shields, providing them with extraordinary protection."

"You've established your point," Diana said.

Ella smiled softly, unintimidated. "I don't mean to belabor the obvious, but it is important. Shields are more critical for stopping certain kinds of weaponry than others. For instance, shields help in forestalling PDD or Particle Discharge Detector missiles."

"You're talking about very special missiles," Briggs said.

"Exactly," Ella said. "A missile outfitted with PDD means less space for warheads. In compensation, a PDD missile targets a ship's engines. Once inside the ship's shield, a PDD missile multiplies the probability that an enemy ship will explode because its engine explodes spectacularly."

"Yes," Briggs said, nodding. "I like it."

"Explain it to me," Diana snapped.

"The Plutonian ships don't have shields," Briggs said. "While they can withstand heavy firepower due to their inhibiter fields and exotic hull armor, they're vulnerable to an older-style weapon: a PDD missile. Thus, as we attack the Plutonian ships, we should saturate them at the end with PDD missiles and blow up their engines to blow up the ships."

"Blow up," Diana said. "I thought we were talking about how to capture one."

"On, no," Ella said. "My idea was how to destroy the Plutonian ships as quickly as possible so as to save Confederation warships from the enemy's deadly particle beams."

"Maybe that will help us in capturing one," I said.

"How?" Ella asked.

At that point, an alarm rang. We all looked up. The main door opened and an orderly ran in.

"Luna Command has spotted a dimensional portal opening," the orderly blurted. "Admiral Sparhawk wants me to inform you that Plutonian ships should begin appearing at any time."

For a second, there was silence.

"Creed," Diana said. "You were saying?"

I told them my idea. Some of them looked at me as if I were crazy. Others nodded.

"Right," Diana said. "General, do any of the battlejumpers have these PDD missiles aboard?"

"There should be a few of them still in storage on each vessel," Briggs said.

"Then, we'll use what we have," Diana said. She regarded those of us at the conference table. "We're going to try Creed's idea. But first I suggest you get back to your ships so we can win this war."

-51-

The Prime Minister's statement was premature, but her sentiment was correct. Earth had gained time since fighting off the first Plutonian attack and had gathered reinforcements. The other side had tried to set up a trap so the bulk of Earth Force would have been caught between two enemy forces.

That had been a plan worthy of Hannibal Barca—Hannibal *Lightning*—of the Second Punic War. Studying warfare from the ancient world, one would be hard put to find a more perfectly executed battle.

At the start of the Second Punic War, Hannibal had left Spain and marched across the Alps into Roman Italia. There, his mercenaries had defeated the dreaded iron legions on two different occasions. Hannibal had been the wizard-general of the ancient world, taking inferior soldiers and creating a nearly invincible force with them, terrifying the fabled Roman legions for thirteen years. Much of his legend derived from the perfectly fought battle of Cannae.

There, with fewer soldiers, Hannibal's mercenaries and Gallic firebrands had butchered the largest host of Roman-born legionnaires ever assembled on a battlefield. Hannibal had baited the legions—the iron soldiers with blood-soaked short swords—into pushing the front-row Gallic warriors back. Through dint of hard fighting, the legionnaires forced the Gauls to retreat in a concave fashion as the barbarians died horrifically, but in return, the Romans and their allies had followed the longhaired warriors into a trap. Like the jaws of a ravenous beast, Hannibal's veterans wheeled around the Romans, hitting them from the sides. At the same time, the superior Carthaginian and Numidian cavalry—who had chased off the Roman horsemen—closed the trap from behind. It was as if the legions had marched into the neck of a bag until Hannibal had them in the sack.

At that point, Hannibal's killers had pushed the legionnaires in against each other until the dreaded Romans had been packed tight and hardly able to draw their swords. Surrounding that mass of screaming men, Hannibal's butchers had slaughtered for hours.

That's exactly what Orcus had planned to do to us. He wouldn't have done it through clever tactical maneuvering like Hannibal, but by having the OT Fleet hang back as Earth Force ships went into battle against the Plutonian invaders. Then, the Plutonians would have continued attacking while the OT Fleet hit us from behind, having neatly sandwiched our ships in the killing ground.

It had been a great plan disrupted thanks to yours truly. Now, we had to tear an advantage from our advanced warning of the current Plutonian attack. There was only one problem.

In the same general region as last time, a dimensional portal opened. Three Plutonian ships—cruiser-sized and with their exotic hull armor—zipped out of the bizarre opening, one right after the other. There was a pause. Then, practically nose to tail, the next trio zoomed out.

Ella, Rollo and I were already in our captured Lokhar Light Cruiser *Thistle Down*, with the GEV in its main cargo hold. General Briggs had charged upstairs into CLP Battlejumper *America*, there to lead his space marines if the chance came. Admiral Sparhawk had overall command of the fleet.

Diana and Spencer had remained behind on Earth.

Even as we hurried up to our respective warships, the Police Proconsul, on the Prime Minister's orders, had instructed the various battlejumper captains about Ella's idea concerning PDD missiles. Thus, munitions officers on the various monster warships hurriedly tried to find the few missiles of that type and get them ready to launch.

Diana had chosen not to tell the people of Luna Command about the plan. They were too near the enemy, for one thing. For another, Luna Command only had newly built missiles—and none of those had been PDDs. There was a third reason. The Plutonians might intercept such a message and take whatever countermeasures they could against PDD missiles. Besides, we didn't want to hit the Plutonians with the PDD missiles until exactly the right moment.

It was possible this wasn't the right battlefield to attempt the PDD tactic. One of the biggest problems militaries had with new inventions—or old inventions used in new ways—was using the tactic piecemeal the first time and giving the enemy time to adjust to it.

We didn't want to give the Plutonians time to study our new tactic. However, the Plutonians had always attacked in these endeavors, never trying to get back home through the dimensional portal. So maybe we wouldn't have to worry about that aspect of the missile assault.

As the first battlejumpers of Earth Force began accelerating out of Earth orbit, the third and last set of Plutonian vessels popped out of the dimensional portal. These were not cruiser-sized vessels. These were larger, battleships, possibly three times the size of the cruiser-type Plutonian ships. That still made them much smaller than our battlejumpers.

Nine highly advanced enemy vessels had come through the dimensional portal before it closed. If this had been nine regular ships against our massed battlejumpers that would have been no big deal. But these were nine technologically superior ships against fifty-three battlejumpers, two captured light cruisers and a hidden GEV.

The Starkien Fleet was far too late to help us. Earth was on its own, again, and the odds were heavily stacked against us.

-52-

The Plutonian ships weren't Lokhar vessels upgraded with a few fancy techs. The Plutonian ships represented old school adversaries that had fought against the First Ones and held their own for a time. That made the Plutonian warships uniquely dangerous.

Yeah, we had the numerical and tonnage advantage, but that could easily fall before technical dominance several factors higher than ours.

Three Plutonian vessels wouldn't have been such a big deal. I figured we could have easily handled them. *Nine* Plutonian ships, three of them ugly-looking bastards from the dawn age, oh yeah, we were in trouble.

The essence of my PDD missile assault plan was killing Plutonian ships as fast as possible. How would that help us capture one? Very easily; we could concentrate on the last mother while I dismantled the detonator from the inside.

But what would it profit humanity if we gained a Plutonian ship but no longer possessed an Earth Force of any size? Nothing. Then the Lokhars could swoop in and finish us with ease. The game would be up. We had two vicious enemies, one always willing to take up the slack of the other.

Well, damned if you do and damned if you don't. If that's the case, do what you want. That was pretty much my life rule.

Luna Command did not have much in the way of missiles. We could thank Orcus and the OT Fleet for that. LC used the light-cruiser drone, peeking around the Moon at the Plutonian flotilla.

Particle beams flashed at the drone.

Luna Command launched several missiles from the handful they had left. The missiles circled the Moon and shot out, racing at the enemy from various directions.

Particle beams swiftly disintegrated them.

There was more peek-a-boo with the light-cruiser drone until three Plutonian ships peeled off from the others, heading for the Moon to take care of the problem.

I had to give Luna Command this: collectively, they had big brass balls and a group heart that refused to count the odds. Were they going to run away to save their skins? No. They were going to die if those Plutonian ships raked the surface installations, which was what Luna Command had been goading the enemy to do to so the enemy would *not* be one united mass when they hit our fleet.

Earth Force battlejumpers moved into formation as they broke from planetary orbit. Light Cruiser *Thistle Down* kept behind them, waiting for our opportunity.

Our battlejumpers were patterned off the old Jelk models. Our first ship had been a battlejumper, the one we assault troopers had torn out of Shah Claath's red grip. A battlejumper was huge, much bigger than a city-block-sized Starkien beamship. During my mercenary dog days for the Jelk Corporation, one battlejumper could launch hundreds of assault boats. The heavy lasers could fire with killing power up to ten million kilometers. That was much farther than a Starkien beamship's measly one million kilometer range.

Of course, that meant the enemy ships were already in range, as the Moon was between four hundred and five hundred thousand kilometers from Earth.

The heavy cannons targeted the larger Plutonian ships first. Then, lasers stabbed through the stellar darkness.

Some lasers hit.

Why not all, you ask? For a simple reason. Each side used electronic jamming, ghost decoys and other defensive systems. The Plutonian defensive systems were much better than ours.

That meant our hit percentage was lower than theirs. We used missiles, as well. The Plutonians launched none.

In many ways, that was the essence of space battle. Two sides slugging it out as hard, fast and as heavy as they could.

Of course, one could just as easily say that that was the essence of old-style naval combat. Vessels from two sides floated relatively nearby and duked it out by means of guns, screaming jets, cruise missiles and submarine-launched torpedoes.

Anyone who has studied the great naval battles of Earth knows it never quite worked out like that. There was maneuvering, superior gunnery, hitting with a fast strike or a heavy strike, or pecking strikes that came in driblets. There was the use of smoke, fog at the Battle of Jutland, great amounts of empty space at the Battle of Midway, fantastic seamanship at the Battle of Trafalgar and Greek cunning at the Battle of Salamis.

The three Plutonian ships raced toward the Moon. Clearly, the Plutonian commander did not want the Moon on one side of his flotilla and Earth Force on the other. Thus, he was taking out Luna Command fast.

"We have to do something to help them," Ella said on the bridge of *Thistle Down*.

I shook my head. "There's nothing you can do."

"So you're just going to sacrifice Luna Command?"

"One," I said. "That is not my decision to make, as I am not in overall command. Two. Even if I could, this is a battle in which our extinction is more than possible. A commander has to make calculated choices if he's going to win and save most of the people."

"That doesn't mean I have to like such sacrifices," Ella said.

"True."

"Oh-oh," said Rollo, who'd kept his eyes glued to the main screen.

I joined him before it.

The three Plutonian ships slowed down, bombarding the Moon's surface. In moments, masses of debris blew outward from one terrific explosion after another from the Moon.

At that moment, the Luna Command light-cruiser drone raced into view, accelerating at the enemy vessels, all cannons blazing.

It made no difference. As if swatting a pesky fly, the Plutonian ships opened up on the drone, disintegrating it with contemptuous ease.

At the same time, the main Plutonian flotilla headed straight into the teeth of massed heavy laser fire. It was galling to watch. The smaller three ships hid behind the larger three. Their inhibiter generators must have been more powerful, as they seemed to shrug off the combined laser fire.

"Missiles," I said. "Earth has to launch its missiles."

Someone on our side must have been thinking like me. I saw missiles launching from the planet. Soon, they rose up into space like swarms of bees, heading for the enemy.

"The missiles are never going to run that gauntlet all the way to the Plutonians," Rollo said.

Even as he said the magic words hordes of missiles began vanishing. Seconds later, they popped into existence in front of the Plutonian ships. Our own beams destroyed some of those appearing T-missiles. Plutonian reactions also proved to be astonishingly fast. They used the particle beams to destroy one T-missile after another.

Still, a few got through, using nuclear and antimatter detonations. Those explosions weakened as they struck the inhibiter field before washing against the enemy's exotic hull armor.

All the while, the enemy vessels spewed their deadly particle beams. This part of the battle proved to be a war of attrition. We pounded them. They pounded us.

A forward battlejumper exploded as entire hull pieces shed off the main bulk. Then, the ship died a fiery death, wounding many of its sister ships with its shrapnel-like debris.

The attrition continued, with two more battlejumpers dying from the savage particle beams.

At that point, the Plutonian vessels began to move away from each other. I knew why, and it gave me hope. If one of those enemy ships took too much damage, the interior self-destruct explosive would ignite the vessel, making it a deadly weapon against the other ships.

The "expansion" maneuver exposed the smaller cruiser-sized vessels. Our side took the bait, concentrating on a smaller vessel, almost immediately doing damage to its hull.

Now it appeared to be a matter of speed and who could pour out the greatest firepower in the shortest amount of time.

Two more battlejumpers went spinning as they exploded with intense multi-colors. Tens of thousands of personnel died in those detonations. It was sickening to contemplate, and I had to compartmentalize it.

Finally, though, a combination of massed laser fire and more T-missiles caused a spectacular explosion as one of the cruiser-sized Plutonian ships exploded violently. Fortunately for their side, that vessel had maneuvered far enough away from its own kind that it didn't hurt any others.

The three that had bombarded the Moon raced to join the rest of the flotilla that attacked Earth Force.

"If we're going to capture one of them…" Rollo told me.

"I still don't like the idea of risking all of you in this," I said.

"Phht," Rollo said. "What risk? We're the Lucky Thirteen."

"The few survivors from the last mission," I said. "How many are going to survive today's mission?"

"Wrong question," Rollo said. "How many of the Plutonians are going to survive?"

"Yeah," I said. "You're right. It's time to get started."

-53-

I'm sure a few of you are wondering why I didn't simply use the GEV and take remote control of the enemy vessels. The easy answer was that I couldn't. Their tech was too good for me to pull a fast one like that.

That meant we had to do this the hard way, risking our own blood to defend what we loved.

The Lucky Thirteen, which included me, piled into the GEV. I launched us from the *Thistle Down's* cargo bay and went into the darkest stealth mode possible. Then, I began to accelerate toward the incoming enemy.

There was a real danger that our own people would inadvertently shoot us down. We were essentially invisible to any sensors. Thus, a stray laser or particle beam or speeding missile could collide with us and wreak whatever damage it was capable of wreaking against my superior hull armor.

That danger was moderated to some extent by the extreme openness or emptiness of space. Even between the Earth and Luna there was a lot of space. Still, bad luck happened, and it could happen to us. It was simply another risk we had to endure if we wanted to keep on living free.

The ranges closed as the two sides headed at each other. The Plutonians were suicidal fighters, and Earth Force couldn't afford to let them reach orbital space. They might bombard the other continents and wipe out human life before the battle ended.

I gave Ella the piloting chair and left to get my phase suit. I would not take the metallic loops along this time, as I would not live through another hyper-speeded state right now. I did take Abaddon's old force axe, though. If one wanted to destroy something immediately, it was the weapon of choice.

I wondered if the Plutonians had been this suicidal during their war against the First Ones. I rather doubted it. What made them so kamikaze-like now?

The best answer I could come up with was Jennifer. Had she taken on Abaddon's worst characteristics? I believed that was likely. She lacked the First One's former power and ability. Maybe racing to the Plutonians had been one of her ways to fix that.

Ella used shift-speed to get us close to the Plutonians. Then, all while in deepest stealth mode, I had her decelerate and then accelerate so she followed close behind the enemy flotilla.

The Plutonians definitely had the better tech compared to Earth Force. The ancient slime bastards did not, however, possess better tech than the Galactic Effectuator.

Now, I had Ella accelerate even more.

Earth Force knew which Plutonian craft I wanted. They would target it last.

"It's time, Creed," Ella said over a comm.

"Got it," I said. "Wait for my signal."

"Don't get killed," she added.

"Good luck to you too, darling," I said.

With that, I began to run, going out of phase as I did. I ran through the GEV bulkheads until I reached the outer hull. Once through, I gave myself thruster power.

This thruster pack was smaller than before, and it contained a lot less fuel. Even though I was out of phase, I had the velocity of the GEV. Even now, Ella was supposed to be decelerating enough so the stealth craft didn't reach the enemy ships too soon.

I did not ghost up to see where I was going. I was dealing with Plutonians. I expected them to have something to sense ghosting. Thus, I used dead reckoning to tell where I was.

The AI had made the computations before I'd left. Now, I was risking everything on those computations working. That included not having the Plutonian ship jink or juke out of my path.

Time passed. It was lonely out of phase. I could hear myself breathe. Out there, I knew, we were slaughtering the slugs and they were slaughtering us in return, just as they had butchered Luna Command.

How many thousands of soldiers had died through no fault of their own? They had done exactly what they were supposed to do, but somewhere else, someone on their side made a mistake. Or the enemy did something really smart. Then, ten thousand soldiers marched upon one hundred holding a fort. Those one hundred died with hardly a murmur because they were totally out of position. That was what had happened to the people of Luna Command. Its occurrence was inevitable. How did one make sure he wasn't in that crowd?

Luck? Good sense? An act of God?

I don't have the answer to that one, just a lot of questions.

In any case, my time out of phase neared its end. This would be dead reckoning phase movement.

I put the chronometer up on my visor. I had a decision to make. Should I ghost up just a little and take a look, and then use the thruster pack while out of phase again? Or should I decelerate now and trust to dumb luck that nothing bad would happen to me?

It was a hard decision. Obviously, as a friend of mine used to say, I should do the prudent thing. But this wasn't so obvious here. What if the Plutonians—?

I decelerated while out of phase, trusting to the AI's computations, trusting to some divine justice for our side and crossing my fingers.

I saved just a squirt in the pack, and felt gravity take hold, as I no longer floated.

I let out a giant sigh of relief. I was in a place with gravity. That implied I'd reached the target.

Even so, I did something a few of you might think stupid. I shed the thruster pack from me, held onto it with one hand and got out the force-axe handle with the other. I took several deep breaths. Then, I released the thruster pack. For a second, it remained out of phase with me. A second later, it disappeared from my sight, heading in-phase the hard way.

I took several steps back, readied the force axe—but did not make the red power glow yet—and let myself phase into the present reality…

-54-

I phased in as two big Orcus-looking dudes used a special, weird-sounding type of gun, blasting the thruster pack that had materialized in their midst.

The sight of them shocked me. Luckily, I was so pumped up that the surprise did not cause any hesitation. My fingers blurred over the buttons in the correct sequence. As the saying goes, I could have done that in my sleep. The red force axe sizzled into being even as I chopped at one of the Abaddon clones.

The force axe lived up to its horrible reputation. It sheared through the clone, cleaving through flesh, muscle and bone with equal ease, hacking off part of his shoulder and chest from his torso. He bled—a LOT—and toppled over onto the deck.

The second clone looked up with a what-the-hell expression. It was pure gold as far as I was concerned. The expression began changing as I shoved the force axe into his face like a spear-point. I destroyed his face in a spray of gore and added his melted head to the mess.

I jumped aside as he also toppled to the floor, making a meaty thump that I heard through my helmet pickup.

I looked around, finding myself in a large chamber with tons of munitions I didn't recognize. No one else was in here.

I frowned. How had I managed to enter the only chamber with two Abaddon clones?

The answer, of course, was I had not. I let the force axe zip back into the handle and slapped it to my phase-suited side.

The suit had a second useful function of shedding all blood. Theirs hadn't stuck to me.

Anyway, I picked up an item that had tumbled from one of the clones. It was a box of some kind, a tracking device.

Son of a gun, I got it. They had been tracking me, able to see where I was while out of phase.

Had they been able to track the GEV too?

I didn't want to call the GEV yet, as that might cause Ella to begin the assault.

"Right," I said. I didn't have time to ponder this. I was on a mission. Two Abaddon clones had possessed a phase tracker. Did that mean the other ships had Abaddon clones with phase trackers?

"Not necessarily," I muttered to myself. If the clones could teleport, and I'm sure they could, they could have teleported from ship to ship.

I laughed. It was an outburst of pent-up emotions and relief that I'd dodged a terrible problem by killing these two in time. Now, I had to get it done.

I took the phase tracker and ghosted down so everything seemed faint around me. Then, I began humping it through the battleship-sized vessel. I had to find the ultra-detonator and destroy it, and then I had to make sure the slugs didn't destroy their ship manually, giving the rest of the Lucky Thirteen time to storm the vessel and capture it.

-55-

I had no idea how the battle was going outside as I searched for the ultra-detonator inside. It wasn't easy. For one thing, the Plutonian ship proved to have a nasty environment.

Instead of regular-sized corridors, it had these metal tunnels with slime tracks in places. The slugs had been as big as cows when I'd seen and killed them before, but apparently, they could wiggle through these tight, tubular corridors.

Whenever I ghosted up to look around carefully, I noticed the weird drippy walls and the stench of the place. I opened my helmet visor several times. The stench made a Starkien ship seem like a perfume store. The worst smelling were fogs drifting here and there. Plutonian creatures stood in the fogs with their bizarre slug-like skin rippling as if with delight. Sometimes, there were groups of them doing that, touching their disgusting skin against each other.

I had a powerful desire to draw the force axe and start chopping, but I didn't want to give myself away until I had to.

Surely, the two Abaddon clones had checked in periodically. Why hadn't I sensed alarm among the slugs due to their lack of check-ins? Maybe the Plutonian captain figured the clones had teleported to a different ship.

Finally, I reached a reactor area. Thank goodness, it was larger, so I didn't have to crouch down to keep my head out of bulkheads.

I studied the setup, going from reactor chamber to reactor chamber. Certainly, they could blow the engines, but that wouldn't produce the same fantastic explosion as came from the ultra-detonator.

Then, I saw the machine that must have done the special exploding. It was a huge pulsating dome with red veins outlined across it. The dome almost seemed to be alive, or a cross between a biological entity and a machine, but in a Karg-like freaky way. It was the size of a typical garbage truck from before The Day.

There were no slugs in the chamber, but it did possess what looked like communication devices and cables hooked from it into the nearest bulkhead.

I thought about that and decided on an Effectuator answer.

Moving to an out of the way alcove, I phased in and set up a scrambler. That should cut the communications without immediately making the dome or the slug command crew go crazy.

I phased out again, moved to the dome and phased in. At the same time, I used the force axe and hacked like a Viking berserker.

It was fitting in a way. I used to be a Star Viking. The old-time berserkers had ripped off all their clothes, racing into battle naked. Usually, they used an axe, but a heavy sword would do the trick almost as well. Some of the berserkers had tied tight ropes around their limbs. That way, if an enemy warrior lopped off an arm or part of an arm, they wouldn't immediately bleed to death. Vikings considered berserkers consecrated to the All-Father Odin, the king of the Viking gods. The bear or the wolf had been their special totem.

Berserkers had fought as madmen, attacking in a frenzy and often howling like beasts. Most sane Vikings kept out of a berserker's way—he often had a hair-trigger temper, flying out of control on a whim.

Odin had touched them, the others said.

Well, Odin hadn't touched me, but I flailed at the pulsating, veiny dome just the same. The force axe hacked out entire chunks. I could see electric sparks in the slimy substance even as green blood gushed from it.

This thing was alien, all right. It made me think the Plutonians were indeed originally from a different space-time continuum than ours.

I waded into the torn dome in order to hack out even more. I had no idea how much of the dome—

My fingers tightened around the force-axe handle. I kicked against solid stuff on the bottom. Looking down, I thought I could see numbers flickering, numbers like those on a ticking bomb.

I cursed wildly and phased out, forcing myself down into the thing under the floor.

Right. The dome had been the trigger. This down here was the explosive. I wasn't sure how to dismantle the bomb. I sensed that a timer was ticking and would soon detonate the bomb and foil my plan.

I found a tiny area beside the explosive and phased in crouched over like a human cannonball. I activated the force axe and hacked out more area. Then I tunneled with the force axe, trying to slice the terrible bomb into harmless pieces. If it went off now, I was dead. I would not be able to phase out in time to escape.

If I thought I'd gone berserk earlier, it was nothing compared to this. I used the force axe like a true berserker with no thought for tomorrow. I panted. I growled. I stomped my feet in frustration.

Finally, I ceased hacking because I needed a breather. Sweat poured off my body, the phase suit's conditioner unit working overtime to cool me.

The flickering numbers had stopped moving, or what I'd taken to be alien numbers. Did that mean I'd dismantled the ultra-detonator and its bomb?

I was going to guess yes and summon the GEV. We had our opening. Now, I had to get to the bridge and make a way into the vessel for my people. The slugs could still destroy their ship the hard way, by blowing the engine or having the other Plutonian ships beam it.

We'd have to pirate this ship under their very noses if we were going to be successful.

-56-

This time, I took stims. I needed energy even if it was going to cost me later. The others were counting on me. If I didn't do my part, the rest of the Lucky Thirteen plus N7 wouldn't be able to capture the Plutonian battleship. They would most likely die.

I raced up the decks in ghost phase. I did not kill any stray slugs along the way because I needed to get to the bridge pronto.

The vessel shook. I didn't feel it, but I saw things shaking and shivering around me. Did that mean I was too late? Was I going to have to try for a different vessel?

The shaking intensified. Explosions began around me.

This was bad. I didn't have a thruster pack anymore. I could not easily transfer to another Plutonian ship.

"Think, Creed," I told myself.

I pivoted in ghost phase and headed to a compartment I'd seen earlier. As the bulkheads continued to shake, as explosions ripped through the battleship, I reached a largish chamber. I studied the machines.

I'd seen machines like this on Delta Magnus IV, an inner galaxy world where I'd gone on a mission on the Curator's behalf.

"Right," I said.

I phased in as I dug out a universal chip. The decking rocked under my boots. I heard more ship explosions and felt waves of some kind pass through me. They made my teeth ache.

Shoving the chip into a slot in the machine, I hoped this piece of Curator tech worked like it was supposed to. The chip sparkled. That was good sign.

The worst explosion so far shook the deck, panicking me. I ripped out the chip and phased all the way out. I wanted to be sure I survived the explosion.

I hadn't summoned the GEV yet. I had a feeling that now I wouldn't get the chance for this battleship.

I—

The box attached to my waist began to flash.

Since I was out of phase, there was only the gray void around me. The flash—a yellow one—caught my eye. I unhooked the box from my phase suit, realizing this was the phase tracker flashing.

I saw an image in a circle: the circle was like an old-style radar screen. A yellow dot blipped in and out, moving across the top part of the circle.

Was that someone else in a phase suit?

I started in that direction and checked the box, finding the dot moving away from me. I reversed my direction, hurrying the opposite way. Soon, the dot blipped closer to me.

"Who are you?" I muttered to myself.

A second dot appeared near the first.

I swore, put my head down and began to run in that direction. I ran hard as the dots came closer and closer.

I must have tumbled out of the Plutonian battleship or the vessel had broken up under me, for I was weightless, without gravity to move me. Surely, I drifted in the direction I'd traveled.

But the dots did not. They veered off at an angle.

I ghosted up until the stars were extremely faint points of light. Ghostly ships moved around me. The battleship I'd been on lost chunks of itself as explosions ripped through it.

I strained to see the ghost forms, but saw nothing.

I checked my phase tracker. The two dots neared a circular edge. They moved away from Earth and from the Moon. Was there a hidden ship out there for them?

I could not tell.

Abruptly, the two dots went out of range and off my tracker. They were gone, two phased-out intruders, their identities hidden to me.

I growled with frustration. Who had that been? I had to know. Had that been Jennifer? Where had she gotten a phase suit?

"You idiot," I told myself. She must have stolen one from the Fortress of Light.

But I'd seen *two* dots, *two* individuals. Could Orcus have a phase suit? Did I know for sure it was Jennifer? Was there another player in this game?

I scowled and told myself I couldn't worry about them now.

The space battle raged around me. The battleship I'd been on, where I'd worked so hard so we could capture it, continued to explode. The thing was breaking up. I'd failed to stop them from self-destruction.

I was less than a flea on the battlefield, with no way of getting off unless I called the GEV for a lift.

I looked around, trying to determine what I could do. The trouble was that despite the small battleground—the area between Earth and its Moon—naked eyesight wasn't enough given the relatively smaller nature of spaceships.

With a sigh, I brought myself a little more into phase. I used my helmet comm, but all I got was static. With all the beams flashing back and forth, I couldn't get through with a small comm signal.

For the moment, at least, I was stuck out here.

If this lasted too long, I'd run out of oxygen.

-57-

I didn't suffocate, but I had to wait as the battle entered its final phase. It took a strange turn, too, which helped to explain a few things about the Plutonians—or at least as to how they interpreted their present orders.

The strangeness related to the last moves of the Plutonian vessels, a battleship and two of the cruiser-class raiders.

They might have tried to press through and survive the massed assault of the remaining battlejumpers long enough to unload their hellish cargos onto the Earth's surface. Our side had run out of PDD missiles, although the slugs surely didn't know that. Instead, the enemy battleship attempted to shield the two cruisers as they used presser and tractor beams to collect all the undestroyed pieces of Plutonian hull armor into one general zone.

During that time—as our massed laser beams dug into the last battleship's hull—one of the cruisers self-detonated. That vaporized much of the collected debris, but flung a few pieces of hull armor and other assorted junk elsewhere.

The last cruiser worked furiously, and one could almost say valiantly. But could one use the word valiant toward a suicide soldier or suicide ship?

Before The Day, we'd had Muslim suicide bombers of assorted kinds. Some strapped TNT chest-vests or homemade pipe bombs to themselves and detonated among crowds of Muslim heretics or unbelievers. Some, of course, took over the infamous planes on 9/11 and crashed them into the Twin

Towers of New York City. Others climbed into a truck and mowed over people walking on a sidewalk.

The idea that any of those fanatics could be valiant would infuriate many people. Others believed that some of the suicide bombers had, at least, shown a perverted courage to die for what they believed in.

That was the old question: was a man willing to die for his country or for his god, big or little G? We esteemed as heroes those who had sacrificed themselves on the field of battle. Why not esteem a suicide bomber as a hero?

Because he'd murdered hordes of innocent people, many would argue. And maybe they're right to say that. Hero might be the wrong word for a suicide bomber. Still, dying for what you believed in seemed like it might take some form of courage.

I'll tell you, though, I preferred George Patton's old saying on the subject. "No dumb bastard ever won a war by going out and dying for his country. He won it by making some other dumb bastard die for his country."

In any case, the last Plutonian cruiser attempted to gather those pieces of debris. And when it did, the ship detonated, vaporizing the assembled junk with it so we could never study the composition of the pieces.

At that point, the battleship did likewise—self-detonated—and the second Battle of Earth against the Plutonians was over. We'd won, even if we hadn't gained all of our objectives.

I could finally phase in and call for help from Ella. Without all the beams flashing, my call went through this time. She piloted the stealth ship to me, and I floated into a small locker hatch and into the GEV.

"What happened?" Rollo asked, as I exited the locker and removed my helmet.

What happened was that I slumped onto a steel bench, exhausted and depressed.

"We waited for a call," Rollo said. "Then the targeted battleship blew up. Why didn't you try for another one?"

I looked at him.

"Oh," he said. "Something bad happened?"

"You think?"

Rollo paused before saying, "They hit us hard."

I took the bait. "How hard?"

"We lost twelve battlejumpers for sure. Luna Command is gone, the people and all the installations with it."

"Twelve battlejumpers for sure?" I asked.

"Others were hit hard but didn't blow. Some of those might not be worth much anymore. We'll have to wait and see."

"That's just great," I muttered.

"Ella thinks the Plutonians might not have vaporized all their hull armor. Our scientists might get a look at it and see if they can duplicate it anytime soon."

"Good luck with that," I said.

"Otherwise, we got zippo. This was a huge bust, Creed."

I inhaled through my nostrils several times. I was exhausted. I'd been out of phase too long. That always disoriented a guy, and I knew as well as Rollo that we'd failed in our objectives.

"I found a few things," I finally said.

"Anything interesting?"

I told him about the Abaddon clones, the weird tunnel system in the battleship, the blips on the phase tracker—"

"They have a phase tracker?" he asked.

"Had," I said. "It's mine now."

"You don't think they have more?"

I removed the boxlike device from a waist pouch and examined it. "This strikes me as center galaxy tech, maybe even Fortress of Light tech. They may not have any more of these."

"That's something, at least," Rollo said.

"But they have at least two phase suits of their own."

"What?"

I told him about the bogeys I'd witnessed on the tracker.

"Any idea who they were?" Rollo asked.

I gave him my thoughts.

"Huh," he said.

It was at that point I recalled the universal chip that I'd shoved into a Plutonian machine.

I stood up and began marching for the hatch.

"You were holding out on me, Creed," Rollo said, trailing behind. "You found something interesting out there, didn't you?"

"Maybe," I said. "It's time to find out."

-58-

Earth Force licked its wounds and honored its tens of thousands of brave men and women who had died in the battlejumpers and on the Moon.

We didn't fight the same way the Jelk Corporation had done. Our battlejumpers were primarily firing platforms instead of launch pads for masses of assault boats. The Jelk masters had used slaves and mercenaries by the millions, and their lizard-like Saurians as whip-drivers. The Jelks hadn't cared if their soldiers died. We most definitely cared about our soldiers, and that made a huge difference as to the type of battles we chose to fight.

Despite the best efforts of the Plutonians to do otherwise, Earth-Force sensors discovered pieces of exotic hull armor drifting in space.

Shuttles roared out, and pilots returned with the precious cargos. The hull pieces went post-haste to laboratories down on Earth.

Now, our top scientists had to figure out what in the heck this stuff was and if they could duplicate it and how fast and in what kind of quantity. This was reverse engineering time, if—a big if in these sorts of things—our smart boys and girls could figure out what the hull armor was composed of.

All the while, my AI analyzed the chip I'd brought in.

After seventeen hours of waiting—I took a nap and a regular sleep during that time—the AI was still silent.

The GEV was in a low Earth orbit with only N7 and me aboard. I no longer housed the stealth ship inside the former Light Cruiser *Thistle Down*. The vessel had taken damage during the battle and was on the waiting list for the orbital repair yards.

More important battlejumpers were in the docks, with welders and others working overtime to repair the damage. Earth had become like an overturned anthill, boiling with frantic activity.

Fortunately, the Starkien Fleet arrived, so we didn't fear a quick repeat attack by the Plutonians.

After waking up, I went to the stealth ship's galley and put on some coffee. Then I walked around with a full mug, sipping and thinking. Finally, I found N7 poring over battle reports.

"What have you found so far?" I asked.

"Many things," the android said, looking up from the table.

"What strikes you as the most important?"

"The Plutonian vessels at the end attempting to gather hull debris and vaporize it," he said.

I sipped, thought about that, and said, "They failed."

"Given the nature of the operation they were bound to fail. Thus, I ask the question, why did they attempt it?"

"Trying and failing was better than not trying at all."

"That is not the answer, Commander. The Plutonians should have driven home their attack and bombarded Earth. On every other known occasion that is what they have done against a terrestrial planet or livable moon."

"Sure," I said. "But we also know how important keeping the composition of their armor from us is to them."

"I do not believe that is the answer," N7 said.

"What is it, then?"

"They want us to study the hull armor."

"Reverse psychology?" I asked.

"Precisely," he said.

I sipped more coffee, thinking that through. "Do the slugs strike you as sophisticated thinkers?"

"They do not," N7 admitted. "I believe another mind was the genesis for the order."

"Jennifer?" I asked.

"Or Orcus."

I shook my head. "Orcus must be Jennifer's slave."

"I find the concept difficult to fathom." N7 held up a hand as I opened my mouth to retort. "I understand Jennifer could have installed mental safeguards in Orcus. Remember, I was once your instructor when you wore a shock chip for Shah Claath."

I rubbed my neck, recalling those sorry days.

"There is another consideration," N7 said. "Jennifer suffered under Abaddon and she became like him. The First One had tricks within tricks. I deem it likely the DNA clone revival was originally an Abaddon concept of last resort. He would wish to be born anew given the unlikely occurrence of his defeat and death. Would he program Jennifer to revive his clone with implanted control devices?"

"Abaddon was a clever bastard, I'll grant you that. We still killed him, though."

"That is not germane to my argument."

"I know. But I like saying it. Makes me feel good."

"Yes. You are a true killer. It is your first love."

"Hey," I said.

N7 cocked his head. "Do you not accept that about yourself, Commander?"

"I would if it was true, sure, no big deal."

N7 did not comment further on the topic.

Would Abaddon want a clone to appear after his death? The clone would not be the individual that had died—it would not be the same him, but a copy. I suspected Abaddon had been so self-centered that he would gain no satisfaction thinking a clone would win where he had failed. That being so, he would not have programmed Jennifer to make Abaddon clones.

Still, given his failure, he would want to pull everything down in an orgy of destruction. The Plutonians were indulging in mass destruction. Maybe N7 had a point after all.

But I didn't want to get into that right now. I was on a different trail.

"Maybe the hull-armor-debris destruction wasn't a Plutonian decision," I said.

I told N7 about the phase suits I'd detected, how the two had departed the battlefield during the fight. Surely, one of them could have given the Plutonians whatever orders the slugs had followed.

N7 cocked his head the other way. "We did not see a dimensional portal reopen," he finally said.

"Why does that matter?"

"Is that not the point of your observation? The phase-suited individuals were observers, returning to the pocket universe with the results of the attack."

"That's an interesting idea. You think that's what they did?"

"No, as we did not see a dimensional portal reopen."

I sipped more coffee.

"It would be good to know who those two beings were," N7 said. "It would be even better to know where they went, if anywhere."

"Whoa. You think they're still in the Solar System?"

"It is possible."

"Right," I said, finishing my cup. "I'm getting the phase tracker. It's time to find those two."

-59-

With the GEV, I returned to where I'd first spotted the two phase-suited beings and then headed in the direction they had gone. The phase tracker did not scan a large area. Thus, I set up a search grid, moving back and forth, waiting to see a yellow dot on the round screen.

I never found anyone by using the tracker, not even after a day and a half of tedious searching. However, by that time, the AI had made a discovery from its analysis of the Plutonian machine I'd hacked.

The discovery was primarily strange mathematical formulas translated into gibberish English, as far I was concerned. I brought the collected data to Ella aboard the Light Cruiser *Thistle Down*.

The GEV and the light cruiser were in low Earth orbit. I transferred between them via my flitter.

Ella inserted the data into an e-reader and began studying, trying to absorb the meaning of the formulas.

I went back to the GEV and bed.

In the morning, I ate a large breakfast of bacon, eggs and hash browns. Afterward, I headed to the light cruiser. When I found Ella, she looked up with bloodshot eyes. Had she been reading all night?

"Anything?" I asked.

It took her a second before she said, "I want to take this down to Earth."

I'd been wondering what exactly the formulas were. Maybe there were advanced techs that would seriously anger the Curator. I mean techs that this Civilizational Zone shouldn't have. I was willing to give humanity the dimensional portal, superior hull armor and maybe even the particle beam. Otherwise, Earth wasn't going to survive repeated Plutonian attacks combined with a massed Lokhar invasion. But what if the formulas represented something else?

There was another thing. Why hadn't the AI been able to crack the codes and just tell us what it had found, a summary, as it were? Maybe it could summarize now.

"Give me an hour," I said, "and I'll give you an answer."

"Fine," Ella said, rising unsteadily. "I need a break anyway." She stumbled out of the room while I glanced at her notes. It didn't help in the slightest; they were in Russian.

I returned to the GEV, brewed a pot of coffee and went to the AI. It still lacked an opinion on what it had translated. I asked it to go over the formulas.

"What does it all mean?" I asked later.

"That is an insufficiently precise question," the AI told me in its robotic voice.

I tapped my fingers on the console. "Give me a summary concerning the data."

"It is too much and varied to summarize easily."

That was an odd and even illogical reply. "Give me what you can, then."

"I am unable to comply with your request."

"Why's that?" I asked, growing suspicious.

"I do not know," the AI said. "I am unable to present a coherent reason for my statement."

I sat back, scratching the top of my head. There was something weird going on here.

"Have I stumbled onto a Curator-installed failsafe?" I asked.

The AI did not respond.

"Is it impossible for you to reply to that?" I asked.

The AI still said nothing.

"By your silence," I said, "are you agreeing that the Curator installed a directive into you concerning this issue?"

None of the extra lights embedded in the console blinked for even a second to show that the AI was thinking about the question.

I scratched my head again. This was most—

I froze. I had seen a faint gloved hand lift just a fraction out of the AI main frame. I don't know how, but one of the ghosted beings—a being with a phase suit—was hiding inside the AI.

I looked away slowly, trying not to react to what I'd witnessed. I had no idea why the phase tracker hadn't spotted the other phase suits earlier—maybe the two had been in phase then and now were out again. I had to don my suit in order to investigate this while out of phase.

"Have it your way," I said, getting up.

"Where are you going, Commander?" the AI asked.

"I need to freshen up my cup."

"Please explain," the AI said.

Now I knew they'd tampered with the AI. It knew my habits. I shouldn't have to explain adding coffee to my cup.

"Give me a minute," I said. "I'll be right back."

"Commander, I believe I have found evidence—"

"Save it," I said, interrupting. "You can tell me when I return."

I headed for the hatch. As I did, a massive being phased in right in front of the exit. His height and the breadth of his shoulders left no doubt. An Abaddon clone blocked my escape.

-60-

I should have kept the force axe with me. But it was simply too powerful a weapon to just carry around. I should have kept my blaster on, too, but I hadn't. I did have a trusty force blade, a regular one, in lieu of the giant Bowie knife I used to keep on my person.

I'd been in the slammer at a young age, and had learned to carry a shank at all times.

There had been two bruisers in my youth who had caught me in the bathroom alone. They had some funny ideas about what constituted kicks and giggles, and had insisted I strip and give them satisfaction.

Well, that was the first day I had my new shiv. It hadn't been much, a thin piece of carefully sharpened steel with a cloth handle.

I'd cut them up pretty bad. The key had been a little deception on my part and striking without hesitation when I'd gotten the window of opportunity.

As the Abaddon clone appeared, I grabbed my force blade, clicked on power and stabbed at his suited midsection.

At the same time, something slammed against my shoulder blades from behind. It struck hard enough to knock the air out of me, and it caused my hand to open. The force blade hit the deck and winked out—the force of the blade retracted. It was a modern safety feature on the latest knives as manufactured on the Fortress of Light.

I didn't go down, but I reached for my knife. I needed something against this Abaddon clone—and against the sucker who had attacked from the rear.

The phase-suited clone caught my wrists and held them with viselike strength. Since I couldn't break free, as much as I tried, I used his hands as a pivoting point, jumping up and mule kicking him in the gut. He stumbled, but he also hung onto my wrists. I tried that again—and an even more powerful force slammed against my back. It drove me against the Abaddon clone, and he put me in a bear hug, squeezing me against his giant torso.

I struggled in vain, an enraging sensation.

"AI," I said. "Sound the alarm."

"No, no," a wheezy voice said from behind. "You misunderstand the scenario. This is not what you think it is."

I twisted my head as best as I could, but couldn't see anyone or anything behind me to have spoken.

"AI," I said. "Sound the general alarm throughout the fleet."

"Are you certain about this, Effectuator?" the AI asked.

"Effectuator?" the wheezy old-timer voice said. "You are an Effectuator, as in a Galactic Effectuator working for the First Guardian of the Fortress of Light?"

I twisted my head more, and thought to finally see someone. I twisted the other way. Yes. I saw a white-haired humanoid wearing a phase suit with the visor to his helmet open. He had a shotgun-type weapon aimed at me. That must have been the device he'd been firing at me.

"Tell the clone to let me go of me," I said.

"Please, Effectuator, do not call him that, I implore you."

"You implore? Who are you, old man?"

"Before we chat, be so good as to tell your AI to desist in its warning."

"Why should I?"

"Saul," the being said; "Release him."

The Abaddon clone removed his huge arms.

I landed on my feet and took a deep breath, arching my back and gingerly twisting it. The clone had torqued it with his bear hug. Then I shuffled around, looking at the white-haired humanoid.

I realized he no longer spoke in a wheezy way. Had he faked that?

Whatever the case, even though he stooped, he was taller than I was, had wrinkled skin, a beak of a nose and filmy green eyes as if he might be half-blind.

"Who are you?" I asked.

He grinned evilly. "Think of me as an interstellar hitman."

I squinted at him. "You're an assassin?"

"Not precisely."

"But you just said you're a hitman. What's the difference?"

"Plenty. An assassin implies a political connotation. A hitman is for hire, a killer for profit."

"You don't look like a hitman," I said.

"Exactly. My perceived feebleness helps me work in close to the target. Not that that matters in this case."

I stepped to the side so the Abaddon clone—this Saul—wasn't behind me, while I kept the old hitman in front of me. He tracked me with his weapon.

I shook my head. "This doesn't make sense. You have phase suits."

"They come in handy in my line of work."

"That's not my point. Phase suits are the ultimate in technology."

"Not quite the ultimate," he said, "but I know what you mean."

"Where did you get them?"

His evil grin widened into a smile.

"What's your name?" I asked.

"You can call me Ifness."

"Just Ifness?"

"For the moment."

"How is it you know English?"

"Jennifer speaks it. So I thought it useful to learn."

"Uh-huh," I said. "You know Jennifer?"

"She's the one who hired me."

"To take me out?" I asked.

Ifness snapped his gloved fingers. "Creed," he said mockingly. "You must be the Creed she hates with intense loathing."

"You already knew that."

"Tsk, tsk, don't play the martyr, Creed. It doesn't become you."

"You still haven't said. Are you here to kill me?"

From within the helmet, Ifness smile turned crafty. "That would seem to be the case—the logical deduction. However, nothing could be further from my mind."

"Why's that?"

"For the simplest of reasons. I desire sanctuary."

I searched Ifness's filmy green eyes and couldn't tell if he was serious, pulling my leg or wanting to work with me so I could give him a ride back to the center of the galaxy. If Ifness the Hitman wasn't gunning for me, his target should be the Curator. Surely, Jennifer hated him, too.

"I like you, Creed," Ifness said. "You're suspicious. Not only that, but you neatly thwarted the latest Plutonian raid. I noticed that you saw us during the battle and gave chase. Lately, you've been making our lives hell, trying to find us with the tracker. We lost our ride home because of that."

"Look," I said, "If you want sanctuary, I'm going to need weapons, some of my friends here, and you're going to have to surrender to me."

The filmy green eyes hardened. "Creed, Creed, Creed," he said in a sinister voice. "You think my white hair makes me stupid. I resent that, as one professional to another. If you were just another fool, I wouldn't care. You're going to give me sanctuary on my terms or I'm going to kill you and take over your little stealth ship. I could use a vessel like this."

I shrugged. "Fine. You have sanctuary. What do we do next?"

"I thought you'd never ask," Ifness said.

-61-

First, via comm, I ordered N7 off the GEV. The android used the flitter and headed to the light cruiser.

I hadn't given N7 any coded messages. I didn't think there was anything he could do to help me right now, other than threaten the destruction of the GEV. Ifness and Saul would just phase out and, presumably, escape. So what was the point? I'd die for no good reason.

I wondered if Ifness had wanted me to give N7 coded instructions. Or maybe Ifness planned to kidnap me and take me to Jennifer. I realized too late that I'd been a fool and possibly played into Ifness's hands. If I disappeared now, no one would know the reason. They might think I'd just defected and gone back to the Fortress of Light.

I swiveled around at the comm, facing the two. We were in my piloting chamber, with Saul in back with folded arms towering over Ifness watching me carefully. He'd put away the shotgun-like weapon. They both wore their phase suits, although each of them had taken off his helmet, hanging it from the back of his suit.

I'd cast sly glances now and again at Saul. He did not seem like Abaddon or Orcus. I do not mean that he didn't look like the original First One. Saul most certainly did in feature, if not in form.

Think about yourself. If you had a perfect clone, but he was a drooling idiot, would he look like you? Yes and no.

Saul didn't drool nor did he seem like an idiot. He simply did not have the devilish cast to his eyes. He did not seem satanically cunning. He seemed like a big strong brute that would listen to Ifness and do exactly as he was told. You've seen the old cartoon with the two thugs, one little and smart and the other big and dumb. In a way, that was these two. Since Saul was massive, Ifness, only a little bigger than normal, still seemed small beside him.

"Are you confused?" Ifness asked me. "You look confused."

"I'm waiting, if that's what you mean."

"You're confused. I can see it in your bearing. That's fine, though. You should be confused, as this is a confusing situation. By the way, I know what you're thinking. No. This isn't an elaborate setup. I'm not here to kidnap you or lull you into a trusting state so I can screw you later at just the right time."

"You mean like Baron Visconti tried to do to us earlier?"

"The baron," Ifness sneered. "He was Orcus's dupe. I thought you knew that. Oh. I see you already do."

I frowned. I hadn't changed expression or altered my position in any way. So what was Ifness talking about that he could tell I already knew that?

He smirked. "You don't like the shoe on the other foot, do you?"

I said nothing.

"I'm a hitman and you're an effectuator. We're practically in the same line of work, but I do it for profit and—why do you do it, Creed? Why did you consent to becoming the First Guardian's errand boy?"

"You've used that name before," I said. "I know him as the Curator."

"That's a nickname. I thought you knew that."

"There's a lot you think I know that I don't."

He said nothing, but the smirk evaporated, so that was something. The smirk had started to annoy me.

"Saul's different from Orcus," I said.

Ifness waved that aside. "Never mind about Saul. It's sanctuary I'm after. I haven't decided yet if you can provide it."

"I said I'd give you sanctuary."

"You said. You said. What has that to do with it? Can you provide it? That's the question."

"Oh. You mean can I keep you safe from…" I raised an eyebrow.

"Let's see," Ifness said. "Saul and I stowed away in the largest raid force so far. A team of soldiers tried to track me down but you killed them. That was neatly done by the way and gave me my first glimmer of hope. Then you chased me. 'Good, good,' I told myself. 'The boy has brains and balls.' But the Plutonians detonated their ships before you could storm one. I found that disappointing, as I'd been counting on your side capturing one. Now…now I've had to move openly. The only reason I did was because the alternative was worse."

"You're afraid of Jennifer?" I asked.

Ifness laughed, shaking his head. "I'm petrified. She's a monster with delusions of out-performing the worst fiend in our galaxy's history."

"You're referring to Abaddon?" I asked.

"That I am."

"Did Jennifer hire you?"

"Listen to me, son. Don't get personal. Don't pry into my history. I've been doing this a long time, a lot longer than you've been breathing. I bet you think you're something special. Well, you're not. The First Guardian always thought he could get by with second-rate talent. I know you're better than the common ruck, but that don't mean you're shit compared to the real professionals like me."

"You're that good?"

"I'm the best," Ifness said.

"That's why you're running scared?"

He stared at me. It was a flat study and showed me the man was a stone cold killer. He could turn his charm on and off at will, depending on what he wanted. He had a phase suit, and he'd dodged the tracker. He'd been doing something to my AI—

I threw up my hands.

That made him smile. "You give up?"

"Decide, Ifness. Accept our sanctuary and work with us or do what you have to."

"That might mean killing you," he said.

"I know. You probably can, too."

"Do you doubt it?" he asked.

I said nothing.

"Listen, son, it was my plan that freed Jennifer from the Fortress of Light and made sure she grabbed some first-rate effectuator tools on the way out."

"That means you're from the galactic core."

"My goodness," he said sarcastically, "you're a freaking genius."

My jaw dropped as it hit me. I closed my mouth quickly enough, but he stared frowning again.

"Spit it out," he said. "What are you thinking?"

"You were trapped on the Fortress of Light," I said. "You wanted off just as much as she did. How come I never heard of you?"

He shrugged querulously

"Were you a Galactic Effectuator?" I asked.

He stared at me again, and then a grin broke out. "I worked for that old fart so long in the past it would take your breath away if you knew the timeline. I did some side work, though. I slipped up once, and that was all it took. The First Guardian might seem like a tolerant duffer. That just ain't so."

"You're human," I said. "You're a little killer."

"'Little killer' is an insult, not a term of respect or endearment. So don't call me that."

"How long ago did you—?"

"No!" he said, interrupting. "I'm not going to tell you when I did the old fart's dirty work. The point is he woke me up for a spell to keep your little girl company. Then, he would put us both down again. Well, I started whispering to Jennifer and she started getting ideas of her own. She's a smart girl. And she's learned how to delve into her hatred. With most people, hatred weakens them in all sorts of ways, particularly health wise. Not so with Jennifer. She thrives on her hate."

"Did you two have a falling out? Is that why you tried to escape the pocket universe?"

"She's crazy, Creed. Worse, she's started shooting people when she doesn't like something. If an aide reports about a loss, she's as likely to whip out a gun and shoot him as to nod and go back to her planning. She's becoming unpredictable in a bad way."

Ifness shook his head. "I'm not hanging around that kind of ruler. One day, she'll aim a gun at me. Her hatred has driven her mad for vengeance against the universe and against you."

"Why not bring me in and win her permanent favor?"

"I've thought about it, but decided against it for the reasons I just stated. With Jennifer, nothing is permanent."

"Uh-huh," I said. "So, you're going to help us capture her?"

"No."

I gave him a look.

"I'm going to help you kill her," Ifness said.

-62-

I hid my consternation with a grin.

"You don't believe me?" Ifness asked.

"It's more of a question of how we're going to do it."

"I'll tell you when the time is right," he said with a wink.

"You must realize how unconvincing that is."

Ifness gave me that flat stare again, finally saying, "You don't trust me?"

It was my turn to snap my fingers and then point at him. "There you go, Ifness. You hit the nail on the head."

"I'm here, aren't I?"

"That you are."

"Creed, Creed, you're a suspicious bastard. I can see why Jennifer hates you so much."

I waited, tiring of his act, wondering what his game really was.

Ifness glanced at Saul before regarding me more closely. "I know how you think, Creed. That's the problem for you and me. You think I'm here to trap you in some slick way. I could, if that was my idea. But this is a straightforward proposition. You let me hole-up with you for a time, telling no one, and I'll give you the key to killing her."

"And if I say no?"

"Oh. Well. Then Saul will kill you here and now."

I glanced at Saul. The clone's expression never changed. He was the dumb brute, ready to obey whatever order Ifness gave him.

What did I really think about this? Did I buy Ifness's story? I considered it from several angles until I realized the hitman was a first-rate liar. He would feed me whatever story he thought I'd buy. But he had an ulterior motive. Heck. He probably had *seven* ulterior motives. That way, he could produce the one that succeeded and call it a win.

Sometimes, the best lie was the truth, for a time. The switch-up, the misinformation, would come later. It would be like a tiny movement on a track-switcher that would still derail the train and kill thousands.

"What if I told you I had a T-suit?" Ifness asked me.

The idea was intoxicating. Not stealing one out of the Fortress of Light before I'd left had been my greatest regret so far.

"The T-suit is here?" I asked.

"Hell, no," Ifness said. "But's it's where I can get it when I need it."

That made sense.

I jerked a thumb at Saul. "Can he do the regular teleportation of his kind?"

"Show him," Ifness said.

Saul blinked out—and reappeared on the other side of the piloting chamber.

"He's a—?"

"Don't say it," Ifness warned me.

I nodded, and I grew curious. "Have him blink outside in the corridor a moment."

"You heard the man," Ifness told the clone.

Saul teleported away, leaving just Ifness and me in the piloting chamber.

"He's the clone of a First One?"

"Correct," Ifness said.

"Is he…dumber than the others like Orcus?"

"Correct again," Ifness said.

"Did you cause his…stupidity in order to make him more malleable?"

"Three for three," Ifness said. "You're on a roll."

"Did you—or your expedition, anyway—find an accelerator on Acheron in order to grow the clones fast?"

"Boy, you're starting to impress me. You've been paying attention to what's been happening."

"Where did you accelerate the clones?"

Ifness shook his head. "That's not a statement. That's a question. Can't you guess?"

"You'd need something to turn the DNA strands into fetuses."

"That's not the guess I wanted, but I like it. Keep going."

"Was that right?"

"You're five for five," Ifness said.

I scratched my cheek. "You'd want adult clones before you reached the pocket universe. So, you cloned and grew them in our space-time continuum."

"I'm not going to count that one, as it's too obvious and easy. But now it's my turn, hot shot. How do you propose to get into the pocket universe without a dimensional portal?"

"With your help," I said.

"Oh," he said. "And I'm just going to give you such priceless information?"

"I don't know, are you?"

"Creed. Let me explain something. I don't work for free. It goes against my ethics, my principles as a mercenary. I have to get paid or I can't take an action."

I merely nodded, as something had just struck me. Ifness the Hitman had told me he had a T-suit. I remembered hearing someone teleport while I'd crept to Jennifer's stasis quarters inside the Fortress of Light. That must have been him. And if that was true…his entire story seemed suspect. The timing was wrong for one thing. Why had he been teleporting there?

I almost gave away my thoughts. Back then, had the hitman done that for my benefit, noticeably teleporting while I'd been headed for Jennifer's stasis chamber? If that was true, this had to be a setup, right?

I didn't trust Ifness. How could I? He was slippery, double-dealing and maybe too clever for a straight shooter like me. Maybe the best thing would be to kill him and Saul after I got the needed information from them and then get on with the primary task.

"What were you doing in my AI?" I asked.

"Strengthening my hand," Ifness said. "You almost pulled it off, Creed. That was a slick move using a universal chip. You might have gotten the dimensional portal out of it. But right now, you don't have jack."

I'd gotten the formulas Ella read. Didn't Ifness know that? It would seem not. And if he didn't know something so basic—

"You've been making mistakes, Ifness, one right after the other. The Abaddon clones with the phase tracker weren't hunting for me, but for you and Saul. I just happened to stumble onto them. No… they stumbled onto me, thinking it was you. When they saw two blips—when my thruster pack dropped back in phase, they must have figured it was Saul. That's why they were so busy firing and not realizing right away that it was just a piece of equipment."

"Is that what happened?" he asked. "I've wondered how you took them out. Those two—" Ifness shook his head "—were bad mojo, Creed. But I don't get it. You saw Orcus, right?"

"Saw him? I talked to him."

"What did you—?" But Ifness didn't finish the question. Saul popped back in. The clone looked disturbed.

"What is it?" Ifness asked the clone.

"People are coming in the flitter," Saul said.

Ifness looked at me.

I shrugged. "That's not my doing," I said.

"Hmm…"

"Look," I said, realizing N7 must have known something was off. Ella or Rollo might be with him. I wasn't going to sacrifice them to this scoundrel, or sacrifice them to his whims. "I'm not hiding you, Ifness. Either you come out in the open and help us or it's off."

"You that eager to die, boy?" asked Ifness.

"No," I said. "I just know that you're desperate for help, and I'm your best bet."

He looked away and seemed to be calculating. I could almost see the wheels turning in his head. Finally, he regarded me again.

"Smart boy," he said. "We'll try it your way for a time and see where it gets us. I just hope you know what you're doing."

I didn't tell him the real reason I thought he wouldn't kill me. He was here to get me to the pocket universe. The more I thought about it, the more I didn't believe he'd run out on Jennifer. This was a setup, a trap. They'd tried it once with Baron Visconti and Orcus, and failed. This was the second try…right?

That was the problem with this: I thought I was right about Ifness, but I didn't know for sure.

-63-

Rollo, Ella and N7 climbed out of my flitter in the small hangar bay inside the GEV. The two humans wore their second skins. They all had weapons and tried to look everywhere at once as I greeted them.

"N7 said there's trouble," Rollo told me.

"I didn't give you any code words," I told the android.

'I have become an expert in body language," N7 said. "You did not have to."

"Well, you're right," I said.

"I know," N7 said.

I gave them a quick rundown on Ifness and Saul.

"And you let them lose in your GEV?" Ella asked.

"I didn't have a choice," I said. "They got the drop on me."

"But you just sent N7 away," Ella said.

"He did it for you," Ifness said.

I hadn't heard him, but he'd phased in on my left. Saul must have materialized to my right, because Rollo's Bahnkouv came up and I saw he'd covered the giant humanoid.

"Tsk, tsk," Ifness said, "this isn't very friendly."

Ella glanced at me. I minutely shook my head. She lowered her rifle. A second later, N7 did likewise. Rollo kept his laser rifle centered on Saul's chest.

"We have to come to an agreement that will work for both of us," I said. "After Baron Visconti, we're finding it harder to trust you."

"Do you believe Orcus or Jennifer has altered my mind?" Ifness asked.

"No," I said.

"But you're wondering about my real motives?" he asked.

"Yes," I said, knowing that any other answer would make him suspicious.

"Let's make it simple," Ifness said. "Saul and I will stay aboard the GEV. While we're here, we'll store our phase suits in whatever locker you like."

"On the *Thistle Down*," I said.

"Negative," Ifness said. "On the GEV."

"Saul can teleport to the locker and get the suits at any time," I said. "How does that help me trust you?"

"Keep your robot here with us," Ifness said.

"I am an android, not a robot," N7 told him.

"I believe you," Ifness said. "A robot wouldn't be so touchy about it. What do you say?" he asked me.

"Saul can teleport," I said. "That's going to be a problem. If you're roaming around in your phase suits…I can't trust you."

"Take our phase suits," Ifness said. "I'll take the GEV."

"Forget it," I said.

"Then we're leaving," Ifness said.

"So leave," I said.

"After we kill you and your friends," Ifness said. "I was just waiting for them to get here so I could off them with you."

"Jericho," I said.

"What was that?" Ifness asked.

A sonic blast hit us. It was loud and long, and incredibly debilitating. Ella dropped first, unconscious. Rollo went second and I succumbed third.

After that, I don't know what happened.

***

N7 shook me awake to a pounding headache,

The AI had hit all of us with a sonic blast at my order. 'Jericho' had been the code word. In that area, at least, the AI had functioned one hundred percent.

N7 had worked fast while we'd all been unconscious. He'd put Saul in the stasis tube. As long as the Abaddon clone was asleep, he couldn't teleport anywhere.

Ifness wore a special container suit. He wasn't in stasis, but he would sleep for a while.

N7 had divested them of their phase suits and other paraphernalia. These, he had stashed in a special vault.

I woke up Ella and Rollo. They were in a worse state than I'd been.

"What happened, Creed?" Ella whispered from on the deck.

"Come on," I said. "I have something for that."

N7 and I helped Ella and Rollo to the galley, where I served sandwiches and beers, and gave each of them a pill to take away the ache in their heads.

As we ate, I told them all of what Ifness had told me. The three listened raptly.

"Do you believe him?" Ella asked.

"Maybe about three quarters of what he said is true," I answered.

"Is that enough for us to trust him?" Ella asked.

"I don't know."

"Kill 'em both," Rollo said. "Those two are dangerous. At this point, we can't afford to take any chances."

"You have a strong argument," I said. "I'm tempted. But I could be wrong about them."

"Better safe than sorry," Rollo said, with murder in his eyes.

"True," I said. "But we may need them in order to gain the ability to make a dimensional portal."

"Clearly, that is our first priority," Ella said. "Let us see what we can do on our own. They're our last resort."

-64-

The days passed in a blur.

The scientists worked on the formulas I'd gleaned from the Plutonian machine with the universal chip. Others tested the pieces of hull armor. Neither gave us any answers.

I went back to my AI. While it had successfully implemented Jericho, it still couldn't give me a summary on the Plutonian data. Whatever Ifness had done to the AI, I couldn't find or fix it.

I even went in it with my phase suit, but that didn't help.

The scientists went into overdrive, having a worldwide, computer-linked symposium concerning the Plutonian formulas.

According to what I've read, once you knew something was possible it was supposed to be easier to figure out how to do it. We had the formulas. We had the best scientists on Earth. What was wrong?

The scientists had also failed to unlock the secret of the exotic hull armor. They called it adamant armor, but none of them had a clue as to how to manufacture some of our own.

While all this was taking place, missile factories pumped out PDD missiles. If we faced Plutonian ships again, we'd have a ton of them. The PDD missiles had proven their worth during the Second Battle of Earth. If there was going to be a third battle, we'd kick serious butt.

I told Diana about Ifness. She automatically distrusted him. Spencer listened but kept his opinion to himself.

"Could you break him?" I asked the Police Proconsul.

"Given enough time," Spencer said, "and if he didn't commit suicide first."

"You think Ifness would kill himself? He doesn't seem like the type."

"I try to cover all possible options," Spencer said dryly.

My estimation of the Police Proconsul went up. I also distrusted him more. He could keep his own counsel and he tried to anticipate every angle. I kept hearing trickles of information about the police stranglehold on Earth and Confederation politics. Did that mean Spencer had ulterior motives? There was a rumor he'd tried to install political commissars in the military. If that was true, it showed vaulting ambition on his part.

I wanted to investigate the rumor, but I simply didn't have the time.

Rollo trained more former assault troopers, using the Lucky Thirteen as platoon leaders, increasing our numbers of bio-suited soldiers until we had around two hundred and fifty combatants ready for action.

Later, I had Rollo come upstairs to the GEV and trained him to use a phase suit. N7 had used mine before; he was the obvious second choice.

Clearly, I did not intend to give the suits back to Ifness. I viewed them as priceless gifts for our side.

Finally, though, I realized I needed to wake Ifness. We had PDD missiles. We had ready battlejumpers. We did not have the new adamant hull armor, but the scientists discovered that graviton beams set at a lower frequency than usual would have greater penetrating power. There wasn't anything we could do yet about the special inhibiter field except pound Plutonian ships relentlessly and hit them with PDD missiles.

I brought sleeping beauty to *Thistle Down* as a precaution and had Ella pilot the light cruiser into Luna orbit. The GEV remained in Earth orbit.

I wheeled the special tube into a large cargo bay. I didn't want Ifness to feel as if I'd trapped him in a prison cell. I had a band of troopers working on assault boats in the background to give the place a homey feel.

Then, I revived Ifness while I sat at a table, studying stellar charts and cracking sunflower seeds, spitting the shells into a cup.

I heard Ifness stir but left him alone. Soon enough, he grunted and levered himself out of the tube.

"Hungry?" I asked.

The hitman rubbed his face. He had white stubble, making him seem even older than before. He wore a metallic garment but was barefoot.

"I'd like to shower and shave," Ifness said in a rough voice.

I pointed to a nearby "stall" specially set up for him.

He gave me a steady look before shuffling to the stall. Two assault troopers quietly took up station there.

When a clean-shaven Ifness came out, the troopers politely insisted on frisking him. It didn't seem possible he had anything on his person, but they found razor slivers and a small broken handle with a jagged end that he could have used as a makeshift shiv.

Ifness returned to the table afterward, sliding his chair as far from me as he could. He hunched over the plate I'd ordered him, gobbling the omelet like a wolf, demanding more when finished.

I had a trooper bring him more.

Ifness wolfed that down as well, drank several cups of black coffee and ate twelve slices of buttered toast.

"How do you keep so slender?" I asked.

"My hunger has nothing to do with that," he complained. "I've been in stasis—"

"Not exactly true," I said, interrupting. "It was enforced sleep."

"That only makes it worse," he said. "I've obviously been out for days. I'm ravenous, is all, and thirsty."

"Do you want some water?"

He nodded.

A trooper brought a jug and a cup. Ifness picked up the jug and began to chug until all the water was gone.

"More?" I asked.

He shook his head as he wiped his mouth.

"Feeling better?" I asked.

"Feeling double-crossed," he said. "Where's Saul?"

"He's fine."

"That's not an answer."

I spit out the rest of the seeds in my mouth. Sipped from a glass of orange juice and regarded him.

"We need to come to an understanding," I said. "You wanted sanctuary. You have it. Now, we want a few things in return."

"Like what?" he asked.

I smiled indulgently. "First, you have to convince me you really want to help us. If you can't, you're going back to sleep."

"No. That's a bad tactic. You're not giving me any choices. If you force me to help you, how can you trust what I say?"

"I don't trust you, and I doubt there's anything you can do to make me trust you."

"Then we're at an impasse."

"Not necessarily," I said. "You can help us, and I'll pay you for it, but I'm not going to do anything with or for you that demands I trust you in any way."

"What will you pay me for helping you?"

"What's your price?" I countered.

"To begin with, I want my phase suits back."

"Nope," I said. "I'm keeping the suits. They're the Curator's property after all, and I'm still his agent."

Ifness's filmy green eyes burned for just a moment. "You're using the honesty tactic," he said, while hooding his rage. "But that's all it is, a tactic. You plan to kill me after I'm no longer of use to you."

"Why should I do that?"

"Because I'm more dangerous than you are," he said.

I raised a sardonic eyebrow. He was my prisoner. I wasn't his.

"You got the drop on me," he said. "That proves nothing."

"On the contrary. That proves everything. Now, what's your price?"

"Saul's release, as a start," he said.

"Out of the question," I said. "I'll never trust an Abaddon clone."

"Hmmm…" Ifness said, studying me. "You say that with barely concealed hatred. Your fight with Abaddon seared you."

"What Abaddon did to Jennifer seared me," I said with genuine emotion.

Ifness watched me closely, nodding shortly. "I see. I made a mistake. You don't want to kill Jennifer."

"No."

"You want to save her somehow."

"Yes," I said quietly.

He snorted and shook his head. "I made a critical miscalculation. She hates you, Creed. I assumed that you must hate her just as much."

Ifness scrunched his brow, seeming to cudgel his mind for an answer.

"I feel guilty for what happened to her," I said.

His head swayed back as if in shock. Could that be genuine surprise?

"You love her," he said. "That's what this is all about."

I shrugged.

He chuckled softly. "An effectuator in love," he said. "Boy, in our line of work, that's not an emotion you can afford."

"That's not an emotion a person can afford to be without," I countered.

"Oh, boy," he said. "You really don't understand what you are. You think you're better than me? No. You're a disaster waiting to happen."

"What's your price?" I asked, already tired of his psychoanalysis.

He seemed to become all business. "After we defeat Jennifer and company, I want a Plutonian cruiser, a crew and permission to set any coordinates I want with a dimensional portal."

"Your price is reasonable," I said. "But I have to capture Jennifer first, not just defeat her."

Ifness shook his head. "You might not capture her. She might slip away, or she might—she's deadly, Creed. You really have no idea. Killing her is the smartest play for all of us. Trying to capture her while taking out the Plutonians—forget about it."

He had a point, and Ifness wasn't responsible for my success. I was buying the opportunity from him.

"Just for the record," I said, "is Jennifer in the pocket universe?"

"Last time I checked she was."

I nodded. "I accept your price. I'll pay it."

"Great. Now, what do you want from me?"

"Tell us how to make a dimensional portal and what to expect once we reach the pocket universe."

"I'm going to need a guarantee first."

"What guarantee can I possibly give that you'll accept and I can grant?"

He looked me over, rubbed his leathery chin and finally grinned. "Give me your solemn word."

I could hardly believe it. A liar would doubt another's word, wouldn't he? Had Ifness been telling the truth the whole time? Or was he even more cunning than I realized?

If I were in his place, I'd play along until I got an opportunity to make a move for what I really wanted. He'd said before that he wanted to kill Jennifer.

The truth was that I didn't know what to believe.

"You have my word," I said, "provided you play straight with us the entire time."

He thought that over, finally nodding. "Done," he said.

"Let's shake on it."

We both stood and shook hands. Ifness had a surprisingly powerful grip. I hadn't expected that.

"First things first," I said, "the dimensional portal."

He sat down and gave me instructions on how to fix my AI. It sounded easy enough. How had he known to bollix the AI in the first place?

"I'll try that as soon as I'm done with you," I said.

"Sure."

"What are we going to find in the pocket universe?" I asked.

"Well," Ifness said, "you're never going to believe me, but here goes…"

-65-

"Are you familiar with the concept of a pocket universe?" Ifness asked

"A little," I said.

"More than a little," Ifness chided. "I've spent a lot of time with Jennifer, remember? She told me about your expedition to the Karg space-time continuum."

"Then why ask me about the pocket universe?" I asked, exasperated. "Are you trying to test me?"

"Why bother asking if you're going to supply your own answer?" Ifness replied.

I silently counted to three before saying, "It's a pocket universe…"

"A pocket universe is just like a different space-time continuum in this one particular," Ifness said. "The properties of the other reality can and often are different from this one."

I nodded.

"The Plutonians were originally from a different space-time continuum," he continued. "I don't know when or how they crossed over to ours. I'm sure they made the crossing long before Abaddon ever went to the Karg reality. Maybe the Plutonians' coming goaded Abaddon to try a cross-continuum exploration. But like I just said, I don't know and haven't been able to find out.

"It isn't like I've been trying real hard, either," Ifness said. "Jennifer doesn't like much speculation on the subject and the

Plutonians almost broke their conditioning when asked about it."

"Wait," I said. "The Plutonians are conditioned?"

Ifness eyed me.

I closed my mouth. I'd given away some of my ignorance. That was a bad move. The less I said, the less Ifness could deduce what I knew and what I didn't already know.

"Yes," Ifness said, in answer to the question. "I'll give you a freebie to show you my honest intent. We found the dimensional-portal tech on Acheron. We found plenty of what we needed on that old world. If we hadn't gone to Acheron first…"

Ifness shook his head.

He waited for me to comment on what he'd just said.

"You can ask," he finally said.

"What, in particular, can I ask?"

He sighed. "You keep thinking I'm stupid or not as bright as you. That's a mistake, Creed. I'm five times smarter than you are. There's only one way you outclass me."

"Yeah?"

"You have shifty animal cunning. Jennifer warned me about that, but I guess I thought my natural heightened intelligence would help me run circles around you. Granted, you'd never figure out how to form a dimensional portal without me, but your shifty animal cunning—"

"Enough about that," I said, interrupting.

"It must be a lowbrow ability," Ifness mused, "the reason I don't have it."

I drummed my fingers on the table.

Ifness chuckled. "You can't take a joke, can you, Creed?"

"Ha-ha," I said, flatly.

"All right already," he said. "Here's what you're dying to know. How did we defeat the guardian machine in orbit around Acheron?"

"Earl Parthian helped you."

"Hey," Ifness said, jerking back. "You're not going to make this bloody simple, are you?"

"What are you babbling about now?"

He smiled. I must have blushed, because he chuckled next.

"*You* have the low animal cunning," I said. "That was all smoke meant to set me up."

"Maybe you're not quite as dumb as I thought," he muttered.

He'd wanted to know if I known about Purple Tamika. Well, now he knew. I did. I wished he would stop playing hitman games and just get on with it.

"You went to Earl Parthian with Holgotha?" I asked, trying to get him back on track.

"Indeed. The Forerunner artifact has been critical to all of this. The galaxy-ranging teleportation is a fantastic power. But you already know that, don't you?"

"I've worked with Holgotha before, yes."

"You're a pip, Creed. Why you work for the Frist Guardian is beyond me. You should be Galaxy Emperor by now. Instead, you're an errand boy."

"What about you?" I asked. "You're so smart, and you're the hitman for a madwoman."

"First things first," Ifness said. "Remember, I've been stuck on the Fortress of Light for a long time. Been out of commission, you could say."

"You really expect me to believe that part of your story?"

"You don't?" he asked, seeming genuinely surprised.

I waited. I was tired of this cat and mouse game.

Ifness shrugged. "We used Holgotha and overawed Earl Parthian. The artifact also helped defeat the Acheron machine and helped us locate the hidden caches on the ancient world. Soon thereafter, the new Emperor-to-be took his cut of the planetary treasure and we took ours.

"Jennifer began the DNA stamping right away, using the accelerator to form adult First Ones. The Acheron implants seemed to hold, and she has the greatest soldiers in history.

"How many adult clones are there?" I asked.

Ifness shrugged. "I'd say an easy sixty."

I shuddered. "That's madness. She's created *sixty* Abaddon clones?"

"That's what I said."

Sixty Abaddon clones! Sixty First Ones. Sixty beings with the same potential for evil as Abaddon. He'd been the worst monster in galactic history, and now Jennifer had made sixty more?

She must be mad to think she could control all of them. Heck! Shah Claath hadn't been able to control us humans with the shock chips and by having every advantage. Whatever Jennifer had become, she lacked the same potential for greatness, good or bad, that each of her clones possessed. Well, not all of them.

"Was that when you made an idiot Saul?" I asked.

"No, I did that later," Ifness said abruptly.

I looked at him. What did that mean? "You...you trapped an adult clone and turned him into Saul?"

Ifness shrugged.

I shuddered again thinking about what Ifness had done. "I'll have to check Saul's cranium, see if there are any surgery scars," I said as nonchalantly as I could.

"I'll save you the trouble," Ifness said. "There are cranial scars."

"You cut out some of his brain?" I asked, unable to keep the horror out of my voice.

"Does it matter?"

I wanted to push away from the table in disgust. The hitman wasn't just ruthless; he was vile. But I needed him. Therefore, I needed to bury my outrage, at least for the moment.

"You were telling me about the pocket universe," I managed to say.

"Brain surgery to an Abaddon clone troubles you?" Ifness asked.

I said nothing.

"Huh," he said. "Who would have guessed? Then again, look what Abaddon did to Jennifer."

"Yeah," I said. "Exactly."

"One of Abaddon's clones got his just desserts. So what?"

"A clone shouldn't pay for the sins of his father," I said.

"You have a better way of getting revenge?" Ifness asked.

"I do."

"I'd like to hear it."

"You reverse what the criminal did."

Ifness snorted. "You're too softhearted, Creed. Abaddon wasn't a criminal. Ultimately, he was a failed conqueror. Everyone hates those, while everyone reveres the victors. It's the same old story throughout the universe. Losers are bad, and winners are good."

"Why not tell me about the pocket universe?" I said.

Ifness shook his head. "Maybe that's why you're an effectuator and I'm a hitman. I don't have any illusions."

I said nothing, hoping to wait him out.

"The pocket universe," Ifness said, seemingly switching mental gears. "Without Holgotha, we never would have made it through to it. I won't bore you with the technical details. Your brainiacs can figure that out later from your AI. We made a dimensional portal and crossed to the other side."

Ifness exhaled, shaking his head in remembrance of what seemed to have been an ordeal. "Their void or space is nothing like our space. Here, it's a vacuum with particles of dust or bits of debris. There, it's like the middle reaches of…" He plucked at his lower lip. "What do you call your largest gas giant?"

"Jupiter," I said.

He snapped his fingers. "The void in the pocket universe is like piloting a submarine through the gaseous substance of middle-level Jupiter. Gas giants are—"

"I'm aware of a gas giant's composition."

"Oh. Sure. I wasn't trying to say you weren't."

I nodded.

"Anyway, that's what the pocket universe's space is like. The Plutonian planet floats in that. That means the planet is much denser than ordinary. It's not as dense as a neutron star, but it's damn dense and rather small."

"Wait a minute. You're saying space there is like traveling…underwater on Earth?"

"No. Not that much pressure and not through a liquid. I said gas, thick gas in some places. For instance, if a spaceship tried to go too deep in an Earth ocean, the outside water pressure would crumple the bulkheads."

"Plutonian ships are more like submarines?" I asked.

"I seem to have given you the wrong idea. The gaseous pressure doesn't grow or become greater as you travel through the substance. It's like your space, only over there it's filled with gas. Think of it as an extra-thick nebula."

"What gas?" I asked.

"Its own Plutonian gas," Ifness said. "The gas isn't found on our periodic table. I think that's why Plutonian ships don't have force fields. No one's force field—I mean your battlejumpers—is going to work in the pocket universe's heavy gas void."

"That's not good," I said.

"Not good for you," Ifness said. "It's great for the Plutonians."

"What else?" I asked.

"It's easy to get lost there, much harder to use your sensors. Sonar works best. Of course, missiles aren't as useful. It takes a lot more push to travel through the compacted gas. Many beams will fizzle over distance there, especially lasers."

"That's just great."

"On the plus side, it's hard teleporting over there."

"Come again," I said.

"Your T-missiles will be useless. The Abaddon clones can teleport some but not nearly as far as they can here. That's good, because they'll find it difficult to swarm one ship at a time through teleportation. Even Holgotha is severely limited in his teleporting abilities over there."

"Oh," I said.

"And you don't want to be too close to an explosion," Ifness said. "The gas helps spread shockwaves. The Plutonian explosive device is far deadlier in their space-time continuum than here."

"It sounds like a horror show over there."

"Now, you're understanding. Now, you're starting to see why I wanted out of that madhouse. It's a strange realm, Creed. It's warping Jennifer. It's warping her elite guards, too."

"You mean the Abaddon clones?" I asked.

"Of course. They're her chosen ones."

"And the Plutonians?" I asked.

Ifness pursed his lips. "Jennifer has only woken a fraction of them. There are millions more on their planet. There are many more of their spaceships in mothballs."

"What about Holgotha? Is he still there?"

"He is," Ifness said.

Something about the way he said that alerted me. I tried not to show it, though. "Is Holgotha still in Jennifer's good graces?" I asked.

"As far as I know," Ifness said.

My gut told me the hitman was lying. Why should he lie about that?

"So…how do we win?" I asked.

"Depends on what you think winning is."

"Destroying the Plutonian ability to keep striking our worlds," I said.

"Easiest way to do that is to kill 'em all."

"Suppose Earth Force agrees with you?"

"Then you nuke their planet from a safe distance. You don't want the gaseous void to take the explosions and rebound them against you."

"How big is the Plutonian defensive fleet?"

"Maybe twice the mass of what you faced a few days ago, and…"

"And?" I asked.

"The mother of all Planetary Defense Satellites," he said. "You've seen nothing like it anywhere. If you think Plutonian warships are bad, this thing is one hundred times worse."

"Is that an exaggeration?"

"Since you don't believe me, you'll have to see for yourself."

"You think we're going into the pocket universe after what you've said?"

Ifness scoffed. "Creed, if you don't go, you're going to lose eventually. It's either kill the Plutonians or be killed by them. You have no other options."

I sat back, realizing it was time to talk to Diana and the others about this.

-66-

Ifness asked if he could join me. I told him no. He said it would be better if he came, but he declined to provide a reason why.

That made me suspicious. I had the damaged light cruiser travel to Earth orbit, while I instructed N7 to remain in stealth mode on the GEV until further notice.

Did I have a premonition? Maybe. I don't know. I left the *Thistle Down* and headed down to New Denver in a regular shuttle. Halfway through the atmosphere, an emergency alert blared inside the cabin. I was sitting up front with the pilot. It was proving a bumpy ride through the atmosphere. Then the comm squawked.

"Creed? Creed, are you in the shuttle?"

The voice sounded familiar, but I couldn't quite place it.

The pilot looked at me, a young woman fresh out of the academy.

I switched on a viewer. It showed an awful sight. A huge, donut-shaped Forerunner artifact was less than half-a-kilometer from the OT light cruiser *Thistle Down*.

I cursed. I couldn't believe this.

Worse, huge missiles lofted from Holgotha's hull. The missiles sped for Earth. Jennifer, or her side, anyway, was using the artifact as we'd used it as Star Vikings over ten years ago. I did not like this reversal.

"Creed," the voice said over the comm.

Then it hit me. It was Jennifer. I knew it was a trap, but I answered anyway.

"This is Creed," I said.

Jennifer's image appeared on a small screen. She'd braided her long hair, and her dark eyes seemed to stab into my soul.

"So, Ifness did not lie," Jennifer said.

"What are you talking about?"

Orcus, or his brother, stepped into visual range, holding aloft a beat-up looking hitman. Ifness's eyes were puffed shut, he was bleeding from several cuts and was missing most of his left arm. There was a tourniquet on the stump.

"He's going to tell me everything," Jennifer gloated. "So, his treachery is not going to help you in the slightest."

"Jennifer," I said, "don't do this."

She laughed in a sinister way, and I heard something behind me.

I whirled around in my seat, and two Abaddon clones wearing dark garments appeared. They had teleported, obviously. And just as obviously, Jennifer had used the comm to pinpoint my location.

The pilot looked back, too, and screamed. Fortunately, for me, the pilot lost concentration, or she made the most perfect choice of her life.

The shuttle plunged for Earth.

The two clones fired at me, one beam punching through the shuttle's skin from the inside. The other shot shattered shuttle controls. Then both clones, who had already been on their way up due to the plunging shuttle, struck bulkheads.

I don't think I'd ever thought faster in my life. I'd taken to wearing the super-tech Abaddon force axe. I tore it from my hip, unbuckled from my seat and launched myself at them. As I flew through the cabin, the activated force axe sizzled with red power lines.

The first Abaddon clone shouted a warning to his brother. The red power lines seared against the first clone so blood and gore sprayed everywhere, including against my face. The blood blinded me. I slashed all around, cutting—

I tumbled head-over-heels from the shuttle cabin, having created an opening with the axe.

Then, the craziest thing happened. An Abaddon clone appeared near me, trying to strike a blow as we fell. I don't know how I dodged, but I did.

The clone teleported away, and appeared above me for a second try.

At that moment, the pilot must have regained control of her vessel. She beamed against the clone's back. The massive creature arched in pain. That stole his concentration.

I made a full-eagle spread with my body, slowing my descent just enough, and seemingly rose toward him. In reality, I just fell to Earth slower than he did. While passing him, I hacked with the force axe, killing the clone.

At that point, a beam slashed through the heavens, hitting the shuttle, destroying it as a coherent vessel as pieces tumbled away.

Luckily for the pilot, she ejected in time.

I waited for another beam to stab from space, killing me. When it didn't come, I expected more Abaddon clones to teleport near me, trying to capture me for Jennifer. That did not happen, either.

Instead, with the force axe in my hands, I plummeted to Earth, with no parachute on my back to help me. Given a few more minutes, I would strike the surface and end my existence in this present reality.

-67-

I deactivated the force axe, slapping it back onto my hip. Then I spread myself as wide as I could, hoping to buy myself a few seconds more of life.

I was over land and couldn't spot any large body of water. Not that striking water would help much given my velocity. Still, I was hoping for a miracle.

My eyes watered even though I kept them slit and used my fingers to shield them, peeking between two fingers.

I was over the Rockies. Well, at least I'd die in the old United States of America. I'd started out as an American and would die as one. Then I noticed specks. They seemed to zoom up at me from the ground.

I turned around to look up at the clouds. I couldn't spy any beams or missiles racing down. I did not see any more Abaddon clones popping into existence around me.

I'd like to be able to teleport like that. Once, with a Ronin 9 T-Suit, I'd done just that in space.

I rolled around to look at the nearing mountains. The specks had grown. They seemed humanoid. Then I realized that space marines wearing jetpacks were zooming up to save me.

The wind tore away my laughter. I might survive this yet. I waited as they grew larger.

Soon, two jetpack-suited marines reached me. One grabbed me, steadying me in the air. The other quickly fit a parachute onto my back, only snagging the straps once. I helped him out.

They tugged, slapped my back. I nodded. Each of them jetted away from me. They must be running low on fuel.

I pulled the ripcord, and the most beautiful chute in the world spread into existence. It yanked me up short, and then I began to float and sway toward the approaching mountains.

I kind of lost it, then, lost it in a good way. I started whooping with laughter—all my pent-up emotions at dying so young gushing out of me. Winston Churchill had once said there was no greater feeling in life than being shot at, and having the shooter miss. Well, I could top that. There was no greater feeling than plunging to your death, and having space marines zoom up and slap a parachute onto your back so you floated down light as a feather.

It was awesome.

I touched down, running down a slope, tripping and rolling around and around. I was entangled in the parachute lines, but soon worked free. I was in a glade between spruces. A startled deer took off.

As quickly as I could, I gathered the parachute, bundling it up and putting it to the side. I sat on the grass afterward, taking delicious gulps of air.

It felt good to be alive.

I looked up at the clouds. Jennifer was up there, and she'd just tried to capture me.

I cursed, jumping to my feet. Had Ifness told them about the GEV and Saul in the stasis tube?

If Jennifer grabbed my GEV—

"Come on," I said to myself. Someone needed to pick me up.

On a screen, I'd seen the missiles launched from Holgotha. Those had looked like big missiles meant to carry hell-burner warheads. Had Earth Force intercepted them in time? Was the world burning or about to burn?

As much as I loved being alive, I was starting to die from the curiosity of it all.

I saw a shuttle—a new one—zooming toward me. Did they see me? I started waving. Then I wondered if the better question was if they were good guys or more bad guys.

I kept waving anyway. If it looked like they were going to make a strafing run—well, I hoped they didn't. I waved like a fool. The shuttle's stubby wings wobbled back and forth.

I stopped waving and plucked my longish handle.

In minutes, the shuttle was above me, using VTOL jets to land on the slope. My gut clenched. What if Abaddon clones stepped out?

That's not logical, I told myself. They would have already teleported to me. Heck. They could have teleported to the pines, set up sniper rifles and shot me.

The shuttle thumped onto the ground. My stomach tightened even more, and a ramp extended and a hatch opened. Three marines wearing combat armor clanked down. Police Proconsul Spencer followed. He had a gun in one hand, pointed at me.

The marines circled around, each with a Bahnkouv laser rifle aimed at me. These were probably part of a police SWAT Team, not military space marines.

I wondered what had happened to the jetpack marines.

Spencer came a little closer to me, but not too close. I'd already put away the longish handle in order to seem less threatening, and so he wouldn't realize I had a priceless weapon on my person.

"I've been waiting for a chance to talk to you alone," Spencer said.

I waited.

"Hands up, please. I don't want any misunderstanding between us."

-68-

I raised my hands, still waiting, wondering about his angle. Was he a traitor to Diana, to Earth?

"What just happened?" he asked.

"You saw it," I said. "You tell me."

Spencer shook his head. "The time for games has ended. Holgotha appeared. It launched missiles."

"That's wrong," I said.

"Interesting," Spencer said. "Explain, please."

"Whoever is using Holgotha launched the missiles."

"How do you know that?" Spencer asked.

I opened my mouth, but then I closed it with a snap. "You have a point. I don't know. I'm guessing."

"You believe *Jennifer* is responsible?" he asked.

"Why ask that so sarcastically?"

He waggled the gun, although his eyes remained on me. The SWAT members, by the way, never moved a muscle. I couldn't see their eyes behind the visors. I didn't have to. Their Bahnkouvs would kill me just as dead if they beamed.

"This all seems too…contrived," Spencer finally said. "I think it's a trick. You got tired in the galactic core. No one knew you out there. So, you decided to come home and take over. What better way to do that than to manufacture a crisis that only the great Commander Creed could solve."

"Spencer, you're a genius. Only you could see through my falling through the air like I just did as a ploy on my part."

"Please," the Police Proconsul said. "Your allies turned on you. It's happened before."

"Oh. Sure. No wonder you're so good at your job. You invent the danger and fix it. How do I know that's your special MO? Easy—because you suspect in others what you're most prone to do yourself."

The Police Proconsul frowned. "Enough of your word games, Creed. Give me the force axe."

"What?"

"It's on your hip. Give it."

"Are you—?"

As I spoke, a huge Abaddon clone appeared behind a SWAT marine. The clone jabbed the armor suit with a prod of some kind. A huge electric spark zapped the armored marine. The marine in his suit flew ten feet, striking the ground in a jumbled heap.

The other two SWAT marines turned toward the clone. One laser rifle beamed. At the same time, Spencer's pistol barked.

Neither man hit the clone, for he'd teleported behind another marine. The clone jabbed the marine, and the same mighty shock catapulted the man into a heap ten or eleven feet away.

Once more, a SWAT member and Spencer fired. The clone teleported again, and the marine whirled around, beaming as he did so.

That was smart thinking, but the clone did not appear.

"Stop!" Spencer shouted. He took several steps toward me, aiming at my head. "If you—"

The clone appeared beside me. Spencer fired. The clone dove and tackled me, knocking me down. The bullet hit the dirt beyond me. Then, the two of us disappeared—

And reappeared behind a clump of pine trees. I tried to grapple the clone—he popped away again. I sagged to the ground.

I heard air rushing as he appeared several feet from me.

I looked up from the ground. I recognized the clone. It was Saul, and that baffled me. Saul panted, and his eyes were bloodshot. He looked beat, as if he might faint at any second. He had the zapper, a big prod weapon with a power-pack on his back and a line linking them. He must have taken that from my armory of special weapons on the GEV.

He let go of the prod and shrugged off the pack so they both hit the dirt.

"You're not going to zap me?" I asked.

Saul shook his head.

I climbed to my feet. Part of me said to use the force axe and kill him while he couldn't teleport away. Another part suggested he'd just saved my life, or saved me from some intense interrogation.

"What gives, Saul? Why did you do that?"

"N7 woke me," Saul said slowly.

"Is N7 dead?"

Saul frowned, possibly trying to understand why I'd ask something like that.

"N7 is still alive?" I asked.

"When I left he was alive," Sault said. "But I thought N7 was an android."

"You don't think androids are alive?"

Saul shrugged his massive shoulders.

"Did Holgotha, or the people on Holgotha, go after N7?"

"No."

"They only went after the light cruiser?"

"First, the light cruiser," Saul said slowly. "Before they could find the GEV, N7 went into deep stealth mode. He woke me up afterward. N7 intercepted Jennifer's message to you."

"And...?" I asked.

A little of the exhaustion left Saul's features as anger appeared. "They hurt Ifness."

"You don't like that?"

"Ifness is Saul's best friend."

I almost started coughing. The hitman seemed to have done a number on Saul.

"Wait a minute," I said. "That's why you're helping me? You want my help in getting Ifness back from Jennifer?"

"Yes. Saul needs help. Ifness will die unless Saul acts fast."

"Why didn't you teleport to Jennifer?"

Saul shook his head. "Jennifer is strong. Jennifer has powerful guards. They would have killed Saul or captured him and made him evil like them."

Whoa-boy. I didn't know what to think. I might have seriously miscalculated concerning Ifness and Saul. Had the hitman done brain surgery on Saul or not? If he hadn't, why had Ifness lied to me about doing surgery?

"Saul, can I check your scalp?"

"Why?" the clone asked suspiciously.

"I want to see what kind of surgery they did to you."

"What do you mean? No one do surgery on Saul. I am the strongest, fittest First One in the universe."

"Can I check anyway just to make sure?"

"We are out of time. We must save Ifness."

"Is Holgotha gone?"

Saul looked up into the sky. He stared for a time. His shoulders sagged.

"We are too late. Holgotha is gone. They go back to small planet. Now, Ifness scream for days. I lose my best friend."

I must have been out of my mind because I believed the Abaddon clone. First, though, I wanted to see his scalp.

"I have a plan," I said. "First, I have to check your scalp."

Saul shrugged, walked to me, bent down on one knee and lowered his head. Like a baboon looking for lice, I moved the thick dark hair on Saul's scalp. I found no evidence of surgery scars, none at all.

"No one ever performed a lobotomy on you," I said.

"No! Why you think so?"

"Uh…forget it, Saul."

Why had Ifness lied about that? The hitman had told me he'd had surgery done to Saul. Had Ifness said that to make himself seem tougher? I couldn't figure out his angle. But maybe that wasn't so critical right now.

"Look, Saul," I said, "you need to teleport us to New Denver. We have to attack the pocket universe as soon as possible."

"The small planet surrounded by weird gas?" Saul asked.

So Ifness had been telling the truth about that. Maybe the hitman really had had a falling out with Jennifer. She'd come to the Solar System to seize her errant hitman. I needed to reach New Denver before Police Proconsul Spencer did.

"This is important, Saul. I have to get to the Earth capital right away."

Saul stared at me. He didn't seem quite as tired as before. "Yes," he said. "I see what I can do."

-69-

Before Saul teleported us there, I reconsidered. It would be better to show up in New Denver in strength.

"Can you see the spaceport at New Denver?" I asked.

The clone nodded. How else could he teleport to a place unless he had some mechanism to see where he was going? The same had been true for Holgotha.

"Do you know what Ella looks like?" I asked.

Saul shook his head.

I described her.

The clone got a faraway look in his eyes. I learned this was his pre-sight. Much as Holgotha did with an interior machine, Saul—or a First One—could do with their mind. I didn't know the range limitation, but I guessed it must in hundreds or possibly thousands of kilometers, but not thousands of light-years like Holgotha.

In any case, we waited until Saul spotted Ella, Rollo and other assault troopers piling out of several landed shuttles at the spaceport.

"Take us there," I said.

Saul did, creating a surprising commotion among the troopers.

I explained as quickly as I could. Rollo informed me about the bad news. The captured Light Cruiser *Thistle Down* had been destroyed. Three of the Lucky Thirteen had been aboard it. They were all dead.

The subcontinent of India had taken a hell-burner. Everyone there was dead or dying. Another hell-burner had slashed down between Australia and Antarctica. The sea boiled there. Billions of fish would have already died. Radiation poisoning was likely going to kill millions more humans.

My knees seemed to unhinge. I crashed down onto my butt. Rollo and Saul both hauled me back to my feet. Rollo glared so viciously at the clone that Saul released me.

"You okay, Creed?" Rollo asked.

"Jennifer," I whispered. "She murdered millions."

"She is a monster," Saul said.

"Shut your yap," Rollo told him. "Don't you know she's his woman?"

Saul peered at me strangely. "Why does she hate you if she is your woman?"

"Creed?" Rollo asked.

I shook my head. I knew what Rollo was asking. Should he kill this Abaddon lookalike for me?

"I still don't understand certain aspects of this," Ella said. "Spencer—"

"Forget about Spencer," I said. "He tried and failed to pump me of info."

"The Police Proconsul wanted to do more than that," Ella said.

"It doesn't matter," I said, still sick to my stomach at the thought of all the murdered people. We had to put a stop to the genocide by taking out the Plutonians once and for all and stopping Jennifer and her band of center-galaxy outlaws. That meant putting aside minor differences among ourselves. Spencer was an opportunistic bastard, but he wasn't a genocidal maniac.

"Are we ready?" I asked.

"What if Diana decides Spencer has it right?" Ella asked.

"I don't know."

"We need a plan," Ella said.

"That's why we're going to meet Diana."

"We need a plan about dealing with her," Ella said. "With Spencer's latest stunt…"

"We don't have much choice anymore," I said. "Neither does Diana. We have the dimensional portal data and knowledge about the pocket universe. They have the battlejumpers. We mix and trade and join forces."

"I hope Diana still feels the same way," Ella said. "Millions, tens of millions of people have died today. That has a way of changing people's minds."

"I know," I said. "Now, let's go."

***

Our troopers wore their second skins as we piled into cars and vans, heading toward the main Government House in the middle of New Denver.

Soon, we found one hundred hover-tanks waiting in the nearby streets and around the building, with several thousand space-marines in combat armor to help them. General Briggs and Spencer were at the main checkpoint where we stopped the cars.

"Wait here," I told Rollo before exiting our car.

"You know they could fire cannons at us, right?" Rollo asked.

I detached the longish handle, giving it to him. "Hold onto this, would you?"

Rollo looked at what he held before nodding stiffly.

I climbed out of the car and walked with a thousand lasers and a hundred cannons pointed at me. I was a dead man if Spencer gave the word. Behind me were two hundred assault troopers, including Ella and Rollo. N7 was upstairs in the GEV. I'd told Saul to teleport back to him, but the clone had said he couldn't because he couldn't find the stealth ship right now.

The clone was hidden in a van. I'd told Saul to keep his head down.

I halted by the barricade, with marine laser-rifles pointed at me. I had a force-blade knife-handle and a sidearm pistol at my waist. I could see the main spire of the Government House from here.

"Spencer, General Briggs," I said.

Briggs said nothing, looking at me stiff-lipped. Spencer looked peaked, winded, as if he'd rushed to get here, which was no doubt the truth.

"You must surrender to us, Commander," the Police Proconsul said.

"Did Diana order this?"

"Your woman appeared on worldwide TV," Spencer said. "She told us that Earth will cease to exist unless we hand you over to her. She said that she will attack again, in a similar manner, within the next five days. You tell me, Commander. What would you do? Hand you over or watch millions more die in hell-burner holocausts?"

"Do you know what will happen if you hand me over to her?"

"We will survive," Spencer said.

"Nope," I said. "She'll bind me and make me watch while she annihilates Earth. I'm the last chance you have to save the planet. Jennifer knows that. She's running scared. She wouldn't have made the threat otherwise."

"You don't know that."

I surveyed the hover-tanks, the space marines and then Spencer with his red-suited security people behind him.

I snorted. "You know what I'd do in Jennifer's place?" I didn't wait for the Police Proconsul to ask. "I'd have a teleporting sniper somewhere and shoot you and Briggs. Then, all the space marines and tankers would kill the assault troopers and me. The only reason that isn't going to happen is that Jennifer wants me alive. Do you understand the importance of that? If you really want to stay alive, capture me and tell Jennifer that you'll kill me if she launches another hell-burner."

Spencer became thoughtful. "You could be right. Will you come peacefully into custody?"

"Under one condition," I said.

He nodded sharply.

"After we have a strategy session in the Government House with Diana," I said. "Or are you and Briggs staging a coup and taking over?"

The hatch to the nearest hover-tank opened. The Prime Minster in all her Amazonian glory stepped down.

"Spencer and Briggs are not staging a coup," Diana said, as she approached the barricade. "The Police Proconsul and General have been acting on my authority regarding you. I don't like anyone trying to push me," she added. "But your idea…I like it. I'm going to keep you under lock and key for a long, long time, Creed."

"First, though," I said, "we have a strategy session in the Government House."

Diana studied me. She looked at the cars and vans filled with assault troopers. "You sure do believe in brazening it out, don't you, Creed? You've always had the biggest balls of anyone I know. Yes. Let us talk. I'll listen. I'll ponder your daring plan, and then I'll lock you away where not even Jennifer's teleporting giants can find you."

-70-

I told them what Ifness had told me regarding the strange pocket universe, the gaseous quality of the void around the planet and star.

"How does the star work?" Diana asked.

"I don't know," I said. "Probably the way our Sun works here."

"That doesn't make sense," Diana said. "Wouldn't the star ignite the gas?"

"That's an interesting point," Ella said.

Diana had agreed that I could bring two of my people with me. I suspect she liked that I'd picked Ella and Rollo, believing the other troopers less dangerous without them there.

"Maybe the gas is less dense near the star," Ella said.

"I'd think denser," Diana said.

"Why?" asked Ella, sounding intrigued.

"No particular reason," Diana said. "That just seems right."

"We won't know until we go," I said. "Ifness's explanation gives a concrete reason for the inhibiter field, as electromagnetic shields won't work over there."

"Good point," Ella said.

"How can we go there?" Diana asked. "We don't have a dimensional portal."

"I know how to construct one," I said.

Diana and Spencer traded glances.

"When did you learn this?" Diana asked.

"Ifness told me how to fix the damage he'd done to my AI." I told them about the universal chip I'd inserted into a Plutonian computing machine. "Once I fix the AI, we'll have the data we need to construct a dimensional portal."

"What do you suggest we attempt to do after that?" Diana asked. "Are you thinking we go through the portal with the Earth Force battlejumpers?"

"What else?" I asked.

"Maybe with the Starkiens, too," Diana added.

"Yes," I said. "That would be the smart move."

"And if Jennifer pops near Earth with Holgotha while we and the Starkiens are gone?" Diana asked.

"Then we lose the Earth," I said.

Spencer struck the table with a fist. "Suppose, against all the odds, we win. Why won't Jennifer escape on Holgotha and burn Earth to the ground for what we've done?"

"We'll capture Jennifer before that happens," I said.

"How?" asked Spencer.

"I have three phase suits."

"She has teleporting soldiers," Spencer said. "That trumps your three phase suits. And don't say what other choice do we have. We can grab you and hold you—"

"Are you daft?" Rollo shouted, rising from his chair. "That's a coward's strategy. You said yourself that Jennifer has teleporting soldiers. Sooner or later, if you hold Creed hostage, they'll find and kidnap him. Then you've lost anyway. The only way to win, to save Earth, is to destroy the Plutonians, the Abaddon clones and..." He looked at me. "Capture Jennifer."

"Kill Jennifer," Diana said. "She's clearly a genocidal maniac."

"Kill or capture," I said, "the key is in attacking."

"I've been thinking," Briggs said. "The pocket universe has a gaseous medium. Maybe we should convert submarine torpedoes. If missiles work sluggishly there, torpedoes might be better. We could even take submarines along as well."

Silence filled the room.

"That's a good idea," I said, pointing at the general. It sounded dumb, but I wanted the general on my side. "Rig subs for the pocket universe. We can put them in the battlejumpers' assault-boat cargo holds."

"That's crazy," Diana said. "Submarines are a silly stunt."

She was right, but I said, "It's a way to add to our ship power. Massed torpedoes, massed PDD missiles, graviton-beam cannons. We know how to fight, where to go, how to get there... All we need now is the desire to roll the dice for humanity's fate."

"They have Holgotha," Diana said. "Holgotha."

"I know," I said. "But we have pure hearts."

"Meaning what?" Spencer asked.

"That we have no freaking choice," Rollo told him. "That's obvious. This jabbering is a waste of time. What do you say, Diana? Creed always came through in the past."

Diana glanced at Spencer.

The Police Proconsul shook his head.

The Prime Minister turned to Briggs.

The General nodded. "I'm for it. We have to fight."

I was gladder than ever I'd backed his silly idea of using subs.

Diana glanced at Admiral Sparhawk.

The old man frowned for a time, examining his hands. Finally, he faced the Prime Minster, "Fight," he said. "We must exterminate the Plutonians before they exterminate us."

Diana seemed forlorn.

"I'm glad we actually have the chance to win it all," I said. "We'll soon know how to make a dimensional portal. We know something about the terrain ahead. We know the enemy fleet's approximate size and that they have the mother of all PDSs there. We have some tricks of our own, with three times the phase suits than before."

"Three altogether," Diana said.

"Like I said," I told her, "three times as many."

"This is a mad gamble," Diana said.

"But it's the only way that assures human survival over time," I said.

"I think you're right," Diana said. "Police Proconsul, will you stand by my decision?"

Spencer paled, slowly rising to his feet. "Prime Minster, I regret to inform you that—"

From where I sat, I detached my force blade from my hip, clicked it on and locked it into place, and threw hard and fast.

Before Spencer could finish his traitorous speech, the force blade sizzled into his throat. He catapulted backward, hitting his chair and going down on the rug.

At the same time, the doors flew open and red-suited security police covered us with their pistols. Spencer had clearly signaled them in some hidden way to make their move.

A major of the security police noticed the Police Proconsul on the rug. He hurried to him and looked up in alarm—he'd withdrawn the knife and clicked it off so it powered down.

"He's dead," the police major said.

"On my orders," Diana said into the shocked silence.

"Your orders?" the major asked her.

"Yes," Diana said. "Please take him away in honor." She turned to Briggs. "Summon your marines."

The General looked at the police major. The major hesitated, always a bad thing to do at a time like that. Then Briggs spoke into his wrist comm.

The major looked at Diana once more, looked at me and then summoned some security people to carry the dead Police Proconsul outside.

By that time, armored space marines entered the chamber.

"You're right, Creed," Diana said. "It's time for us to attack the Plutonians on their home ground."

-71-

Earth Force went into high gear. Clearly, we dreaded another Holgotha-launched assault. Two hell-burners had done dreadful damage to the planet.

Diana wisely and quietly nixed the submarine idea but went ahead with the torpedo possibility. Thus, torpedo-constructing factories churned around the clock. The battlejumpers took aboard more PDD missiles, torpedoes and graviton cannons where they lacked them.

I fixed my AI and it gave us the data as Ifness had said it would. Constructing the giant dimensional portal was another matter. For various technical reasons, the workers and welders started construction a little beyond Mars.

The days ticked away as people worked at a frantic pace.

Saul grew increasingly anxious for Ifness, but there was little I could do about that yet. We were all working as hard as we could.

Then, Holgotha reappeared near Earth.

We'd been waiting for that. Silent drones roared toward the Forerunner artifact, leaving huge tails behind them, making them easily visible.

To escape from the fast closing drones, Holgotha teleported onto the other side of Earth.

Now, though, Earth Central was on high alert. An equally hot reception with more waiting drones pressed in hard against the appearing artifact.

Huge missiles launched from Holgotha. It almost took too long for them to leave, though. Several drone warheads ignited, using aiming rods at the tip of the detonating warhead to direct gamma and x-rays at the artifact.

One hell-burner exploded in orbital space, spewing radiation and a giant EMP in all directions.

I was in the GEV, far from the action but straining to see past the momentary whiteout from the hell-burner. Finally, I saw what everyone else must have. Holgotha had teleported to a different location.

We didn't know it right away, but the artifact teleported near the half constructed dimensional portal way out by Mars.

Naturally, Earth Force had war-gamed such a move. Waiting battlejumpers opened up with heavy graviton beams. The giant artifact didn't have a chance to launch any hell-burners. It barely teleported away in time…for good, it turned out.

"Jennifer has to know we're coming," Diana complained the next day in New Denver.

I shrugged. I was still in my GEV, training with Rollo and N7 in the phase suits. "We do what we can," I said over the comm.

"Going to the pocket universe feels like a trap," Diana said.

"Jennifer has a lot of cards," I said. "But in the end, she's going to have to face our fleet."

"We're going to have to face the Plutonian Home Fleet," Diana said. "I still don't understand why she doesn't just wake up more Plutonians."

"Because she lacks enough control devices," I said as patiently as I could. We'd been over this. "That would be the worst thing for Jennifer. She'd have a mass rebellion on her hands. She'd have to flee with Holgotha while she could."

"There's something else," Diana said. "It's been bothering me for some time. If Jennifer is losing, she could just teleport far away into another part of the galaxy to start again."

"No plan is perfect," I said. "You should remember, though, that according to Ifness, teleportation over there is harder than in our space-time continuum. Maybe Holgotha can't get away as easily as that."

"Jennifer could wait ten years to hell-burn Earth in retaliation," Diana said, apparently having heard nothing I'd said.

"She'd have to stay hidden for ten years, then."

"How are you going to capture her, Creed?"

"Leave that to me," I said. "I don't want to say over a comm, even a secure one."

"You have a plan?" Diana asked.

"Absolutely I do," I said, which was a lie. I was still thinking night and day, racking my mind for a way to capture Jennifer.

"I want to believe you," Diana said.

"Good choice," I said, knowing how important morale was in something like this. Others would take heart or not according to Diana's feelings.

On the screen, the Amazon Queen nodded moodily before signing off.

I sped to Mars to inspect the dimensional portal. It didn't look like much, huge struts floating in empty space. In some manner, though, this was going to help us get into the pocket universe.

The Orange Tamika dreadnaughts of old had used black holes to transfer us into hyperspace. This portal had nothing like that. There were big power-units at the end of each space strut. Those would be energized through antimatter explosions. According to the chief technician, the units were still unstable. He wanted to ask my AI a few trouble-shooting questions.

I gave him permission and escorted the lanky Scotsman to the AI. He asked questions I didn't understand. The AI did, though, and answered each one. Finally, the chief technician thanked him.

On the way out, he stopped and said, "Could I buy time to ask the AI more questions?"

"Personal ones?" I asked.

"Business questions," he said.

"I'll think about it."

"I'll pay billions," the chief technician said. "The AI could revolutionize our technology."

I nodded noncommittally.

The man departed, and the work sped up on the dimensional-portal power sources.

Two and half weeks after the strategy session, the great armada of Earth was almost ready to make a stab into the pocket universe.

We had too few battlejumpers. That seemed clear. Earth Force had sixty-three of them packed with PDD missiles, torpedoes and 1,432 fighters and bombers. I don't mean converted jet fighters, although the military people had debated the idea. If gas or an atmosphere of sorts filled the pocket universe, maybe masses of converted jet fighters would work. That was a big if, however. So, all the "planes" were regular space fighters and bombers.

Given our fleet and the nature of our enemy, we were gambling big time.

Could three phase suits change the tide of battle? The three of us would attempt to storm the giant PDS while the warships fought each other. Four hundred and twelve assault troopers would be on call in waiting assault boats to help us.

In some ways, this reminded me of the Jelk Corporation attack against the Lokhar PDS in the Sigma Draconis System. That had been a long time ago, and now we appeared to have come full circle. We'd had a lot more assault troopers in those days, although we hadn't had any phase suits.

The big day finally arrived. Earth Force moved en masse toward Mars and the still untested dimensional portal. We'd decided the first test would be the entire fleet making its move. It might be the stupidest thing we'd done, or it could give us a small surprise advantage.

Yes, Jennifer had to know we were coming. Holgotha had seen the incipient portal. But Jennifer didn't know the exact day we would come through. We'd been watching for Holgotha to appear in the far distance and had never spotted the artifact trying to spy on us, so that was something.

The last change concerned the Starkien Fleet. Diana's worries had grown over time, not lessened. The Prime Minister had become insistent that we should still heavily defend humanity's homeworld. Thus, the baboons would stay behind to protect Earth. That would mean far fewer ships in the pocket universe, but I agreed that it helped to know that Earth would be here if we succeeded.

If we failed—

No, failure wasn't an option.

-72-

The invasion fleet moved serenely past Mars, heading toward the giant struts in space. There was a lot of space between the struts that had been joined in a vast circle.

I was in the GEV, inside a vast hangar bay in a battlejumper. There were old-style assault boats for my troopers, all five hundred and twenty-two of them. During the last few days, a few more troopers had reported for duty with working second skins.

Ella commanded our battlejumper, named the *Demetrius*. Rollo would have taken command, but I needed him as a phase-suit specialist.

N7, Rollo and I were all inside the GEV. We had no plans to depart unless we did so in the phase suits.

It was funny, the assault troopers and I were such a tiny part of the entire fleet. We weren't even enough to call us the spear-tip. We might be the very tiny point of the spear-tip. Yet, if Earth Force were going to win this battle, it would likely be up to us in some fashion.

How was that for being elite?

I knew that feeling well as the Galactic Effectuator. Now, it was time to pull out all the stops regarding my trade.

Admiral Sparhawk commanded the fleet. General Briggs had political authority as granted by the Prime Minister. The police were noticeably absent, as no red-suited security people were anywhere in attendance on the battlejumpers.

From his flagship, the Admiral gave the order.

I sat before my main GEV sensor board, watching the proceedings by means of center-galaxy-level tech.

The antimatter energizers activated. I actually saw them shake. Seconds later, a red glow emanated from them. That glow climbed along the long struts. Soon, all the struts glowed red and shook. The space between the struts started to swirl and change color.

"Ominous," N7 said. The android stood behind me, watching over my shoulder.

"Challenging," I countered.

"I have never liked traveling from one dimension to another," N7 said. "The possibility for trouble intensifies exponentially."

"Exactly," I said.

"You cannot mean to state that you are enjoying this."

I swiveled around. "Are you kidding me? This is an adventure. This is why we're alive, to do new things."

"I challenge your basic assumption," N7 said.

"Save it," I said, swiveling back to the sensor screen.

The power units glowed with a deeper red color. They shook more than seemed possible without breaking apart. The struts shook and glowed. The swirling between the struts worsened and the space turned an orange color.

The first battlejumper of the fleet entered that mass. The others followed. We were doing it.

Maybe this was a gigantic trick of Jennifer's devising. Ifness was actually fine and Saul would teleport away, laughing as he went. Earth Force would disappear in some tragic accident, and nothing would stop Jennifer from her awful quest of human extinction.

And yet, that couldn't be the case. I was the reason. If the fleet died, I died. And one thing I knew: Jennifer wanted to torment me for as long as she could. That would be Abaddon's long reach from the grave, against me.

"I'm going to finish this once and for all," I muttered.

"What was that?" N7 asked.

"I'm going to finish this," I said. "I'm going to rescue Jennifer from Abaddon's evil and put a stop to this genocidal romp."

"You truly have grandiose dreams, Commander. I have missed your megalomania. It is refreshing in its difference."

"You're welcome," I muttered, wondering if N7 should go somewhere else for a while.

The swirling colors encompassed more of the fleet. It was our turn now as Ella ordered the *Demetrius* to follow the others.

N7 cocked his head. "Do you hear that?"

"You can hear noise from the portal?"

"I think I do."

"What's it sound like?" I asked.

"An ethereal whine," the android said. "It is almost beautiful. It has harmony and…"

"And what?" I asked.

N7 said nothing.

I turned around. The android had frozen like a statue. What could have caused that? For a second, I wondered again if this was another of Jennifer's secret plots.

Then I heard a heavenly sound. It was ethereal, and eerie all at once. Sound could not travel in space, so how was this happening? It must have something to do with the dimensional portal. The sound increased. I had to force myself to breathe because I listened enraptured to the sound.

Suddenly, it seemed as if a thousand violins joined in with an awful Charlie Daniels' screech. Don't get me wrong. I liked Charlie Daniels CDs. But there was one about Georgia that had a special sound.

I clapped my hands over my ears, but it didn't make any difference. The sound grew. I opened my mouth to help ease the pain in my ears. The sound became a bedlam of scratchy, devilish noises as if we'd opened a gateway into Hell.

Maybe we had.

Abruptly, the noise ceased. I looked at the screen. It was blood red with swirling black colors. The swirls went faster and faster and suddenly, everything seemed to tear open. Streaks of bright light lengthened and there was a terrible sense of movement. It seemed as if our ship hurtled through time and space across a vast gulf of nonexistence or other nebulous realms. I made gobbling sounds. The speed increased, and we hurtled through places, realms, realities that stunned my senses. Had we not calibrated the dimensional portal correctly? I had an awful sensation of falling into the depths of an evil abyss.

And then—

I felt as if I was caught in a terrible time loop that would repeat over and over again. Someone had to stop this. Someone—

I felt like a kid on the greatest roller-coaster ride ever invented. We sped along in the car, and we stopped on a dime with bone-jarring suddenness.

My head went forward, cracking against the console. That hurt like the dickens. I rubbed my forehead and squeezed my eyes closed.

Wait a minute.

I opened my eyes, and I couldn't believe it…

-73-

We'd made it—we'd reached somewhere, anyway, that wasn't our space-time continuum. A great murky "sea" of gases spread out in all directions. A diffuse light glowed strongest in one direction.

That must have been where the pocket universe's star shined.

The gases were mainly purplish with orange streaks drifting like fog. It was like a Halloween universe.

What a truly dreadful feeling. We were in a place utterly new to humans.

Battlejumper captains began passing shortwave messages to each other. Like a hesitant school of tuna, we turned away from the brightest area and moved toward the darker region.

That had a sinister feeling all its own.

I shook my head and flexed my fingers, starting to run analyses of the outer gas. It was five percent helium, thirty-four percent hydrogen and one percent water vapor, ammonia, nitrogen and other gases. The other sixty percent was an alien gas with unknown properties. Was it flammable in some way? Did it dampen certain explosions? We didn't know.

More than ever, I believed the old conquering First Ones have given the defeated, "sleeping" Plutonians their own kind of realm. The First Ones had shown mercy for reasons I could not fathom. Why cause the enemy to sleep for centuries, maybe even for eons, in their own home-style realm?

It made no sense.

I shrugged, remembering N7.

I swiveled around. N7 blinked slowly as if coming out of deep freeze.

"You feel okay?" I asked.

The android looked at me. "I feel…strange," he said.

"We're here."

"I see that on the screen."

"Any…comments?" I asked.

"Give me time."

I turned back to the screen and listened to comm chatter.

The fleet assumed traveling formation, sending out small probes, testing how far they could send transmissions.

Some captains asked permission to test the graviton cannons and various missiles. Others said that was a terrible idea. We could give ourselves away.

Admiral Sparhawk finally came on an open channel. "We will make tests," the old man said. "We must know the capability of our weapons if we're going to make wise combat decisions. We will direct the tests toward the light, assuming the enemy is not in that direction."

It was smart thinking, as far as it went. We really didn't know enough, though, to be sure what was best. Yet, Sparhawk was right. We weren't going to win if we didn't know anything.

N7 tapped my shoulder.

I got up and let the android take my place. He was going to test the atmosphere—the void.

I went to other controls. I felt tense, but I'd felt tense many times on effectuator missions. This was different. This was personal.

I thought back to the expedition to the Karg space-time continuum. That had been a shrinking universe. This one was a pocket universe. What did that mean in actual terms? Was the pocket universe round? Could one come in "behind" the planet by first traveling to the star? How hot did the gases heat up near the star? I'd guess plenty hot.

I shivered. I didn't like this place. I didn't like Plutonians. I dreaded facing fifty-plus Abaddon clones. There weren't sixty anymore, as I'd slain a few already.

"There," N7 reported.

Graviton beams fired. They did not go far before dissipating. That was interesting, and possibly lethal to us. Would the Plutonian beams fire farther? I would bet so.

That meant we had to rely more heavily on our missiles and torpedoes.

"Has any captain tested torpedoes?" I asked.

N7 made some manipulations on his board. "Yes, two," he said. "The propellers are useless in the gas."

"That's just great."

"But," N7 said. "One of the captains suggested we use them as mines."

I cocked my head, soon nodding. At least we could get some use out of the torpedoes.

"Sir," N7 said. "Admiral Sparhawk is on the comm. He wants a word with you."

"Sure," I said.

The android vacated the seat and I sat down again. Sparhawk came on. He was older with white hair, blue eyes and an intense way of staring straight at you.

"Sir?" I asked.

"I'd like some recommendations, Commander."

"Bore in and attack," I said. I told him my thoughts concerning the graviton beams and how missiles might have jumped in importance for us.

"Attack just like that?" he asked.

"Yes," I said.

"And if it's a trap?" he asked.

"We fight our way through it with a relentless willingness to trade lives and ships to destroy the enemy. We have one chance, sir. We have to nail them hard and fast. We have to destroy Holgotha if possible. We don't have time to finesse this."

"I thought you were going to soften up the enemy for us with your phase suits."

"That's just for the PDS," I said. "First, we have to take out the fleet. We have to take out Holgotha."

"If I were Jennifer, I'd keep Holgotha behind the PDS."

"Yeah," I said. "So would I. We're hoping she makes a mistake."

"And when the Abaddon clones strike at us?"

"Frankly, if you want my advice, sir, you blow the battlejumper the second teleporting clones appear in it. You don't give them any hint about what you're doing."

"And take all those thousands of Earth Force personnel with the Abaddon clones?" Sparhawk asked.

"The crew is likely dead if the clones appear on their battlejumper anyway. This way, they take the enemy with them."

"Ruthless and bloody," the Admiral said.

"Do you have a better idea…sir?" I asked.

Those bluest of blue eyes stared into mine. Slowly, the older man shook his head.

"Any more questions?" I asked.

He opened his mouth as if to ask one, and then reconsidered. "That's it," he said. "Anything you want to tell me?"

"Yes," I said. "We're expendable as long as we can win."

"We're agreed there, son," he said.

I almost did a double take. I hadn't expected that. Instead of showing my surprise, with everything in me, I kept a calm demeanor, waiting.

The Admiral's eyes narrowed.

I kept waiting.

"Well?" he said.

"Well what, sir?" I asked.

"You seem agitated."

"You're right there," I said. "This place gives me the willies."

"Do you still agree we should bore in and attack?"

"More than ever, sir," I said. "I want to finish this as fast as I can."

"Fine," he said, his manner softening. "You know, I just had a thought. I'd like to talk to you in person."

"When, sir?" I asked.

"Now, if you can."

"Not yet," I said. "If you could give me a few hours first."

"We might be fighting in a few hours."

"I doubt that," I said. "I want to make a few tests here first."

"Very well," the Admiral grumbled. "In three hours, then."

"Yes, sir," I said. "Three hours it is."

With that, we cut communication.

I stood and faced N7. "Get Rollo," I said. "We're going to don our phase suits."

"For what reason?" the android asked.

"Because I think our Admiral is an imposter," I said. "Now quit jabbering and summon Rollo on the double."

-74-

The three of us traveled through the void while out of phase. We used heavy thruster packs, passing through and passing by one battlejumper after another.

The Admiral's battlejumper was in the center of the formation, theoretically, the best-protected vessel.

The fleet as a whole had stopped while the captains assessed the results of the various tests. This state of affairs would not last long. Once the battlejumpers started accelerating again, they would leave us far behind.

I had the Abaddon force axe. The others hefted state-of-the-art Fortress of Light weaponry. Both Rollo and N7 moved deftly. They were almost as good thruster-pack pilots as me.

Saul was in the battlejumper that kept my GEV. I hadn't alerted Ella about the clone's possible connection to this. I wasn't sure Saul was in on the game.

The three of us had donned phase suits because the last word, "son," had given it away. No one but Ifness had ever spoken to me like that. The idea that Jennifer had nabbed Ifness to substantiate his statements seemed like a super-elaborate trick to lure the bulk of Earth Force's battlejumpers into an annihilating trap in the pocket universe.

Think Hannibal *Lightning* and the Battle of Cannae. Think of any of a number of U.S. Cavalry raids against Indian camps while the braves were away.

How had Ifness done it, though? Did the enemy possess hundreds of phase suits? Had the notion that Abaddon clones couldn't teleport too far out here been a fat lie?

I wanted to thrust faster and get to the Admiral's battlejumper sooner. Had Jennifer tricked me all along the line? It would have been easy for Ifness to fake his beating. Yet, why leave Saul behind?

Soon, I motioned to my companions. We ghosted up until Rollo pointed at the Battlejumper *Quebec*. N7 and I nodded.

We went fully out of phase again, applied thrust, soon rotated around and braked hard. A few minutes later, there was an abrupt jar. We stopped floating and had to walk. We'd reached the *Quebec*. We were under gravity again.

Once more, we ghosted up to faint beings. We all shed our thruster packs in a storage compartment. Then, we began to run up one level after another, heading for the bridge.

Finally, without anyone noticing our faint passage, we entered the last bulkhead and eased to the other side of it. Through the edge of the bulkhead, each of us watched the Admiral. Was that Ifness in disguise, or had the hitman taken control of the Admiral in some nefarious fashion?

I gave Rollo and N7 the signal for "stay here." Then, I went fully out of phase and walked to the back of the Admiral's chair, counting out the steps. I'd become very proficient at judging distances through years of practice as the Galactic Effectuator.

When I reached the estimated position, I ghosted up to the faintest possible degree. The Admiral was barely visible to me, as was the rest of the bridge. I could see them much easier than they could see me, as I knew they were there. It was harder to spot a "ghost" when you weren't looking for it.

I studied the Admiral's scalp. It told me nothing.

I unhooked a device from my belt and brought it up to my eyes. It was like an old-fashioned magnifying glass. This one didn't magnify anything, but it made the Admiral ordinarily visible to me instead of staying faintly ghostly. I used the device to search his scalp and neck.

There was nothing out of the ordinary. It did not seem like a flesh disguise, either. Was Ifness a shape-shifter?

I silently debated the idea.

I had a new thought. I pushed the "magnifying glass" through his skull and peered at his—

Whoa. I saw a wire right away. It was like a neon signal. Yeah. That made more sense. Now, who was operating the Admiral? Why had the oldster called me "son?" Did Ifness have a way to speak through Sparhawk via brain wires?

I withdrew the "magnifying glass" and went fully out of phase. What would I do if I were Ifness controlling the admiral of an enemy fleet? Where would I hide so no one found me? I'd have to have access—

I snapped my fingers. I knew where I'd hide. Now, it was time to see if I were right or not and if a hitman truly thought like an effectuator.

-75-

While in ghost mode, the three of us went from one assault shuttle to another in the battlejumper's hangar bays. Each of the shuttles was empty of people and filled with—

Wait a minute. It was possible someone would board one of these for any of a number of reasons. In an emergency, personnel would race onto the shuttles.

I signaled Rollo and N7. We sprinted across one huge hangar bay after another, racing through the intervening bulkheads. Finally, I slowed as sweat poured down my face. The suit's conditioner unit worked overtime, difficult to do in ghost mode.

We neared big drones. I studied them. None of them looked different from another.

The last one, I thought. *That's where I'd hide.*

We hurried there. The last one looked no different from the others. Its only uniqueness was its rank for launching; last.

I turned to N7 and Rollo. I took my longish handle from my side and held it up, shaking it.

They got the message. Rollo grabbed his Globular Blaster, a heavy pistol that ejected balls of disintegrating force. N7 had a long rifle that fired a purple disrupter ray. They flanked me. I nodded.

Together, we pushed through the drone's hull and entered living quarters.

We glanced at each other.

My chest tightened. I couldn't believe this. Admiral Sparhawk had almost led us into the ambush we'd feared all along. A lone word had given it away.

I took the lead and crept in ghost mode through the living quarters, through a restroom and into a control chamber where Ifness sat at a panel, speaking into a unit.

I hesitated, thinking about this.

Ifness stiffened and jerked around.

I acted immediately, phasing in, lunging at him. His eyes widened, and he yelped with surprise. That only lasted a second. He fast-drew a gun, aimed it at me—I was still too far from him to use the axe—a purple ray speared the gun. The metal melted into a molten lump, dripping to the deck.

Ifness yelled this time, snatching his hand away from the disrupted weapon. Before he could do more, I hit him square in the face, smashing him back against the controls.

He bounced off the controls, wobbled and tried to grab something else. I hit him again. He went down. I released the inactivated axe, dropped on him and used a cage-fighting technique, hooking his legs with mine and pinning his arms behind his back. I wore a phase suit, so it was harder to do. He'd taken two shots to the face and must have been woozy or stunned, at least, so that helped.

Rollo and N7 had phased in like me. The android covered Ifness with his rifle while Rollo started searching the man. Ifness was like a joker with a thousand weapons and devices on his person. Rollo kept taking another and another item from him and dumping it onto the deck.

"This is crazy," Rollo said. He spoke past his lowered visor.

I'd also lowered my visor. "Hello, Ifness," I said.

He struggled and did not stop struggling to get away from me.

"It's useless, Ifness," I said. "We have you."

The interstellar hitman panted and tried to twist around to peer at me.

I gripped him tighter. "Why did you do it?" I asked.

"It was the 'son,' wasn't it?" Ifness asked me.

"Yes," I said.

"I knew it as soon as the Admiral said it."

"You can speak through him?"

"Of course," Ifness said.

"This was all an elaborate trap?" I asked.

He laughed hollowly.

"Was this your idea or Jennifer's?" I asked.

"Mine, you idiot," he said. "But it doesn't matter. You're all dead. You're all going to die. The Plutonian Fleet will annihilate you. I beat you, Effectuator."

"Why do it like this?" I asked.

"To prove to Jennifer that I'm five times the man you are."

"I don't understand," I said.

"I do," Rollo said heavily. "The fool is in love with Jennifer."

I looked up at the man I held on top of me. I asked in his ear, "Is that true, Ifness? Do you love my girl?"

"Your girl," Ifness sneered. "She hates you, Creed. But she hates you with such loathing that it proves she loves you more deeply than is decent. You failed her. I would never fail her. She's going to see that."

"She loves me?" I asked, softly, in amazement.

Ifness tried to twist around as he said, "Can't you understand a damn thing? I said she hates you."

"Yes. Hates me so much it proves she actually loves me. Hate isn't the opposite of love, indifference is."

Ifness cursed me.

"What about Saul?" I asked.

"Forget about him," Ifness said. "Let me go, and I'll help you escape this realm."

"The Holgotha-launched attack before, when the hell-burners slaughtered millions—"

"That was my idea," Ifness said, interrupting. "It gave the deception a real feel of authenticity."

A cold feeling of rage swept over me. With a heave, I hurled Ifness off me. I scrambled to my feet afterward. He did the same and whirled around.

I picked up the force axe, activating it. Ifness produced a small gun Rollo hadn't found. I lunged. Ifness fired. The pellet failed to penetrate my phase suit. The force axe sheared through the hitman. He toppled in two bloody halves, pumping blood everywhere.

Rollo aimed and fired the Globular. A glowing ball burned the two halves in a sizzling discharge. Ifness was no more.

-76-

Rollo, N7 and I phased in on the bridge of Flagship Battlejumper *Quebec,* startling everyone. In short order, I convinced Admiral Sparhawk to take a medical exam.

The results proved my allegation. Sparhawk had wires in his brain.

Soon, space marines tore into the fake drone. They found living quarters, food and banks of controls. Technicians confirmed the worst. The controls directly stimulated the Admiral. A test proved that a controller could actually speak through the Admiral.

"This is outrageous," Sparhawk whispered.

The old man seemed to have aged ten years or more. He sat in the Officer's Lounge on the Ninth Deck. The evidence was clear. The *Quebec's* captain and chief medical officer were in attendance, together with General Briggs and his Master Sergeant Marine bodyguard.

Sparhawk looked to Briggs. "I don't know what to do."

"When could this have happened?" the *Quebec's* captain demanded. His name was Laval and he had a squat, bulldog body with a flat face.

"It doesn't matter when," I said. "It happened. Nothing else counts. The fleet is in terrible danger."

"We must retreat," Sparhawk said. "There's no going on now."

I glanced at Briggs.

The General looked away, shaking his head.

"The Admiral is right," Captain Laval said. "We must return to Earth."

"Begging your pardon," I said, "but how do we know that's what the Admiral really thinks?"

Sparhawk stared at me openmouthed as the realization donned that someone else might be controlling him.

"That's uncalled for," Captain Laval growled at me.

"No," Briggs said. "It *is* called for. We've been duped. Ifness's data has become meaningless."

"I wouldn't go that far," I said. "So far, everything he told us about the pocket universe has proven true."

"He must have lied about something," Briggs said.

"That does not hold," N7 chimed in. "The key is the fleet. A spy led it. Clearly, Ifness meant to lead us to our destruction and the Commander's capture."

"That means the Admiral is correct," Laval said. "We must retreat back to Earth."

"The Admiral is not correct," I said. "Everything he suggests is suspect. He has wires in his brain. Maybe they tampered with his brain. Maybe he has fail-safes installed in case anyone discovered the wires."

"He's the Admiral," Laval said.

"Are you that dense?" I demanded. "Admiral Sparhawk is the unwitting tool of Ifness, the hitman for Jennifer. We cannot trust anything the Admiral suggests."

"Until the wires come out?" Briggs asked.

"No," I said. "Ever. The enemy has tampered with his brain. Don't you see what that means?"

Admiral Sparhawk seemed to shrink inward. It was an awful process. I did not mean to demean him. But I didn't want to lose the war in order to save his feelings.

"What do we do then?" Briggs asked me.

"Exactly," I said. "The answer is that it depends. Who runs the fleet now?"

"We have to form a committee," Laval said.

"You can't be on it," I told him, "because that's an asinine suggestion. One man has to run the fleet, not some *committee*."

"You?" Laval demanded.

"Why not, Creed?" Rollo demanded. "Creed's led us to victory on more than one occasion."

"Never!" Laval snarled. "I'll never serve him. Half the captains here will never serve him."

"Fine," I said, "since I don't want the command anyway."

"You're suggesting *him*?" Laval asked, pointing at Briggs.

"No," I said.

Briggs scowled. He held the political authority as Diana's representative.

"No offense, sir," I told Briggs. "But you're a general. You're not an admiral. This is a fleet action. We need a fighting admiral."

"We don't have a fleet admiral," Laval said.

"You are wrong," N7 said. "Rollo Anderson used to serve as the First Admiral of Earth Force."

Everyone in the room looked at the hulking brute that was Rollo Anderson.

"No," Laval said. "That is out of the question."

"General," I said. "What do you think?"

Briggs shook his head. "I don't know what to think. This is demoralizing. We've been led by a spy."

"We have to fight," Rollo said. "We're here. Now, we have to finish it."

"We're here as part of a trap," Briggs said.

"How else do we win?" Rollo asked.

We all looked at each other.

"To win, you have to destroy the enemy," Rollo said.

"How do you propose to destroy the enemy when he knows our plans?" Captain Laval demanded.

"I've been thinking about that," I said. "Given the nature of the pocket universe, I have an idea that might turn the tables on them."

"What does that even mean?" Laval asked.

"Consider what we know," I said. "Ifness controlled the Admiral."

The old man looked more stricken than ever.

I cleared my throat. I needed to be more circumspect with my words. "We don't know that Ifness has been in contact with the enemy since we've arrived here," I said.

"That would be difficult given the nature of the pocket universe," N7 said. "According to our tests, we can only send messages fifteen to twenty kilometers away."

"That's more than interesting," I said. "It proves my point."

Laval snarled quietly, saying, "I still don't see what you're driving at."

"The enemy expects us to follow a certain path," I said. "Ifness is supposed to lead us a certain way. Well, Ifness is dead. Now, we have to hit the enemy in a new way. Our only real advantage is that the enemy doesn't know that we know he tricked us."

The bulldog-looking Laval seemed to think that through. He finally nodded.

"That's where the nature of the pocket universe comes in," I said.

"How does that help us?" Briggs asked.

"The pocket universe is the size of a small star system," I said. "That's what I learned in the Library of the Fortress of Light. That means it's a limited universe. So, what happens? When we reach the limit, do we bump up against a wall?"

"That seems unlikely," Laval said.

"Agreed," I said. "I think instead that one travels *around* the universe. It's like a man sailing around the Earth. If he sails long enough, he'll come back to where he started."

"Meaning?" asked Captain Laval.

"Meaning we head for the star," I said. "We pass the star and eventually come in behind the enemy. The PDS will undoubtedly be on the other side of the dense planet, waiting for our attack in the other direction."

"I'm with you so far," Laval said.

"We rush the planet, circle it and hit the PDS from pointblank range. We board it if we have to. We beam it to death with massed graviton rays. Once it is destroyed, we grapple with the enemy fleet. It might even be that we'll capture Jennifer on the PDS. That will cripple the enemy, and we'll hold all the advantages."

"That's a rosy picture," Laval said. "How do you know it will work?"

"I don't," I said. "But it's what Hannibal *Lightning* would do. A Great Captain of history—Alexander, Caesar, Genghis Khan or Napoleon—would dare to take the road less traveled in order to surprise the enemy. If we falter now, Earth will perish."

"Or we'll all die in a fruitless voyage," Laval said.

"Have some courage, man," I told him. "Think about it. We have a chance to surprise the enemy. That's instead of walking into a perfectly laid trap. Or would you rather run home with your tail between your thick legs?"

Captain Laval glared at me, but only for a moment. Maybe some of the words sank through his skull. Finally, he slumped into a chair and threw his hands in the air.

"I don't know what to do," Laval admitted.

"Briggs," I asked, "do you know what to do?"

The General shook his head.

"Doctor?" I asked.

The medical officer hurriedly shook his head.

"Admiral Sparhawk?" I asked.

"What?" he whispered.

"What's your suggestion?" I asked.

Old Sparhawk stared at me until a tremulous smile appeared. "I thank you for asking me, young man. I'm unfit to command. That is clear. I say…I say do as you suggest. It's bold. The only real way to handle a fleet is boldly. We're here to fight. Well, by damn, let us fight."

"Yes, I agree with that," Laval said. "But who will lead us?"

Sparhawk looked around the room until he pointed at Rollo.

"I agree," I said.

"I second the motion," N7 said.

"Yes," Briggs said. "I will stand behind the former First Admiral and accept his orders."

"Very well," Captain Laval said. "I agree with the majority. We might as well make it unanimous."

And that's how Rollo came to command the expeditionary force into the pocket universe.

-77-

The fleet decelerated, came to a dead stop and began accelerating in the opposite direction. We were on a mad gamble to surprise the Plutonians. Our only real hope was that they expected us to follow an exact pattern of Ifness's devising. Could we turn the tables on them?

We gained velocity, plunging through the murky gases as they swirled past our mighty battlejumpers.

One day turned into two, three and then four. The light increased in our direction of travel. So did the outside heat. We were clearly nearing the pocket universe's star.

I interviewed Saul each day, questioning him subtly about Ifness. The Abaddon clone did not appear to be part of the cabal of spies sent against us.

I also began to run T-tests with Saul. The clone could easily teleport anywhere within a battlejumper. It was harder for him to go from ship to ship. He would concentrate and then abruptly teleport. We found that distance made no difference until the two battlejumpers were eleven kilometers from each other. At that point, Saul shook his head.

"I cannot see the way," the clone said.

"Can you teleport into a dark room?" I asked.

"Of course not," he said.

"Can you teleport to any place that you can't see?"

"Maybe to a few close places, but that would be foolish."

"You might teleport into an object then?" I asked.

"Yes," Saul said, yawning, tiring of the interrogation.

Under First Admiral Rollo's orders, the captains launched staggered probes toward the brightness. The probes found several interesting properties. The gases began to thin out ahead, allowing one to see several hundred kilometers. The closer the probes came to the star, the longer the distances they could see with their teleoptics. Finally, they could see thousands of kilometers, tens of thousands of kilometers and then several hundred thousand.

It is good to keep in mind stellar distances. Luna was only a little more than four hundred thousand kilometers from Earth, right next to each other in Solar System terms. That meant even at these new sight ranges, we would practically have to be on top of the enemy to see him and fire our beams.

Missiles were different. Missiles were interesting. Maybe the best way to fight the Plutonians would be through long-range missiles that took several days or even a week to crawl to the enemy position.

Through the murk of swirling gases, we saw the diffuse brightness of the star far, far away, like a bright light surrounded by fog. Thus, we never actually saw the star itself. The fleet changed heading so we would skirt the star, circling wide around it.

The days became a week, then two, and then three. By now, the star was far behind the fleet and receding more every day.

Did Jennifer wonder what had happened to us? Had Plutonian cruisers made more attacks on various regular star systems? Had they attacked the Earth again, or made contact with Emperor Daniel Lex Rex? Clearly, the main Earth Force Fleet had vanished. The enemy also would not have heard a peep out of Ifness.

It was strange in a way. The Plutonian pocket universe was tiny, but the thick and, in a sense, stifling gases made the reality seem much larger than it really was.

The weeks of travel as we sailed back into the gassy thickness taught our personnel how to act while here. It taught our sensor techs the best way to track. We became accustomed to the murk. Tacticians thought up plans, tricks and ploys. As practice, we staggered the fleet into a long thin line. Later, we spread out into a wide row. We changed formations constantly, testing theories. We had war games and refined our tactics. It was lonely. It was instructive. We were in our own tiny universe, and we had yet to find a way to leave it and return home.

I worried about that for several days. What if Jennifer only had a single dimensional portal here, used to it leave and caused the portal to self-destruct afterward?

Finally, Ella pointed out that there were supposed to be millions of sleeping Plutonians on the planet. They would have the tech to make more dimensional portals.

Ella had been demoted from being the *Demetrius's* battlejumper captain to a phase-suited commando with N7 and me, as she had taken Rollo's place. The three of us practiced constantly, honing our silent, phase-out signals and various special tactics.

The assault troopers also trained diligently, particularly on boarding tactics.

It was interesting. The continuing weeks of travel and constant practice turned us into a more cohesive fleet with greater trust in each other's abilities.

At the end of that time, First Admiral Rollo issued our first slowing of velocity. The gases ahead had increasingly thickened and actually produced greater pressure against our hulls. Soon, it was like plowing through icy water, the gases dragging against the hulls.

"This is a vile realm," Ella said one day while we put away our phase suits in the GEV. "We can hardly see a thing. Why would anyone want to live here?"

"I have a theory," N7 said. "Creed once thought the First Ones did the Plutonians a favor by building them such a pocket universe. It would seem to have been what the Plutonians had once escaped. Maybe that is the wrong idea. Maybe the First Ones were punishing the Plutonians by putting them in this place, returning them to their previous awful existence. Maybe the Plutonians realized they had come from a…a strange and even sinister space-time continuum."

"Whatever the reason," I said. "It doesn't matter now. The pocket universe is dreadful."

The fleet soon slowed again, as the gases continued to thicken. Perhaps we approached the small, dense planet, the single one in this infernal realm.

The coming space battle would be with ships practically on top of each other. That wasn't normal—for our universe, anyway. If the gases became too thick, could our graviton beams even work?

Several days later, the fleet slowed to a dead stop.

Rollo ordered probes launched and had them travel in a growing string, one right after the other. He was using up almost the last of our probes for this. Finally, word raced back from probe to probe to probe.

One probe had found the planet. It was six hundred and ninety-eight thousand kilometers from the fleet. The probe had almost immediately withdrawn.

We had a council of war several hours later. There was debate. Rollo asked for advice, and every captain, every marine lieutenant agreed: we must attack at once and annihilate the enemy. The sooner we did so, the sooner we could leave this awful universe.

-78-

The fleet began to move two hours later, heading in the direction of the single planet.

Rollo had ordered a retraction of all the probes. The enemy mustn't have any advance warning of our approach and attack.

I paced in my GEV as the fleet crept toward the strange planet.

It's crazy how the imminence of danger focused a man's thoughts. There was a saying about that—how death, or waiting at the gallows to hang, wonderfully concentrated a man's thinking. The decisive moment had a way of burning away the excess.

As I paced back and forth through the piloting chamber, a truth penetrated my thinking and grew stronger the more I thought about it.

Jennifer was no one's fool. She had known me once, had understood my thinking better than almost anyone else I'd known. Our fleet had disappeared. It had not returned to Earth. She must have established that by now. Could the invasion fleet have brought a dimensional portal with us? I suppose that was possible. I guess what I was hinting at was the truth that she had to know we were still in this Hell dimension with her. Jennifer must realize that I would try a daring attack. Since we hadn't shown up at the ambush site, she must have figured out by now that we'd discovered Ifness's trick.

Was Jennifer waiting even now behind the strange planet? Was she waiting for us to pull a fast one? The more I thought about it, the more certain I was that we were sailing to our destruction.

The Plutonian ships were made for this weird realm. Their beams would likely slice through the thick gases better than our recalibrated graviton beams. Our missiles—the enemy's fantastic self-detonations and the gases that would carry the shockwaves for possibly tens of thousands of kilometers—Jennifer had all the advantages here, not us.

I paced and kept going over and over and over again in my mind—I whirled around and dashed to the comm. Soon, Rollo in his First Admiral's chair regarded me.

"This could be a trap," I said over the comm.

"I don't agree, Creed. We've tricked them. You've said so yourself more than once."

I told him my new reasoning.

Rollo examined me, finally nodding. "I congratulate you, my brother. You've stolen my confidence. Now, I have no idea what to do."

"I do," I said. "I'll slink ahead in the GEV and do what I do best: effectuator tactics. This place is made for it. Think about it. Jennifer uses control devices in her Plutonians."

"If—and it's a big if—what Ifness originally told us is correct," Rollo said.

"That's true. But Ifness's descriptions have been accurate so far. His only "lie" was that he was double-crossing us and controlling our commander, leading us into an ambush."

Rollo leaned forward. "We're on their freaking doorstep, Creed. This isn't the time to get squeamish. This is the time to harden our hearts against fear and head into the lion's den."

"You can still do that, *after* I've had a chance to grab Jennifer and decapitate them, so to speak. If she has controls or wires in the Plutonians, maybe I can get them to do something incredibly stupid that will give us an easy victory."

"That's a lot of ifs, Creed." Rollo scowled. "It's time to roll in with battlejumpers blazing and kill them all."

"I'm right," I said. "I know I'm right."

Rollo hunched his massive shoulders, staring at me as if he planned to rip off my head and finish it with a pissing contest. Soon, however, in spite of himself, he began to nod.

"You're the man, Creed. I've seen you pull off a miracle play more than once." Rollo sighed. "I'll go with your hunch. But if you're wrong and give away our presence…"

"I know. It's always a roll of the dice."

Rollo grinned, but it had a false feeling. He was finding this hard to do, as it went against his basic instincts.

"How soon are you ready to try?" the First Admiral asked.

"Give me an hour."

Rollo turned away, thinking, finally facing me again. "I'm going to take the fleet in closer during that hour. I'll let you try your way, but I'm not waiting long to unleash some whoop-ass against these bastards. My gut is churning, Creed, and the only way I can get it to stop is killing them and burning their planet to the core."

"Right," I said. "We each do what we gotta do."

-79-

The GEV slid out of one of Battlejumper *Demetrius's* hangar bays and began the lonely trek to the small, dense planet hidden out there in the thickening murk. There were three occupants in the stealth ship; Ella, N7 and me. We had the three phase suits.

I heard a familiar rush of air, and found Saul standing beside me in the piloting chamber.

"What are you doing here?" I asked.

"Creed, he has a gun," Ella said.

My heart sank as I realized Saul had a heavy caliber pistol in his huge paw. It was Rollo's unique .55 hand cannon. I couldn't believe it.

I looked into Saul's eyes, but to my surprise, I didn't see any murder there, did not see my death. The big guy held the gun beside his right thigh.

"You're not here to kill us?" I asked.

Saul frowned. "Why would I kill friends? I want to kill enemies. I find this." He raised the hand cannon. "I like it very much. Do not leave me behind, Effectuator."

This was a quandary. Could I trust Saul? I did not see how. He would be alone in the GEV while we went on the mission. Could I subdue him? I suppose I could grab a trank gun and fire a dart into him. Would the Abaddon clone trust me after that? Did I care?

I found that I did. Despite everything, I'd learned to like Saul. Did that mean I could trust him?

"You shouldn't have teleported here," I said.

"I should have," he said. "I have…" He seemed to concentrate. "I have quest against…evil Sauls."

"What?" I asked.

"Quest against evil Sauls," he said.

"You mean the other Abaddon clones?"

He shook his head. "Evil Sauls. They look like me. They big, but they not act like me. They murder. They laugh at thought of evil. Saul hates that. That is why Saul likes Ifness. Ifness in big trouble. Saul save friend."

Oh, boy, did he have things backward, at least in some areas.

"Creed," Ella said, motioning to me.

"Stay here," I told Saul.

"Where else I go?" he asked.

"Right," I said.

I went to Ella, and she pulled me even farther aside. "You can't let him stay," she said.

"That's it?" I asked. "You had to pull me all this way to tell me that?"

"He's got ears like a cat," she said. "I think his dumbness is a trick. He's just waiting to take us out."

"Why didn't he do it a moment ago?"

"N7 wasn't in here."

"All the more reason to strike," I said, "taking us out piecemeal."

"You can't be serious letting him stay. He's a menace to everything."

I rubbed my neck. As I'd said earlier, the near threat of horrible danger wonderfully concentrates one's thoughts. We were on our way to the mother of all PDSs. The thing was supposed to be massive. If we were going to complete our mission in time…

I turned around and walked thoughtfully to Saul.

"Tell me, big guy," I said. "Have you ever been on the PDS before?"

"You mean Jennifer's Fort?" Saul asked.

"Does it orbit the small world?"

"Yes. The Fort is huge. It holds millions of sleeping Plutonians."

My eyes widened. "The Plutonians are not on the planet?"

Saul shook his head. "Ifness tells me. Planet is big trap. You can go down, but no one can ever leave. It is…dense and has great gravity."

"The planet is a trap?"

"Ifness says so."

I looked at the giant mug more closely. He did not seem to be putting on an act. He seemed—damnit, but Saul seemed good. Did lower IQ equal goodness? I didn't believe that. High IQ meant a high potential. How one used the potential determined their degree of good or bad.

Why would Saul's heart be good while Orcus's heart was bad?

Could it have something to do concerning their genesis? I didn't know enough to make the call.

I grinned to myself. Did it matter how Saul had become a good guy? Wasn't it more important whether he *was* good or not?

"You're not seriously thinking about letting him stay?" Ella asked.

"Why not?" Saul asked her.

"Because we can't trust you," Ella told him.

"That not make sense," Saul said. "I have always helped. I have always been good."

"Maybe to trick us just like Ifness tricked us," Ella said.

"That is a lie!" Saul said angrily. "Ifness is a good man. He be very good to Saul."

"Sure," I said. "No one is going to tell you otherwise. Now, Saul, I want you to sketch out the PDS and tell us everything you know about it."

"Yes. I can do that. Saul has great memory."

"Later," I said, "you're going to have to go into the stasis tube for just a while. Will you agree to that?"

"On one condition," Saul said. "You let me fight to free Ifness."

"Sure," I said, lying through my teeth. "It's a deal."

-80-

N7 piloted us in extreme stealth mode as we slowly eased through the thick gases. That gave us time to listen to Saul and study his sketches.

He drew ten times better than I would have thought he could. Maybe this moron Abaddon clone was brighter than he seemed.

"I heard Ifness say this PDS blow away any enemy fleet," Saul said as he passed us another sketch. We sat around a table in the galley. "The heavy gas means only pointblank-range firing works. The PDS super-thick hull armor and massive inhibiter engines give it fantastic power."

"Does Jennifer stay in the PDS?" I asked.

"When she here," Saul said.

"Where is Holgotha?"

"Who?"

"The donut-shaped Forerunner artifact," I said.

Saul shook his head. "The artifact hates it here. He never stays. The artifact checks in from time to time. Then he goes before the place…" The clone frowned. "I forget how Ifness said it."

"Don't worry about it," I said.

I gathered the sketches strewn across the table. One of them showed a square-like oval with jagged edges along the sides. According to Saul, there were vast beam cannons embedded in the super-thick, dense hull. The cannons could fire farther through the murky gas than any Plutonian warship. Jennifer and her crew stayed in the central node in the very center of the PDS.

I figured it would be like that.

"Any comments?" I asked Ella.

"None that I haven't made before," she said, gloomily.

"Right," I said. I kept studying the sketches until Ella got up and left. Saul made himself a meal of five big hamburgers and a mound of fries an hour later.

I returned to the piloting chamber, spelling N7.

Time passed as we crept through the thickening gases. I detected flashes of lightning in the distance. This was like heading deeper into the gas giant Jupiter. The conclusion seemed obvious. The dense planet attracted more gas, causing it to compact. Why hadn't the same thing happened by the star? Presumably, the heat forced the gases away, or maybe the star devoured the gases, chugging them like a thirsty man in a desert. Yet, if that were the case, wouldn't the star consume all the gas in time?

I nodded. Of course, it would.

That showed this pocket universe wasn't very old. Given enough time, there would be no gas. Unless the planet or some other mechanism created more gas.

It was interesting to speculate and frustrating because I didn't know. My lack of knowledge might lose me the coming battle. However, the more I learned about the PDS, the more I believed our fleet would face annihilation if we attempted to attack it en masse and head on.

My way might be the only way to victory.

I piloted us through the gas and became more nervous as time passed. If the gas became thick enough, the stirring gases caused by the passage of my GEV would give us away to watching defenders.

I had to take us closer, though. My thruster pack wouldn't take us as far as in our universe.

I reduced velocity and watched my passive sensors. It was like driving through a thick fog at night. High beams helped me less than low beams, as the brighter light reflected off the thick fog.

Finally, about two hours later, I detected a faint signal.

I leaned closer to the panel, waiting for—

I jerked back as I heard alien screeching. I had no doubt it was Plutonian communication. I did not like it, but that should mean we were closing in on the planet.

After that, the weird screeches increased. The longer I had to listen to the alien noises, the worse they sounded to me. Soon, the sounds began getting on my nerves. I tried to analyze that. I think the sounds caused it to hit home with greater clarity that I was in an alien dimension.

Would I go to Heaven if I died in the pocket universe? I decided yes. If there was a Creator—and I believed there was—He would have created *all* the dimensions. Thinking otherwise would have taxed my morale to the limit.

I used the Plutonian signals, guiding our stealth ship nearer the small planet. The signals thickened. I veered away from the loudest clot and strove with all my might to pierce the darkness ahead.

I strained—

"There," N7 said, peering over my shoulder again.

"What?" I asked.

He pointed.

I saw what he meant, a dot out there that didn't move.

"You think that's the planet?" I asked.

"What else?" N7 said.

Like a one-eyed man in a dense fog, I turned the GEV ever so slowly. We crept toward the dot. It never wavered. It never shifted. It seemed to grow the closer we came.

Then, I realized N7 had to be right. It wasn't a moon, an asteroid or a meteor. That was the small dense planet of the Plutonians, a trap, according to Saul.

Soon, now, we would have to leave the safety of the stealth ship and see if we could storm the mother of all PDSs by our lonesome.

As we closed in, I crept around the planet. It was the size of Luna. By its pull on the GEV, it had to be thirty times as dense as our Moon. It was a Hell-world if there ever was one. It had an atmosphere, a heavy one, of course, making the surface invisible to any of my sensors.

For the time being, I ignored the planet.

Our fleet was behind me. If I took too long, they would come roaring in, trying to wipe out everything.

"Take over," I told N7.

The android sat at the controls, guiding the GEV with a delicate touch.

I went to the galley, telling Saul it was time to sleep.

The giant shook his head, although he did not reach for the .55 lying on the table.

"Are you going to give me trouble?" I asked.

"I am going to help you," he said.

"You know we're going in with the phase suits."

"I know," he said.

"I can't leave you behind on the ship."

Saul picked up the .55 hand cannon. He seemed crestfallen. He looked away and made a deep sigh. I almost felt bad I'd hurt his feelings. Before I could say so, he disappeared.

"Saul," I said.

There was no response.

"AI," I said.

"Here," the AI replied.

"Where is Saul?"

"I do not know."

"Is he on the ship?" I asked.

"Negative."

I spoke a one-word curse and clutched my face, shaking my head. So now what should I do? Turn around? Keep going?"

This was a disaster. I'd just told the clone our plan.

I muttered another curse and jumped up, racing to the piloting chamber.

-81-

We crawled around the planet at a distance. The gravity was even worse than I'd feared from the last scan. The greater gravity meant even denser gases. The denser, thickening gases acted as a natural shield against "invisible" ships like ours by revealing our position more easily due to gaseous stirrings.

"I see it," I said, from the piloting chair.

Beside the planet was a massive PDS. The artificial station was almost the same size as the world. That made them companions and the station almost as big as Earth's Moon.

"The PDS is like the Curator's Moon-ship," Ella said.

I nodded mutely, wondering why Saul hadn't told us about that aspect of the PDS. I knew the reason, of course. In the end, the Abaddon clone had been just as treacherous as his master Ifness.

I manipulated the controls, as I said, "All stop." I didn't dare go deeper into the densest gases. Even at a crawl, I'd give away our position.

"So now we're a submarine?" Ella asked.

"No more negativity," I said. "We're as close as I'm taking the ship. We'll add extra thruster tanks and head to our destination by suit. This is it. It's time to gather our—"

"Please," Ella said, interrupting. "No more speeches, Creed. I'll go. But no more speeches."

I nodded. "No speeches. We'll let our actions speak for us."

"That's another speech," Ella complained.

"No more *long* speeches," I said, trying to lighten the grim mood.

Ella didn't respond.

Okay. She didn't have to. It was enough that she was going. Once we were on the way and she saw we could do it, everything would be fine. I realized my own morale was low. But I had a life rule: fake it until it was real. I would fake enthusiasm and a belief in victory until it happened or until I was dead.

To that end, it was time to get ready.

I won't bore you with the details. We donned our phase suits, the thruster packs and tanks, and our respective weapons—Ella had the Globular Blaster—and set out for the PDS while fully out of phase.

We checked in at a timed interval and found ourselves much farther away than I'd expected. I did not like that.

The next run, we moved out of phase for twice as long, ghosting up afterward.

The Planetary Defense Station loomed hugely in the near distance. It looked even more menacing than before. N7 spied movement around the vast station, pointing at it.

I used a zoom function in my visor for a close-up and felt awe. Those were battleship-sized Plutonian vessels. There were docks for thousands of them. The free battleships accelerated away from the PDS and planet, heading obliquely toward us. Were they sallying in order to attack our fleet? I would bet so. Of course, that had to be the case. Saul had certainly told Jennifer Earth Force was here. Now, the Plutonian battleships raced to join other, hidden enemy fleet elements. This was turning into a vast disaster. Rollo had been right after all. Our entire invasion fleet should have come in firing. If the entire enemy battleship fleet left those docks—

A grim certainty filled me. In order to give Rollo any kind of chance, we had to destroy the PDS. Given the thousands of docked battleships... I could not allow the massed Plutonian navy to sweep aside our fleet, to invade our space-time continuum. These weren't Karg numbers, granted, but still, with all those docked battleships coming out, it would be a mass invasion that could possibly destroy a quarter of the galaxy before the last Plutonian vessel was destroyed. By that time, the human race would be extinct.

That meant the three of us had to finish what we'd started. To that end, while out of phase, we continued toward the PDS. The closer we got to the appointed target, though, the more attraction I felt tugging at me, causing me to drift away from target. That had to be the planet's fierce gravitational pull, which obviously reached into out-of-phase enough to influence us. The only thing for it was greater thrusting power. Slowly but steadily, while consuming fuel at a prodigious rate, we neared our target.

There was a new negative to the mission: according to my gauges, we would not have enough thruster fuel to get back to the GEV.

Did the PDS have the needed fuel for our tanks? We would find out. If we died or lost, it wouldn't matter. Heck. Maybe we could steal one of those battleships later and fly back to the GEV.

That gave me another problem. How long would the GEV stay in its present location? Wouldn't the planet's gravitational pull yank my stealth ship to it?

I shook my head. I couldn't worry about such minor details now. I had to mentally "burn my ship" in my heart in order to focus on the coming mission.

We thrust toward the PDS and finally ghosted up for another look. The vast station loomed before us. I could no longer see it as a whole, but just the nearest hull. We hardly moved toward it, though, as we did not thrust at this point. That meant the planet was pulling us toward it.

I made an arm-hand signal, as I didn't dare use the helmet comm for fear of giving away our coordinates. The other two nodded. We phased out again and headed for the PDS. It took longer than I liked, but finally, we stopped drifting and had to use our feet to walk, as we'd passed through the outer hull into the PDS.

I soon found a hiding place for our thruster packs and tanks—a cubby in a low-ceilinged vault near the outer docks. We'd saved most of the tanks this time instead of letting them go. I'd try to find thruster-pack fuel later and refill the tanks. I snorted to myself. Given the vast size of the PDS, would I ever find my way here again to pick up the packs?

I had my doubts. But I shoved those aside. Now wasn't the time to give myself more and possibly needless worries.

I grabbed a tablet from a phase-suit pouch, typing out the words: Are you ready?

The other two looked at the screen and nodded.

This was it. We were here. It was show time.

Unfortunately, the next problem proved to be the PDS's size and our motive power of walking while out of phase. It would take us days, maybe even weeks to reach the center of the station. By that time, the coming space battle would have long been over.

I gave the signal, and we phased in, this time deeper inside the station. I expected the place to be honeycombed with narrow Plutonian tunnels. Instead, we stood in a regular-sized—human-sized—corridor. That was a surprise, and it meant something. At the moment, I didn't know what.

We plugged attachments into to each other's suits, hooking a comm-line between us so we could talk in safety.

I said, "We need a faster means of locomotion while out of phase if we're going to get to the center in time to influence the battle."

"I agree," Ella said. "Logically, there have to be elevators or something that acts like elevators. We should commandeer one, using express speed to go down."

"What do you think of that, N7?"

"I suspect all such elevators will be monitored," N7 replied. "That means Jennifer will know we are coming, especially if she sees no one riding in the elevator as the three of us are out of phase."

"Jennifer already knows we're coming," I said. "Or have you forgotten about Saul?"

"I have not," N7 said.

"Saul is why we should ride express elevators to the center," Ella said. "They know we're here. So let's hit them as hard and as fast as we can."

Before I could respond to that, a huge Abaddon clone teleported into our corridor. He was wearing dark garments, gripped a massive .55 hand cannon in one hand and held onto a tall, stooped, badly beaten-up Ifness with the other.

There was a strange light in Saul's eyes. I expected him to aim the hand cannon and start firing. Instead, he moved the nearly limp Ifness toward me as if passing him off.

I was so startled by the action that I failed to attack. I guess the same was true of Ella and N7.

Slowly, the hitman raised his battered head to peer at me. He seemed surprised at what he saw, and he grinned with cracked lips, showing that he was missing teeth.

At that point, I realized that neither Saul nor Ifness wore breathing gear. That meant normal Earth-breathable air must have been circulating in the corridor.

My helmet motor whirred as my visor slid open.

-82-

"What's going on?" I demanded.

"I found Ifness," Saul said in an altered voice. "They have tormented my friend for many weeks, although he said they regrew his mangled arm."

Ella and N7's visors came down.

"This is a trick," Ella warned. "We must phase out immediately."

"I disagree," N7 said. "Saul, how did you find us?"

"What do you mean?" Saul asked.

"The PDS is vast," the android said. "How could you possibly have found us in all this mass?"

That was a good question, and it made me doubly suspicious.

"You not understand," Saul said. "I…fixate on that." The clone pointed at the Abaddon force axe at my side. "I sense it here, look, and find you."

I traded glanced with N7.

"Can others sense this weapon?" I asked Saul.

"Maybe," the clone said. "I do not know."

That was just great. I was carrying a veritable beacon.

Ifness began to cough, and his lanky body shuddered.

"Ifness has been cloned," Ella said, as if figuring out the answer to a complex problem. "Jennifer must have cloned your hitman friend with her DNA stamper," she told me. "Jennifer must have made a least one more Ifness and used the accelerator to turn the clone into an adult. You killed the Ifness clone—an Ifness clone, as there could be more. That Ifness clone was controlling Admiral Sparhawk from the drone in the *Quebec*."

The obviousness of the deduction struck me hard. Yes. Jennifer hadn't only fashioned Abaddon clones, but Ifness clones as well, at least one. But if that was true—

"You've been telling the truth all along," I said to Ifness.

"Bright boy," the hitman wheezed.

"I could be wrong," Ella said. "This Ifness could be a clone meant to trick us."

"No," Saul said, angrily. "This is Ifness. He is the original. He is why I came to this place, to rescue my friend."

I made a hard and fast decision. I decided to believe Saul and thus Ifness. Yet in a way, I hardly had a choice. If they had tricked us, we were dead anyway. If they were friends, and we were too distrustful to use their help, we would likely lose as well. The one way to win was to use what Saul—and possibly Ifness—represented.

Saul could teleport and likely "see" just about anywhere in the PDS. Ifness must have specialized knowledge. We were going to need both if we were going to save our fleet.

"Listen to me," I said. "Ifness, you once said you had a T-suit. Is it here?"

"On the PDS," he said, "yes."

"Can you direct Saul to it?"

Ifness gave me a beady bloodshot study with a single eye. The other was almost puffed shut. "The T-suit is my most priceless possession," the hitman said. "You think I'm going to just hand it over to you? You've already stolen my phase suits."

"Those extra suits are the reason we're here to help Saul rescue you," I said.

"Nice try," Ifness said, weakly. "Saul did the rescuing by his lonesome. You didn't do a thing."

I turned to Saul. "Did I give you a ride near the PDS?"

"Creed helped me," Saul told Ifness.

"Inadvertently is all," the hitman said.

"Fine," I said. "What's the price for the T-suit?"

It only took Ifness a second to decide. "We kill Jennifer," Ifness said in a cold dark voice.

I only hesitated a second. "No," I said. "I haven't come all this way to kill her. I'm going to save her."

Even as I said it, I winced. This would be a perfect moment for Jennifer to appear or maybe all fifty Abaddon clones to appear and attack. I actually looked around as I put a hand on the longish handle.

Nothing of the kind happened. That surprised me, and it told me I'd guessed right about Saul and Ifness.

"At least you're not lying to me," Ifness said, sourly. "If you'd agreed to kill her, I would have known you were snowing me. What do I want? I want my phase suits back to start with."

"After the mission is over," I said, "they're yours again."

"That works for me," Ifness said.

"Anything else?" I asked.

Ifness eyed us, finally saying, "I want the Globular Blaster, the Disrupter Rifle and the Abaddon Force Axe."

I studied the hitman. Even though he was barely standing, he still had fire in his belly, willing to dicker at a time like this.

"You can choose one between the Globular Blaster and the Disrupter Rifle," I said. "The axe is not for sale no how, no way."

"I want the guns or the axe," Ifness said.

"*One* of the guns and two phase suits is a bargain for a Ronin 9 T-Suit. It is a Ronin 9, isn't it?"

"Of course it is," Ifness said. "I should point out, you stole my two suits. You're only giving back what is already mine."

"The suits are mine at the moment," I said. "Besides, it doesn't matter how I got them. I'm willing to bargain with them—that is the point."

Ifness glanced at Saul, but the Abaddon clone was no help. The hitman eyed me again. "Fine," he muttered. "I'm getting ripped off. You'd better not welsh on the deal, though. I'm giving you everything beforehand while you—"

"What's wrong with you?" Ella shouted, interrupting. "Saul just rescued you. He needed our help to do it. And you're here complaining and bickering about giving us the tools so you can escape? Are you crazy?"

"I have to be paid," Ifness said, stubbornly. "It's my code. It's who I am. Live with it."

"Let's shake on the deal," I said, hoping Ella would shut up about it already.

Ifness struggled to raise an arm. I stepped up to him to make it easier. He leaned near, whispering, "This is hitman to effectuator honest, right?"

"My yes is yes and my no is no," I said.

"Quoting the Good Book, are you?"

I nodded.

"I accept," Ifness said.

The two of us shook hands in an outer corridor of the giant PDS in the pocket universe.

"One thing," Ifness said, as we let go of each other's hand.

"What's that?" I asked.

"The T-suit will be heavily guarded. It's questionable whether you can fight your way to it."

"How far away is it anyway?"

"Deep in the PDS," Ifness said.

"How do we get there in time?"

Ifness nodded slyly and grinned so his cracked lips began to bleed. "You're not going to like it, but here's the plan…"

-83-

In order to do this, we had to trust Saul. Just as the Abaddon clone had grabbed Ifness from his cell and teleported away with him, Saul could do the same with each of us—one at a time.

Ella, N7 and I had a short council of war. We agreed to the plan, as it was the only way to move fast enough inside the moon-sized PDS in order to win in time—if winning was possible.

"What do we do once we have the T-suit?" Ella asked me.

I shrugged. "Seems like we attack and grab Jennifer."

"Just like that?" Ella asked.

"Do you have a better idea?"

"I do."

"Let's hear it," I said.

"First," Ella said, "we need the T-suit. I say we do this one step at a time."

I shrugged and turned to Ifness. "We're ready. Let's roll."

Saul stepped near, picked me up in my phase suit and the corridor disappeared. Another corridor that looked exactly like the first one appeared. The one difference was that that Ifness, Ella and N7 were gone.

"Are you sure this is the right place?" I asked Saul.

The big guy had let go of me and panted as if from exertion. He nodded, and then Saul was gone.

I phased into ghost mode and backed into a bulkhead to hide. As I did, I checked a sensor. If this reading was correct, I was hundreds of kilometers deep in the PDS. I waited—

Saul appeared with Ella. He released her, and did a double take as he looked around.

I stepped out of the bulkhead and phased in. "Right over here," I said.

Saul whirled around as he raised the .55. He checked himself a second later. Wiping his forehead with the wrist of his gun-hand, he disappeared.

Ella and I both went into ghost mode and backed into a bulkhead.

Soon enough, we had everyone, included a winded Saul.

Ifness gave us the coordinates for the T-suit. Its storage cell was several bulkheads and corridors to our left. According to him, Plutonian soldiers likely guarded the suit along with other exotic paraphernalia.

"You're going to wait here?" I asked Ifness.

"Saul will know when you've won or not," the hitman said.

"If that's true, why can't the other Abaddon clones know as well?"

"They most certainly can know," Ifness said. "I imagine at least one of them mentally checks on the T-suit every now and again."

"When were you going to tell me that?" I asked.

"Now," Ifness said, "like I just did. Do you have a problem with that?"

I didn't answer, but turned to Ella and N7. We made our plan, went into ghost mode and began walking through bulkheads and crossing empty corridors.

In less than a minute, we stood inside the final bulkhead and slowly moved forward until the very edges of our visors jutted less than a centimeter out from the inner wall.

The storage room held a familiar Ronin 9 Teleportation Suit among other interesting technical goodies. It also had six Plutonians.

Ifness had told me these were soldiers. Instead of being bigger, as I'd expected, they were smaller, with hard shells like snails and seemingly armored tentacles. They peered around with their eyestalks and held bulbous weapons. I imagined those were guns of some sort.

The Plutonian soldiers did not overly worry me. What really worried me was that they would act as tripwires. Before I killed them, one of them would likely alert an Abaddon clone. If one enemy clone knew, presumably, all could know in short order. Could I defeat fifty Abaddon clones armed with their latest weaponry?

Some of you might be wondering why the other Abaddon clones hadn't yet sensed my force axe and attacked us. First, they must have been concentrating on other matters. Second, they didn't know to search for the force axe. Saul had told me he had to concentrate to find the force axe "signal." Third, I think Saul had grabbed Ifness without anyone else knowing. Finally, I think we had indeed slipped near with the GEV, and slipped onto the PDS without anyone sensing it yet.

In any case, as I stood in the bulkhead of the chamber with the T-suit, I realized we'd give away our presence if we attacked openly. The Abaddon clones would know the location of the T-suit. If I were one of them, while I was donning the T-suit, I'd teleport to the room and release a bomb, letting it evaporate everyone.

I smiled, remembering that the Abaddon clones would not have permission to do such a thing. Still, they would likely T-swarm in, trying to capture me while I donned the suit.

Hmm… Maybe I could use that to trap—to ambush—the clones as they teleported in to grab me. After some quick analyzing of the plan, that seemed iffy. If they could "see" in some fashion before they teleported, they could "see" our ambush. I should have questioned Saul more closely on his teleporting abilities.

In that instant it came to me what I should do. We were going about this the wrong way.

I withdrew back into the bulkhead and motioned the other two. We retreated through the bulkheads and corridors to where we'd left Ifness and Saul. Fortunately, they were still there.

We phased in and opened our visors.

"I don't see a T-suit," Ifness said tiredly.

"Correct," I said. "There's been a change in plans."

"What now?" the hitman asked.

I told them my new idea. Predictably, Ella didn't like it. N7 said it bordered on madness. Ifness hadn't yet made a comment.

"Well?" I asked.

"I'm too tired, too beat-up, to do as you suggest," Ifness said.

"You're not too tired," I said. "Besides, you have the easiest part. I can give you some stims to perk you up if you like."

"I don't like," Ifness said, querulously.

"It's a good plan and you know it."

"Your plan will get you killed," the hitman said.

"I hadn't realized you'd grown so fond of me. Thanks."

"No," Ifness said. "The more I think about your plan, the more…fraught with peril I realize it is."

"Look," I said, starting to get irritated. "This shows the difference between a hitman and an effectuator. You work for profit. I don't have a problem with that. But I work for a different payment. I might die, as you say, but I might finally grab the woman I love and start the process that heals her."

"You're an idealist," Ifness muttered. "No wonder you work for the First Guardian. He must have pumped your mind full of mushy slogans that you bought hook, line and sinker. Okay. I'll do as you ask, but I'm keeping the T-suit if you get killed."

"I know you mean that you'll keep everything if I get killed. But I'm not going to let them kill me. I'm going to win the most stunning melee in galactic history."

"Bragging before the fact gives you bad karma," Ifness warned.

"Whatever," I said. "Are you ready?"

Ifness glanced at Saul before muttering that he was.

-84-

Some of you have probably already guessed my plan. I had a teleporting team once we owned the T-suit. The trick was in grabbing the T-suit without causing a bunch of Abaddon clones to appear and shoot us up before we were ready.

That meant we had to move fast while grabbing the suit and moving to a place the Abaddon clones wouldn't immediately "see."

Saul stared intently into space, disappeared, and reappeared nine second later with a bleeding left shoulder and clutching a Ronin 9 Teleportation Suit. He dropped the suit and staggered back until he struck a wall, sliding down to his butt.

"Leave him," I told Ifness. "We'll take care of him. You get into the T-suit."

Ifness hesitated only a second, shuffling to the suit, picking it off the deck with N7's help. Again, with the android's help, the hitman began to climb into the bulky suit.

Ella and I checked on Saul. The wound wasn't deep but it bled freely. As Ella pressed pseudo-skin to the wound and the surrounding skin to check the bleeding, I studied the clone's eyes.

Saul was possibly in a slight state of shock, but he seemed fully coherent.

"You okay, big guy?" I asked.

Saul grinned at me. "I was hit."

"How bad is it?"

"I can still do my part."

"You're not going to die on us, are you?"

"Saul is tough."

"True."

"Saul is tougher than you, Effectuator."

"Maybe," I said. "But I won't believe it until I see it."

Using the wall for support, Saul began to work his way up.

"Hold it," Ella told him.

Saul ignored her and climbed to his feet. That was just as good, as we probably didn't have much time left before one of the Abaddon clones spotted us with his T-sight.

I started taking off my phase suit. I wouldn't be able to wear it and defeat a chamber full of Abaddon clones.

Once out of the suit—only wearing my metallic-like garment—I donned the heavy hyper-state bands around my ankles, wrists and neck. Once they were activated, I could move at hyper-speed. Combined with the force axe, it was a lethal combination, especially if one had to do the fighting as fast as possible.

Ella quietly picked up my phase suit. "You might need it later," she said.

I nodded, but I was finding it hard to talk, as I was psyching up for the battle royal. I gripped the longish handle with both hands and breathed in and out, in and out.

We had a slight advantage that could evaporate at any moment. Saul knew where Jennifer was and could thus teleport there. We were hidden somewhere on the PDS, hidden at a place that they had as yet been unable to find. The force axe would probably give us away soon, though.

Of course, the Abaddon clones—Jennifer's elite guard—could teleport away from me if I charged them. But if they were going to protect her from me, they had to stick around on the battlefield.

I was proud of the logic and hoped the Abaddon clones didn't grab her and teleport away. Now, I could possibly have had Ifness or Saul teleport in, leave a bomb and vamoose before it exploded. But I had a hindrance, just like Jennifer's regarding killing me that way. I wanted to save my love and return her to sanity. She wanted to capture me for extended torture.

Ifness raised a gloved hand, waggling a T-suited thumb. He was ready. Saul still looked green around the gills, but he expanded his already considerable chest in a strongman's pose. Ella held onto my discarded phase suit. N7 had his Disrupter Rifle out and ready. Both Ella and N7 wore their phase suits and could go in and out of phase as needs dictated.

"Ella, you're coming in last," I said. "Have the Globular Blaster ready."

She nodded her helmet.

"Any last words, anyone?" I asked.

No one had any.

"Saul," I said. "You're taking me. Start firing the hand cannon if you want, just don't get yourself killed while doing it."

"Saul understands," the big guy said.

"Ifness?" I asked.

"I'll come back and get Ella," the hitman said. "Then, I'm staying out of the fight."

"That's your choice," I said. "But if it was me, I'd want to get some serious revenge for torturing me for weeks. But hey, that's effectuator thinking. Hitmen probably don't want payback."

"Keep your junior psychology to yourself," Ifness said. "It means nothing to me."

"Sure," I said.

A second later, Saul stepped near and put a heavy hand on my left shoulder. He squeezed, hanging on tight.

I gripped the inactivated force axe and knew that I might be dead within ten minutes. Even if I won, I might push my body farther than it could go. I wasn't going to quit until I'd done it, though. I wasn't going to—

With terrifying suddenness, the corridor disappeared…

-85-

And I was standing at the edge of a vast, octagonal-shaped chamber that had a cathedral-like ceiling way up there. Lined up along the walls for twenty meters or more were Plutonian slugs at countless stations. Combined, they manipulated thousands of levers, buttons and other devices with their slimy tentacles. There were huge screens even higher up showing all kinds of Plutonian vessels, bustling chambers, possibly engine or beam rooms and strange shots of the murky surface of the planet below, or beside, I suppose I could say, the PDS. Giant cracks crisscrossed the planetary surface. Out of those cracks steamed roiling gases. I guessed in that moment that the planet was the engine or genesis for the pocket universe's gases.

Did I mention two Plutonian Fleets showing on the highest screens? The two fleets moved through the murky gases. I imagined they were trying to encircle our invasion fleet by surprise. Did Rollo even know the enemy vessels were approaching him?

I didn't have time to wonder, as I had my own problems just now.

In the center of the vast, octagonal-shaped chamber was a tiered pyramid. It wasn't massive like an Egyptian pyramid, but around three stories tall. It had six tiers, if one counted the top where various machines or computers did their thing. The rest of the tiers had machines embedded in them. Plutonians worked the bottom two tiers. Abaddon clones worked the other smaller levels.

Jennifer sat up there on top of the pyramid in a throne-like chair. My ex-lover still had braids, wore a dark metallic suit in an evilly sexy fashion and held a baton with crackling energies on one end. The other end had a glowing, ethereal spike.

I took this all in as Saul released his painful grip from my shoulder. The clone disappeared with a rush of air, and reappeared on a pyramidal tier beside a different clone. Saul raised his hand cannon and fired.

The booming blast had no discernable effect, as the targeted clone vanished an instant before Saul pulled the trigger. In retaliation, the vanished clone reappeared behind Saul, attempting to stab him with a gleaming knife. Saul also vanished before the knife struck home, and he seemed to stay vanished this time.

As the Abaddon clones and the Plutonians began reacting to the shot, a purple ray speared through the chamber, striking a different Abaddon clone in the back. Some might have considered that a dirty blow, but this was war, and that made it fair, right? N7's disrupter ray burned through the clone—he did not have the same awful powers as his father, Abaddon, had possessed. The clone did not have a mental force field, and went down as he gushed golden ichor from the wound.

At that point, I began to run toward the tiered pyramid. N7, meanwhile, fired another purple ray.

I did not run at a sprint, but at a pace to get me there and get things started. I wanted to refrain as long as I could from entering the hyper-speed state that devoured my muscular strength and stamina.

Things were starting to happen, all right. Abaddon clones turned from their instruments, and they began drawing weapons of various kinds. Jennifer stood up, and hundreds of Plutonians began to shriek and screech in their freakishly alien tongue.

So far—

Oh-oh. The Plutonians along the walls produced weapons, aiming at me.

With my tongue, I pressed a switch embedded in a back molar, and I entered hyper-speed. I moved much faster as a host of beams sliced and diced the air where I'd been.

The Abaddon clones and Plutonians seemed to stand still. It was uncanny and delightful. I had to remind myself that I could only stay in this state for a short period. During that time, I had to achieve victory or face—

I wasn't going to think about losing. I was going to get while the getting was good.

As I ran—I must have seemed like a blur to them—I snatched the longish handle from my hip and readied the weapon. All I needed was to press one more switch and the red force would emerge as the deadly axe.

Abaddon clones sparkled on the tiers. I grinned to myself, certain what was going to happen next.

A clone disappeared. So did another.

Around me, sudden sparkles heralded the appearance of a massive, menacing Abaddon clone. More began popping into existence near me. Each held a powerful weapon—pistol, beamer, rifle or crackling energy blade.

I cheated in the worst possible way. I pressed the last button. The red force axe hissed into being and I swung at the glittering sparkles in the air. The axe sheared through one appearing clone after another. This was fantastic. This was murderous mayhem on my part.

In a microsecond, six clones began toppling to the floor in various states of dismemberment. It would take them time—in my frame of reference—to hit the floor.

Even as the six fell in slow motion, I climbed up the first tier. It was pathetically easy slashing, hacking and stabbing the alien blob creatures. This was joy. This was fun. Slimy, hateful Plutonians, with their strange partly mechanical innards began melting from the heat of the ancient force axe passing through them.

I jumped up onto the second tier, creating the same zone of death as I climbed onto the third tier. Two Abaddon clones managed to teleport away before I reached them. The third tried to teleport behind me. He died in a gory ruin of golden ichor.

I reached the fourth tier. It was empty. The elite guard was getting smart in an incredibly short amount of time. But I couldn't quit now. As I scaled up to the fifth tier, massed clone weaponry fired at me from seeming pointblank range.

I barely dodged in time as beams and slow-moving bullets passed over where I'd been. I raced along the edge and jumped up again.

The tier here was empty.

A terrible premonition told me to glance back. Nine clones fired up at me from the main deck. I ran, I dodged and I twisted away from their beams, and I barely missed the ethereal spike driving down for my face from above. At the last microsecond from the corner of my eye, I'd noticed darting movement. Jennifer stabbed down from the top of the pyramid with her baton spike. She moved faster than anyone else here except for me.

She was not moving at hyper-speed. But she was fast enough that we were in a similar realm of heightened movement.

"Creed," she sneered. "You were a fool to come here. You will never escape from this place."

The shrieks and shouts from the others came in garbled slow-motion sounds. Jennifer spoke slower than normal, at least to me, which meant she was speaking super-fast to everyone else.

"Honey-bun," I said. "I've come here to show you how wrong I was long ago to leave you to Abaddon in the Karg space-time continuum. If I could change anything, it would be that moment."

"Foul liar," she snarled. "You never loved me—not that it matters."

"I did," I said. "And I do."

"Prove it. Lower your weapon and bare your chest to me."

I dodged more beam fire from below and another one of her ethereal spike-stabs. As I did, I clambered onto the top tier with her.

"You're a fool with delusions of romance," she spat.

"So sue me."

Jennifer crouched as she twirled her baton like a grandstand master. A second later, she aimed the other end at me. A gout of strange fire burst from it.

Fortunately, I was no longer standing in its path. I moved in toward Jennifer, dodging another gout of strange fire, weaved the other way and swung the force axe. Jennifer blocked with the baton, a poor choice on her part. Yet, to my astonishment, the baton stopped the force axe. Sparks showered from her weapon and the red axe-energy crackled and seemed as if it might short out.

Jennifer laughed, ducked and swung the baton, trying to slash me with the ethereal spike. I wildly parried the ghostly spike, and once again, the axe's red lines of power crackled and hissed.

I dropped the force axe and moved as fast as I could, grabbing both of her wrists as she tried to jab the ethereal spike into me. Jennifer proved dreadfully strong. What had Abaddon done to her? Yet, despite her enhanced strength, she wasn't as strong as me.

I squeezed her wrists and wrenched one as hard as I could. Bones snapped. She paled, and the grip of her other hand weakened.

I tore the baton from her.

"No!" she shouted.

Then a beam from one of the Abaddon clone's rifles struck my side. The metallic suit held for an instant, and that was enough for me to twist out of the beam's path.

"Forgive me, my darling," I said.

"I will never forgive you anything," she hissed like a wildcat.

I cocked back an arm and struck her a sharp blow on the jaw, a strong blow. Jennifer's eyelids fluttered. Her knees wobbled. I'd held back some because I did love her and didn't want to hurt her. But if I failed to win today—

I struck again, harder, and she slumped unconscious.

I caught her, slinging her prone body over my left shoulder. I found the button for the baton, clicking it off, sticking the baton between my belt and body. I picked up the still-energized force axe—it had been busy digging ever deeper in the pyramid—and began to jump down from one tier to another.

I had reverted to type, becoming a Star Viking once again. Like any good raider, I'd selected my prize, a beauty beyond compare, and captured her. Now, I was going to kill anyone trying to stop me from taking my war-booty back to my ship.

I laughed recklessly. I was doing it. I was winning. The question was, could I survive long enough to enjoy the heady feeling of ultimate victory?

-86-

Once I reached the main chamber floor, the remaining Abaddon clones went berserk. I wasn't expecting that. They teleported at me, charging, shouting, clawing, shooting, swinging, trying desperately to either kill me or stop me from taking Jennifer from them.

The massive, towering clones still moved in slow motion. Only their teleportation was fast.

I slew with the force axe. It was unfair because I still moved at hyper-speed. But it was heady and enjoyable to an intense degree. Let them come to me to die. I would happily oblige.

The ferociousness of the attack told me that Jennifer must have programmed them to do anything they could to save her. That programming was now resulting in their slaughter. Perhaps the programming had helped keep them in submission to her. I couldn't blame Jennifer for it. But this evidence of her action helped prove the dictum that dictatorships were among the easiest forms of government to topple. All you had to do was decapitate—nullify the leader—and everything else fell to pieces.

My arm grew weary, and I began to pant. Dead and still-falling clones littered the main chamber floor.

Then, I was alone but for Jennifer still limply draped over my shoulder. No more clones teleported at me to die. No more clones stood in the vast chamber. The Plutonians no longer fired for the simplest of reasons. The slugs had all fled from the chamber.

I looked up at the screens. Something was wrong. I pinpointed it almost right away. More battleships, hundreds of battleships, docked along the outer hull of the PDS were powering up as if to leave the station.

I did not understand, unless the fleeing Plutonians had caused that.

I wondered, in that microsecond, how the slugs had managed to get out of here so quickly. The battle in the chamber had not lasted long in real time. How had they gotten off the higher wall-stations? I hadn't recalled seeing any slugs leaping off or glopping onto the floor.

There was something strange going on.

I raced to Ella, who stood beside a badly wounded Abaddon clone. It was Saul. She'd pasted several pseudo-skins onto his body. Golden ichor pooled everywhere around him. He seemed unbelievably pale and feeble. I feared Saul was dying.

"Where's N7?" I asked.

Ella said nothing, just kept staring at me. Then I remembered that she was moving and thinking at regular speed.

I looked around the chamber a last time, and shut off the hyper-speed bands around my neck, wrists and ankles. As I did, overpowering exhaustion and weakness struck. Intense lethargy threatened to drag me unconscious. I fought the feeling.

"Creed," Ella said, "is something wrong?"

I managed to look at her—and that was the last thing I remembered…

-87-

This time, I almost died from using the hyper-speed bands.

I learned later that Ifness injected himself with stims and used the T-suit to take each of us, one at a time, near the PDS's outer hull. Then, Ifness had one last mission to perform in true hitman fashion.

He was the consummate professional, knowing that an employer could always sour on him. During the good days with Jennifer, he'd learned to the best of his ability the secrets of the giant PDS. He'd wanted that knowledge in case he had a falling out with her, like now.

But more about that later.

From the new location near the outer hull, Ifness in a phase suit and while out of phase carted me, a phase-suited Ella brought an unconscious Jennifer and N7 hoisted the badly injured Saul. The others had garbed Jennifer, Saul and me with spacesuits and extra air tanks so that we might survive the long journey.

Luckily, Ifness knew the PDS's layout. He took the others to a chamber where they refilled the thruster-pack tanks. The hitman also knew a trick that helped them move away in spite of the planet's gross gravitational pull. The trick only worked during out-of-phase flight.

After a harrowing and nerve-wracking ordeal, they made it back to the drifting GEV, depositing me into the stasis tube. The tube immediately began its healing process. They put

Jennifer into a sleep-suit and hooked Saul to a special medical bed.

Afterward, N7 began piloting the GEV back to Battlejumper *Demetrius*.

Unfortunately, Plutonian battleships and cruisers were already passing the stealth ship. The enemy vessels were presumably straining to join the first two fleets that must have almost been in attack position and awaiting the go signal from the PDS.

Finally, Ella revived me in the stasis tube.

I felt like death warmed over, as the saying goes, and it took me a while to even climb out. Leaning heavily against Ella, I shuffled into the piloting chamber. The short journey left me gasping.

Ifness and N7 regarded me. It looked as if they'd been arguing.

Ella filled me in on the relevant details. The murky, gaseous space was filling up with more and more Plutonian warships, ready to pounce on the Earth ships.

"The Plutonians have clearly broken Jennifer's conditioning," Ifness said sharply.

I blinked several times before managing to ask, "How do you know?"

"During our commando strike, the slugs fled the Control Chamber," Ifness said. "Their wall-stations had mini-teleportation pads. That's how they get up there. After you struck Jennifer, they began teleporting away. My suspicion is that the blow jarred the mental domination she kept over them."

"What?" I whispered. "How is that possible?"

"Her domination or that you jarred it loose?" Ifness asked.

"Either, both," I said.

Ifness shook his head. "You have no idea what you've brought onto the GEV. Jennifer is no longer human, not as you conceive of it. Abaddon's alterations changed more than just her physical appearance and mental state, but gave her increasingly mutating mind powers."

"You mean like telekinesis and telepathy?"

"No," Ifness said. "I mean Abaddon-like mental domination and the ability to teleport."

"Jennifer can do that?"

"She's learning."

"She's become a First One?"

"That's astute of you," Ifness said. "Yes. Becoming. She's becoming like a First One."

"How is that even possible?"

"For us to change someone like that, it isn't," Ifness said. "For Abaddon to slowly transform a little killer into a First One or someone like a First One…that is clearly possible."

"How?"

"Right," Ifness said.

"That's not an answer."

"No," Ifness said. "But it's one of the many ways that Abaddon was greater than anyone else. The Abaddon clones were like babies in power and ability compared to their father. None of them would have been able to approach him for a thousand years or more."

"First Ones can live that long?"

"If they can figure out how, yes," Ifness said.

"Okay. I don't have the strength to understand that now."

"You don't need to figure it out," Ifness said. "The point is, because of what you've done, the Plutonians are free from Jennifer's control. That was always the gravest danger. With your blows, you destroyed the delicate balance in her mind. If it's any consolation, you've made it possible for the Plutonians to finally go on their full-scale genocidal galaxy sweep."

"How does that console me?" I shouted, coughing afterward.

"Oh," Ifness said. "My bad. By trying to save your woman—who has already been lost for good—you've ensured trillions of deaths from years of coming brutal war against the Plutonians."

"Surely, you have a plan, right?" I asked. "There's a reason you're urging N7 to hurry back to the fleet."

"Yes," Ifness said, while glancing at N7. "I have a plan. It could get us all killed, *will* get us killed because this android is too stupid to do what needs doing. Now, if he would listen to—"

"What's your plan?" I asked, interrupting.

Ifness gave me a wintery grin. "I'm going to destroy everything in the pocket universe."

"How is that possible?"

"Several months ago," Ifness said, "I preprogrammed the PDS. To be precise, Jennifer had me preprogram the great station. It was one of her holds over the Plutonians. I don't know if they've forgotten about that or if they've already dismantled the programming."

"What?" I said.

"Right after the commando raid, I teleported away and started the doomsday process. Then I returned to the team to get us out of there fast."

"What doomsday process?"

"Didn't I previously mention that I'd built several levels into the doomsday protocols?" Ifness asked.

"No!"

"Oh. Well, the first two secret PDS protocols are there for the Plutonians to find. The third—once they find it, too—is to make them realize I tried to outsmart them but that they were too clever for me. The fourth…" Ifness shook his head. "They're not going to find the fourth protocol in time. If I'm right about that—which I am—the PDS is going to fire cobalt-tipped missiles and heavy beams into the planet. Those missiles and beams will ignite the unstable core."

"And the accompanying explosion will destroy the PDS?" I asked.

"Oh, yes indeedie," Ifness said.

"So…why do we have to race back to our fleet again?"

"You'd better listen carefully so you understand. Are you listening, Creed?"

"Just get on with it," I snapped.

Ifness nodded. "The entire planet will blow up, and that will ignite the special Plutonian gases that have been pumping into the pocket universe during its long existence. Once the gases ignite, they will *burn*, destroying everything in this realm."

"By everything," I said, "does that include our fleet?"

"Our fleet, their fleet, the PDS, *everything*," Ifness said.

I was speechless. This was incredible.

"That's...that's a genocidal plan," Ella sputtered.

"Don't you understand yet?" Ifness asked her. "The First Ones installed that special failsafe. That's why they made this place the way it is. They knew it would be generations before anyone found the pocket universe. It would take the planet that long to manufacture all that special flammable gas and pump it throughout the system."

"I'll be damned," I said, softly.

"No," Ifness said. "If you can't get this ship moving any faster, you'll be *dead*. We all will, including me."

"Uh, one question," I said. "Do you know where the dimensional portal is that will get us out of here?"

"That I do," Ifness said.

"Can we and the invasion fleet reach the portal in time?"

"If we accelerate soon enough, maybe," Ifness said. "But maybe just to be sure, we should already be headed there ourselves."

I turned to N7.

"If we accelerate too fast," the android said, "the Plutonians will surely spot and destroy our ship."

"Maybe not," I said, "not if we accelerate fast enough."

"I know about the mechanism you are implying with your comment," N7 said. "We can't risk it, though, because the gases will impede our travel too much—the gases will cause too much friction and burn away our hull, killing us in the process."

I nodded slowly. "You might be right. But I don't see that we have any other choice than to try."

"It is your call, Commander," N7 said, primly.

"Right," I said. "Let's get this ship ready to move."

"Directly to the dimensional portal?" Ifness asked.

I stared at him. Isn't that what I had done to Jennifer long ago at the portal planet? I shook my head. No. I'd thought Jennifer had been safely aboard and had learned too late that she hadn't.

"If we don't get back to our universe," Ifness said, "how will anyone know that we've—?"

"Hey!" I said with force. "We're saving our fleet by taking them to the portal, and that's final."

Ifness seemed peeved and looked away.

I crackled my knuckles, starting to feel better. It was time to get moving.

-88-

Ella, N7, Ifness and I buckled in. N7 had already secured Saul and Jennifer. Ella and I were in the piloting chamber. The others were elsewhere on the stealth ship.

"Creed, I have a question," Ella said.

"Do I trust Ifness?"

"That's right. Do you?"

"In what way do you mean?"

"You're dodging the question," she said.

I sighed. "The short answer is *some*. I trust him to want to live. From that issues my willingness to believe him—partially, anyway—for now."

"What if Jennifer or someone else has preconditioned him?"

"You think this is part of some sinister plot? All right, tell me this, who's doing the plotting? It couldn't have been Jennifer. I mean, my knocking her unconscious and kidnapping her couldn't be part of a nefarious plot she's hatched."

"No, I suppose not." Ella thought deeply before asking, "I wonder if all the Abaddon clones are dead."

"Do you have any particular clone in mind?"

"Orcus," she said. "I haven't seen him for a long time. I didn't see him in the Control Chamber."

"I don't recall seeing Orcus either, but maybe N7 killed him with the Disrupter Rifle. Oh. I've actually thought of a slim possibility to consider along with all this being a plot. Holgotha still seems to be running loose."

"Yes, *yes*," Ella said, as if revitalized. "The Forerunner artifact might well have—"

"Stop!" I said, interrupting her, wishing I hadn't mentioned Holgotha. "We don't have the luxury of figuring out every angle beforehand. Let's destroy one enemy at a time, and worry about the next one later…"

"Yet more Creed speeches," Ella complained.

From my chair, I focused on the piloting controls, making adjustments. The AI had the coordinates for the last known position of our invasion fleet. Rollo might have moved, though. The First Admiral might have detected the approaching, sneaking Plutonian warships. Might have this, might have that—it was time to make a choice.

"Are you ready?" I asked.

"No," Ella said. "But that's never stopped you before."

I switched on the intra-ship communications. "Get ready, get set, because here we go."

I didn't wait for any replies, but pressed the activation switch. We'd been accelerating slowly. Now, I kicked in shift-speed so that we would return quickly to the invasion fleet—if it was in the calculated spot, and if we survived—

The shift-speeding GEV began shaking, due no doubt to buffeting outer gases. The shaking intensified, causing my teeth to chatter against each other. A klaxon blared—

"Warning," the AI said.

"Can it!" I shouted, with everything shaking around me.

"I do not understand your reference," the AI said.

"That means 'shut up.'"

"Cease giving warnings altogether?"

"Just for the next minute," I shouted.

"Even if enemy warships are firing at us?" the AI asked.

"No, not then. Are they firing at us?"

"Negative."

"Then why did you ask that question?" I shouted.

"My decision parameters are such that—" An explosion inside the ship ended the statement.

I studied a chronometer, waited for it…and pulled a lever.

A loud and insistent interior whine ceased immediately, as did the ship's shaking. Ella and I both jerked against our safety straps.

"What is the status of the hull's integrity?" I asked, winded.

The AI did not answer.

"AI, I rescind the previous order. You can speak again."

"The hull is eighty-three percent intact," the AI said.

That meant gases and friction had breached seventeen percent of the hull. That was far too much. Were stellar gases pouring into the rest of the ship?

"Have you sealed off the rest of the ship to the exposed areas?" I asked.

"Affirmative," the AI said in its robotic voice.

Like submarines, the GEV had fully sealable hatches that kept up the internal integrity of the vessel.

"Creed," Ella said.

I knew what she was going to add. "Is or was anyone in the breached areas?" I asked.

The AI did not answer.

I began unbuckling. Here was more trouble. Had we lost someone?

"There are no biological entities in the exposed areas of the GEV," the AI said.

Why had it delayed giving an answer and why had it been so specific? "Are there any foreign attackers of any kind in the exposed areas?" I asked.

"Negative," the AI said. "May I add, Effectuator, that you appear to be overly sensitive to my semantics?"

"You may not."

"Noted."

"Send robotic repair teams to the exposed areas. Begin repairing the outer hull at once."

"The repair team is on its way."

"Are there any other immediate dangers?" I asked.

"I would have informed you if there were, Effectuator."

"Right," I said. "Can you spot any Earth Force vessels in our vicinity?"

"Negative."

I cursed. Where had Rollo gone—?

"Effectuator," the AI said, interrupting my thoughts. "I have spotted an Earth-built probe. It is emitting a weak signal. Would you like me to translate its message to you?"

"Is the probe's message addressed to me?"

"Yes, Effectuator."

"Let's hear it," I said, deciding that getting angry with the AI was a waste of time.

The AI informed me that the First Admiral had sent a coded puzzle that revealed the fleet's movements. I feared, for a just a moment, that Rollo had decided to make the attack run against the PDS. Instead, to my delight, the message said that Rollo had retreated several hundred thousand kilometers, as the sensor techs had detected enemy ship movement around them.

The weeks in Plutonian Space had paid off for us. The Earth-Force crews had become more proficient and savvy in this realm.

"One more shift-speed," I said.

"Are you sure, Creed?" Ella said. "We've already taken hull damage. How does it help to reach Rollo as a wreck?"

"The gases aren't as thick out here. We should be fine this time."

"Whatever you say," Ella muttered.

I made some swift calculations, asked the AI's advice, informed the others to be ready, and once more risked entering shift-speed…

-89-

We made it to the fleet—barely.

Still, Ella had proven herself a better prophet than me. The GEV not only took more hull damage but lost the robot repair team. I hadn't informed the team and the AI hadn't thought it necessary before we entered shift-speed. I'd have to look into that later, if we survived.

Despite the extra damage, the GEV limped into one of the hangar bays of Battlejumper *Demetrius* amid a raging space battle against the forward elements of the original two Plutonian fleets.

The great battlejumper shivered as we hurried across the hangar-bay deck.

"What was that?" Ella asked.

I shrugged while dragging Jennifer in her sleep-suit. She floated behind me on a mini gravity sled.

The *Demetrius* shook again, harder than before.

"Ifness," I said. "Take the sled. Ella, show him where to stow Jennifer. And don't leave Ifness alone with her. N7, you guard Jennifer from Ifness as well."

"That's not very trusting of you," Ifness told me.

I stopped to look back at the hitman. I shook my head. What kind of fool was I? I looked around, spied a hangar-bay tech and whistled for the woman's attention.

She came running.

I gave her instructions regarding Jennifer. "On no account let anyone wake her," I said.

After receiving the tech's acknowledgement and watching her take the gravity sled, I put a heavy hand on Ifness's shoulder. "You're coming with me."

"I have to look after Saul," Ifness said.

"Now," I said, squeezing so Ifness winced painfully under my grip.

That didn't last. The hitman tried a fancy hold on my squeezing hand. I twisted free of him and used two hands and an arm to put him in a painful headlock.

"We're all going to die if we don't do this right," I whispered in his ear.

"Let go of me," he hissed.

"You're coming with me, as Rollo needs to hear it from the horse's mouth."

Our eyes met. I could see he really did want to kill Jennifer. That wasn't just an act. I also saw that he saw I understood that about him.

"Fine," he said. "Truce?"

"Truce," I said, letting go.

I half-suspected Ifness to make a quick try, come what may. Did I see the thought flash in his eyes? Then the thought vanished. He must have realized I watched him too closely.

"Let's go," Ifness muttered.

I pointed. He went in that direction, and soon we both began to sprint for the main elevator. In time, the two of us reached the bridge exhausted. By that point, neither of us was in the best of shape.

Captain Maddison Rowell stood, vacating her chair.

"No need for that," I said. "You're still the *Demetrius's* captain."

She resumed her place on the captain's chair.

"Patch me through to the First Admiral," I told the Comm Officer. "May I use the main screen for this?" I asked the captain.

"I would have it no other way, sir," Maddison said.

In seconds, I saw the First Admiral on the *Quebec's* bridge. Rollo barked orders, listened to one of his officers, turned and barked more orders. Finally, he faced around, looking through the screen at Ifness and me.

A huge smile broke out on Rollo's face. "You're back. Do you have Jennifer?"

"Yes."

"I knew you'd do it, Creed. What's the situation?"

I told him as tersely and quickly as I could. I pointed at Ifness. The hitman explained fast, adding applicable facts about the PDS, the unstable planetary core and then the flammable gases.

"Run away, huh?" Rollo asked, dubiously. "I can't say I like it. But if everyone and everything is going to burn here…" He chuckled in an evil and vindictive way. "It will have to be a running fight, at least for a time."

"I get that," I said. "The key is to start now. Ifness set the clock ticking. Either we get out in time or we die."

Rollo nodded. "Couldn't have sent a signal through all this gaseous crap, I understand. How far away is the dimensional portal?"

Ifness told him.

Rollo tapped a nearby console. He appeared to be nothing but a bruiser. The bulky muscles kept many folks from guessing he had a sharp mind. He looked up. "You barely made it back in time, Creed."

I nodded. I knew that.

"We need to break away from the enemy," Rollo said. A second later, he smiled like a shark smelling blood. "The missiles—it's time to put our massed missiles into play."

"That's an excellent idea, First Admiral," I said.

Rollo barked the loudest laugh so far and then turned to his command team and began to issue strings of orders. The final contest had just about begun.

-90-

The thick and fumy gases of this realm made it hard to know how everything was going.

Even so, we certainly knew that the forward elements of two Plutonian fleets attacked the rearmost part of our invasion fleet. The enemy had numbers at the point of contact, but we didn't know that right away.

Our main tactic quickly became a standard one. Massed battlejumpers pounded on a single Plutonian cruiser with graviton beams as missile officers remote-piloted missile packs against the beleaguered ship. Invariably, the cruiser detonated violently with its sinister explosive, hurting our attacking ships as badly as it did other nearby cruisers. Sometimes, because of the wicked explosion, a second cruiser detonated.

We lost the *Brazil* and the *Indonesia* because of enemy chain-reaction explosions, as the battlejumpers' outer armored hulls ruptured and enemy beams lashed the innards before the ships could escape.

Rollo kept rotating our battlejumpers, sending wounded ships forward and fresh vessels back to stave off the increasingly heavy Plutonian rushes.

The maneuver wouldn't work forever, as Rollo would soon run out of fresh battlejumpers. Could we get away in time?

As Ifness and I watched from the *Demetrius's* bridge, we saw more and more missiles launching from cargo holds and firing tubes. The amount of missiles the fleet had brought along was impressive.

Finally, the battlejumpers' missile holds were depleted. All that remained in them were the nearly useless torpedoes.

By that time, our invasion fleet had begun to accelerate away from the Plutonians. In the fleet's place was the first wave of massed PDD missiles.

Time passed as PDD missiles sought out enemy ships, and failed almost every time to reach close enough to detonate. Without the battlejumpers' helping graviton beams, the missiles simply lacked the ability to breach the enemy's defensive fire.

The corresponding missile explosions—not the missile warheads exploding but the delivery systems—helped to mask our fleet's increasing velocity. Soon, we lost sight of the lead Plutonian warships. Not long thereafter, we lost contact with the last massed PDD missiles.

We were buying time for as long as the missiles lasted. Would that be long enough?

The fleet accelerated, rushing through the surrounding gases. Fortunately, the gases had considerably thinned as compared to near the planet.

On the *Demetrius's* bridge, I started pacing. The idea of the moon-sized PDS igniting the planet, which would ignite the special gases…It made me thoughtful. What had the ancient First Ones been trying to achieve with that possibility? Had letting the Plutonians live after a fashion lessened their collective guilt for some reason? Why bother putting the Plutonians in a pocket universe? It must have taken fantastic effort to build such a place.

Would the Curator know the answers? Would he tell me if I asked him?

I paused in my pacing. Once this was over—if we survived—was I going to take Jennifer back to the Fortress of Light? I hadn't thought that far ahead. I realized I didn't want to make the decision yet.

"Concentrate," I told myself.

"What's that?" Ifness asked.

I thought about asking for his advice concerning the problem, but decided I'd rather not.

I restarted pacing, letting my worry take over so I wouldn't have to think about ideas that were more painful.

What do you want to hear? It proved to be a harrowing journey, with several surprise Plutonian assaults against the fleet. In the end, we reached the dimensional portal. Ifness told Rollo how to configure the portal to take us back to Earth.

"Don't try any tricks this late in the game," I whispered to Ifness.

He jumped away from me, scowling. Perhaps he hadn't heard me sneak up behind him.

I held the longish handle as I stared into the hitman's filmy eyes. Did he see my thumb hover over the last needed button? Did he realize the red power lines would emerge and I'd lop off his tricky head if he did something...false?

"First Admiral," Ifness said, facing the screen with as much dignity as he could muster, "there is one more thing I'd like to add."

"Oh?" Rollo asked from the flagship.

"Enter these coordinates instead of the ones I just gave you."

"What's that?" Rollo asked. "The first coordinates were wrong?"

I cleared my throat. On the screen, Rollo glanced at me, at the inactivated axe-handle and then into my eyes.

"Oh," Rollo said, before focusing on Ifness again. "We'll use the new coordinates then. What are they?"

Ifness gave them in a cheerful tone. After Rollo signed off, the hitman turned to me. "You can put that away. We understand each other."

I patted the longish handle. "I'll keep this around just in case."

"As you wish," Ifness said. "Now, where is the Globular Blaster you owe me?"

"Once we're safe, you'll get it."

"I'd like it now, if you please."

"I realize what you want," I said. "But you're not getting the blaster just yet."

Ifness fingered his lower lip, finally saying, "You keep insisting I trust you. It's about time you trusted me."

370

"You really want to pursue that line given what just happened?"

Ifness muttered under his breath and finally shook his head.

Outside our battlejumper, the giant circular dimensional portal received the latest coordinates. Soon, the boxes glowed with energy. As the energy built up, Plutonian battleships reached our vicinity. The heavy-class warships bored in against the waiting fleet.

Fortunately, Rollo had been ready for something like this to happen. He gave the order, and massed signals went out to inert torpedoes seeded behind us and now amongst the closing Plutonian warships.

The warheads exploded. I doubt they breached any enemy hulls, but the Plutonian assault did not begin yet. Instead, the battleships slowed or stopped altogether. Then, we detected enemy beam-fire as the battleships undoubtedly sought out any remaining torpedoes.

Rollo's torpedo-mine tactic was buying us time. Would it be enough, though?

Ahead of us, the portal as a whole began to glow and swirl. After another tense two minutes, Rollo gave the order. Our ships surged for the swirling, glowing area—and the sensation of rushing through immense, inter-dimensional distances took over as streaks of light flashed across the main screen. The light-streaks intensified, lengthening—and suddenly, everyone on the bridge surged forward as the battlejumper jerked to a stop.

I must have been one of the first to look up. I laughed. Soon, others looked up and joined with me in laughing, shouting and slapping each other on the back. We were in the Solar System. To be more precise, we were two hundred and forty-seven thousand kilometers from Luna Base. We were home. We'd made it. But had the pocket universe exploded as we'd hoped and destroyed the terrible enemy for us?

No one in the fleet knew the answer. Thus, First Admiral Rollo gave a wise order considering the many possibilities. At emergency acceleration, the fleet roared away from the location. At the same time, battlejumpers issued an emergency alert to the Moon, to Earth and to all nearby vessels.

All such vessels heeded the warning, accelerating at top speed to put themselves behind the Moon or behind the Earth in relation to the location of our initial appearance.

Sixteen and a half minutes later, an opening appeared where we had first entered regular space. The opening was from the pocket universe, of course. Yes. Plutonian battleships began entering our space. First, there were three. Soon, eight had plunged through. Then, seventeen of the terrible Plutonian vessels had reached our space-time continuum.

Next...next was one of the most frightful explosions I'd ever witnessed. A raging fire blew through the opening. The flames expanded and reached one-third of the way to Mars' orbit. The inferno blast incinerated the seventeen Plutonian battleships. The great gout from the other dimension—that surely proved an entire space-time continuum blazed with an end-time fury—utterly devoured the seventeen battleships caught within it.

Thankfully, the dimensional portal snapped shut after that. No more Plutonian ships came through. No more end-time fire raged in our space-time continuum. Likely, no more Plutonians existed over there, as the planet, PDS and every ship had to have fallen in the consuming fury of gaseous destruction.

Had that been the plan of the ancient First Ones all along? Why go to such crazy lengths to save a race and then ensure their total genocide?

I shrugged. I wasn't a First One. I had a woman that might be turning into a First One, though...

Thinking about Jennifer both depressed and elated me. I had completed the first part of my mission. I'd stopped her from destroying humanity. Now, I had to win back her love. Well, I had to restore her sanity to begin with. Could I make her love me afterward?

I stood on the bridge of the *Demetrius*, staring at the afterimages of the terrible fury from a dying pocket universe.

Had most of the energy been consumed in the separate space-time continuum? Or had some leaked out into other places. What was the wall between dimensions? I'd been to two different realms of reality in my life, three if one counted hyperspace.

I sighed deeply. Okay, I'd won round one. What was going to happen with round two between Jennifer and me?

I also had Ifness and Saul to worry about, never mind the Curator. While I could rejoice and maybe relax for a few hours, I still had not reached the conclusion of this particular mission.

-91-

The days drifted together as I debated possibilities concerning Jennifer.

The GEV was in Earth orbit as the AI oversaw internal repairs. I'd added certain features that had allowed the stealth ship to fashion a new robotic repair team. Then, I had given a list of needs to the Prime Minster. General Briggs himself had overseen the shipments of the parts to my vessel.

The AI had assured me I'd be able to begin the journey home to the Fortress of Light in another two weeks at most.

Home. Where was home for me? Home is where the heart is. Where was my heart? That was easy. It was Earth. That meant I was already home. Did I want to go away again to the center of our galaxy?

I hadn't made up my mind yet. Much of the answer would depend on Jennifer.

And what about Ifness the Hitman?

Yes, I paid Ifness with the Globular Blaster. I was a man of my word…most of the time. I also returned to him the two phase-suits.

Diana soon heard about Ifness. The Prime Minister asked if I would come to Earth with him.

I consented, and Ifness left the *Demetrius* aboard a shuttle. I arrived on the surface two days later in my flitter.

First Admiral Rollo kept his rank and post in the fleet. I thus had little worries regarding my safety. The Police Proconsul was gone. Briggs was a good man. Diana—I did not think my old friend would screw me. Even so, I made certain preparations just in case, as she had been with Ifness for two days already. I hadn't become the Galactic Effectuator for nothing.

I went down to New Denver, but this time it was to a mansion built on a mountain slope. It was huge, a veritable Louis the XIV-type palace. This, I learned, was Diana's retreat.

I parked the flitter on a landing pad and followed a liveried servant into the house. There, General Briggs met me in the first living room. A team of burly space marines stood along the walls.

"General," I said.

"I'm glad you came down, Commander," Briggs said, coming forward to pump my hand. After letting go, he said, "The Prime Minister wants your advice on several matters."

I nodded.

Briggs and I spoke about other things for a time. Finally, red-suited bodyguards entered the living room. I wondered who the new Police Proconsul was. I was relieved that it wasn't Ifness. The hitman was a fast talker, and I'd been wondering what he could talk Diana into.

Finally, the Amazon Queen in a Louis the XIV-era gown appeared. The flowing and costly dress highlighted her delightful bosom to awesome effect. I was stunned to see Ifness enter next. He wore a courtier's suit with buckled shoes. It fit him somehow, especially with the powdered wig the men had worn at that time.

"Commander Creed," Diana said. "I'm so glad you came down. Let us go for a walk, the three of us."

Diana took my right arm and guided me from the living room. Ifness followed behind us. General Briggs did not follow. The space marines stayed where they were. Only the red-suited bodyguards followed at a discrete distance.

We moved through a Hall of Mirrors that reminded me of the Curator. For a moment, I wondered if the old duffer had come to Earth in his Moon-ship.

We passed out of the Hall of Mirrors and entered a garden with many fountains and gorgeous flowers everywhere.

Here, Diana stopped, releasing my arm. She flounced her gown and sat on a ledge beside a pool with lily pads, frogs and large, lazy goldfish.

Ifness sat on a small boulder, crossing his legs and letting his left foot move up and down to an internal beat. He seemed at ease, but I doubted that. I wondered what game the hitman had played with Diana.

I spied a chair and dragged it near the two of them, sitting down, leaning back, trying to appear as if I was relaxed.

"You did it, Creed," Diana said. "I congratulate you on a job well done."

I dipped my head in acknowledgement.

"Of course," Diana said, "you never would have achieved success without Ifness."

I waited, saying nothing to that.

"Do you disagree with my prognosis?" Diana asked.

"Not at all," I said.

She smiled, glancing at Ifness. For some reason, that made the hitman uneasy, although I doubt anyone else noticed.

"Earth could use Ifness's talents," Diana said.

"No doubt that's true," I said.

"Do you disapprove of the idea?" Diana asked. "I sense disapproval."

I eyed the slippery hitman. While staring at him, I told Diana, "Not if you take the necessary precautions."

"Such as?" Diana asked.

"He has two phase suits," I said. "If you leave those in his possession while he's serving you…" I shook my head.

"Is that true, Ifness?" Diana asked. "Do you own two phase suits?"

Ifness breathed deeply so his nostrils flared. "I haven't decided if I wish to stay here or not," he said, primly.

"You're changing your mind?" Diana asked.

"Not necessarily," Ifness said. He raised an index finger, aiming it at me. "Uh, are *you* staying on Earth?"

"I haven't decided yet," I said.

"Does Creed's decision make any difference to yours?" Diana asked Ifness.

"No, no," Ifness assured her. "I'm simply curious."

"The present Lokhar Emperor has proven to be quite a nuisance to Earth," Diana said in an obviously hinting manner.

"I could, uh, *manage* the situation for you," Ifness said. "Of course, to do that I would need my phase suits, and Saul's help, naturally."

"That makes sense," Diana said. She asked as if it was a mere afterthought, "What would such *management* cost?"

Ifness glanced at me before answering. "I prefer not to say in front of the Commander. It's nothing against him, just a professional courtesy. You understand?"

"I'm not sure that I do," Diana said. "Creed loves Earth. He helps to protect its interests."

"Then hire *him*," Ifness said, peevishly.

Diana raised her lovely brows. "Are you for hire, Creed?"

"I'm still thinking about it," I said.

"If that's the case," Ifness said, "I should be leaving."

"Should I let him go?" Diana asked me.

Ifness stiffened, opened his mouth, maybe thought better of what he was going to say, and closed his mouth.

"Ifness has two phase suits, as you just pointed out," Diana said, "and a Globular Blaster. I imagine you could use both, could you not, Creed?"

"This is an outrage," Ifness said, exploding with indignity. "Creed does not murder a friend for mere gain, nor does he steal from a companion-in-arms."

"I've been thinking about what you told me a while back," I told Ifness. "Maybe I should reconsider my *Effectuator* ethics, to become more like you."

Ifness's eyes bulged, but he quickly reverted to seeming unconcern. "No, no, that's ridiculous," he said. "You're clearly not hitman material, Creed. Stick to being an effectuator or the savior of the human race. Such noble occupations suit you."

"Diana," I said, coming to a decision, "using Ifness is possibly a double-edged sword. Jennifer lost everything through employing him."

"Lost?" Ifness asked, as if surprised. "Jennifer is on the verge of regaining her former humanity. I would call that a fantastic turnaround for her."

"No thanks to you," I said.

"On the contrary," Ifness said. "I was instrumental in her…rescue. Her rehabilitation I now leave to you."

In that moment, I decided to refrain from further arguing, as Ifness actually had a point after a fashion. He'd also struck a nerve. How was I going to rehabilitate the monster, Jennifer, back into the wonderful woman I'd known years ago?

-92-

The first attempt to rehabilitate Jennifer left me gasping.

A *Demetrius* shuttle had already taken Jennifer in her sleep-suit to a sanatorium in old Nevada near refurbished Lake Tahoe. Today, they were going to revive her, and I would be watching.

I arrived in my flitter, spoke to the chief director and soon found myself behind a two-way mirror looking into an armored cell. The chief director announced my presence to those in the cell and then took his leave.

Ella and two nurses were with Jennifer, still in the sleep-suit and lying on a large heavy table. The Russian scientist flexed her fingers, asked if the others were ready and approached the suit. Delicately, Ella tapped in the code to begin the revival process.

The nurses monitored special machines aimed at Jennifer. Ella backed away, clicked open a holster, drew a dart gun and hid it behind her back. Today, now that she'd entered the code, she was security.

The table was situated at an angle. Thus, from the other side of the two-way mirror, I saw Jennifer's eyes snapping open. That was odd. She was supposed to be groggy, but she was like an awakened bobcat inside a dog pound full of barking inhabitants.

"It's fine," a large nurse said smoothly. "You're with friends."

"Friends?" asked Jennifer, as if tasting the word and finding it sour.

"Yes," the large nurse said. She wasn't fat, but strong—in here because of her known strength.

"Where am I?" Jennifer demanded.

"Near Lake Tahoe," the nurse said.

Jennifer frowned. "That is not on the PDS."

The nurse shook her head. "You're no longer in the pocket universe."

The wariness in Jennifer's dark eyes heightened. "Creed hit me. I remember that. It's the last thing I remember."

"Creed and the others brought you to his stealth ship," the nurse said—Ella had filled her in on the pertinent details.

Jennifer raised her head, again reminding me of a bobcat checking its surroundings. Her eyes darted everywhere, taking in the mirror. She stared at it.

From the other side, even though she shouldn't be able to see me, I looked into her eyes. Jennifer recoiled as if she could see me, or sense me in some fashion. She glared at the head nurse.

"You're with friends," the nurse repeated.

Jennifer spotted Ella, and a snarl curled her upper lip. "What are you doing here?"

"Hello, Jennifer," Ella said in a strained voice.

"You're *Creed's* friend, not mine."

"I'm your friend, too," Ella said.

"Is that why you're hiding a dart gun behind your back?" Jennifer sneered.

Ella did not bring out her hidden hand, but waited.

Abruptly, Jennifer sat up, coming out of the sleep-suit. She wore rumpled garments. She surveyed the cell.

"Yes," she said in a cold voice. "This is a prison."

"No, no," the large nurse said. "We're here to help—"

"No!" Jennifer said, while drawing her long legs out of the sleep-suit. "Don't you think I know a prison cell when I'm in one? Abaddon taught me many things. One of them was to see truly."

"Abaddon perverted you," Ella blurted.

The head nurse, the strong one, looked at Ella and shook her head.

At that moment, Jennifer slid off the table and charged the head nurse. The strong woman tried to grapple with Jennifer. It was like a child trying to restrain an Olympic strongman. Jennifer swatted away the thick arms, grasped the woman by a shoulder and thigh and easily lofted her over her head.

Ella aimed the dart gun, but she was too slow. Jennifer pivoted and heaved in one motion. A dart hissed from the gun, smacking into the nurse's back. Then the large woman struck Ella, sending her flying against the wall.

I'd seen enough. I charged for the cell door. It seemed to take forever. Finally, I unlocked it and stepped into the room.

Jennifer laughed victoriously. All the others were prone on the floor, either unconscious or groaning painfully. In her hand, Jennifer held the dart gun.

"Welcome, Creed," she mocked. "It's wonderful to see you again."

Jennifer fired as she spoke. I charged because I couldn't think of anything else to do. Thus, I took two darts in the chest. I would have taken more, but the gun was slow at chambering a new dart into the firing slot.

The drugs were fast acting, but so was I. I reached my ex-lover and tore the gun from her grasp. She struck me a heavy blow on the face, causing me to stagger backward.

"No foul Effectuator advantages now," she said. "This time—" She swung again. I dodged, and she twirled like a top, connecting with her left foot. I'd barely twisted in time, so I took the powerful shot on my shoulder instead of my face.

I staggered backward and slammed against the wall. As I slid down, my eyesight dimmed from the darts' injected drugs. Jennifer charged. I raised the dart gun and faked firing. Jennifer twisted aside. I shot then, sinking a dart in her side.

"Beast," she hissed. "You'll pay for that."

I heard another dart chamber, and fired again. The dart hit true, and Jennifer crashed headlong into the wall.

She groaned and sank down beside me. I looked into her eyes. They glared with murderous hatred.

"I only have to succeed once," she whispered in a slurred voice. Then her head slumped as the knockout drugs took effect.

I fell unconscious soon thereafter.

-93-

Jennifer was like some feral she-beast, raging at her captors, slavering to sink her fangs into them.

Ella told me of the psychoanalysis sessions while Jennifer was strapped down to a chair. It was a joke, with Jennifer almost ripping free of the restraints.

She devoured her food, paced endlessly in her cell and often stared like Saul used to do before he teleported to a place.

What if Jennifer figured out how to do the First One trick? Was that why Ifness was waiting around Earth? Did he plan to kill her if she managed to escape? Could he kill her?

Diana had declined his latest offer. The hitman had left her palace and was now touring the planet. I knew that he was cataloging many things in case he ever took a contract against us. Rather, in case he took *another* contract against us.

The more I thought about Ifness, the less I liked that the interstellar hitman had free rein on Earth.

I thought about Orcus and Holgotha, too. What if they had escaped destruction by not being in the pocket universe at the time? That would mean Emperor Daniel Lex Rex had two potent allies in the continuing war against us. Who was worse: Orcus or Holgotha?

I couldn't make up my mind on that one.

Still, the Terran Confederation of Liberated Planets was in a much better position now. Plutonians—anyone, for that matter—could no longer just appear from the pocket universe and start attacking. The war had turned into a regular strategical conflict against the Lokhars.

We were the little killers, the most effective soldiers in our galaxy. Did it matter that the Lokhar Empire was bigger and had more friends than we did? Maybe to a small degree. However, especially if I decided to stay a little longer, I put the odds with us.

After a week of depressing reports regarding Jennifer, I asked to join one of the psych sessions.

Several hours later, Ella guided me into a bright chamber with a view overlooking Lake Tahoe. The alpine lake was as blue as I remembered it from before The Day. There was even a large paddleboat like Mark Twain used to write about. I watched the boat from a large window.

It was strange. What would Earth be like if the Lokhars had never nuked and sprayed us with a bio-terminator?

What if, what if... I shook my head.

"They're ready," Ella said, quietly. She paused. "Creed..."

"You don't need to warn me," I said. "I understand it won't be good."

"Don't get your hopes up. Jennifer is like a devil. If she spots a weakness, she exploits it ruthlessly. She burns-out some staff in a matter of hours. The chief director is bringing in other mental health workers to continue the process."

"I've already heard all this."

"I just want you to be ready for it."

"Okay. I get it."

Ella opened the door, and we walked into the next chamber.

"Creed," Jennifer immediately sneered. She laughed in a loathsome way.

Jennifer sat in a throne-like chair, her arms and legs secured by metal bands. She wore ordinary clothes but her eyes seethed with demonic power. It was painful to witness.

Jennifer laughed again, mocking me.

Around her sat several doctors and waiting nurses. There were also two large male orderlies with dart guns. They seemed nervous as they watched Jennifer like hawks.

"Sit down, sit down," Jennifer said. "Let's probe the depths of your evil."

I walked toward her, my eyes focused on her face. I tried to remember the woman I'd known many years ago. I dredged up that memory and tried to overlay it onto this fury.

Jennifer snarled.

I refused to let go of the memory. I moved closer until I could have reached out and touched one of her hands.

"I hate you," she whispered. "I will destroy you."

"No," I said, softly. "This time, I'm staying."

"Is that your guilt talking?" she sneered.

"That," I said, "and my love for you."

"Love?" she shrieked. "You don't know the meaning of the word."

I smiled, but it felt false.

"You left me, Creed. You left me in the hands of the most evil being in any space-time continuum. Do you have any idea what he did to me?"

I tried to speak, but my throat had closed up.

Jennifer squealed with evil laughter. "Cat got your tongue?" she said.

"I'm sorry, Jennifer."

"*You're* sorry. *You're* sorry. How did you think I felt? You deserted me, Creed. You were the great savior and you left me as if it was *nothing*."

"It was the hardest choice of my life."

"No. It was to save your precious skin."

I shook my head. "I had to save the galaxy."

"Oh-ho, the galaxy," she sneered. "How noble you are, Creed. Was it worth it?"

I stared into her eyes. "It was worth it because we'd be dead or under Abaddon's rule now if I hadn't done what I'd done. *That* would be hideously worse. You would likely have faced the same end, or you could already be dead."

"I wanted to die a thousand times."

I nodded. "I failed you, then."

"You are a failure."

"But I'm not going to fail you this time. This time, your healing is my quest."

"Good luck with that."

"Thanks."

"I was being sarcastic."

"I wasn't."

"Leave, Creed. You no longer amuse me."

"Jennifer…"

She stared into my eyes. She stared, and in a moment, she teleported out of her restraints and stood before me.

I acted instantly. Maybe I'd sensed this was going to happen. She stood there, and she attacked with raking fingernails. But I was too strong and too fast for her, catching her wrists, spinning her around and shouting at the two orderlies.

Finally, as Jennifer thrashed, one of them fired a dart. It hit, and soon Jennifer's head slumped. Just before she went unconscious, I heard, "Next time…"

-94-

I took a walk along the shores of Lake Tahoe. I remembered life on Earth before The Day. I missed those days. I also missed my old Jennifer.

Maybe her healing was beyond me. How could I beat the great and gloriously evil Abaddon? I wasn't smarter than he was. I hadn't been stronger, better looking—

He'd defeated me up and down the line. I'd helped kill him, though. Maybe that's all I was good at. I could kill things.

I picked up a flat rock and skipped it seven times across the lake's still waters. Maybe Ifness was wrong. Maybe I was perfect hitman material.

I frowned as the stone sank. Someday, the momentum of my life would be over. I would die.

My scowl grew. I had beaten Abaddon in the end. How had I done it?

I put my hands inside my jacket pockets and quickened my pace. How had I beaten Abaddon? What had been the secret?

It struck me suddenly. I stopped, staring out over the pristine lake. How had I beaten Abaddon? By cheating. I'd brought in stronger forces.

I couldn't defeat Abaddon's process of twisting Jennifer, not the way I'd been going about this. I had to cheat. What did I have to cheat with that could possibly give me victory?

I snapped my fingers. I knew what I had to do.

***

"No," Ella said. "I refuse to do it. That's tampering with things we don't understand."

"It helped with Dr. Sant," I said.

We were eating lunch at an eatery overlooking the lake.

"Things were different back then," Ella said. "Besides, Sant was a Lokhar."

"Jennifer is turning into a First One. You saw what she did. She teleported like an Abaddon clone. In time...we have to save her before she becomes fully like the clones."

"But Creed, what you want me to do, it's wrong."

"Not if it saves her life," I said.

Ella looked away. She shook her head, continuing to do so. "Have someone else do it. I want no part in it."

"N7?" I asked, quietly.

"Are you insane? Now, don't get me wrong. I love N7. But he's an android. He won't have the right feel for it."

"Ella," I said, finding the words hard to say. "I'm—I'm begging you to do this. If not for me, do it for Jennifer."

Ella looked at me with stricken eyes. "Creed..." she whispered.

"This is the last time I'll ever ask you to do this," I said.

Ella kept staring at me. Finally, in the quietest voice I'd ever heard, she said, "Yes. I'll do it."

***

We brought Jennifer upstairs to my GEV. The sanatorium people were glad to see her go. I'd learned that thirteen people had quit since Jennifer had started the therapy there.

Jennifer was in the sleep-suit again. She did not look peaceful, she looked tormented.

My chest hurt. This was hard to do. I fought against Abaddon's cunning and evil, an Abaddon that fought even from the grave. I had my wits, and I had a Jelk mind machine.

I'd taken it from Earth and installed it in the stealth ship. I also had Earth's best practitioner with it: Ella Timoshenko.

We carried a sleeping Jennifer to the Jelk mind machine and strapped her into it. Afterward, we woke her.

Ella began the grim task. Jennifer proved to be her most difficult mind-machine subject yet.

Ella had driven many Lokhars insane using the Jelk mind machine. She had not done it on purpose but because it was a delicate procedure that could easily go awry. Often, she'd failed. As I've said before, Dr. Sant, who became Emperor Sant later, had been her greatest success.

Emperor Sant of Orange Tamika had brought peace between the tigers and humans, for a time, at least.

Ella worked long hours. She twisted dials, made adjustments and whispered endlessly in Jennifer's ear.

I was the Russian scientist's assistant in this. I found the ordeal horrifying. Jennifer screamed, raved, arched her back, wept, cursed foully and chomped her teeth like a madwoman. I'd never seen anything like it.

Ella endured. As long as she could do this, I would assist in any way possible.

The various monitors seemed to contradict each other. Ella's hair became tangled and she spoke as if she was creating the Frankenstein monster. The scientist did not falter, but strove, adding mental safeguards and breaking down others inside Jennifer's mind.

Jennifer glared at us at one point. She spoke in a hideous voice as if Abaddon had reappeared inside her.

"You will die, Creed," Jennifer said in an impossibly deep voice.

I could not speak.

Ella worked with haste, manipulating the board. "We're going to damn her forever, Creed, or—I don't know what will happen."

What happened in the end was the most soul-terrifying scream I had ever heard in my life. Jennifer went on like that for far too long.

Ella's shoulders slumped. "I've failed," she said wearily as Jennifer drew a long, shuddering breath, beginning another wretched howl of despair.

Finally, at the end, Jennifer screamed yet again, stopping suddenly and slumping over as if she was dead.

I raced to her.

"No," Ella said. "Beware. It's a trick."

I didn't believe that. I reached for Jennifer, but something inside me warned me off. Instead of taking her chin, I grabbed a handful of her long hair and raised her head.

For a dreadful instant, I feared that I would see her staring eyes glaring for my death, and an evil smile of purified hatred. No. Instead, Jennifer slept. And it seemed, for the first time, that a glimmer of sweaty peacefulness had descended upon her.

I prayed to God that it was true.

All we could do after that was wait.

-95-

I slept, exhausted. Upon waking, I remembered the horrible night. With leaden feet, I rose, went to the galley and made a pot of strong coffee.

I sat at a table for over an hour. At the end of the time, Ella dragged herself in. She looked terrible, poor woman, with circles under her eyes and slack skin.

She drank coffee and nibbled on toast. "I'm afraid," Ella told me. "I don't know what we're going to find."

"Let me go first," I said.

"But Creed..."

"I'm all out of ideas," I said. "Let me deal with her."

Ella studied me, and she paled. "Are you going to kill her if she's not better?"

"What?" I asked. "Never! I'm going to put her in stasis if everything is the same. Then, I'm going to take her back to the Curator. It will be up to him, then."

"Oh," Ella said. "Oh. This could be it. You might be leaving soon, maybe forever."

I nodded glumly.

After that, we sat silently for a time. Finally, I stood. Ella wished me luck. I nodded, and left for what could be a horrible interview.

***

Jennifer lay sleeping on a cot with straps holding her down. Before bringing her here last night, Ella had put a bright nightgown on her.

I quietly removed the straps. Then, I picked up a stool I'd brought into the cell and set it beside her bed. I sat down, picked up one of her limp hands and gently stroked it.

"I'm sorry, Jennifer. I never should have taken you on that mission to the Karg universe. I made a mistake. I never should have risked you. You have no idea how seeing you hanging from your wrists..."

I stopped speaking because I no longer could.

I had told Jennifer the same thing a hundred times before, maybe even three hundred times. How I'd longed to see her open her eyes and tell me that she forgave me. I wanted to make the world bright and soft for her again. I wanted to hear the woman I loved laugh and then feel her hug me. I wanted to heal the evils done to her.

"Oh, Jennifer," I said. "I've missed you. You have no idea what it's like—"

I stopped because I saw her eyelids twitch. I almost snatched my hand away, but I did not. I wanted to hold onto her hand and hope for as long as I could. I didn't think I would have any hope left if this didn't work. And what a longshot it was. Jennifer wasn't a Lokhar. She was a—

Her eyes snapped open. She looked up at me. "Creed?" she asked, speaking my name as she used to long ago.

"Yes," I said, in a voice I hardly recognized.

She stared into my eyes. "I've had a terrible nightmare, darling."

The words hit. They actually *hurt*. I did not deserve sweet words from her. I deserved curses.

My mouth was dry as I whispered, "The nightmares are true, my love."

Fear entered her eyes. Then her eyes widened with astonishment as if she remembered something hideous. She jerked her hand out of mine. She sat up and brought up her knees, hugging them. All the while, she kept staring at me.

"You left me," she said in a small voice.

"It was the hardest decision of my life. I have...often..." I could no longer speak.

"How could you do that, Creed?"

"Please... Forgive me for a horrible sin that I committed against you and you alone."

Her eyes welled with tears until one by one they trickled down her cheeks. "I can't remember everything...but I think I hated you for a time."

I nodded.

"How did I get here?" she asked.

I told her the truth as I explained about the Curator, Ifness, the Plutonians, everything, including how I'd captured her in the PDS Control Chamber.

"Creed," she said. And although tears still dripped from her eyes, she reached up and tenderly touched my cheek.

I expected her to scratch four long furrows down my skin. But for that single soft touch of her fingers, I would have gladly paid such a price.

"I forgive you, darling," she said. "I understand why you had to do it."

"Jennifer?"

"I forgive you," she repeated.

A thrill I could scarcely believe filled me with power. I stood and swept her up into my arms. I crushed her against my chest and began to shower kisses upon her wet, upturned face.

I wondered if she would become feral again, but she did not. She laughed, cried and hugged me as hard as she could.

Jennifer, my sweet Jennifer had returned after many lonely years. The last attempt—the Jelk mind machine—had worked. It had worked. It had actually and truly worked!

What did this mean for the future? I did not know. This I did know, though. I would stay on Earth with Jennifer. I would help Diana and the First Admiral against the next Lokhar attack. I would make sure Orcus and Holgotha did not bring victory to Emperor Daniel Lex Rex. But most of all, most of all, I would love my sweet Jennifer and treasure the great prize that I had lost but now found anew.

For the first time in many long years, I believe I had peace of heart. For a warrior like me, it made all my battles worth fighting.

Jennifer, sweet Jennifer. How lovely it was to feel her embrace. This had to be the happiest moment of my overly storied and checkered life.

THE END

SF Books by Vaughn Heppner

LOST STARSHIP SERIES:
The Lost Starship
The Lost Command
The Lost Destroyer
The Lost Colony
The Lost Patrol
The Lost Planet
The Lost Earth
The Lost Artifact

THE A.I. SERIES:
A.I. Destroyer
The A.I. Gene
A.I. Assault
A.I. Battle Station
A.I. Battle Fleet

EXTINCTION WARS SERIES:
Assault Troopers
Planet Strike
Star Viking
Fortress Earth
Target: Earth

Visit VaughnHeppner.com for more information

Printed in Poland
by Amazon Fulfillment
Poland Sp. z o.o., Wrocław